PRAISE FOR THE
NOVELS OF J. BARRETT

"Fans of fantasy novels featuring action and fascinating people will inhale this story. Readers will find a gritty adventure full of heart, loyalty, intrigue, deception, and a host of bitter-sweet emotions. This fantasy has the depth to cross genre boundaries and provide a provocative, captivating read. I heartily recommend this read." - *Terri Stepek, Reader Views 5 Star Review (Orabelle)*

"A crackerjack yarn featuring a strong heroine, plenty of action, and genuinely surprising twists and turns. Get it." – *Kirkus Reviews (Orabelle)*

"Barrett's storytelling prowess shines, offering readers a riveting journey into a world where shadows of the past converge with the uncertainty of the future. A must-read for fantasy enthusiasts craving a tale of complexity, heart, and unrelenting suspense." – *Reader's Favorite 5 Star Review (Maialen)*

"An epic narrative unravels through intricate plots and surprising turns. Characters and events come to life, offering readers a cinematic journey. The author's words skillfully paint each scene, making it enthralling to imagine. For enthusiasts of fantastical tales, this story is sure to enchant." – *Author's Reading (Blaise)*

"An exciting new world filled with elemental magic and political intrigue. This is an excellent start to an epic new fantasy series." – *Reedsy Discovery (Orabelle)*

"There was never a dull moment, and I immersed myself in the depiction of another world. The dialog was engaging and the connection between Orabelle and the supporting characters was effortless. Fantasy, family drama, and more await. I recommend Orabelle to readers who enjoy action filled fantasy stories" - *Reader's Favorite 5 Star Review (Orabelle)*

"Orabelle was a unique fantasy incorporating fresh takes on elemental magic and political intrigue. My favorite parts of this novel were the ways it defied my expectations." - *Judge, 10th Annual Writer's Digest Self Published E-Book Awards.*

"A taut fantasy tale of bloodshed and politics with a complex hero battling her own personal demons. Barrett once again weaves together heart-pounding action and complex characters to create an epic tale that tackles themes of grief, forgiveness, and self-determination... Our verdict – GET IT." – *Kirkus Reviews (Maialen)*

"An enthralling journey infused with raw emotions, unwavering loyalty, and intricate webs of intrigue and deception; un-put-downable. Readers hungry for stories of adventure, betrayal, and the unwavering strength of the human spirit won't want to miss this one." – *The Prairies Book Review (The Keepers of Imbria full series review)*

"Author J. Barrett has crafted an exhilarating novel that kept me on the edge of my seat from start to finish...Eolande delivers a satisfying conclusion that will linger in the minds of readers long after the last page is turned, and I would highly recommend it and the series in general to fantasy fans everywhere." – *K.C. Finn, Reader's Favorite (Eolande)*

BOOKS BY J. BARRETT

The Keepers of Imbria

Orabelle

Maialen

Blaise

Eolande

EOLANDE

The Keepers of Imbria Book 4

J. Barrett

Anthem in Art

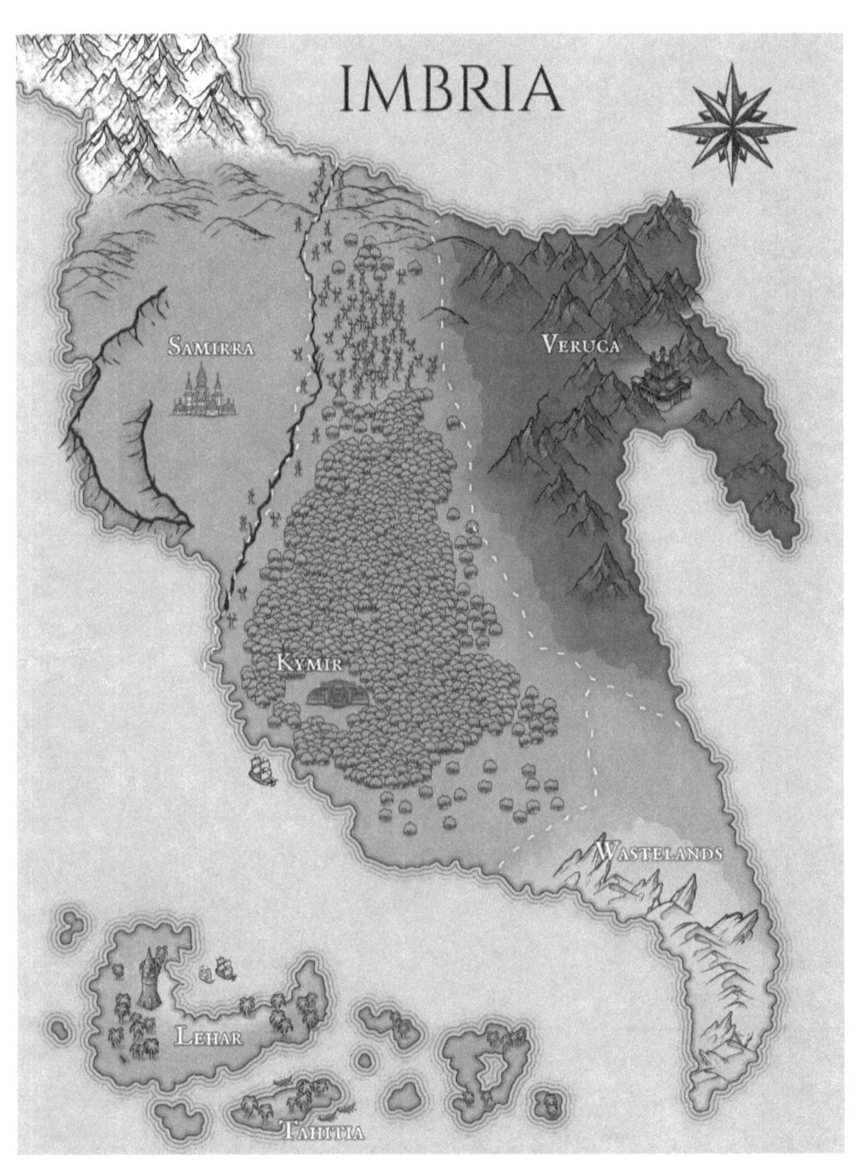

IMBRIA
SAMIRRA
VERUCA
KYMIR
WASTELANDS
LEHAR
TAHITIA

1

My eyes flew open and my body convulsed violently as I tore myself out of the dream that had overtaken my fitful slumber. The chains that bound my wrists were wrenched painfully, their heavy shackles digging into my tender flesh as a metallic rattle reverberated through the hot room. I forced myself to breathe, to relax and lie still. The ache in my arms began to subside, along with the poignancy of my dream, and I moved gingerly, dragging the chains across the filthy mat I slept on so I could roll onto my side. The iron shackles rested uncomfortably against my ribs as I pulled my knees to my chest, my body curling protectively around itself. My dirty hair fell over my eyes and I felt a trail of sweat sliding down my forehead, beading up in round droplets that dripped from my face like molten iron from the forges that raged above my prison. The air in the room was thick and bloated with heat, and it stuck in my throat as if an unseen hand had wrapped feverish fingers around my neck and squeezed. I hated Veruca, and I hated the dreams that made me forget I was a prisoner in this hateful realm. I preferred the nightmares, for those I could endure. It was the sweet, hazy remembrances of my time in the forest, the glimpses back to the idyllic and carefree existence of my childhood, that destroyed me.

Flowers filled my recent dreams, and the image of their delicate stems bending in the wind brought tears to my eyes. I missed flowers. When I was a little girl, Gideon would tuck wildflowers behind my ear, the brightly colored petals tickling my round cheeks as I paraded merrily in front of his indulgent smile. He would reach out and playfully tug one of the strands of cloud-colored hair that escaped my bonnet, making me squeal with delight. I could barely remember what they smelled like, those happy little flowers that grew wild and untamed around our small little cabin in the Kymirran forest. It had been too long since I had seen them, too long since the joy of those days had been ripped away from me. How long I could not be sure. When I was first taken captive, I had not thought to count the days. I was a child then, and I foolishly believed that someone would come for me. Someone would save me. I waited, heedless of time, for a rescue that never came. It was not until much later that I understood why. There was no one to come. My parents, my true mother and father, Tal and Orabelle, had been dead for years, one slaughtered before I was born and the other killed in battle soon after. As a baby I was given to Gideon, the man I thought was my father, the one who haunted my dreams with happy memories. We had lived in the woods, hidden from the world, until his accidental death at the hands of the Keepers. After that, I was brought to the islands, hidden amongst the Tahitians who wanted me to be the legendary Solvrei. I always hated the way the islanders looked at me, the reverence in their dark gazes. I was a mere child then, scared and alone, with a power that I could not understand. There was nothing about me to revere, and their adoration had frightened me.

There were a handful of others who might have searched for me after I was kidnapped and taken from the islands. The grey-eyed boy and the Fire Keeper, or the strange, ugly dog and the twin brothers who walked with him. Perhaps they came to Veruca and learned from Queen Logaire that I was dead, or maybe they knew someone who had been present in the crowd that gathered to watch my execution. They might have seen for themselves the macabre show Logaire had put on, staging my death and pretending to hang me in front of half the realm. There was no reason for anyone to search for me after that twisted act of deception. I was dead.

It was after my supposed hanging that I was thrown into the lonely, dark depths of the Verucan dungeons, locked away like a rabid dog until the Verucan Queen wanted something from me. There was fear in Logaire. I could see it in her golden eyes and the way she shrank away from my touch when she was near. She was afraid of me, and she was not a woman who could tolerate being afraid. That was why she was cruel to me, why she kept me isolated in the desolate dungeon. It was there, in the castle keep, in my lonely cell, that I finally began to count the days, to draw subtle marks on the wall of the room I was kept in. I counted the times I was fed to guess the days since I could not see the sun, but they soon became so many that I could no longer bear the sight of them. Each mark represented a day of pain, of loneliness and heartbreak, agony and degradation, and they filled the black walls of my prison, horrid reminders of the desolation my life had become. And so I had torn bits of cloth from the ragged dress I wore and rubbed them away, scraping my hands and tearing my nails on the rock as I desperately tried to erase those days. I had cleaned the marks from the wall, but I could not erase the memories or the emptiness that filled my soul.

I tried to escape many times, planning it in my head for thousands of hours, but every time I came close, someone stopped me. I would be dragged back, beaten and thrown into my cell, left alone in the darkness. Eventually, I had given up, and the foolish hope of my youth died away. There were times I still considered it, wondered how far I could get if I broke away and ran when they came for my blood. In my mind I ran forever, until there was sunlight and wind and the cool blue ocean lapping around my ankles, but I knew that was just another spiteful dream. I would not even reach the end of the hallway, let alone see the ocean again.

It was better in Halig, my other prison, where I was under the care of the Oracle. Logaire shuffled me back and forth between the two locations as it suited her whims, and I was always happy to return to the quiet temple. I dreamt less when I was there, hidden from the world in the farthest chambers of the Oracle's mystical palace. Sybylla, the Oracle, was kind to me. She would bathe me, clothe me in soft robes, allow me to wander through the temple at night when no one was awake to see me. Sometimes the other man came to visit me. His name was Vishram, and he always brought me little gifts, books and poems and sometimes an apple, always trying to atone for what he was a part of and what he had done to me. When I was first taken captive, Vishram was the one who held me down and carved open the skin of my back, shoving the Warding Stone into the wound and sewing it shut so that I could not use my power against them. Though he had done so at Logaire's command, he carried an immense weight of guilt for the barbaric act, and he believed that one day his small acts of kindness and mercy would add up to forgiveness.

The heavy iron door that led into my cell creaked on unoiled hinges, pulling me from my thoughts of Halig and returning me to the dark corners of Veruca's dungeon. An orange glow spread over the floor, pooling around me and illuminating the stifling room. The light crawled up the black walls and rolled across the low rock ceiling, worming its way in and out of the stone crevices of my prison, bathing me in its unwelcome glow. I squeezed my eyes shut, my body tensing, metal chains pressing against my fragile ribs. I waited anxiously for the sound of their voice, to learn which captor I would be facing this time.

"What do we have here?" a man's voice asked, curiosity lacing his acidic tone. There was something familiar about the voice, something dark and haunting that echoed faintly in the back of my mind. I had met this man before, a long time ago.

I pushed myself upright, hugging my knees to my chest and blinking up at him through the fringe of matted dark hair that hung over my eyes. He had an unpleasant face, with a silvery scar carved through his chin, curving up into his bottom lip. His eyes were small and set deep beneath heavy brows, and his forehead rose in two broad peaks around closely shaved auburn hair. He was dressed in black, a soldier's uniform, with a conspicuous golden crest on the collar. I had seen the emblem before. I felt the memory of it crash over me like a tidal wave. I remembered screaming and fighting to pull myself from his vice-like grasp. He was the man who had taken me from the island of Tahitia all those years ago, the one who had brought me to Logaire and Veruca.

He smiled, sensing my fear, and knelt before me, shoving the torch he carried close to my face so he could see me better. I shrank away from the unwelcome heat, and his smile widened. "I knew Logaire was keeping something from me. Tell me who you are."

Panic thundered in my chest with every beat of my heart. I could not tell him who I truly was, that I was the one they called the Solvrei. I closed my eyes and for a moment I wished I could hear them again, the Element Keepers who had come before. When I was a little girl, I hated the voices that shouted at me from the amulets, but ever since the Verucan Queen had embedded a Warding Stone in my back to dampen my power, the voices had been silent. I found myself longing to hear their insistent cries. They would have helped me, told me what to do, told me who to pretend to be. But they were silent, so silent, and I was alone, my mind clamoring desperately for an answer to give the leering man who stared at me expectantly.

Tell him something say something he cannot find out who you are he is cruel I see it in his eyes do not tell him the truth hide hide hide what do I say what do I tell him?

"Well?" the man prodded, squinting his deep-set brown eyes. "You seem familiar. Why is the Queen hiding you down here? Come here, come closer and let me look at you."

He took a step towards me and I edged away, pressing myself against the wall behind me, but there was nowhere for me to hide. When he reached out his hand, fear flooded through me. I moved without thinking, grabbing the chain that bound my arms and throwing it over his neck, twisting him to the ground and squeezing with all my strength. The torch clattered to the floor, the garish light of its flame wavering madly around the cell. The man was gasping, gripping the chain and trying to pull it away from his neck. He rolled, crushing my frail body beneath him and breaking my hold. He leaped up, gulping in air with great heaving breaths as he backed away from me.

"You little wretch!" he snarled, rearing back his hand and slapping me soundly across the face. I fell back, pressing my palm against my stinging cheek. He grabbed my hair, jerking me towards him, then he abruptly let go, staring at the smears of black soot on his fingers, the dark powder that hid what I really was. "Your hair... you are Leharan."

A smile spread over his face, malevolent and sinister, and I wondered if he was going to kill me. I looked around desperately but there was nothing, no one to help, no weapon I could grab. The torch was still lying on the ground. If I could reach it, then I might be able to hit him with it, but then what? I was still chained, bound to the iron ring that was embedded in the wall.

"I know who you are," he said, his hateful voice now filled with smug satisfaction. "Your eyes give you away, no matter how much Logaire tries to cover your hair. You are that little brat from Tahitia. Tell me, has she kept you here this entire time? What has it been, nearly ten years now? Longer, perhaps?"

Ten years. The passage of time was like a blow to my stomach. I felt the air knocked out of my lungs, the world spinning as if he had struck me again. Ten years. I had been a prisoner for half my life. Ten years that no one had cared, no one had come. I wanted to cry, to scream, to shout until my voice was hoarse, but now was not the moment to mourn my lost years. He was coming towards me again and I saw him glance at my hands, his eyes wary. He remembered my power and what I could do. He had no idea there was a Warding Stone embedded under my skin.

"I know who you are, too. Touch me again and I will kill you," I whispered. It was a vain threat, but he did not know that. His name was Akrin. The Oracle had spoken of him often, her face drawn and clouded whenever she mentioned his name. She told me to be grateful he did not know I was alive, warned me he was dangerous, that if he ever found me, he would hurt me. I believed her. One look into his eyes and I knew that everything she said about him was true.

"You can try," he mused, picking up a strand of my hair and rubbing it between his finger and thumb. "But I will probably kill you first."

He let go of my hair, stepping back and crouching down so we were eye to eye. I looked away, avoiding his piercing gaze, wishing he would leave, wondering if he would try to hurt me. It had happened before. The men who guarded me were not always good men. In Halig, at the temple, I was safe. I could sleep without fear of someone coming, protected by the Oracle, but not here. Here, I had to be vigilant. I had told the Oracle of what happened at the castle, and she had tried to keep me with her, but as powerful as she was, she was not the Queen. When Logaire sent for me, I was forced to go. I remembered overhearing an argument they once had about it. I was hiding around the corner as they debated my fate, eyes squeezed shut, listening intently and praying that the Oracle could convince the Queen to return to the castle without me.

"She is not safe there. Leave her here with me. I can send you all the blood you need," Sybylla was saying patiently, using all the powers of persuasion that she had garnered over the years. I could imagine her tawny eyes round and earnest, her smile soft and encouraging.

The Verucan Queen had laughed, a sharp, brittle sound like glass breaking. "I need to be sure the blood is hers. You are too sentimental when it comes to this girl, my dear. Perhaps I have left her in your care too often."

The Oracle paused for a moment, considering, wanting to find the right thing to say. She had learned to speak slowly, not to rush or be impatient with her words. "If she dies, then you will have nothing left of her. I fear that bringing her back to the castle will destroy her spirit. Let her stay with me. You know I would never betray you, and Vishram is here to attest to that."

"It is the ones closest to us that hurt us the most, dear Sybylla. I am taking the girl and that is the end of it. If you keep persisting as you are, then I will keep her at the castle permanently. Your attachment to her is dangerous."

I had opened my eyes at the Queen's final words on the matter, my breath and prayers leaving me. I felt hollow, empty, and my hands trembled as I wrung them together. At least the Oracle tried. It was more than anyone else would have done for me. I hurried down the long hallway of the temple, past the archway that led to the main courtyard where a giant fountain bloomed with hot water from the springs below. I reached the small door that led to the back chambers, the rooms of the Oracle and her devotees, and I slipped through, shutting it quietly behind me. The Queen would not be pleased to see me roaming freely and I did not want her threat of keeping me at the castle to have any further justification.

I passed an open door, seeing the heavy figure of the Queen's advisor, my only other friend in the world, as he bent over a busy table full of scrolls. Though maybe friend was the wrong word to use. Vishram was perpetually repentant for what had been done to me, for what he himself had done. He spent years trying to atone for his part in my misery, but trying to assuage his guilt did not make us friends.

Vishram had glanced up from his mountains of parchment as I went by, a hopeful expression lifting his cumbersome features. He knew Sybylla wanted me to stay with her, and he had even promised to do what he could to help convince the Queen that it would be best, but it seemed Logaire did not care for either of their opinions on the matter. I gave him a curt shake of my head, hurrying on before he could stop me, not wanting to see the resignation on his face.

I never knew how long I would be gone when I was summoned to the castle, and this time it was the Queen herself who had come to collect me. Months of misery and loneliness could lie ahead. Whenever I had to leave the temple, Vishram would always find a moment before I left to whisper to me that one day someone would come for me, that I just had to endure a little longer. As the years dragged on, we both knew they were just empty words that neither of us believed, and I did not think I could bear to hear those futile words again. The advisor's heavy sigh floated through the air behind me as I hurried to go and change into the wretched rags Logaire preferred me to be clothed in. Tears stung my eyes, but I wiped them away quickly. I had learned long ago there was no point in crying.

My mind returned to the present, to the stifling, sweating cell and the man who stood looming over me. Akrin's eyes strayed to my arm, seeing the tiny scars that crisscrossed my skin where it was visible beneath the sleeves of my tattered gown. "Logaire has been taking your blood? What does she do with it?"

I refused to answer.

There was a slight twitch in the corner of his left eye. It was obvious he did not like to be challenged. "It is impossible that you have been here in the dungeon this entire time. I have been down here. I would have found you. Where else has she been hiding you? Halig? I always knew that wretched wench Sybylla was a liar. We will see how self-righteous Logaire's precious Oracle is when I go there and remove her deceitful head from her shoulders."

My stomach churned. I felt like I was slipping down a dark hole, every move I made causing me to fall further. Sybylla had been kind to me, and I did not wish her to die, especially not at the hands of this twisted monster. I shook my head stubbornly. "I know nothing of Halig, and I will not help you."

Akrin laughed at my meager defiance. "I am impressed that you still have any spirit left in you after all this time. Have it your way, then. Stay here and rot. I will find out what I need to know with or without your help, and in the meantime life will be very unpleasant for you down here. Whatever you have been through, I promise you I will make it a hundred times worse."

I felt panic stealing the air from my lungs, my mind sliding further into the dark pit he was pulling me into. I had already suffered through countless cruel degradations and I could not imagine enduring worse.

"I do not know what she does with the blood! I swear," I promised desperately.

His brooding malevolence faded, a cold smile playing at his lips, but there was still a slender thread of anger running through him at being kept in the dark, betrayed by the Verucan

Queen. He stood abruptly, turning and striding out of the cell. "I will be back."

"Wait! Please, let me go," I begged, lurching forward as he began to swing the door shut. I knew it was a vain plea. No one in Veruca would ever help me, but I could not stop myself from asking, no matter how pathetic I sounded, even to my own ears.

"You are not going anywhere," Akrin said, his voice now playful, toying with me as I tried to keep up with the dizzying swings of his mood. "Not until I see who will offer the most for you. There are quite a few people on Imbria who will be very interested in finding out you are still alive, girl, and the prosperous Queen of Kymir is among them."

2

I could not tell how many days had passed since Akrin left me there in the oppressive emptiness of my cell. It could have been weeks for all I knew. The passage of time had blurred into an ephemeral filament, an intangible thing that I was always clutching at but could not grasp as it slipped by me. I waited in the darkness each day, waited for the door to open, each time expecting Akrin to come for me, each time feeling my anxiousness mounting until it nearly overwhelmed me. But it was not him, never him. Every time the key scraped in the lock and the door creaked and my stomach turned, it was not him. Guards came with food, emptied the bucket in the corner of my cell, went in and out as if I were not even a person, barely glancing at me, their eyes filled with disgust. It began to wear on me, the constant waiting broken only by brief, fleeting moments of relief. After a time, I wanted Akrin to come. I wanted him to stop the endless march of meaningless time, to end the constant cycle of dread and relief. Perhaps I would die at his hands, but at least it would be the end of something, a halt to the infinite circle of misery I was trapped in.

My thoughts strayed to my mother, as they often did on the days when hope was hard to hold on to. This had all begun with her. Logaire had told me some about my family, her trilling voice at odds with the dizzying complexity of their betrayals and deceptions. Orabelle had been betrothed to the Fire Keeper, but her heart belonged to my father, her Guardian. Chronus, who was supposedly my grandfather, was the one who orchestrated Orabelle's engagement to Blaise, a way to punish her for being the bastard daughter of another man. He then had my father killed, framing the Fire Keeper for the heinous act. This ultimately brought them to war, and it was at the battle of Queen's End that my mother was bitten by a blooddrinker and killed by the Air Keeper, Astraeus, her sister Maialen's husband. As for me, my mother had given me up as soon as I was born, tasking the Guardians Gideon and Damian with keeping me safe. She was told by the Tahitians that I was the prophesied Solvrei who would save Imbria. I always wondered if she had truly believed the prophecy and given me away to protect me, or if she was merely unable to bear the sight of me, a painful reminder of my father and all she had lost.

I dragged my mind away from the question of my mother's love, for it did not matter down here in the dungeon. Nothing from that life mattered anymore, not even the Tahitian's prophecy. I lifted my finger in the darkness, placing it against the stone wall and dragging it across the obsidian surface. I wondered what it would feel like if I did not have the Warding Stone buried in my back, if I could still feel my power. Would the walls tremble beneath me? Would I be able to call to them, to pull them down on top of me?

I sighed. It would not feel like anything because there was no one here to feed it. The power that ran through my veins, the power of the Solvrei, could only be harnessed with an amulet or another person to draw from. And I had neither of those things. I was helpless, with or without the Warding Stone. I dropped my hand and settled back into the bleakness of my thoughts. Then the silence of the dungeon was broken by a distant shout.

My eyes flew open and I pressed myself towards the door of my cell, straining to hear. For a moment, part of me doubted that I had heard anything at all, and the sound was merely a fabrication created by my fracturing mind. I had been alone one day too many and I was finally going mad.

There was a frantic scratching on the other side of the door. I was not mad. Someone was trying to open the lock. I backed away, gathering my chains in my arms, fear swelling in my throat until I thought it would choke me. The door was flung open and a man stood there, a Verucan soldier. I could barely make out the shape of him in the flickering light of the candle he carried, but I could see that his eyes were wild and his face pale beneath his auburn beard.

"We need to get out of here!" he cried, motioning me forward.

Inside my mind, my thoughts were screaming at me, a chaotic mess of words that pounded against my skull.

Out of here out outside is freedom do I run what if he is lying what if they find me I don't care I don't want to die here in the dark alone I have to try run Eolande run run run.

I lifted the chains I was grasping in my arms, showing him that I was still shackled, that I could not do as he commanded. A stricken look passed over his face, and he glanced down the hallway as if tempted to flee without me. He cursed under his breath, then set the candle on the ground and fumbled with the ring of keys in his hand, coming into the cell and trying frantically to unlock me from my bindings. There were more noises from the hallway, more shouts, the sounds of heavy footsteps falling on stone. Wiping the sweat from his face with the back of his hand, the man cursed even more vehemently, fumbling at the lock with clumsy fingers.

"Give them to me," I said, surprising myself with the steadiness of my voice. He put the keys in my hand and turned back to the doorway, leaning out to peer down the hall.

"Hurry! We must get you out of here. They are coming for you," he hissed back at me.

Sweat soaked my skin and I felt the warm metal slipping in my grasp, but I somehow managed to find the key that fit the lock. I turned it and the shackles fell apart with a metallic tang. I yanked them off and dropped them to the ground in a clatter, looking up at the relief washing over the man. It had to be a mere fraction of the relief I was feeling. My arms felt light, hollow, unused to moving without the laborious weight of chains. The soldier reached out and grabbed my hand, unceremoniously dragging me behind him down the darkened corridor, away from the shouting and calamity. My bare feet struggled to keep up, stumbling along blindly as he led me through a labyrinth of twists and turns. We came upon a door and he rattled the handle fervently, trying to open it but finding it locked. He cursed some more before turning to me and demanding the keys.

"I... I do not have them," I confessed. I had dropped the keys back in my cell, along with the heap of discarded chains, not knowing we would need them again.

There was a moment of silence and I could feel his frustration radiating out from him, even if I could not see his face in the dark corridor. He once again grabbed my wrist and pulled me along behind him.

"Where are we going?" I asked, my voice barely a whisper. It was quieter here, in the dark bowels beneath the castle. Whatever the commotion was above us, it had not yet reached this part of the keep. I was trying to think, to reason, to decipher what was happening around me, but I felt lost, stumbling through the darkness of the world with no clue where to find the light.

"The Queen has ordered me to keep you safe until the usurper has been dealt with," he muttered, as if he were not at all grateful for the task he was assigned.

"The usurper?" I repeated, unfamiliar with the word, for I had never seen it in any of the books or poems that Vishram had leant to me.

"General Akrin. He has tried to assassinate the Queen."

"Assassinate?" I once again repeated the word he had used, not knowing what it meant.

"Kill her. He tried to kill her," he said, his impatience obvious in his brusque tone. "We need to hide you, whoever you are, until this is all over."

"Hide me?"

He sighed in annoyance. "Are you daft, girl?"

I felt my face flush, was glad it was dark so he could not see my embarrassment as I stammered, "N-no, I do not think so. Though I suppose I would not know if I was... What happens when this is over?"

"You go back to the dungeon and we never have to-"

His words broke off in a cry of surprise as I threw myself at him, clawing viciously at his face with my jagged fingernails. He backed away from me, trying to stop my unexpected assault, and I turned and ran, fleeing into the darkness beyond him.

Run run run just keep going Eolande do not go back don't go back don't let him take you back never go back just keep running.

I ran as fast as I could, terrified that I would crash into a wall, or worse, into another soldier or Akrin himself. I could hear the man's footsteps behind me quickening in pursuit. He was faster than me. I had been locked away for too long, not allowed to run, barely allowed to move. My legs were unsteady beneath me, and I was unsure how far they could carry me. I would not be able to get away, he would catch me. I stopped, taking a heaving breath, backing up until I felt warm stone behind me, pressing myself flat against the wall. The man was faster than me, but I was quiet. Over the years, I had learned to be silent, to hold my breath and not make a sound so that I would not draw attention to myself. I was silent now, waiting, hearing him come closer, his breaths loud and panting, his feet stomping on the ground like thunder. He ran right past me.

I waited until the echo of his boots faded into the distance before I finally allowed myself to breathe again. A flare of triumph rose in me, a bright, burning moment of light in the darkness. The unfamiliar shape of a smile pulled at my lips, a strange expression for me to feel. I slowly started to move, following the edges of the wall, grateful for my bare feet, which made no sound as I moved. I could hear the clamor of fighting coming from above, and the noises were getting louder, closer. I needed to find a way out of there.

"Quick, this way. Hurry!" I heard furtive whispers from up ahead and for a fleeting moment, I thought they were speaking to me. I almost ran back into the darkness, then I saw the orange glimmer of torchlight and a group of Verucans huddled together. A woman was motioning for them to follow her. A maid, most likely, or one of the cooks. The others with her also looked like servants, their faces terrified as they shuffled after the woman. I felt hope rising within me. They must be fleeing the fighting in the castle. The woman knew a way out. I just had to follow them.

I hung back, staying in the shadowy darkness beyond the reach of their torch, creeping after them as they made their way to a door. The woman pushed it open and moonlight poured in, a rush of air that smelled of sulfur and smoke.

Outside.

It was just beyond that door. My heart was pounding in my chest, the noise deafening, and I was sure they would hear it. I tried to breathe, to be calm, but I could not stop the elation that was threatening to overwhelm me. I was so close. So close to outside. I had no chains, nothing to bind me. I could go. I could escape them.

"Someone is coming!" one of the men hissed in fear.

"Quickly, go! I will lock the door behind us," the woman promised them, ushering the Verucans through to their freedom. I felt the heart-pounding elation in my chest turn to terror at her words. If she locked the door, then I would be trapped there forever. I had to go. I had to get out with them. There was no other choice.

"Please! Wait for me," I called out, running forward. I was just a girl, a dirty wretched girl, they had no reason to fear me.

The woman looked at me in surprise, eyes rounding, then she motioned with her hand for me to hurry through the doorway.

"Thank you," I whispered as I moved past her, stepping out into the glorious night.

I took a few steps and stopped, my face turned up to the silvery moon, the cool breath of night tickling my cheek. I felt something wet on my face, wiped a tear away with my dirty fingers.

"There, there," said the woman who had led us out, her voice kind and gentle as she patted my shoulders. "You are safe now, child. I have heard whispers of the vile things the General does down in the dungeons. Whatever happened tonight, at least you were able to get away from him. Have you somewhere to go? Family that you will be safe with?"

I stared down at my hands, at the wet streak on the side of my thumb where I had wiped away the tear. Family. I rolled the word over in my mind, trying not to let my emotions show on my face.

"Yes, of course," I replied quietly. I could not tell her the truth, that I had no family who loved me, that I was alone in the world.

"I always knew it would come to this," one of the men said, his tone full of righteous bitterness. "That woman was never meant to be the Queen. We would have been better off in the desert wastelands, outlawed with the Fire Keeper. At least he protects his own."

"Well, no one is stopping you now," the woman retorted. "By all means, go and join the Keeper. Though if you ask me, they are all poison and you will just be trading one set of problems for another."

They began to move away, drifting apart like shadows passing beneath the moon. I stood there, hesitating, looking around me in confusion.

"Do you know the way home, girl?" The woman stopped a few feet away, turning back to look at me curiously. I kept my head down, my sooty hair hiding my face from her, lowering the eyes that would show her who I really was.

"I am just disoriented," I murmured. "Can you tell me which way to Halig?"

She pointed and I hesitated, looking in the direction she was indicating. Part of me wanted to run the other way, to go south to the desert they spoke of that was ruled over by the Fire Keeper. I remembered him. Blaise. He had been kind to me as a child, despite what everyone said about him. And he had no love for the Verucan Queen, his cousin who had stolen the throne from him. It was possible that he would help me, but I could not be certain of it, and I could not forget the threat Akrin had tossed at me, his promise to kill the Oracle. It was foolish, I knew that in my heart, but I could not live with myself if I did not try to warn Sybylla. She and Vishram were the only people who had shown me any mercy in ten long years, and I could not let them be slaughtered if there was something I could do to prevent it. I looked up at the sky, at the bright swathe of stars that were scattered across the darkness, and I began to walk.

3

I stopped to rest, shading my eyes from the glare of the sun. The row of small wooden houses seemed no closer than they had been an hour before, and I wondered miserably if I would ever reach them. I could just make out the faded earthen tones of the once happily painted boards, the color peeled away like flaking skin to reveal the rot underneath. Some of the houses sagged in the middle, as if the weight of their existence was too much for them. I wondered if that was what I looked like when people saw me, if I was something bowed and nearly broken by the heaviness of what I was supposed to be. The Solvrei. The divine child, descendent of the gods and the last Water Keeper. Laughter bubbled in my throat as my stomach rumbled loudly, reminding me that all I had to eat that day was a handful of grub worms I had dug out from a rotten tree trunk. I wondered what the gods would think of me now, eating worms and trudging across Imbria on bloodied feet that were scraped raw from days of walking.

Keep going Eolande you have to keep going you cannot stop they will find you they will take you back move your feet ignore the pain it is not that bad you can keep going.

I began to move again, trying not to think about the soreness of my poor feet. I walked as long as I could before I had to stop, sitting in the tall grass and rubbing the aching muscles of my legs, wincing at the sight of my torn, blistered feet and the flaps of skin peeling off. The houses were still so far away and I began to doubt that I would ever reach them. I would just walk and walk and walk for an eternity, till all the flesh fell from my bones and my skeletal feet made dark, deathly imprints in the damp earth and still I would walk, never reaching anywhere.

Stand up no more sitting you have to keep moving you must keep going you must warn the Oracle you cannot let them find you they will take you back you cannot go back keep walking.

I stood shakily, nearly collapsing as my feet took my full weight and a wave of nausea rolled over me. I choked on a sob of pain and stubbornly swallowed it. I had felt pain before. I could tolerate pain if the prize was my freedom. Gideon had once told me that pain was the offering we gave for living. I was a child and we had been walking along the riverbank near our cabin. I had fallen and scraped my knee, wailing dramatically and cupping my hands around the raw skin because I knew he would come to comfort me. He moved my hands aside, so tiny in his giant, gentle grasp, and he smiled at me, tilting his head to one side. He had told me then about pain, how it was the price we paid for the beautiful gift of living. Looking back on those words I could see that he was warning me, but that day in the forest, amongst the peaceful sounds of the rushing river and chirping birds, still full of innocence with flowers tucked in my hair, I could not have known what he truly meant.

I somehow managed to reach the first of the dilapidated houses. I rubbed the foggy glass with my sleeve and peered into the window, unable to decide whether I was relieved or dismayed. The house was empty, abandoned. There were a few broken pieces of furniture scattered about and a scrap of cloth hung sadly from one window, pale pink and green, like a wilting flower.

My stomach rumbled again, and I hugged my arms to my-self. My stomach would have to wait. My feet could go no further. I needed to rest.

I made my way to the door, pressing my thin body close to the walls as I moved in case someone should see me, though the silence was so complete that I could not imagine anyone was nearby. I turned the door handle, giving it a hard push. It swung open easily, and I stumbled inside, having expected more resistance. Dust swirled up around me and I began to sneeze. I pulled my filthy sleeve over my hand and held it to my nose as I looked around. The house was only a single room with a raised loft for sleeping. The ladder that had led up to the loft was broken into pieces and there was no way I could climb up there in my condition.

I curled myself into the corner behind the door. Anyone who came barging in would not see me at first glance, and I would have a few moments to do something before they caught me, though what I could possibly do was a mystery to me. I laid my head on my hands and slept fitfully, my aching stomach waking me every few minutes with pangs of hunger. My throat was dry and my head pounded horribly, vying with my feet to be the greatest cause of my suffering.

Several hours must have gone by before I heard a voice in the distance. The rosy glow of sunset filtered in through the dirty window, causing the dust in the air to shimmer like flakes of gold. For a moment I watched it glitter, thinking how beautiful the shabby hovel had become in the dying light, then I moved on hands and knees to peer out the grimy panes of the window. Two men stood outside the next house, one of them gesturing wildly as he spoke. They were Verucan, but they were not soldiers, their clothing simple and homespun. I could not make out the words they were saying to each other, but one man finally stopped ranting and seemed to give up in the face of the other's resolve. His shoulders sagged a bit in defeat and he turned, marching into the house while the other waited out front. He emerged a few moments later with a pack slung over his shoulder. He was holding something in his hand that he lifted to his mouth and took a bite of. I could hear the sound of it crunching, see him chewing as the two men moved off, following the unkempt dirt road that snaked between the houses.

Food they have food there was food in that house there might still be food I am so hungry so hungry.

I was practically salivating at the thought of food being close by, and I watched them with growing agitation. Their journey down the path seemed to last for an eternity as I waited, hearing the satisfied crunch of his bite over and over in my head like a cruel taunt. Their distant figures finally faded against the horizon and I slipped out into the evening, hurrying as fast as my injured feet would allow. I pressed my ear to the door of the second house. There was nothing but silence from within. I twisted the handle, but it was locked, so I moved around to the shuttered window. These too had been locked, latched from the inside so I could not open them. I struggled vainly with the shutters for a few moments, trying to pry them open with my weak fingers, but they would not budge. There was no other way in. I went back to the front of the house and tried the door again, jerking on the stubborn handle, kicking ineffectually at the shabby frame, tears streaming down my face from frustration and from kicking with my injured feet. I gave up, my chest heaving from my efforts, and I sat on the dirty straw mat that lay before the door. Perhaps if I rested for a moment I could try again.

I might have fainted from hunger or simply fallen asleep, I could not be sure which, but I opened my eyes to find myself staring at the toes of a sturdy pair of boots caked in mud. My heart leaped into my throat and I pushed myself up slowly, lifting my chin cautiously till I was face to face with the man. He was older, perhaps the age my father would be had he lived, and his face was weathered and pock-marked, with heavy jowls dusted in grey stubble. His brown eyes widened a little upon seeing my own blue eyes, for he clearly was not expecting to find a starving Leharan sleeping on his doorstep. He opened his mouth to speak, but before he could say a word, I swung my small fist at his head with all the strength I could muster. He ducked out of the way of the ineffectual blow and I toppled forward, falling sideways into him.

"No!" I screamed, shoving my dirty fingers at his eye sockets as he grappled with me. He twisted me around, pinning my arms as I continued to scream and claw at him desperately, tearing at the dusty fabric of his shirt. "Let go of me!"

"Whoa, there. Calm down, girl. Stop screaming," he said steadily, giving me a small shake. "You'll need to be quiet now."

Don't hurt me let me go let me run I should have run I was foolish how could I fall asleep will he tell them will he send me back will he hurt me what do I do how can I get away run run run.

"Calm down. Do not cry. I will not hurt you, but I can't let you go if you keep attacking me like that." He stepped back, releasing my arms and I backed against the door, hugging myself tightly and trying to control the trembling that was wracking my body.

"Are you calm now?" he asked with a wary glance around, holding his hands up before him so that I could see he meant no harm. I nodded, then flinched when he stepped forward, reaching out. He backed away quickly, once more holding up his hands in peace. "I was only going to open the door. You have had a bad time of it, I can see that, but we cannot stay out here. There are soldiers from Veruca heading this way, and we need to get inside before they come. No use provoking them by standing out in plain sight."

"Soldiers? Coming here?" I pressed my clenched fists against the sides of my head.

They are coming for me they are coming to take me back Akrin is coming he will take me back and I will die there alone in the dark I don't want to die don't want to die alone.

The man reached past me and opened the door and I backed in, not taking my eyes off him. He lit a candle that sat on a wobbly table. The furnishings were meager and there was no fire burning in the hearth, but there was a small, sturdy wooden cot in one corner with a thin red blanket tossed over it. I wanted more than anything to curl up under that blanket, to close my eyes and just let everything fade, to hide in a safe cocoon and pretend that no one wanted to hurt me anymore.

I tore my eyes from the bed reluctantly and the man motioned to a small closet near the fireplace. He opened the slatted door, and my elation nearly overwhelmed me as I looked at the bounty that lay before us. There were bushels of oats, pears, raisins, a few leeks and cabbages. I forgot about the soldiers and everything else that was happening. I snatched one of the pears without hesitation and bit into it ravenously.

"Help yourself," the man said with irony. I felt my cheeks flush, but I did not care about my embarrassment or how feral I must have appeared to him. All I cared about was stopping the gnawing hunger in my gut. I reached out again, shoving a handful of raisins into my mouth.

"I can make a stew for us later, after the soldiers have gone," he offered me. "I saw them coming up the road and so I turned and came back here. Last time they came through and I was not here, they raided the place, stole my best horse and most of my goods. They don't come around too often and when they do, it is usually because they are after something. And I am guessing by that look in your eye you know what that something is, don't you?"

I gazed up at him, wiping my sticky mouth with the back of my hand. I did not answer, just stared with my wide Leharan eyes, so obviously out of place in their kingdom. He had to know it was me they were after, had to know that it was no coincidence I was here just as they were coming through. I wondered if he would give me to them, shoving another handful of food into my mouth as I pondered my fate in the hands of this stranger.

"Quiet, now." The man pressed a finger to his lips and I nodded, hearing the pounding of hooves beating the road outside. I fought the urge to press my hands over my ears at the jarring, metallic rattle of armor that shattered the quiet stillness of the evening. There was a loud whinny from one of the horses and their steps slowed to a walk. I could hear the soldiers dismount and then there was a moment of silence before a familiar voice called out.

"If there is anyone in this village, I order you to make yourself known!"

I could not stop my breath from coming in shallow gasps as panic churned and swelled in my stomach. It was him. Akrin was here. The man beside me made a gesture with his hand, urging me to be calm as he pushed me gently inside the pantry. I had to crouch to fit into the space, the fragile muscles of my aching legs screaming at me as he shut the slatted door.

"I am looking for a prisoner who has escaped!" Akrin continued to shout. "You there. Has any stranger come through here?"

"He is talking to some of the others," the man reported from the window where he had unlatched the shutter and let it fall open a fraction. "I will be back in just a moment."

"You cannot go out there!" I whispered desperately.

"I have to, or they will come in and search the house. I swear I will not tell them you are here," he vowed, his drooping face somber, distorted by the broken lines of the slatted door I watched him through.

"No, please. Please don't go out there," I begged.

He is going to leave me he will leave me and they will find me he will tell them even if he does not tell them they will come they will look they will find me and he will take me.

The man's tone was firm as he reached for the door. "Unless you want to make a run for it, which I do not recommend in your condition, this is the best way. Stay quiet."

He stepped out, leaving the door slightly ajar behind him to show he had nothing to hide and so I could hear what was said. Heavy boots came forward to meet him. I tried to see what was happening, squinting through the slats into the darkness outside, but the world was broken into fragments of light and dark that I couldn't make sense of and I was too afraid to move. My back ached where it was bent and I could feel my legs start to tremble with the effort of holding me up.

"Why did it take you so long to answer my summons?" Akrin demanded. His voice was so loud, so close. I could not breathe through the sound of his voice, it was suffocating me. It was as if the dungeon of Veruca was there in his voice. The chains, the filth, the misery. He had brought all of it with him in the angry and spiteful twist of his words. There was nowhere to hide. He would find me. He would walk up and open the door and find me and then he would put his hands around my throat, so small in his hands, and the black armor he wore would press against my skin and I would try not to look at his awful eyes, full of nothing but darkness. The only bright spark of hope I could hold on to was the knowledge that if Akrin was here, then he had not made it to Halig yet and the Oracle was still alive.

"I was washing up," the man said to the Verucans. "Just returning from a long ride."

"Is that so? Where were you riding from?"

I hated the way Akrin's voice sounded, the nasal bitterness of it laced with condescension. He knew the man was lying and Akrin was going to trap him, to taunt him and make him slip. Then he would find me.

"I went out to meet with some of the hunters. The herds are too thin and we are trying to save the ones who are left from those who kill without conscience," the man said, making it obvious that he was referring to the Verucan soldiers.

"The herds belong to Veruca. The hunters should know that, and so should you. You say you were washing yourself?"

The man must have nodded, for I heard no response from him. I was clenching my fists so tightly I felt my nails digging into my palms, trying to distract myself from my shaking legs. My thighs were cramping, the pain so immense that it brought tears to my eyes.

Akrin made a noise of disbelief. "You do not appear to be very clean for a man who was washing himself."

"Most likely because I was interrupted by your shouting."

Someone chuckled and my fear rose another notch.

Don't laugh at them who is laughing do not laugh at them they will get angry.

"I don't believe you," Akrin snarled. "Get out of the way."

There was a shuffle and a thump which made me wince. Then the man said, his firm voice but for the finest thread of fear, "You have no reason to enter my home."

"I did not ask for your permission." There was a scraping sound and I pressed my hands over my mouth, squinting through the narrow slat to see that Akrin had drawn a jagged black knife. "Get out of my way or I will cut your heart out and feed it to you."

"I have done nothing to provoke this violence and I will protest to the Queen," the man insisted stubbornly.

Akrin laughed, a dark, wicked sound. "Please do. And when you see Logaire, be sure and give her my warmest regards."

I felt as if my heart was in my throat choking me. He was coming. He was coming and there was nowhere for me to hide. He would open the door and I would just be standing there, waiting, pathetic and once again his prisoner. I wanted to squeeze my eyes shut, to not see the heavy boots that stomped into the room, causing the boards of the floor to creak and sending dust motes swirling around, like tiny sparkling creatures fleeing his cursed presence.

"You can see there is nothing here. If you would like to be on your way and leave me be, I would appreciate it," the man said. I wanted to yell at him to stop talking, to just remain silent, to not antagonize the horrible General any further. Akrin passed close to the door I was pressed against, his shadow snuffing out the angled strips of candlelight from the slats.

I thought I would die of fear. It was too much. He was too close. He would smell me. I could smell him. The sharp tang of Veruca clung to him, blood and sulfur and smoke. My legs were barely able to hold me, and I fought to keep from collapsing, my whole body shaking from the effort, every second that passed surely the last that I could stand.

"I was about to make a stew. Perhaps you would like some?" the man asked, sounding annoyed.

"We did not come here for food."

"Yes, well, I already told you I have not seen any prisoners running around here. So unless you would like to stay for my supper, I really cannot help you. Perhaps she went south to the coast, or into the forests of Kymir."

"I never said it was a woman." Akrin's voice lowered dangerously.

The man wiped his forearm across his face where he had begun to sweat, the fabric of his shirt scraping across his stubbled jowls. His eyes strayed to the pantry door and I willed him to look anywhere else, praying Akrin did not notice the glance. "He, she. It does not matter to me if it is a man, a woman or a horse, as it is none of my affair."

There was the sound of a scuffle and then Akrin's voice like hot metal, "Tell me where she is!"

"I swear I do not know," the man rasped. Akrin was holding him by the throat.

"Lie to me again and I cut out your tongue."

"She crossed through the fields behind us. Going south," the man choked out. I felt my own throat closing, as if that heavy fist was tightening around my neck instead of his.

"Why did you not say so sooner?"

"I did not realize that was who you were searching for when you asked about a prisoner. She was just a girl, and she seemed quite mad, kept blabbering to herself. I did not bother with her. I have troubles enough of my own."

"Perhaps I can help you with your troubles," Akrin offered. His voice was generous now, pleasant, as if he were offering a pretty gift wrapped in paper. It was more terrifying than his anger.

"No, I do not need your–"

There was a sound like a heavy, wet cough, and Akrin let out a hollow parody of laughter. "Now you will have no more troubles in this life. You, bring my horse. If she is wandering around the plains then we will find her soon enough."

I listened to them leave, still afraid to move, my body in so much pain that tears were streaming down my face. I had bitten my lip so hard I tasted blood. I expected the slatted door to be thrown open at any second, for the looming figure in black armor to leer down at me. My eyes searched the stripes of light, but there were only faded walls and empty air. I reached out, pushing open the door, lowering myself to the ground while I silently screamed in agony, trying not to collapse or make a sound. I stretched out my legs, the knotted muscles spasming in protest as I rubbed at them viciously, trying to stop the pain.

The man was slumped against the wall, a trail of blood smearing the wood behind his back and pooling on the floor surrounding him. His throat was cut from ear to ear and his drooping eyes were open and staring straight at me.

"I am so sorry," I whispered, clenching and unclenching my fists, not knowing what to do and feeling grief overwhelm me. He had tried to help me and now he was dead and I was alive and I did not know if I was awake or dreaming and I did not even know his name. "I am so sorry."

I scooted closer to him, not trusting my legs to hold me if I stood. I reached out with shaking fingers and averted my eyes as I pushed his eyelids closed. He was dead because of me. I had killed him. I pulled the tattered red blanket off the bed and wrapped it around myself, then I sat beside his lifeless body, leaning my head on his shoulder as I waited to wake up from the nightmare.

4

Logaire smoothed down the gossamer fabric of her gown, wincing as her hands passed over her bruised ribs. The woman who stared back at her in the mirror was not the proud and radiant Queen she was used to seeing. Instead, she saw a fearful, haunted woman she did not recognize. A woman who had almost died just a few hours before. Logaire closed her eyes, not wanting to see the unsettling visage that stared back at her. She took a breath, chastising herself for her weakness, willing herself to be strong. She had come so far, overcome so much to get where she was. She would not let that little weasel Akrin, of all people, take it from her.

The blood pulsed in her veins as she thought back to the night before. It felt as if a lifetime had passed since the attack, but it also felt like it had been mere seconds. If not for Jerric, she would be dead. Logaire felt a brief stab of remorse for the man who had sacrificed himself to save her. Jerric was a warrior, a soldier in the Verucan army. He was a natural leader and a vigorous lover, both qualities that Logaire appreciated in a companion. Jerric was younger than her, his senses sharper. He had heard a sound from the corridor, risen from her bed and picked up his sword, going to the door.

"Something is wrong," he said, glancing back at her, his handsome face drawn with worry.

"I'm sure it is nothing, darling. Come back to bed," she purred, tilting back the bedcovers in invitation.

"You should get dressed," he said. He made an impatient gesture, ignoring her enticing seductions.

Logaire flung the bed coverings off her naked body in irritation, but she did as he asked, hurrying to the wardrobe and wrapping herself hastily in a silk robe.

"Come. We need to take you somewhere safe," Jerric commanded, even though she was the Queen and the one who should give the orders. He reached out his hand and she took it, his skin warm and damp with sweat. She could not help the flutter of doubt that crept over her, and she wondered if this was it, if Akrin was finally coming for her after all these years.

"It could be nothing," Logaire protested again, more because she did not want it to be anything of consequence than any actual knowledge of the situation on her part. "One of the servants could be drunk again."

"These are not the sounds of a drunken servant," Jerric insisted. He cracked open the door and she knew instantly that he was right. The clatter of metal and armor echoed through the castle. The sounds of men fighting. She glanced in horror down the hallway as Akrin appeared from the shadows, his beady eyes fixed on her.

"Logaire."

She shuddered at the sound of her name on his lips, at the satisfaction that laced his voice. Her initial fears had been correct. Akrin had finally come for her.

"Go, run!" Jerric shouted at her, dropping her hand and gripping his sword, spreading his feet apart in a fighting stance. Logaire did not hesitate. Turning abruptly, she fled down the hallway, her mind racing to determine her next move, where she could go that would be safe. If she tried to hide in one of the other chambers and Akrin found her, she would be trapped. She could keep running, searching for more of her soldiers to shield her, but the uncertainty of their loyalty to the man who led them made her hesitate. Akrin was their General, some of them would undoubtedly align themselves with him and she would have no way of knowing who they had pledged their allegiance to until it was too late.

Logaire screamed aloud, not out of fear but frustration. She should have killed Akrin a long time ago. Sybylla had practically begged her to, and even Vishram had finally agreed. The Oracle was powerful enough. Logaire no longer needed Akrin to inspire loyalty through fear. But Logaire had hesitated. Though she would never have admitted it to anyone, she was jealous of the Oracle, of the mindless devotion of Sybylla's followers. She worried that putting all her faith in the woman would turn out to be a mistake, that Sybylla would betray her, or worse, the Oracle would grow more powerful than her. It was the same reason Logaire refused to leave the girl, Eolande, in Halig. She could not trust anyone with such power, and so she had waited, hesitated, kept Akrin at her side, knowing what a monster he was. Now she would pay for that mistake.

Logaire stopped running at the end of the hallway, dared to look over her shoulder, shoving her mane of copper hair out of her face. Jerric was fighting with the General, his sword slashing furiously. Logaire felt her throat tighten as she watched. It was obvious Jerric was no match for Akrin. She turned away. She could not help him and there was no point in both of them dying. It would only render Jerric's death meaningless. She gave them one last look, then she turned the corner and nearly collided with a group of soldiers rushing at her.

Logaire halted once more, her eyes raking over the men, trying to read their faces beneath the black helmets. Were they loyal to her? Had they come to protect her, or were they Akrin's men sent there to kill her?

"Get her out of here! Protect the Queen!" one of them suddenly yelled, reaching out and shoving Logaire roughly behind him and knocking her against the solid black armor of another soldier. Akrin was coming.

"Logaire!" he called out, his voice taunting, playful. She looked up, past the men who were now guarding her, seeing the red blood dripping from his sword, the gore splattered across his chest. Jerric was dead at his feet. A grotesque smile played on Akrin's face and his dark eyes shone with malice. "Enough of these games. I want to speak with you about your little prize you have hidden down in the dungeons. You have been keeping too many secrets and now I want the truth."

He knew about Eolande. Panic swelled in her. If he took Eolande, the most powerful being on Imbria, there would be no stopping him. Logaire turned to the man she had just collided with, praying that he could be trusted. "Go to the dungeons, now! There is a girl there. You must protect her. Whatever you do, do not let anyone take her. If you cannot protect her, then kill her before you let them take her. Go!"

The man broke away from the other soldiers, his footsteps echoing down the corridor as he rushed back the way they had come. Logaire spun to face Akrin once more, debating if she should run, if the soldiers would hold him off long enough for her to get away.

The General made a sound of disapproval. "There is no use running from me, Logaire. The time has come for you to reap what you have sown. All these years, all these lies. You must atone for what you have done."

"You are making a mistake, Akrin!" Logaire shouted at him, her voice imperious despite the waver in it. "If you try to kill me, I promise you will not leave here alive!"

He laughed, a dark and malevolent sound that sent a chill down her spine in spite of the heat that blanketed the castle. He was about to say something more when a cacophony arose behind her. The sound of voices reverberated in their direction, and the soldiers protecting her shouted back in response. Reinforcements were coming. Logaire thought she would cry, so great was her relief. She watched as Akrin's horrid face darkened with the realization that he would not be killing her this night. His lip curled in disdain and she would never forget the look on his face at that moment. It was the look of pure evil, of a hatred and darkness so immense that no light would ever reach it.

"I will come back for you, Logaire," he swore. "This is not over."

He and his men retreated down the corridor, Logaire's soldiers swarming after him as they flooded around her.

She learned later that Akrin had escaped, and it infuriated her beyond reason. The man who delivered the news to her had flinched at the string of curses she had hurled upon him. His name was Yaran, one of her newly appointed advisors selected for her by Vishram himself. Yaran had a shaved head that gleamed in the torchlight and a hooked nose that sprouted a robust mustache beneath it. The mustache was currently quivering ridiculously as he tried to find the words to assuage her anger, but in the end he simply lowered his head and waited in silence. Logaire rose from her dressing table and crossed her chambers to stand before one of the tall windows that overlooked her kingdom. She flattened her hands on the stone sill, pressing them against the black rock to stop them from shaking. If Akrin was alive, then it was not over.

"And the girl?" she asked. Her stomach twisted in knots.

Yaran's eyes lifted briefly, then swept back down to the ground, and she knew the answer before he said the words. "We cannot find her."

Logaire pressed her hands harder onto the stone sill, wanting to crush it beneath her fingers. "Find Akrin and kill him. I want his head on a spike for this! Send a hawk with a message to Halig. Make sure the Oracle knows what has transpired here and tell them we will send soldiers to protect her."

Yaran blanched at her words, and she felt the knots in her stomach tighten. He wrung his hands together, clearly wishing that someone else was there to tell the Queen of Veruca all the things that she did not wish to hear.

"My Queen..." he began, hesitating. "The General... the messenger..."

"For the love of Imbria, say it already!" she snapped at him, her voice shrill. She took a breath, brushing back the strands of hair that framed her face, feeling the lines deepen between her brows, inwardly cursing Akrin for being the reason for the depth of those lines. She needed to be calm. To remain in control. The people needed to believe that what had transpired in the castle was a minor incident, that their Queen was still in command and in power. "I am sorry, Yaran. Please, proceed with what you were saying."

Yaran rubbed a hand over the gleaming dome of his head, his mustache trembling. "Perhaps I should show you."

She wanted to throw something at his shining skull, but she refrained, smiling instead and nodding in encouragement. "Very well. Be quick about it."

"Of course, my Queen."

He ushered her out of her chambers and she was instantly surrounded by a dozen soldiers who were now posted outside her door. They moved with her, forming a protective wall around her as Yaran led them to the outer terrace where the falconer kept his flock.

Logaire nearly screamed again, barely controlling her temper as she stared down at the dead falconer with her lips pressed tightly together. The corpse of the handler was ringed with the carcasses of his dead birds, their necks broken, the floor littered with feathers and blood. They would be sending no messages to Halig or anywhere else.

The Queen spun to face one of the men who guarded her. "Go and gather men to ride to Halig. We must protect the Oracle at all costs."

5

I stood staring at the smoking ruins, tears streaming down my face. I knew when Akrin had ridden out from the tiny village on his powerful horses that there was no way I could reach the temple first, but some tiny part of me had still hoped. That flicker of hope had kept me going, mercilessly plodding along the well-worn road, flinging myself down to the ground and ducking behind large rocks whenever I thought I heard anyone coming. I refused to stop until I reached Halig and warned the Oracle. Now I stood on the little hill that overlooked the temple courtyard, knowing that I had failed and I would find only death inside those gilded walls.

I watched and listened, seeing nothing moving in the ransacked courtyard. Akrin and his men must have already departed. I began to make my way down the hill, avoiding the road and pressing myself into shadows and crevices as I drew closer to the temple. The majestic statue that stood before the entryway had been toppled, and I stepped over the shattered hand of whatever god had inspired the marble creation, approaching the open doorway.

Run run away Eolande do not go in do not go in there turn and go leave do not go in there is death in there only death.

I shook my head, wanting to silence the thoughts that were tearing at my brain. I slipped in through the doorway, paused, listened again, my eyes adjusting to the dark interior. There were bodies everywhere and I pressed my hands over my mouth as my feet felt the cool, sticky edges of the pool of blood that had collected on the floor. I backed away from it, retreating into the narrow swathe of light that angled in through the open door.

"Sybylla!" I tried to call out, but my voice was nothing more than a rasping wheeze. I wanted to turn, to listen to the voices in my head telling me to run, but I forced myself to stay. I took a breath and wove my way through the bodies. There were temple guards strewn among the corpses of the acolytes, their bodies hacked apart viciously and without mercy. I did not bother to stop and see if any remained alive, for there was no way that anyone could survive what Akrin had done to them.

I made it through the sea of bodies to the interior of the temple, where I followed the long hallway that led to the Oracle's private chambers. Sunlight filtered in through the skylights that had been cut into the temple roof, the colorful glass throwing a kaleidoscope of dazzling beams around the room. My heart twisted, aching in my chest as I picked my way over the pile of temple guards who must have gathered inside the doorway to protect Sybylla. Blood was everywhere, splashing the walls, painting everything in dark streaks that seemed to swallow the dancing sunlight.

I found her lying on her side and for a moment, hope flared within me and I believed she had survived. There was no blood on her, no wounds, and her face was peaceful and serene, as if she were sleeping. Then I saw the cup that had rolled from her hand when she fell, and the tangle of herbs stuck to the inside, still damp from the tea she had mixed them with. She had poisoned herself, knowing that death by her own hand would be swift and painless. I knelt beside her, rolling her onto her back and smoothing her bright orange hair away from her face. My fingers touched the skin of her neck and it was cold. There was no heartbeat, no trick of the herbs hiding her life. She was gone.

I stared at her for a long time, this woman who had been a captor of mine, but who had also been the closest thing I had to a friend. I wondered if she deserved to die for the things she had done, or if the gods would forgive her for her lies and her mistakes. Would they forgive any of us? Did they even care?

I remembered a time Sybylla had come to me in my small chamber, a piece of sweetmilk cake in her hands. She held it out to me, as if she was bestowing a great honor upon me. I took it from her, more out of curiosity than because I wanted it. I did not like sweet things. There was something about the cloying taste that I found unsettling, as if the flavor was from another world that I was not a part of.

"I made it myself," the Oracle announced, her tawny eyes sparkling. "It has been years since I have cooked anything for myself. I did not realize how much I missed it."

She sat on the hard bed beside me, motioning for me to eat. I took a small bite, the flicker of a smile touching my lips for her benefit as she watched eagerly. There were deep lines that creased her face, and her chin seemed to have sunk even further into her throat, causing her to constantly lean towards whomever she was speaking to in order to compensate for it. Sometimes she reminded me of one of the hens the gamekeeper kept on the little farm beside the temple. I was never allowed to go to the farm, but I would climb on top of the gaudy furniture that littered the sacred chamber, pulling myself up and standing on the tips of my toes until I could see through the skylights. I would find the clearest pieces of stained glass, watching the world below with a longing so intense that it was physically painful. I felt a kinship with the animals of the farm, trapped by their fences until it was time for them to be slaughtered.

"I have been clever lately, and I have given the nobles some tasty morsels of information that will make them pester our Queen for days, if not weeks," Sybylla had told me, speaking in hushed tones and craning her face towards me, as if we were two sisters whispering secrets so our parents would not overhear.

I took another bite of the cake, trying not to be repulsed by the sticky sweetness of it on my tongue and watching her with a guarded expression.

Sybylla laughed, patting my leg. "That means Logaire will be too busy dealing with them to think about you. You will be safe here with us for a while longer, Eolande."

She stood and left, leaving me holding the unwanted cake, wishing I could be grateful for her efforts but knowing that it was not enough. Eventually, I would have to go back, but it was kind of her to try to delay the inevitable, and to bring me the cake. They were rare, those moments when we were alone and she treated me like someone who mattered, but they had been something for me to cling to. Without her and Vishram, I was sure I would have gone mad years ago, unable to silence the roaring of my own thoughts that overwhelmed me in my desolation.

I brought myself back to the present, returning to the horror of the massacred temple. I folded Sybylla's cold hands over her chest, then turned, pushing away the stiff limbs of the dead soldiers so there was a hallowed space around her. I stood looking down at her, wanting to feel something more than the numb emptiness that settled over me. I whispered goodbye, touching her hands one last time before leaving the chamber. There was nothing left for me there, no reason to linger. I paused outside the door, then ducked back in, scurrying back over the bodies and sliding the Oracle's soft slippers off of her feet. She no longer needed them, but I did.

6

My entire body filled with loneliness as I watched a caravan of wagons tumble down the road. I was hidden among the tall stalks of brown grass that bordered their path, close enough that I could have reached out and touched the travelers had I been brave enough. A small child laid its head in the warm curve of a woman's neck and I experienced such an intense longing for companionship, for love of any kind, that my chest ached with it. I wondered what would happen if I stood and went to them, asked them for help. They seemed like kind people. They smiled at each other as they bumped along the pitted road. I imagined walking up to them, feeling the young mother put her arms around me in comfort, knowing the sweetness of being held close. I nearly wept with the desire to stand and call out to her, to feel her soft hair on my cheek and her soothing voice in my ear. But I did not stand. I remained hidden in the grass till they were gone and then I stepped back onto the rough dirt road in the Oracle's tattered slippers to continue my solitary journey.

I thought about my childhood home as I walked. I would have given anything to go back to the place where I had briefly known happiness as a small child, back to our little cabin in the woods, where Gideon had been my whole world and we had laughed and sang. Even though I knew that home was gone, that Gideon was dead and our world was a sweep of ashes, part of me desperately wanted to believe that he would be there, our beautiful little cottage still intact and smelling of fresh bread. He would be waiting for me, sitting at the table with supper ready and wondering what was taking me so long.

It is not real he is dead they are all dead everyone who cared about you is dead.

I was trying to shake the visions out of my head, to remind myself they weren't real. It was too easy to get lost in those waking dreams.

I kept walking, slipping in and out of the living dreams until my head pounded with the effort to remember what was real and what was not. I kept seeing the Oracle on the floor in the temple, her bright orange hair spilling around her. Each time I pictured it in my mind I would feel a rush of panic, worried that she had merely been asleep and I had abandoned her. I would remind myself of how cold she was, how I had let my hand linger over her lips, wanting to feel the faintest touch of breath but feeling nothing. Sybylla would fade and then I would see Akrin, his small, dark eyes gleaming with his perverse desire for pain. I kept imagining him behind me, sneaking up on me as I plodded along, and I would spin around, searching the vast plains in terror.

The food I took from Halig had run out quickly. I was small and weak; I could only carry so much. I was once again hungry and fatigued, worn down beyond endurance, yet somehow I kept going. I was standing in front of our cabin. It was such a lovely little house in a lovely village, small, with three steps leading up to the door. But we did not live in a village, we lived in the forest. I shook my head, trying to clear my confused mind. My mother was inside, waiting for me. I had no mother. I reached for the door and pushed it open, my face breaking into a smile as I waited for the solid embrace of my father to envelop me. I opened my mouth to greet them and suddenly the world fell apart. There was a woman, but she was not my mother and she was screaming. There was also a man who was not my father. He was not trying to help me. He was knocking me down to the ground, and there was a child crying, a little child with red hair and eyes like warm tea, his round little mouth forming a perfect pink circle as he wailed. I tried to tell them it was a mistake, but I could not speak. My breath had been knocked out of me when the man had shoved me onto my back. I turned over, crawling on my hands and knees, tumbling down the shabby front steps and landing in a heap in the dirt. Then there were more hands grabbing at me, hateful hands with chipped and broken nails. Someone splashed cold water on my face and I heard gasps, felt the soot that had darkened my hair sliding down my skin. I was trying to untangle their voices, to sort out what was happening, the sooty water burning my eyes. One word seemed to stand out, and I heard it cried out repeatedly as they hauled me to my feet and pushed me forward. They were yelling "Leharan" over and over as if it were an insult.

"No, no, please, I have to keep going," I mumbled. It was as if a fog had fallen over my mind and I could not grasp what was happening fast enough to prevent it. They were tying my hands and I was sobbing, the rope tightening on my scarred wrists until I screamed, not from pain, but from the memories it brought rushing back. I was right, I had been dreaming and now I was finally waking up and I was back in the dungeon and they would hurt me and I screamed and screamed with everything in me, with rage and terror and longing and shame. The people surrounding me fell back in shock at my wild howling, but then one of them mustered his courage and stepped forward, punching me solidly in the gut. I gasped for air and hit my knees, my screams silenced. They jerked me back up and continued to push me forward, and as the haze lifted, I looked back at the village. The houses seemed to shrink and darken, the luster of my tortured mind fading to reveal a cluster of poorly built shacks, patched together with mismatched pieces of wood and dried mud bricks. I was shoved through a doorway and forced into a dim corner. It smelled of livestock and there was hay strewn over the ground.

The villagers were momentarily silent, seemingly at a loss as to how they should proceed with me. They turned, backing out of the stable where I had been deposited and speaking to each other in frantic whispers. I was too tired to care what they said. I pulled my knees to my chest, resting my head on them and closing my eyes. It seemed like only seconds had passed before I was shaken awake.

"What are you doing here? What have you come for?" a man demanded. He was squatting in front of me, regarding me as if I were a strange animal he had never seen before. I could not tell how old he was. He had the weathered, aged look of someone who had toiled hard for most of their life, the years of strife masking any semblance of youth from his harsh countenance.

"Water," I gasped, trying to clear the confusion from my mind. I thought I had just rested my head for a moment, but I could see through the stable door he had left ajar that it was morning and I must have slept for hours. The man seemed disgusted by my meager request and he motioned to where a woman stood watching. It was the woman from the cottage, the one who had screamed when I entered her home. I wanted to apologize to her, but her lips were pressed into a thin line that offered no sympathy for my plight, so I remained silent. She came forward begrudgingly, tilting a clay jar to my lips.

The water was disgusting, tepid and thick, with the smell of animal hide lingering on it. I drank anyway, swallowing huge gulps as it dribbled down my chin, staining the dirt floor in a dark circle.

"Enough," the man said, pushing the jar away from my grasping hands as I tried to hold on to it. He grabbed a handful of my matted hair, jerking it back to expose my face. I could tell from the look in his eyes that he wanted me to be afraid of him, but he carried none of the darkness that I had learned to fear. His voice was weak and powerless. It echoed with its own futility, trying to be something that it was not. It was the voice of someone who had given up on life a long time ago, who trudged bitterly through the monotonous days of their existence.

"I did not mean to intrude," I tried to tell him, knowing it was futile. He did not care what I had done or why I had done it. The only thing that mattered to him was having someone beneath him, someone he could frighten and intimidate, so that he could feel alive again.

"Leharans are not welcome here," he practically growled.

"Then let me leave. I have no wish to be here."

He was amused, glancing over at the woman who smiled knowingly, as if she held a treasured secret. "We have heard the Verucan soldiers are searching the countryside for someone, and we have already sent men to the nearest town to tell them about you. With any luck, you will fetch us a handsome reward, girl! Queen Logaire loves to put a price on people's heads and I have heard that she pays her debts fairly!"

They seemed delighted by the idea that they had found a new source of wealth, and I had to wait a moment for my panic to subside before I could respond, pleading, "You have to let me go. It is General Akrin who will come, and he will kill everyone here. He will kill you just for laying eyes on me. You don't understand what has been happening at the castle. Let me go. Tell them you did not see anyone, that it was a mistake."

The man laughed, slapping his hands down on the threadbare knees of his worn trousers. "So, it is you they are after."

"I told you!" the woman was smug.

"That you did," the man relented. He looked me over, squinting one eye, his face creasing into deep folds. "Go and fetch her something to eat. We cannot have her dying before we collect our reward!"

7

The villagers came back the next day, gathering around the decrepit little stable where I was locked away. I could hear them whispering to each other, growing bolder as the day dragged on.

"We should just send her on her way. The Verucan soldiers will bring trouble, they always do," someone said, a thread of fear weaving through their voice.

"Burn her!" another voice rose.

"Not until we find out what the reward is and what this Leharan wants from us."

"I will get it out of her."

The door to the stable opened and the slack-jawed group of villagers crowded into the narrow opening, leering at me.

I closed my eyes. I knew what was coming. One last beating and this is how I would die. Tied up and a prisoner, just as I had always feared. Perhaps it was my fate to die this way. It did not matter if I was here, or in a dream, or if I was in Veruca or where I was, the end was the same. I wondered what it would feel like. Would the pain stop? Would I forget about my blistered feet and my raw throat and my tortured, starved stomach? Would there be blissful silence?

One of the men came forward, grabbing the ties that bound my wrists and hauling me to my feet. He did not seem to know what to do with me once I was standing, and he looked around for inspiration, clearly not having thought his plan all the way through. He finally seemed to decide on a course of action, and he shoved me through the crowd and out into the glaring sun. I blinked rapidly, trying to adjust to the blinding light as I was led to a tree, pressed against it while he looped another rope around me.

The man grabbed my hair, demanding to know who I was and wrenching my neck at an awful angle that made speaking nearly impossible. I shook my head to try to dislodge his hand, and he shoved my face into the rough bark of the tree trunk. I could feel it scrape my skin and blood pooled from my bottom lip.

I tensed, waiting for the blow I was sure was coming and steeling myself not to cry out. I wanted my death to be quiet. Gideon would be proud of a quiet death.

The first blow felt like fire across my skin and I managed to swallow my scream. I could not tell what he was hitting me with, but by the third assault I could not hold back any longer and an agonized wail burst from my lips. I slumped forward and closed my eyes, waiting for the next blow and the one after that and however many more would lead to the silence I longed for.

"Do not strike her again," a new voice spoke. It was a woman's voice, but it was different from any I had ever heard. I lifted my head and my eyes flew open. This was not the voice of a life-worn drudge or a toiling villager. This was not a voice that held fear or weakness. This was the sound of violence and promise, like a sharpened blade as it slid from a sheath.

"You would do well to be on your way, stranger," sneered the villager who had been beating me. I was struggling against the bindings that pressed me to the tree, desperate to see who this new sound belonged to. At the edge of my vision I could see two figures, thin cloaks pulled up to obscure their faces in shadow.

The gathered crowd began to rumble in protest at the interruption, and the woman's voice rose again, silencing them and demanding to know, "What has this woman done?"

"She tried to steal my children!" It was the woman from the house. The one who had smiled knowingly at me in the stables, gloating over the reward I would soon fetch.

One of the hooded figures approached me and I wriggled my body again, scraping my cheek against the trunk so that whoever it was would not see my wretched face, stained with tears and dirt. I did not know why, but I felt shamed before them, these strangers I had yet to see but who had stopped me from being beaten.

"Did you do as she accuses?" the other stranger asked me. It was a man, his voice clear and violent.

"No," I whispered.

"Why does she think you were stealing her children? Were you trying to hurt them?"

I felt tears burn in my eyes. "I was confused. I have not eaten for days, and I only slept for brief moments. I did not know what I was doing. I thought it was my father's house. I just wanted to go home, but I forgot he was dead and I have no home."

The hooded figure turned to address the small throng of gaping villagers, focusing on the man who was my assailant. "You would beat and accuse a starving woman who needed help? You are disgusting. Cut her loose, you pig-headed coward!"

"Who are you to order us? This is our land, and she is a trespasser! A filthy Leharan one at that."

"You would do well to shut your foul mouth and heed his words as they are accompanied by my sword," the woman threatened, and I heard the metallic scrape of a weapon being drawn from its scabbard.

"Besides, I am a filthy Leharan myself," the man said, pushing back the hood of his cloak. There was a collective gasp from the villagers and they looked around, as if expecting the entire Leharan population to come swarming into their midst. I craned my head back to look at him in awe, never having expected another Leharan to come to my aid. He was tall, virile, his pale hair cut short on the sides but left long on the top, a shock of white that fell over his forehead. He had high cheekbones and full lips, the angular features that were so distinctive of the islanders.

The woman beside him also threw back her hood, relishing in the shock that her Tahitian appearance caused amongst the villagers.

"You may kill them," the young man offered with a gallant bow at the terrifying woman who was his companion. "I know how much you enjoy slaughtering vermin."

She grinned, and I could see that her eyeteeth had been filed to sharpened points, standing out in stark contrast to her darkened skin. Her black eyes glittered as she assessed the villagers. She shook her head, stepping back and waving an arm at the young man. "They are not worthy of me. You may kill them. Besides, it has been days since you have taken a head. I killed the last group on my own, if you recall."

Her companion shrugged. "That was because it would have been over too quickly if I had joined you. Please, I insist. Today, you may do the killing."

The villagers began to back away in fear and I wanted to laugh at the whole ridiculous scene, but I was distracted by the subtle shake of the Leharan's head. His pale hair parted for a moment on the left side of his face and I saw the dark leather band that covered one eye. His other eye met mine, grey like steel, and I gasped aloud. I knew him. I could never have forgotten him. Kaeleb. It was the boy from the islands, the boy who had fought so hard to save me all those years before.

I know you you were supposed to help me I wanted you to come for me but you never came no one ever came you forgot me and I was alone for all those years alone alone alone but I know your face why are you here how did you know to come for me now after all these years why now.

"You," I breathed in awe, only able to form a single word from the cascade of thoughts that were tumbling through my mind. Kaeleb grinned, clearly pleased at my recognition.

"So, you remember me?" he asked, leaning on his sword as if he were not facing an angry mob.

"You were just a boy... you were supposed to protect me."

His face clouded over and then darkened. He opened his mouth to say something else, hesitated, closed it again.

"Fine, I will kill them," the Tahitian woman announced, interrupting us. She lifted her sword and the villagers scattered, fleeing in fear, all except for the man who had beaten me. He hesitated, looking around for help, though there was none to be had. His mob of bullies had retreated and he was left alone, facing the two warriors.

"Did he hurt you?" Kaeleb asked me quietly. There was something in his voice, a calm that was so deadly, so intense, that it was like a storm rolling in on the horizon. I stared at him, wide-eyed, and he repeated the question.

"Eolande, did he hurt you?"

There was no need to answer. He could see my split lip, the blood on my face, the bruise darkening my eye.

The man from the village was visibly shaking as he hurriedly worked to free me from the tight grip of the rope that was pressing me against the tree. I felt the pressure on my waist ease and I stepped away, kicking off the coil of rope that fell at my feet. His sweaty hands gripped my bound wrists before I could run, as if he could not bring himself to relinquish such a prize. "I did not know she was with you. I swear it. I barely touched her-"

His voice was cut off in a wet gurgle as the Leharan side-stepped and spun, his sword slicing through the space between us, severing the man's head from his neck. I looked down in horror, then quickly looked away, squeezing my eyes shut.

"Pathetic," the Tahitian woman said, spitting on the headless corpse as it collapsed. The dead man was still holding onto me and my arms were nearly wrenched from their sockets as he fell. I managed to pull myself out of his morbid grasp, stumbling forward before the young man caught me with a gentle arm. He pulled a curved knife from his belt, cutting my bindings, and his fingers lingered on the abraded skin of my wrist, as if he wished to wipe away the marks.

"You killed him," I whispered, feeling tears fill my eyes.

He looked confused, dropping his hands, his grey eye narrowing as he tried to understand why I was upset. "Did you not wish him dead?"

"No," I said, my voice barely a breath. "I do not want anyone to die because of me."

The woman scoffed. "That is a foolish sentiment, girl, and one you should rid yourself of quickly. You are the Solvrei. If the prophecy is true, then most of Imbria is going to die because of you."

I was stricken, staring at her in horror. That was not what Vishram had told me.

I can save people I am supposed to save them to make things better not hurt them I don't want to hurt anyone else I am the Solvrei I am supposed to help them I don't want any of this.

The woman frowned back at me. "Do you think she is mad?"

"She is not mad," Kaeleb spoke with quiet confidence as I wiped at my eyes, choking back the sob that was caught in my throat. "We need to leave. Those villagers will be arming themselves or sending someone for help, and the last thing we need are Verucan soldiers showing up here."

He reached out his hand and took mine, though I saw the wary look that crossed his face just before he touched me. He remembered my power.

His grip was warm and solid, his fingers strong and callused, rough from the use of a sword. I jerked my hand away from his grasp, irrationally angry at the feel of his skin against my own. I tried to walk, despising my own weakness and the pitiful condition of my feet, hating it when my knees buckled beneath me. He nonchalantly watched, his eyebrow raised above the one seeing eye, then he extended his hand once more. I glared at his proffered hand, but despite my insensible anger at him, he was better than the murderous villagers who had wanted to burn me, or the Verucan soldiers who would soon be there. I begrudgingly took his hand, letting him pull me behind him to where their horses waited. He lifted me onto the saddle, swinging up to sit behind me.

"Perhaps she wanted to ride with me," the Tahitian woman said, amusement coloring her words. She gave Kaeleb a knowing look and laughed. Then he spurred his horse, galloping over the rolling fields to the south.

8

"We will be safe here," Kaeleb murmured near my ear. I could feel the muscles of his legs working to guide the horse into the dark thicket. We were at the border of Kymir, and there was an air of desolation that hung over the forest like a thick fog. It was almost as if the world itself was trying to scream at us to stay away, the massive tangles of thorny vines warning us away from whatever lay within.

"These are the Earth Keeper's lands," Chaote said from ahead of us, practically spitting the words through gritted teeth. Kaeleb had told me who she was as we were riding away from the village, and it was obvious that the former leader of the Fomori held no love for the woman who was my aunt. "She has poisoned everything with her corrupt power."

"How can we be safe here?" I asked with a shudder. As we passed beneath the canopy of trees, I noticed they were not as they should be. The branches were gnarled, warped and twisted, with great spiked protrusions and strange, hideous pulsing lumps. I was horrified. I had grown up in the forests of Kymir, and I had never seen trees like this.

Kaeleb sensed my unease and started to draw a protective arm around me, an instinctive gesture of comfort that was halted when he felt me grow rigid beneath him. He relaxed, resting his hands lightly back on his thighs, the reins loose in them. He smelled of dust, of trees and campfires and sand and snow, as if he were part of all of Imbria and I did not know why I found it so infuriating.

"Maialen never comes here," he said lightly. "Veruca is an ally. They are no threat to her and she considers them weak, beneath her. She does not bother wasting resources on patrolling the border. Besides, this time of year she is usually in Samirra."

"With her traitor husband," Chaote added bitterly.

"The Guardian?" I asked.

Chaote spun around in her saddle to glare at me with a look so full of malice that I flinched beneath it. Her dark features carried an immense wrath and I could see her fists were clenched tightly on the reins of her horse. "Do not mention that man in my presence, unless it is to deliver me his head."

I nodded, swallowing hard, wondering what the Samirran Guardian had done to provoke such a savage response in the warrior.

"Don't mind her. She is not as awful as she likes people to believe," Kaeleb whispered to me with a chuckle. Chaote shot him a glare of her starry eyes, then settled back into the saddle.

"It will be getting dark soon. We should make camp," she tossed over her shoulder. She began to lead us away from the overgrown path, her horse picking its way through the thicket until we were completely surrounded by the forest, a dark cocoon of trees enveloping us.

Kaeleb swung himself off the horse, reaching up to help me. I ignored him, clambering awkwardly down from the saddle on my own and nearly falling flat on my back as one of my feet caught in the stirrup. I managed to steady myself as the sun faded behind the trees and the small clearing was stained with blots of color from the sky, red and purple that dappled over the dark green foliage. I watched the way the fading light shone off Kaeleb's pale hair and proud features. The golden tint of his skin, the high cheekbones and hooded eye, so distinctly Leharan. I had not seen many of my people, certainly not for several years, and I was surprised by how much I wanted to continue staring at him. He noticed my scrutiny, mistaking my gaze.

"It is not as bad as you'd think," he said, tossing me a grin. "Having one eye, I mean."

"He kept your eye. Akrin. He used to show it to me when he wanted to make me cry. When I was a girl. Before they killed me," I told him, my face flushing at how ridiculous it all sounded, wishing I had not said it aloud.

The grin faded from Kaeleb's face. "Eolande, if I had known you were alive all these years, I would have come for you. I was there when you died. We tried to stop them but we were too late and after it was over, I even made them show me your face. I had to make sure you were really dead."

A knot choked my throat. "You were there?"

He nodded and shadows of guilt passed over his proud features. "My father and I tried to save you."

"Your father... the Fire Keeper?" I asked. He nodded, the edges of his hair parting to reveal a glimpse of the leather band that covered his eye. What had happened back then was not his fault. He had been a child himself. I knew that in my heart, and I wanted to tell him so, but I could not bring myself to say the words. I was still so angry and there was nowhere else for me to direct the pain and the rage that burned inside of me for having been forgotten for so long. Instead, I told him, "The Queen made me drink something, herbs that would put me into a deep sleep so I would appear to be dead."

He continued to watch me, his face unreadable. Then Chaote unceremoniously dumped a sleeping mat between us.

"You can use mine. I will sleep on the ground," she said. I started to protest but she cut me off with a sharp wave of her hand. "I am the Mother of the Fomori, the greatest warrior on Imbria, the one who conquered Samirra. Do not question me when I give an order."

Kaeleb laughed. "Bacatha would be quite displeased to hear you claim the title of the greatest warrior."

Chaote shrugged, her golden armor gleaming beneath the thin cape as she removed it from her shoulders. "The Leharan is skilled, but I am still the greatest."

She rolled the cape and placed it behind her, leaning back on it. Kaeleb spread his blanket on the ground, motioning for me to do the same. Then he rummaged in his pack, proudly displaying a wrapped bundle of food and opening it between us. There were a few apples, salted meat, a potato, and a handful of carrots. He distributed them amongst us and Chaote ate in silence, fixed on the darkness as if we were not even there. I could hardly see her as night fell over the forest, the barest edge to her perfection visible in the faint light of the stars that echoed her eyes.

"Why did you not try to escape?" Kaeleb asked me suddenly, speaking over a mouthful of apple.

I swallowed the bite of carrot I was chewing and looked down at my dirty hands, the nails cracked and brittle. I wanted to scream at him that I did try, to hit him over the head with something for believing I had not. "I tried many times. They always caught me."

"But your power," he began. I lifted my head, my blue eyes meeting his one, grey like steel.

"They put a Warding Stone in me."

Chaote was suddenly attentive, whipping her gaze around to stare at me with avarice, as if I were something to be devoured. "You have a Warding Stone?"

I nodded slowly, wondering if I had made a mistake in telling them. Perhaps this was all a mistake and I was a fool to trust them, to trust the boy.

You do not know him you barely knew him ten years before it is too long too much time you have no idea what sort of man he has become and she is the halfbreed the one sent to kill you will they kill you will they take you back to your prison take the stone from you leave you there bleeding leave you there to die alone always alone.

"Eolande." My name on his lips pulled me out of the rising panic of my thoughts. I stared at him, wide eyed. He spoke as if he could hear the voice that clamored insistently inside my head. "We will not hurt you."

"Where is it?" Chaote asked. I motioned to my back. She stood and walked over to me, waving at Kaeleb. He obediently turned away from us as she commanded, "Show me."

I glanced at the back of his head, barely visible in the rising light of the moon that filtered through the trees. Then I slipped off the shoulders of my ragged dress, clutching the front of it against me as it fell down, revealing the knotted scar on my back. Chaote reached out and her fingertips were warm, the sensation strange against my skin as she ran her gentle touch over the wound. It was almost like a caress, something I would not expect from the fierce warrior who seemed so cold. Then she pulled up the back of my dress and returned to where she had been sitting.

"It is buried deep beneath her skin. We will take her to Gula," Chaote announced.

Kaeleb turned to us, his eye narrowing slightly as he watched me lower myself back onto the blanket. He seemed displeased, his face pinched and his eyebrows drawn together. "Gula is on Tahitia."

"I am aware," was Chaote's quiet reply. "But this is the Solvrei and we must be careful. We can trust Gula."

Kaeleb sighed heavily. "And if Maialen finds out that my mother is helping us, there is no telling what she will do."

Chaote laughed and it was a rich, throaty sound that wrapped around you like an embrace. "The Earth Queen's jealousies cannot dictate our actions any longer. It is enough that she has forced your mother and father apart. We must do what is best for Imbria, not for her."

"Your mother?" I repeated, curious. I had never met his mother, only the man he called his father, the Fire Keeper.

Kaeleb rubbed the toe of his boot against the dirt for a moment, his thoughts far away. Then he folded himself down on his sleeping mat. "I am an orphan. Gula is not my birth mother, just as Blaise is not my birth father. She is a Tahitian healer and for a while, after the islands were destroyed, we were a family of sorts. She looked after us, cared for us. Gula loved my father, accepted him in a way that few ever had, and he was happy with her. They used to laugh and dance all the time, and she would comfort him when he did not even know he needed comfort. I loved watching them together, how at peace and content they were in each other's presence, even though I pretended to find it completely disgusting. Then rumors of their relationship reached the Earth Queen and my father feared for my mother's safety, so he sent her away, back to Tahitia. At first, my mother refused to go, wanting to remain with us. I worried that I was the reason she insisted on staying, and so I left, going north with Thyrr to broker a peace treaty with the Fomori."

My head was spinning as I tried to understand all the nuances of the past that had led us to this moment. "Why would the Earth Queen care about your parents?"

Kaeleb rolled his one eye. "She has an obsession with my father. She always wanted him to love her, but she couldn't accept that he had once been in love with her sister. Your mother."

"Yes, I have heard about that," I murmured, remembering the few crumbs Vishram and Logaire had tossed me over the years concerning my family.

Kaeleb looked mildly embarrassed. "Blaise is not the same as he was then, when your mother was alive."

"How did you two find each other?" I asked, realizing that I had no desire to speak of my parents. The mere mention of them was like an aching hole within me, a void as deep as the Warding Stone. I knew who they were, Orabelle and Tal, knew what they were supposed to have been, the Keeper and the god, but aside from the few brief moments when I had heard my mother's voice speaking to me through the Pearl, they were meaningless. Nothing more than ideas. Faraway things that I had reached for but could never hold. Dead long before I was ever able to know them. It was easier to put them away, to not think of them.

"We found Chaote when we went north," Kaeleb was telling me.

He and Thyrr, my uncle, had been traveling with several other Leharans, making their way to the mountains that bordered the northern edge of Samirra. The home of the Fomori. The beasts, which they called blooddrinkers, had dwelled in the tunnels beneath Imbria for hundreds of years, and now those tunnels were to be the new home of the Fire Keeper and the wayward Leharans. But there was no point in trying to build a kingdom if it was just going to be ransacked by the vicious tribes from the north. Blaise wanted them to secure a pact with the Fomori that would allow the vagabonds and refugees of the islands to make their home in the Southern Wastelands and the tunnels that ran beneath it. The underground realm that had once belonged to the Fomori named Carushka, my great-grandfather.

"The Va'Kul, the leader of the Fomori, always liked me, in her own brutal way," Kaeleb said. "So I was able to convince father to let me go with Thyrr. He knew the Va'Kul would be more likely to listen if I was among them, one of the few humans that she would not slaughter on sight. Or so we hoped."

They had made it to the northern edge of Kymir and were about to cross the giant span of the divide on the makeshift bridge they had erected when Chaote appeared on the other side. She was just as impressive as Kaeleb remembered, strong and imposing, a true warrior. She stood there, glowing in her golden armor, her skin dark like the night sky. So imperious was her demeanor that they did not notice the dried blood on her clothing or the dirt that was caked in the crevices of her breastplate. She had threatened to kill them, to set their bridge on fire if they tried to cross it. Thyrr offered to go across first, on his own, to speak to her and see if he could convince her to allow them to pass peacefully.

"I will only allow you to cross if you promise to help me," Chaote had told him with finality, leaving no room for negotiations.

"What would you have us do?" Thyrr asked her, wary. He had seen her cruelty and her viciousness firsthand in Samirra, and he was leery of making promises to her.

"The Samirran Guardian murdered Damian. He shot him with an arrow as we were walking away from their cursed land. It was cowardly, a disgusting way for a Tahitian warrior to die. I cannot allow it to go unavenged."

Thyrr's countenance fell, pulled down by sorrow, and his strange blue-gold eyes had shimmered with tears. Damian was his friend, had been a companion, someone who believed in Thyrr when there were very few who did. He was devastated to hear the Tahitian's death confirmed. "I feared something happened to him when he never returned to Tahitia, but Blaise said there was something between you two, and we hoped that Damian had gone off with you to live a better life."

"We went nowhere. He is dead," was her flat response. Thyrr sighed, looking back at the group who waited on the other side, the boy among them, scowling impatiently.

"As much as I want to avenge my friend, we cannot go running back into Samirra. Favian is under Maialen's protection now," Thyrr explained to her, pushing a hand through his golden disarray of hair.

She scoffed, her black eyes gleaming. "I have heard about this sham of a marriage between them. The Queen merely wishes to consolidate power."

"It was a shrewd decision on her part, even if we all know that Favian will never be a true husband to her." Thyrr paused, considering his options. His gaze shifted downward, caught by a flash of movement, and he couldn't help but groan internally when he saw the boy standing between them.

"We have no quarrel with you," Kaeleb had said to the Tahitian warrior. "We wish to make peace with your people."

"I have no people." Chaote regarded him, her face inscrutable.

"She says that Damian is dead, that Favian killed him in Samirra. She wishes for us to help her avenge him," Thyrr explained.

Kaeleb had lowered his head, digging his toe into the dirt. It was late spring. The frost was gone and the land less treacherous, though the burnt forest still remained a ghostly crypt of ash. "Damian was in Samirra because of me. I will help you."

Thyrr sighed again. He had not wanted to take the headstrong boy with him, and this was exactly why. The last thing they needed was for Blaise's child to go running off again, or worse, get himself killed while under Thyrr's supervision. No one wanted to incur the Fire Keeper's legendary wrath, least of all Thyrr, not when they were trying to rebuild a kingdom from the ashes Maialen had left behind. "He is a child. He cannot make these decisions for himself and he cannot go with you."

"It seems this boy has more courage than the rest of you," Chaote sneered derisively.

"We need him with us to ensure an arrangement with the Va'Kul," Thyrr explained to the woman.

She lifted one of her dark brows. "If you seek an audience with the Va'Kul, then you are wise indeed to bring the boy. She likes him. She will listen to what he has to say."

Kaeleb was pleased to hear this, smiling from ear to ear. His face still held the youthful innocence of a child despite all that he had seen, and he was happy to be playing an important role in the events that were transpiring. Chaote smiled back at him, a haunted phantom of the expression that did not reach her eyes, as Kaeleb said to her, "Let me go to the Fomori, then I will take you to my father and tell him I have given you my word to help avenge Damian. He will understand."

"This is a waste of time, young one," the Tahitian countered.

"If you want to get to Favian, then you will have to go through Maialen. You cannot fight the Earth Queen alone, and you know it. You need us." Kaeleb was remembering that day in the winter woods, not far from there, when he had sat across the fire from the dog called the Fenris, the god who had told them to find the halfbreed. To find Chaote. He could not let her walk away now, not when they needed her.

She relented. "Very well. But I will not go with you to the Fomori. As I have told you, they are no longer my people. Five days from now we will meet again in this same place. That should give you plenty of time to find the Va'Kul. Knowing her, the negotiations will be brief."

Kaeleb had sworn to it, and he had kept his word, eventually joining her on her quest for vengeance. Neither of them could have imagined that it would take so long.

"Maialen has made Samirra nearly impenetrable," Kaeleb explained. "She has collapsed the ancient tunnels the Harbonah used, and the Earth Queen has banished all islanders from her realms. We have tried to get into Iriellestra but we have continued to fail, and so now we must settle for making their lives as miserable as possible, however we can."

There was so much I did not know, so much I could not understand. A lifetime of experiences, of changes, of circumstances that I would never be a part of, and yet all of it was a part of me, because of me, shaping who I was and who I would become. "Why does the Earth Queen not kill you? Or destroy your lands like she did to Lehar?"

"She has tried to kill us," Chaote confessed, "but we are not so easily killed. As for the other, well, that is Kaeleb's truth to tell."

There was a nuance of disapproval in her tone and I looked at him, questioning. Even in the darkness I could see he was uncomfortable, fidgeting with the edge of his thin blanket.

"She is afraid that if she attacks the Wastelands, she will inadvertently harm her son."

This was something I had not expected. I did not know Maialen had a living son. Someone who was my cousin. If he was in the Wastelands that meant he was not on his mother's side. I felt a flare of hope, asking eagerly, "Who is this son? Will I meet him soon? Does he know about me, that I am his cousin? Why is he with you and not with his mother?"

Chaote lay back on her rolled up cape, clearly finished with our conversation. Kaeleb took the hint from her and said gently but firmly, "That is enough for tonight, Eolande. Try to sleep. You need the rest."

I wanted to protest, to ask a thousand more questions, but I did not want to pester them or make them see me as a burden, and so I laid down, tucking the thin blanket around me as I curled my knees to my chest. I listened to the sounds of the forest, the nighttime hum of life I had grown up with. The sounds that sang me to sleep when I was a child, safe with Gideon in our cabin in the woods, unaware of the world around us and all that it would soon take from us.

9

The dawn rose early, though in our shadowed alcove I could not see the sun as it lifted into the sky. Day reached us in silvery threads that wove through the thicket of trees. I was stiff, my legs sore from riding and my feet were still aching from the torture I had put them through in the last few weeks. Kaeleb was already awake when I pushed myself up, and he was regarding me thoughtfully, as if trying to decide something. His shock of hair hung over the left side of his face, and even in the shadowy grey light of dawn I could see that the leather band was gone. My eyes met his and I did not flinch or look away as he brushed the white hair away from the dark, empty hollow where his eye had once been.

"I like you better without it," I said quietly.

He smiled. "That is what my father says."

"Do you two need a moment?" Chaote asked, her tone dripping with amusement. She had just returned from the woods, pointing to where I should go to relieve myself. I felt my cheeks flush and I quickly ducked into the overgrowth, not sure why I was embarrassed that she had come upon the moment between me and Kaeleb. Perhaps it was because it was something solely between us, something that he and I shared that no one else could. I had been there when he lost the eye. I was the reason he lost it. It was only right that I should be able to look upon it without judgment or disgust.

I returned shortly to discover they had already dismantled the camp. Kaeleb tossed me an apple and a dry piece of bread, and I ate them ravenously, wondering if there would ever be enough food on Imbria to fill my stomach. I took the drink of water he offered, then climbed onto the horse, wincing as my bruised thighs settled into the saddle.

"You are not used to riding," he noticed with a sympathetic look.

"It is better than walking," I admitted ruefully. He was pleased by my response and laughed, swinging himself up behind me. I felt my breath catch at the warm feel of him against me, once more feeling the flush of embarrassment. I was dirty and smelly and covered in grime. Sooty black dirt still clung to my hair, which was a matted mess around my head. Kaeleb was accustomed to women like Chaote, whose strength and beauty shone like a beacon. I doubted she had ever smelled bad in her life, let alone been covered in filth. They both probably saw me as a wayward orphan, a weak and wretched thing to be pitied.

We did not stop riding till the sun was blazing overhead. Sweat was running down my face and I could feel the ragged dress clinging to me, my skin damp. I was grateful for a respite, my legs aching with only the thin gown to cushion them in the saddle. Chaote brought her horse to a halt in front of us and for a moment I was afraid something was wrong. Then she led the animal through a tangle of vines and disappeared.

"Where did she go?" I asked Kaeleb, whispering in case there was danger nearby.

"The same place we are going," he told me. We followed her through the same tangle of vines and suddenly I was drenched in cool air. Before us, a monstrous cavern loomed, water dripping from two massive stalactites that flanked the entrance to the cave like jagged teeth. We climbed down from the horses and he passed his reins to the Tahitian woman.

"This is the way home," Kaeleb said. "You and Chaote will wait here. I will go see my father and arrange for us to get passage to Tahitia."

"Why can't we go with you?" I asked, panic suddenly rearing its ugly head within me. I did not want to be left alone with the terrifying Tahitian woman. I knew who she was, what she had done. Cossiana and the Tahitians had warned me about her when I was a child, and Logaire had whispered her name to me as if she were a demon that would come in the night and slit my throat. The halfbreed, Chaote, who would stop at nothing to destroy me. Yet I had seen nothing in the woman's behavior towards me to make me believe she would harm me, and I had to remember that it was Logaire who had said the worst things about her. Logaire, the woman who had kept me captive, who would lie and cheat and steal and do whatever she had to in order to protect herself.

"Your Warding Stone," Kaeleb explained. "My father does not allow them in the Wastelands. He needs to be able to use his power to keep everyone safe. You and Chaote must wait here. I promise I will be quick. I will only be gone for a day or two."

"But..." I trailed off. I could think of nothing valid to say that would give reason to my unreasonable fears. Just like Kaeleb, Chaote had been instrumental in saving me. There was no cause to question her trustworthiness.

The insensible anger I felt towards the young man had dissipated on our journey, but now it flared back to life, as potent as ever. It did not matter who he was leaving me with, or how trustworthy they were. He was leaving me. Again.

"Chaote will protect you with her life. There is no one on Imbria you would be safer with," Kaeleb assured me. Then he glanced at his companion, teasing her. "Except perhaps Bacatha."

Chaote snorted at this. "Send the Leharan to me. We will see who is stronger."

Kaeleb turned back to me. "I promise I will return. In the meantime, there are clothes and supplies in the cave, and there is a spring where you can bathe."

"There is something else you should tell your father," I said, stopping him. "In Veruca, before he attacked the castle, Akrin told me he was going to offer me to the Earth Queen. He will tell her I am alive."

"Let her come," Chaote snarled. "We have two Warding Stones now and I should like the chance to carve her open."

Kaeleb tossed me a grin, as if the Tahitian's response was all the evidence I needed of my assured safety. He abruptly vanished into the dark interior of the cavern, leaving me shaken by his sudden departure. I stood watching him go, then Chaote cleared her throat, recalling my attention back to her.

"I believe you should take his advice and bathe."

My cheeks flushed yet again and I nodded, rubbing my hands together and feeling the layers of dirt that caked my fingers. She tied the horses to the iron rings near the cave entrance, then led me through the mouth of the darkened cavern. Reaching out to her left, she grabbed a torch from a bundle that had been left there, lighting it with the quick spark of a flint. The orange glow danced across the massive rock ceiling and I looked around in awe, realizing the magnificent size of the place. Tunnels stretched off in every direction, a labyrinth of stone hallways. She strode down one, and I hurried after, nearly running into the back of her when she finally stopped. We had just entered another enormous cavern, and this one was filled with warm steam that wafted up from a black pool. A ledge had been carved out along the edge of the pool and Chaote placed the torch in a notch on the wall, stripping off her armor and clothing and stepping onto the ledge.

"Come along, then," she ordered before sliding into the water. She groaned aloud, closing her eyes blissfully, and I hurriedly shed my ragged gown, eager to feel the elation she was conveying. I touched the water gingerly with one toe, then stuck my foot in it so that the hot liquid swirled around my ankle. Chaote dived in, ducking under and gliding across the black water with smooth, easy strokes. I clung to the ledge, lowering myself slowly, my feet trying to find the ground beneath me.

"You do not swim?" Chaote asked, joining me at the ledge that I was clinging to like a drowning rat. I shook my head. She guided my hand, helping me grasp onto a cut that had been made in the rock. Then she shoved my head under the water.

I pushed myself frantically up, breaking the surface with a sputtering gasp, clinging to the cut in the rock with all of my strength. She was watching me, her dark eyes flickering with reflected torchlight and a smile playing at the corners of her lips.

"Now you know you will not die. There is no need to be afraid," she said, as if she had done me a great favor.

"I was not afraid to die!" I snapped back at her, surprising both of us. She shrugged her shoulders, treading water and watching me carefully. I began to rub at the dirt that caked me, and she pointed to the piles of scrubbing sand that were placed around the pool. I grabbed a handful, scouring my skin until it felt raw.

I watched as the filth from my body radiated out into the dark water and disappeared. If I held still, I could see myself on the glassy surface of the water, my face hollow, the skin stretched over thin cheeks. I touched my chin, feeling along the edge of my jaw, my hand moving to my cracked lips, swollen and full. My face was unfamiliar to me and I stared at its reflection, distorted by the water but still fine-boned and delicate as I tried to commit every detail to memory so that I would recognize myself the next time I saw it. I had not expected to see a woman's face. The eyes that watched me in the rippling pool were a deep blue, the color of the sea as it pulled away from the shore. They were tinged with redness, and there were long lashes circling them. They were eyes that had already seen too much of the world, guarded and haunted at the same time. My skin was golden brown, distinctly Leharan even after years spent locked away from the sun. Strands of shoulder-length pale hair clung to the angular lines of my face and floated on the surface of the water. I tried to run my fingers through the matted mess, but it was nearly impossible, so I gave up. At least it was clean.

"Did they tell you I wanted to kill you?" Chaote asked suddenly. Steam swirled around her across the pool.

"Yes. The Tahitian Elder, Cossiana, when I was a child. And Logaire, the Verucan Queen," I answered honestly. "They told me who you were, that you wanted me dead. Logaire claimed it was one of the reasons she had to hide me and keep me prisoner."

Chaote continued to watch me, her gaze unwavering, and I felt a knot of tension forming in my stomach. The silence between us seemed to stretch on forever, and I tried to imagine what it was like for her to be there with me after so many years of searching, after the centuries she had spent locked away in her own prison beneath the icy mountains in the north. Her life had been taken from her, just as mine had, and she devoted what was left of it to finding me and destroying the Keepers. I wondered if I was a disappointment to her, if she was sorry that after all these long years, it was me she had found. Finally, the Tahitian spoke, lifting herself out of the water so I could see the long scar of the Warding Stone embedded in her chest.

"We are not so different, you and I. Though mine was of my own doing. I have no desire to kill you. My only wish is to destroy the Keepers, to rid this world of the plague that is the amulets and their power."

"And what of me?" I asked her, voicing the question that echoed through my thoughts. "I have the same power. Why do you not wish me dead?"

Her smile widened, the sharpened points of her teeth showing. "Your power comes at a price, Eolande. That is what makes you different. Now finish cleaning yourself. I will bring you fresh clothes."

She pushed herself onto the ledge and strode away, her body glistening like a polished statue. When she returned, she was already dressed and had brought a clean cloth for me to dry myself with, along with a pair of dark blue linen pants and a matching tunic. There was also a soft pair of boots for my feet and I nearly cried at the sight of them.

"The Leharans prefer these garments," she informed me, indicating the blue clothing and looking at me up and down as I dried myself, as if she were assessing a piece of cattle. She noticed the scars on my arms, the others that crossed my back. "They hurt you."

I did not answer, pulled on the clothes she had given me. She stepped close to me, so close that I could feel her breath and all I could see was the endless night in her unwavering gaze.

"You are the Solvrei. This will not be the end of your pain. Everyone will want something from you now. I cannot speak for many in this flawed world, but the boy is honorable. You can trust Kaeleb. He will never hurt you," she said. There was more than a promise in her words. It was a warning, and I felt a shiver of unease pricking along my skin.

She brought me back to the cave entrance, made me sit and wait there while she went to find food. I expected her to come back with a carcass of some sort, and I was surprised to see her return with her saddlebag filled with plants. There were berries, a few mushrooms, dandelions, and some other roots I was not familiar with. She brought them all into the cave and led me to another room, this one boasting a large fire pit carved into the floor. There was a pot on one wall and she ordered me to fill it with water from the pool. I did as she commanded, struggling to carry it back to her. Several times I had to stop and set it down, for the weight was too much and I was afraid I would drop it, but I finally wrestled the heavy pot into the room where a fire was now blazing, my arms trembling with the effort.

"Well done," she murmured, and I felt myself beaming beneath her meager praise. I knew I had passed some sort of test, though I could not be sure what exactly the test had been.

"How did you know where I was?" I asked suddenly, giving voice to the question that had been gnawing at me since the village.

"The Fenris told us."

I stared at her blankly. "Who?"

Chaote regarded me skeptically, clearly surprised that I was not aware of who this Fenris person was. "The dog."

I felt my blue eyes open wide. The dog. I had forgotten about the dog, the animal who spoke to me in my head, whose thoughts I could hear as clearly as my own. The dog who was a god and wanted to die.

"How did the dog know?" I asked.

She shrugged. "He is the Fenris. Much of what is happening is because he has spent centuries manipulating the world so that these events would transpire."

I wanted to ask her more, but she threw me a warning glare, and I knew she was finished speaking on the matter. She made a soup from her forest gatherings and we ate in silence in the main cavern, watching the entrance as the daylight faded once more from the sky above the trees. Then she stood and walked over to me, settling herself behind me on the floor and running her fingers through my tangles of hair that barely reached my shoulders. I sat still, rigid and unsure of what to do. No one had done this sort of thing for me since I was a little girl and I was not accustomed to feeling another's touch without fear. Chaote began to hum, gently untangling the strands of pale hair with nimble fingers and plaiting them into a loose braid.

"My mother and sisters used to do this for me," she said softly.

"I never had a mother or sisters," was my quiet reply. "But Gideon used to put flowers in my hair. Yellow ones. Like the dandelions you gathered."

She finished my hair, tied it off with a strip of cloth, and scooted forward to sit beside me. I found I was grateful for her presence, for the comfort it gave. Though I could not have explained it to anyone else, I knew in that moment we were fated to meet. We sat in silence, watching the stars as they filled the night sky, two women bound by destiny, sisters not by blood but by circumstance.

10

It was late the next day when we finally heard someone returning from the dark hollows of the cave. Chaote stood, her sword in her hands, always a warrior before all else, always ready. I was beside her, brushing back the wayward strands of hair that escaped my braid and wondering if Kaeleb would be pleased to see me again. I quickly banished the thought, chastising myself for caring, even though I still held my breath in anticipation as the echoing footsteps from the dark cavern drew nearer. Part of me had expected him to never come back, the part of me that spent the last ten years being so lonely that I could not imagine having someone in my life who was pleased to see me.

"Thyrr," Chaote said, her flattened tone all the greeting she would muster for the man who was my uncle. I watched him curiously as he entered the giant cavern, my mouth falling open slightly at the sight of him. He walked up to Chaote and gripped her shoulder in a friendly gesture and she frowned at him, stepping out of his grasp. They were like two beings from another world, one night and one day, both of them so incredibly beautiful that I wanted to look away. Vishram had told me the old fables that claimed the half-bred children of the Fomori were creatures of great beauty, and I could not help thinking that the fables had underestimated the reality. Thyrr was golden like the sun, his countenance so vibrant that it seemed as if the light of that solar orb shone out from within him. He had blue eyes flecked with gold, the color of the sky overhead on a clear day. He turned to me, giving me a crooked smile, and I withered beneath his gaze, wondering how such a magnificent being could be related to me.

"So, you are my niece!" he said, coming to stand in front of me and gripping my hands between his own. "It is good to meet you, Eolande."

I had thought I would feel some sort of elation at meeting one of my relatives, that I would be wrapped in the comforting embrace of family, finally knowing what it felt like to be part of someone else. Instead, I felt nothing. The man before me was a stranger.

"Where is the boy?" Chaote interrupted. She was clearly not pleased that Thyrr had appeared out of the darkness instead of Kaeleb. Several other Leharans accompanied my uncle, and I stared at them in wonder, for it had been so long since I had seen a group of my people together.

"You know how Blaise can be," Thyrr said dismissively with a wave of his hand. "He wants more time with his son. We will meet Kaeleb at the coast or on Tahitia. In the meantime, I thought I would get to know my niece. We are to escort you to the shore."

"Why?" Chaote demanded. I wondered what caused her to distrust my uncle so much, but then realized she very likely distrusted everyone.

An imposing Leharan woman stepped forward. She was taller than the others, clad in silver armor, and her blonde hair was pulled back from her face in a severe knot that accentuated the starkness of her features. There were tiny white lines crisscrossing her skin wherever it was visible and it took me a moment to realize the faint marks were scars, and that I remembered the day she had received those scars. It was ten years ago, on Tahitia. *The day I was taken.* She had tried to stop Maialen, and the Earth Queen had ensnared her body in thorns.

Her hands held a weapon I had never seen before, a massive, curved blade atop a wooden spear. She looked me over with eyes the color of a frozen lake, then turned to Chaote and said, "We are here because we do not trust you with her, halfbreed. Eolande is Leharan, the daughter of Orabelle, our last Queen. Her safety will be entrusted to the Leharan Guard."

Chaote smirked. "The Guard that let their last Queen get slaughtered on the battlefield? That harbored a traitor for years amongst them? The Guard that allowed the Kymirrans to destroy their entire realm? This is the Guard that should protect the Solvrei? Come now, Bacatha, you know I will not allow that, nor will the boy."

"Kaeleb does not speak for us and neither does the Fire Keeper. The Leharan Council decides, and this is what we have decided," Thyrr countered, coming between them. There was an edge of repressed anger in his voice, as if she were scratching the surface of feelings that he had long ago buried.

"Council," Chaote said contemptuously. "Your Council is a sham. Masterless fools hiding behind a Keeper, just as you have always done. Your illusions of power are just that, Thyrr, illusions. Blaise holds the real power over your miserable band of cave dwellers, and you all know it. That is why you wish to take this girl, because you want to take control from him."

"Is that not what you have spent your entire life trying to do?" Thyrr asked her pointedly. "The Solvrei is here, Chaote. She is finally here, alive and well, and with her we can stop Maialen before she destroys the world. We can put an end to the reign of the Keepers."

"You know that her power comes at a cost. Are you the one who will pay it?"

Thyrr was not sure how to respond. He shoved a hand through his disarray of golden hair and paced back and forth. "She cannot do anything with a Warding Stone in her back. Let us get her to Tahitia and remove the stone, then we can decide what to do with her."

I wanted to scream, to run, to shout at them that I was a person, not a weapon to be used at their whim.

This is a mistake I should not have come here they will use me just like Logaire used me they will keep me locked away just like before I need to get out of here to run away to get away from them she said I could trust the boy only the boy but where is he why did he not return why is he not here what do I do can I trust Chaote is she lying too they are all liars.

I felt Chaote's hand on my arm, the firm pressure of her fingers, realized that I was trembling. I tried to stop, silencing the thoughts that were racing through my mind.

"I will not leave you," she promised me, and I believed her, finding comfort in her presence. We had already been alone together. If she wanted to hurt me or kill me, she could have easily done it before the Leharans had come.

"Then we all go together," Thyrr said, as if they had just agreed upon a stroll through a garden. "We leave for the coast first thing tomorrow."

Chaote was less than thrilled with this arrangement, and I saw her hand tighten on the hilt of the golden sword that hung from her waist. Bacatha also saw it and she gave a shake of her head, warning the Tahitian that her violence would not be tolerated. Chaote was outnumbered and I did not know how to fight anyone, so I would be useless to her. She finally seemed to relax, releasing the sword hilt with great reluctance.

That evening I sat at the cave entrance, watching the stars emerge from their daytime lairs to shimmer in the black sky and wondering if I should just run out into the forest. The moon was narrow, barely a sliver. I could hide easily, especially in the dark blue clothing Chaote had given me. Perhaps that was why she had given it to me.

"Bacatha says you look like your father," Thyrr said, folding himself down to sit beside me. I tensed, uncomfortable with his presence. To me, he felt like an outsider, like someone who was pushing his way into a world that did not belong to him. "I think you have the look of your mother about you."

"What does it matter who I look like?" I muttered. "I never knew either of them."

He seemed surprised by my morose response. "You do not wish to talk about them? You are among your people now. There is plenty the Leharans could tell you. There are even those still with us who knew your mother well. Bacatha's own father served in her personal Guard."

I looked at him, at the achingly perfect features of his face, so unlike my own, so unfamiliar. "They mean nothing to me."

Thyrr sighed. "I understand that sentiment. Sometimes the shadows of the past can be too dark for us to want to see."

"What do you want from me?" I asked him, deliberately blunt. Perhaps being around Chaote was having an effect on me.

He leaned back on his palms, shaking his golden hair out of his face. "I want your help. I want to do what is best for Imbria. To restore Lehar-"

"So that you may rule it?" I interrupted him.

"Things cannot continue as they are, Eolande. Our existence in the Wastelands is just that, an existence. Our lives are difficult, painful, full of hardship. There is barely enough to eat. You have not seen how we are forced to live, scared and frightened, underneath the ground. You have not seen what the people have become. Now that you have returned there is hope, hope that we can take back the land that was once ours, that we no longer have to be trapped underground."

"Like Chaote and the Fomori were trapped by the Keepers?"

He laughed, but there was no humor in the sound. "From what I have learned of your mother, you are definitely her daughter. Be careful pitying the halfbreed and her kind. She has done things you cannot even imagine. We all have, if I am being honest. I am also part Fomori, Eolande. I have their tainted blood coursing through my veins, just as you do, but I learned long ago that despite that blood, we have no kinship."

I simply looked at him, hoping he could sense what I was thinking without me having to say it. That I felt about him the way he felt about Chaote and the Fomori.

He stood then, leaving me alone. I did not see him again until the morning when we were preparing to leave. Chaote was arguing heatedly with Bacatha, the two of them standing on either side of Kaeleb's horse.

"It is his, and you will not take it," Chaote was insisting. "The girl can ride it, but not you."

Bacatha scoffed. "You are being ridiculous. Let me ride ahead and I will secure the other mounts. The Solvrei can ride with you."

"If you touch this horse, I will cut off your hand," Chaote threatened, lowering her voice menacingly.

"Enough you two!" Thyrr practically bellowed, his impatience echoing in the monstrous cavern. "Chaote, if you do not wish to lend Bacatha the horse, then go fetch the other horses yourself."

Her black eyes rounded and her nostrils flared. "I am not your dog to be sent to fetch!"

"What are you fighting about?" I asked the Tahitian woman. I heard the word *Solvrei* thrown about, knew that I had something to do with the altercation. Chaote bristled, whipping around to face me.

"We keep our horses nearby, somewhere they are safe," Thyrr said, joining us as he laid a hand on my shoulder. The weight of his palm felt strange, heavy, and I found him watching me intently as he spoke. "We cannot keep them in the Wastelands. It is too dangerous. They would be stolen, sold, or killed for food. They are not far. It will not take long to retrieve them."

"I am not leaving her here with you," Chaote told him with finality.

"Then let Bacatha take the horse. You know full well she will return," he said with a sigh, tired of dealing with the petulant warrior women and their immense pride.

Chaote flung the reins at the Leharan, stomping away and settling herself against the inner wall of the cavern, glaring at everyone hatefully. Thyrr gave my shoulder a friendly squeeze, then he moved to speak to Bacatha, who was swinging herself up onto Kaeleb's horse.

"Whatever you do, do not let anything happen to that damned horse," he muttered. The severe woman nodded and rode off, disappearing through the dense curtain of foliage. I moved away from my uncle, coming to stand near Chaote, not sure why I felt more comfortable in her terrifying presence than in his.

"I do not trust them," she said to me in hushed tones. "This feels wrong."

"Do you think something happened to Kaeleb?" I asked her, feeling a knot form in my stomach.

"No." She shook her head. "No one would dare harm the boy while the Fire Keeper still lives. Perhaps I am just being overly anxious. Your presence has us all on edge, it seems."

I felt a flush of relief at her admission that no harm would come to Kaeleb. Despite my fluctuating emotions towards him, the young man was my only genuine connection to the world, the only tether I had that was binding me to both the past and to the future.

Chaote reached out and pressed something into my hand. It was the small, curved knife that Kaeleb had used to cut my bindings in the Verucan village. It was a beautiful object, the decorative hilt adorned with jewels and the silver of the blade bright and sharp.

"It is his. Take it," she commanded. "He wanted you to have it, but feared you would not accept it from his hands."

"I do not know how to use it," I admitted, feeling helpless. I was surrounded by warriors, and here I was, not even sure how to hold a knife.

"You stab them with the pointy end," she responded.

I started to laugh. It was a soft sound, an unfamiliar feeling. Her own lips curved into a smile and I marveled again at how incredibly beautiful she was, despite the vengeful wrath that shrouded her every movement. I tucked the knife into my pants, securing it with the leather belt that encircled my waist and covering it with my tunic. Chaote nodded, satisfied, and we returned to waiting.

Bacatha returned, as promised, leading a handful of horses behind her. Chaote insisted on being the last in line as we headed to the coast, and I rode before her on Kaeleb's horse, trying to distract myself from what lay ahead. An intense dread washed over me each time I thought about the Warding Stone being removed from my body. I remembered the way my power had felt, how the Fire Keeper's face had looked after I used him to draw it, draining moments of his life from him. How Kaeleb had looked. I spent years yearning to have my power back, and now that it was so close, I was terrified of it, just as I had been when I was a girl.

I tried to put the thoughts of what would happen on Tahitia out of my mind. More than anything, I wanted to enjoy the intoxicating sensation of my newfound freedom, but even though I tried, I still did not feel free. How could I be free when I was constantly sought out and hunted? When the course of my life was already chosen for me? When I was forced to be the savior of the world, the magnificent divine child born of legendary parents? I would never be free, not truly. Not as long as anyone believed I was the Solvrei.

I looked around at the forest that arched over our path. The trees were not as warped in this part of the woods, and their limbs were draped with moss, fresh green leaves sprouting from their fingertips. The forest floor was covered in a carpet of vines and shrubs, but it was not the snarled tangle of foliage we had come through before. I wondered what my aunt had done to make it that way, if she had used her corrupt power, distorted from trying to control two Elements at once. Had she tried to bring forth life from the earth and those disfigured forests of trees were the result? I tried to recall all that I had learned about her over the years, most of it gathered from small bits of overheard conversations. Maialen was the younger sister of my mother, Orabelle. I knew she had something to do with Gideon's death; the dog had told me that much when I was a child. I also knew that she destroyed Lehar in a jealous rage born of hatred for my mother, though if I had not seen it for myself, I would not have been able to fathom such a thing. I had forgotten her face over the years, for I had only glimpsed it briefly as a girl when she and Blaise had come to our home seeking Gideon, but I remembered the impression she left on me was one of gentleness, of calm and kindness. I had not seen the monster that lurked within her.

I slowed my horse, bringing it beside Chaote. She was resplendent in her golden armor, the sun glaring off her like a halo. She turned her chin slightly in my direction, a gesture I took as an invitation to speak.

"Do you know my aunt? The Earth Queen?" I asked her.

She let a slight frown mar her face. "I suppose you could say I have met her. I faced her in battle, the day she and the Fire Keeper created the divide."

"What did you think of her?"

She was surprised. "That is a peculiar question to ask."

"Is it?" I murmured. "I know nothing about her, really, about any of them."

Chaote pondered this, found it a satisfactory explanation for my line of questioning. She went on, "The Earth Queen was a rather soft little thing. Timid, like a mouse. Or so I thought at first, before the battle. She faced me bravely and I was impressed. Then I watched her slice open Kaeleb like he was her next meal and I knew there was much more to her than I had first seen."

My blue eyes widened. "Why would she do that? Why would she hurt Kaeleb?"

"She thought he was you."

I was confused for a moment, then I remembered what the old Tahitian woman had told me. The Guardians had pretended another child was the Solvrei in order to keep me safe. It must have been Kaeleb. I felt a wave of guilt bearing down on me. Maialen had tried to hurt him because of me, because of what I was. And still he had helped me, still he had protected me, or tried to.

"He would not want you to feel pity for him," Chaote informed me, discerning my thoughts. "He is not that sort."

I nodded, falling back into my thoughts as our horses trotted beside each other. Chaote glanced at me occasionally, as if to make sure there was nothing amiss and that I was still there, healthy and whole beside her. I enjoyed her attentiveness, how it felt to have someone looking after me. I liked her, though I knew I could never tell her that. She would hate it.

"What of my uncle?" I asked after a long while. He and the Leharans were far enough ahead that they would not hear our conversation.

"Thyrr?" She hesitated, considering her words. "The so-called great leader of the Leharans, who is neither Leharan nor possesses any actual power. His only claim is being the long-lost brother to Orabelle and her fallen throne. He is her brother, a symbol for the islanders, a reminder of what they once were, I suppose. That sort of thing matters to the Leharans. Bacatha could tell you more about your family than I am able to. Ask her your questions. All I really know of Thyrr is that he prefers to find a way to appease all parties, to avoid bloodshed whenever necessary. He is not a man who relishes in killing, but to avoid it he makes too many concessions."

She stopped talking, pulling on the reins of her horse and bringing it to an abrupt halt. Her finger lifted to her lips, a gesture for silence. Thyrr and the Leharans were several yards ahead of us and did not seem to notice that we had halted our progress behind them. For a moment I thought we were going to run from them, but then Chaote pulled her golden sword from its sheath, turning her horse quickly in a circle.

"I heard something," she hissed to me.

I looked around wildly, seeing nothing, hearing nothing amiss. Then Thyrr's voice shouted back to us. "What has happened?"

"Imbecile," Chaote muttered under her breath. "He gives away his position to anyone in earshot."

She waited, sword ready, but there was nothing, only the sounds of the summer forest. Birds chirping, the hum of insects, the wind moving gently through the trees. Bacatha was frowning, her hand on the massive weapon strapped to her saddle. Her eyes met Chaote's and she gave a slight shake of her head. Chaote shoved her sword back into its sheath.

"No more talking," she said to me as we resumed our journey to the coast.

The forest finally ended and we crossed a flat, muddy plain. I could see a shimmer on the distant horizon and my heart was in my throat. The ocean. I felt so many things all at once that it was overwhelming and I did not know whether I wanted to scream or curse or run towards the water or away from it. Tears slid down my cheeks as I stared at that faint glimmer, unable to explain why it made me cry. Perhaps because I never thought I would see it again. Or because the ocean was so much a part of my mother, because there was no escaping who I was or who she had been when I was here, so close to all that mattered to her. I wondered if she would have been happy to see me, if in another life she would have been waiting for me with open arms on her island across the sea, my father beside her. I wondered if they would have loved me, if my mother could have loved me more had Tal not been taken from her. If she would have kept me with her and never given me away.

"Eolande." It was Thyrr's voice that broke through the wrenching sorrow of my thoughts. "I cannot imagine what you have been through, but you are almost home."

I stared at the haunting glimmer on the horizon. Home. What was home to me? It was not Lehar, a place I had never been. Lehar was my mother's home. It was the place where I could imagine another life for us, where I could pretend that my parents had cared about me enough to stay with me, but it was not my home.

"Come, child," Chaote said, nudging Thyrr aside with her horse. "We must keep going. It is not safe here."

I nodded, wiping my eyes with the dark blue sleeve of my tunic, seeing the stain of my tears on the fabric. It was nearly dusk when the marshy plains gave way to sandy dunes that rolled down to the edge of the sea like a string of mottled pearls. The water beyond was fading to grey in the waning light, and waves broke gently against the shore with a rhyth-mic heartbeat that once more brought tears to my eyes. The breeze lifted loose strands of pale hair from my neck and pulled them away from the sea, as if warning me to turn back.

I saw movement from the corner of my eye as Kaeleb came striding down the beach to meet us. He was wearing a new set of clothes, two swords strapped to his waist in leather sheaths. His missing eye was still uncovered, and his pale brows were drawn together. He was clearly unhappy. He barely glanced at me as I dismounted clumsily from his horse, storming straight up to my uncle.

"An earless fish could have heard the lot of you coming," Kaeleb said, scowling at Thyrr. "You are supposed to be pro-tecting her, you witless dolt, not leading all of Imbria to us!"

My uncle looked displeased. "I am growing tired of the constant insults the two of you like to throw around. Your wild adventures with that one seem to have quite an impact on your manners."

Kaeleb snorted and Chaote bristled at being brought into their argument. She glared at Thyrr, her dark eyes glittering with something dangerous.

"If you do not like me, feel free to challenge me," she said, her voice lilting, taunting him.

Bacatha perked up at the halfbreed's words, but Thyrr dismissed them immediately. "I am not fighting any of you, and neither is Bacatha. Kaeleb, where is the boat?"

"The Tahitians will arrive as soon as the sun has set. Tonight is the festival of the summer moon, it is unlucky for them to collect us in the daylight. There is something else, as well," he added, his irritation at the state of our arrival dissipating in a thrum of excitement. "My father will be joining us on Tahitia. He wishes to see Eolande for himself."

Thyrr stiffened and none of us could miss the look of displeasure that washed over his arrogant features. "Is that wise?"

"He will bring an eagle and be back in the Wastelands before dawn."

Chaote frowned. "Perhaps I should remain here."

Kaeleb started to protest but she cut him off with a wave of her hand. "You know I have no desire to go to that island. I will wait for you here and watch the horses."

I also wanted to protest, but I knew she would not like it and so I remained quiet. There was a Warding Stone in me. Blaise's power would already be dampened by my presence, so her own stone should not have deterred her from accompanying us. If she wanted to remain behind, there was another reason for it. Her starry eyes flickered over to me and she seemed pleased by my resolve to stay silent.

"Before we part, I would like to speak to Eolande alone," she announced.

"No, you cannot be alone with her," Thyrr said, shaking his head. Chaote looked as if she wanted to murder him. Then her beautiful face cleared and she smiled, the points of her sharpened teeth showing.

"I did not ask you, mutt," she said derisively. Thyrr sighed at yet another insult hurled in his direction as Chaote went on. "I could have killed her before you even showed up, and since then I could have killed you all ten times over if I wanted to. I am not here to harm the Solvrei. Her blood is the one thing that will right the wrongs I have spent my life seeking to avenge. I will not waste it."

"We can trust Chaote," Kaeleb vouched, his one eye turning to my uncle.

"You may trust her, but I never will. Stay in sight of Bacatha," Thyrr warned. He gestured for the severe Leharan woman to watch over us and Chaote turned on her heel, stomping down the shoreline. Bacatha kept a respectful distance, but even in the fading daylight I could still see the glimmer of her icy blue eyes watching our every move.

"There are many things you need to know, child," Chaote said, and there was a thread of something in her voice I had not heard before. She was worried about me. "I cannot tell you all of them just yet, but you must be careful on the islands. Do not let your nostalgia for your mother's realm cloud your judgement. The Tahitians can be corrupted, just like everyone else. The boy knows this better than anyone. Stay near him and he will keep you safe."

I nodded. "I will."

"Take this. You may need it." She pressed something into my hand and I looked down at the object curiously. It was a hard, grey stone, one side of it splintered with cracks that wove through it like a spider web.

"What is it?" I asked her.

"The Air Sapphire."

My mouth fell open and I nearly dropped the rock in the sand, forcing myself to hold on to it. My fingers trembled and the memory of the amulets hit me like a blow. The horrible whispers they contained within them, the constant, terrible pull of their power. Chaote gripped my hands, closing my fingers over the jewel.

"I tried to destroy it without you, but I was not strong enough," she admitted. "Instead, I gave more power to the remaining amulets, made Maialen even stronger. Once the Warding Stone has been removed from your back, you can use my blood with yours to draw the energy back to the Sapphire and use it. I know what your power is like as the Solvrei, that you can only use it by draining the life from someone you touch. Your enemies know this as well. The Sapphire will grant you an advantage they will not be anticipating."

She pressed my fingers harder against the jewel, dragging my thumb over the jagged edge so that a thin line of blood welled up from it. She swiped her own thumb over the shard, then pressed it against mine, our blood mixing into a precious droplet that fell onto the jewel.

"The Fenris does not know how much I know, Eolande, and you must keep this to yourself as long as possible. Only use it if you must."

"Why are you doing this? Why help me?" I wanted to know. The amulets were the most valuable objects on Imbria, the things she had spent her life trying to destroy. Wars were fought over them and now she was just handing me one.

"Because I need you."

With that, she turned and walked back towards the others. Bacatha gave the Tahitian warrior a curt nod as she passed, then returned her pale gaze to me, waiting. I sighed, tucking the amulet into my pocket and following Chaote's footsteps back down the beach.

11

Maialen could find nothing redeeming in the sullen countenance of the man who stood before her. He was beady-eyed, his skin rough and weathered, and he still wore the black armor of the Verucans, his general's crest gleaming on his collar. His hair was cut short, retreating back from his forehead in a way that exaggerated the moroseness of his features, though these were not the reasons she found him so unappealing. There was something dark that clung to him, something depraved and bitter, and it pinched his face as if he had swallowed glass.

Akrin bent forward in a shallow bow, one that was not nearly deep enough to convey the proper respect that someone of her stature deserved. The Earth Queen frowned at him, her fingers brushing the deep green Emerald that hung from her neck. She sat alone at the Council table, in the chair that had once been her father's, presiding over the centuries old block of white marble that was centered in the sacred space. The thrones of the other Keepers had been removed years before, when the Council was abandoned because of the Fire Keeper's unwillingness to be part of it. Though, if she was honest, the death of the revered Council had been a slow bleed, and one that had begun long before Blaise abandoned it, with the first fatal wound struck by Orabelle.

Maialen felt her eyes narrow at the thought of her older sister. She hated being reminded of Orabelle but was forced to constantly endure endless reminders of her. Especially now that Maialen had taken the Pearl of Water and controlled the Element that had once been ruled over by her sister. Every time she felt the urgent pull of the Pearl's power, she saw Orabelle in her mind, felt her presence in every movement. The haughty, proud Leharan who was so confident and self-assured. The woman who inspired loyalty decades after her death. It was as if Maialen were a child again, wearing her older sister's clothing and pretending to be her, and it infuriated the Earth Queen beyond reason. Orabelle was not the doting older sibling Maialen had looked up to as a child. She had been a selfish liar that poisoned everything she touched. There were days when Maialen was tempted to throw the Pearl back into the sea, to once again feel only the calming bliss of the Earth amulet instead of the tempestuous clash between the two. But she never did. The power of both Elements was all that was keeping her enemies at bay. She could not risk the Leharans getting their hands on the Pearl and choosing another Keeper. The first thing they would do was seek retribution against the Earth Queen for the destruction of their kingdom.

"What is so urgent that you have summoned me all the way from Samirra and insisted on speaking with me?" Maialen inquired, turning her attention away from thoughts of her dead sister and back to the man who stood before her.

Akrin shifted on his feet, his eyes raking over her in a way that made her skin crawl. She knew the stories about him, everyone on Imbria knew about him, and she wondered if he had finally killed Logaire. It would not surprise her. The woman had been a fool to keep him alive all this time, and Maialen told her so on plenty of occasions.

"Come now, I do not have all day," the Earth Queen prompted when Akrin did not immediately respond. She would not allow him to toy with her. He was already insolent enough, showing up in Kymir and insisting that Damek summon her without a word of explanation.

Maialen had been in the Samirran palace when she received her advisor's message detailing Akrin's urgent request to speak with her. She remembered standing in one of the high towers of the marble monument, tracing her finger along a pane of glass, leaving a long path in the condensation that gathered on the tall, arched window. Below her, Samirra's capitol city of Iriellestra stretched out like a sweating carcass. If not for the life-sustaining grain the realm provided, she would have let it fall to ruin years ago. It was a constant drain on her. She had come to hate Samirra, detested that she was forced to spend so much time in the wretched kingdom, away from her forests and the comforting embrace of Kymir.

"Queen Maialen." The quiet voice of her husband had spoken from behind her. She turned away from the window to look at Favian and could not help the frown that marred her delicate features. He had not changed much over the years, was older but still wiry and lithe, with a long braid of dark hair that shone like a seal's pelt draped over his shoulder. His eyes were as haunted as ever, the purple smudges beneath them now broken by deep creases. She herself had not escaped the march of time either, though she was still beautiful. There were streaks of grey in her hair and there was a sharpness to her features that had not been there in her youth. The lines that ringed her mouth were deeper, and her eyes seemed to have lost the sparkle that once shone within them.

"What do you want now?" Maialen asked him, not bothering to hide her annoyance. As she smoothed down the folds of her gown, she could feel the weight of the golden cuffs against her thighs, a familiar and comforting sensation. The cuffs belonged to her father, and she recently had them refitted to her own slender wrists as a tribute to Chronus's memory.

"A hawk from Kymir has brought a message for you," Favian said, his tone flat. Despite their marital status, the two of them could barely stand being in the same room. Favian questioned her constantly, challenged her decisions, was always whining about things in Samirra, always demanding that she do more for the withering realm. But he was loyal and honest, and she could trust him. He would always do what he thought was best for his kingdom.

"From Damek?" she queried.

"I have not read it," he answered, passing her the tiny scroll. She snatched it from him, hating the feel of his pale skin, trying not to think about the travesty that had been their wedding night, when those long, thin hands had shaken with revulsion at the thought of touching her. Theirs was the second loveless marriage she was forced to endure, but at least it brought her security and the realm of Samirra.

She unrolled the slip of paper and felt a fleeting wash of relief as she read the precisely shaped words she recognized as Damek's handwriting. The advisor requested she return to Kymir immediately. Akrin had come from Veruca with a message for her, and it could not wait. Maialen was grateful to have an excuse to leave the western realm, to be away from Favian and his haunted eyes that held no love for her.

The next day, she had taken one of her eagles and flown back to her homeland, wishing that she felt something more upon seeing her return. There were no family or loved ones eagerly awaiting her arrival. No one waiting to greet her with a warm smile. She was alone. She had a son, Aracellis, but it was years since she had even laid eyes on him. For a long time, she believed he was dead, lost in the violent upheaval brought on by the halfbreed, Chaote, during her rise to power. Maialen had been told that Aracellis was killed along with her former husband, Astraeus, the King of Samirra and the father of her son. Then one day the Earth Queen had received an unexpected letter from Favian telling her that Chaote and her army had left Samirra, and Damian, Orabelle's former Guardian, was dead. Maialen was not surprised to hear of the Guardian's death, though the circumstances surrounding the incident were kept vague. The final lines at the end of the letter asked if Aracellis had made it back to her. Her son had escaped, fleeing with the Fire Keeper when he had come to rescue the false savior, Kaeleb. Maialen had gone to Blaise as soon as she learned what happened, demanding answers, threatening to obliterate his pathetic little band of cave dwellers in the Southern Wastelands if he did not return her son to her.

Blaise had stood in the sun, his hand shading his eyes, seemingly unphased by the heat that she found almost un-bearable. Maialen watched the way the sunlight glinted off the beard he had grown, how his red hair shone like fire. His skin was tanned a dark brown and there was a faint web of lines around his eyes. His arms were still knotted with well-used muscle as he folded them over his broad chest. She hated the way her stomach still fluttered at the sight of him. Years before, she had fallen for him, convinced she had finally found someone who truly understood and cared for her. But then he callously discarded her, choosing instead to cling to his unrequited love for her dead sister.

"If Aracellis wanted to return to Kymir, I would not stop him," Blaise told her, glancing at the line of archers that were assembled behind her. Not that she needed them. Maialen held two amulets now, the Pearl of Water and the Earth Emerald. There was no one on Imbria who could come close to matching her power, and she had proved that when she destroyed Lehar.

"I want my son," she repeated. Her fingers rose to touch the Emerald, an instinctive gesture, and she saw the muscles of Blaise's arms tense, feeling a small thrill of satisfaction knowing that he was afraid of her.

"Aracellis is not kept here against his will. He was badly treated in Samirra. I am sure it would be difficult to forgive a parent for not coming for you, for not saving you from those atrocities," Blaise said, his amber eyes flashing.

Maialen laughed scornfully. "Do not act as if you care for the children of Imbria, Blaise. I know you too well for that."

There was something in his face that she had not been expecting, a sorrow or a shadow of regret that she had never seen. He shook his head. "You do not know me at all, Maialen."

His words were like a dagger in her chest because she knew they were true.

"I can destroy this land, just like I did to Lehar. Give me my son or I will do it," she had threatened.

He shrugged, grinning at her with his disarming charm. "Do your worst, my dear. Just know that if your son is in there, his death truly will be your fault this time."

Maialen fumed, dangerously close to using her power to crush everything that mattered to him. She could feel the Elements calling to her, the crashing insistence of the Pearl of Water, so much more tempestuous than she could have ever imagined. Her fingertips trembled against the Emerald and the ground beneath them rumbled in response.

"There will be no going back, Maialen," Blaise had warned her.

She turned, storming off back to the eagle that had carried her there, cursing him thoroughly in her heart. He played the game well, used her son to maneuver her into a position where she was forced to relent to him, and it infuriated her. Ever since then, she had been waiting for the day to get back at him, for the chance to draw him away from the rats' nest he lorded over so she could demand that he return Aracellis to her. Now Akrin was standing before her, and she wondered if this could be the opportunity she had waited so long for.

The brooding general sauntered forward, oozing insolence with every movement. He leaned his hip on the edge of the marble table, his blunt fingers caressing the cool stone. "I have brought you a gift."

Maialen felt her eyes widen slightly while her frown deepened, the long lines around her mouth growing more prominent. She saw a subtle movement from the corner of the chamber where Damek stood, obscured by the shadows in his dark robes, but the elderly advisor remained silent. Maialen focused her attention back on Akrin. "I have heard of your gift giving from Logaire and I must warn you, I am not some powerless woman trying desperately to hold on to a realm. I am the true Solvrei, the first Keeper to control two Elements."

Akrin leaned toward her, his face a grotesque parody of a smile. "This is a gift of knowledge, Earth Queen, and one that I think you will gladly accept."

She forced herself not to back away. "Then, by all means, impart this wisdom onto me so that I may judge its value for myself."

He traced a long vein in the marble, his small brown eyes fixed on her throat, on the little throb of her pulse that was visible beneath the edge of her chestnut hair.

"Logaire has kept a secret from you," he said, tempting her. "You claim you are the Solvrei, but the other who goes by that name still lives."

Akrin watched as the Keeper's face paled, feeling satisfaction curling within him at the sight of her fear, for he knew that was what she felt in that moment. If there was one emotion he could always recognize, it was fear. He saw it in the way her jaw clenched, how the tendons in her delicate throat tightened. The Earth Keeper's eyes darted to Damek, who remained expressionless, like a withered statue skulking in the hallowed recesses of the chamber. She touched the green stone that hung from her neck and the lines on her face smoothed, the fear receding back to hide behind her power.

"It is impossible," Maialen said, her words clipped short.

"I have seen her for myself." He paused, knowing the Earth Keeper's weakness, relishing the moment while twisting his words like a knife in her gut. "Orabelle's child lives. The one the Tahitians boast is the true Solvrei."

The Earth Queen's nostrils flared at his use of her sister's name and she felt an incomprehensible anger swelling in her. Orabelle had ruined her life and now she was ruining it again, bringing her cursed bastard child back to life for Maialen to deal with. She forced herself to remain calm, taking a deep breath and trying to ignore the rising power of the Pearl of Water that pressed like a weight on her chest, clamoring to be used.

"Logaire has her?" Maialen asked the sullen Verucan general.

"The girl has escaped. I have heard rumors while searching for her that I am not the only one seeking her out."

"Blaise." Maialen did not need Akrin to confirm, and the weight of her rage grew heavier within her. Of course, Blaise would go after the child. Even decades later, he was still obsessed with Orabelle. It was pathetic. "Find this girl, bring her to me."

Akrin pretended to be surprised. "What are you offering me in exchange, Earth Queen?"

Maialen looked him over, suppressing the shudder that ran along her spine. Akrin was the last person she wanted to align herself with, but he was the one person who would do anything to hurt Blaise, and she needed that kind of single-mindedness if what he said was true. If the child did indeed still live, then Blaise and the islanders would use her to come for the amulets and Maialen needed to protect herself.

"When I take Veruca I will need someone to oversee my rule there, just as I have Favian in Samirra. I will grant you that task," Maialen offered. There was a rustle of dark robes, like the shivering of an insect's wings. Damek emerged from his silence, his sagging face pulling down into a deep frown as he regarded the Verucan.

"Perhaps the Queen and I should discuss things in private before we make any agreements," the old man said smoothly. His voice was surprisingly rich and oily, completely at odds with his chalky, cracked exterior.

Akrin leered at the old man, thinking how easy it would be to crush his frail bones. "Give me your support and I will find the girl and rid this world of her. We can discuss my payment later."

"You have it," Maialen said quickly. She wanted to laugh with delight. Akrin was just as big of a fool as Logaire claimed he was and she leapt at the chance to get what she wanted while promising nothing in return. No matter what else happened, she knew she could not allow her sister's child to survive.

"Give me enough men and I will ride to the Wastelands tonight and raze it to the ground," Akrin promised, a feverish glint of violence lighting up his morose features.

"We should not be too hasty," Damek warned. "There are other ways to find what we want besides riding into a battle with the Fire Keeper that will cost both sides greatly."

Akrin scoffed. "You speak of your network of spies? Those imbeciles were completely unaware that the Solvrei was rotting in the Verucan dungeons for the last ten years."

"I am the Solvrei!" Maialen practically shrieked, her cheeks turning pink.

"Of course you are, my dear," Damek assured her, laying a skeletal hand on her shoulder. He turned back to Akrin. The general was a useful tool to have at their disposal, but only if he were employed to just the right task. A full-on assault against the Fire Keeper in the south would only lead to wasted Kymirran deaths. They knew nothing of the deserts or the tunnels beneath them. The disadvantages of a battle on that terrain would be too great. "Give me a few days. My spies may not be able to infiltrate the Verucan dungeons, but they know the rest of Imbria well. If this girl really lives, we will hear of it soon and we will know exactly where she is."

12

The faint lights that floated in the sky grew clearer, and I could see they were fires burning in deep pits dug out along the Tahitian beach. As our boat drew near, I could just make out the glistening forms of the dark-skinned islanders as they moved between the fires, swathed in brightly colored fabrics with strings of shells and pearls adorning their wrists and ankles. I felt something stirring within me at the sight of them, a sort of excitement mingled with familiarity. I had been there as a child and lived on the island for a time, and I had loved the Tahitian's wild celebrations, losing myself in the pulsing beat of the drums and the balmy darkness of the island's nights. I watched now as they danced along the shore, my lips slightly parted in anticipation, my heart pounding in rhythm with the drums.

Someone touched my back and I flinched, the spell of the island broken. It was Thyrr, and he was offering his hand to help me out of the boat. I looked at it in awkward silence, not sure what he expected me to do. Then Bacatha was beside me, grabbing my arm and hauling me unceremoniously out of the small vessel. I splashed through the shallow water and onto the sand, bathed in silver and gold, the cool moonlight mingling with the orange glow of the fires. Bacatha released me just as a child ran up to us, slipping a bracelet of glossy white shells onto my wrist. I stared at it, turning my hand over so that the string of tiny objects shimmered in the veils of light.

"Eolande," a woman's voice broke through the din of drums and chanting. I remembered the woman. She was the island Elder, Cossiana, the one who had tried to force me to take the Pearl. "We are honored to have you among us once again."

The old woman bowed low, the long braids of her grey hair sweeping the sand. There was something regal about her, more regal than Logaire had ever been, as if this woman knew she was a queen without needing such a title. Her black eyes danced with memories and she laid a hand along my cheek. Her fingers were warm and dry, and I resisted the urge to turn my cheek into the motherly gesture and rub my face against her palm.

"Come," she said, pulling me towards the revelry on the beach. "Enjoy the celebration."

Panic flared up, overcoming any sort of comfort her presence had given me. I heard Chaote's words in my mind. *Stay with the boy. You can trust him.*

I spun around, jerking out of Cossiana's grasp and startling the old woman as I searched frantically for Kaeleb. I could not find him. My breath was starting to gasp in my throat and I felt sick to my stomach. Then Bacatha stepped aside to say something to Thyrr and suddenly Kaeleb was there, standing behind her, his one eye fixed on me. Relief flooded in, quickly replaced by embarrassment as he slowly grinned at me, delighted that I had been desperate to find him.

"I am here. I will not leave you," he promised, coming to stand beside me.

I looked up at him, at the way the dancing light angled off the edges of his features, at the dark emptiness where his eye had been. I wanted to tell him that I did not care what he did, that I could take care of myself, but we would both know it for the lie it was. He grabbed my hand and before I could protest he was hauling me down the beach, waving back at the others who were clearly not pleased by our abrupt departure.

"We cannot wait for them," he told me. "If we do, then all the best food will be gone."

He released me just as abruptly, throwing his arms around a tall Tahitian man as they clapped each other heartily on the back. Once their pommeling was done, the man bent down and passed Kaeleb two steaming, folded banana leaves. Kaeleb opened his, shoving the contents of it into his mouth with a blissful groan.

"Eat it," he said as I stared at him, bewildered. I unfolded the leaf, revealing a cloud of spices and coconut that made my mouth water. I lifted a piece of the steamed fish to my mouth, tasting it gingerly. It was delicious. Not that I had much basis for comparison when it came to food. I had spent the second half of my life eating mostly slop and gruel.

"Come on, Eolande, there is no time to waste," he chastised me, and I obediently stuffed the rest of the fish in my mouth, barely able to chew the giant mouthful as he hauled me down the beach to our next meal. This continued until I was quite sure I would be sick if I ate anymore, and Kaeleb flung himself down on the sand, folding his arms behind his head.

"You can sit if you wish to," he offered, gesturing to the sand beside him. We were near the far edge of the revelry, where the pounding of the drums was less intense and I could feel the shadows of the night like cool breaths at my back. I folded myself down on the sand next to him, careful not to sit too close. He noticed the deliberate distance I left between us and raised a pale eyebrow. "You don't have to be afraid of me."

How could I tell him I was not afraid he would hurt me, but of something else entirely? I was afraid of his smile, of his eye, of the feel of his hand on mine. There was something about him that made me apprehensive in a way I had never been before.

"Is your mother here?" I asked him, looking at the islanders as they danced among the fires, lifting their hands to the moon in tribute as they moved.

"She is here somewhere. Do not worry, she will find us soon, and I am sure she will give me a stern scolding for one reason or another," he answered with a laugh.

"Did you do something wrong?"

"I do quite a few things my mother does not approve of, but no, that is not why she scolds me. It is her way of showing she cares," he attempted to explain.

"That is a strange way to care about someone," I muttered, letting my finger trail in the sand, leaving a swirling line.

"It is more than anyone else ever bothered to do for me," he said with a shrug. "Except for my father."

"I am afraid. Of your mother," I blurted out, my words jumbling as I tried to sort through the thoughts that were racing through my mind. "Not of your mother herself, but of what she will do. Not that she will do anything bad to me, but of her helping me. It has been so long. I don't know what it will be like to feel the power again. What if I can't control it? What if I hurt someone?"

A shadow passed over Kaeleb's face and he looked down at his hands, spreading his fingers as if to reassure himself they were still intact. His pale hair fell over his forehead in a heavy sweep. "I remember what you did with your power. How it felt. It was awful."

"I'm sorry," I whispered. "I was young then and I did not realize... I knew what I was doing, but I did not truly understand what was happening. To be honest, I still do not completely understand it. Sometimes I think it was all a lie, or maybe a dream. My parents, who they were, who I am. I think that one day I will wake up and I will be nobody again, just like I was in the forest with Gideon, an Eolande who no one cares about."

"You will never be someone that no one cares about." His grey eye was hard like steel and there was an edge to his voice that was at odds with his gentle words.

"People only care about me because of what I can do and because they want something from me," I countered.

"I want nothing from you."

I stared at him. He reached a hand towards me and I felt my breath tighten in my chest, his fingers hovering in the air near my face. Then he brought them down quickly, smacking my shoulder with a startling slap.

"Cava fly," he muttered, wiping his hand and the crushed insect on the leg of his pants with a grimace. I wanted to hit him over the head with something, but I was interrupted by someone approaching. The Tahitians nearest to us fell into a hushed silence, parting with deep bows of respect to allow the man to pass through them unencumbered. I knew him instantly. The blood-red hair, the amber-colored eyes, the swarthy features recognizable even beneath the thick beard. It was Kaeleb's father, Blaise, the Keeper of Fire.

He stopped before us, and I expected him to look menacing, threatening, violent, to fulfill all the harsh promises I had heard about him over the years. Instead, he looked at me with eyes that glittered with something I had not expected. Sorrow.

The Fire Keeper cleared his throat as if he were about to speak but could not find the words he wanted. I pushed myself to my feet, brushing away the sand that clung to the dark blue fabric of my pants, and he watched my movements with his unwavering gaze, one brow arching upwards. He radiated power and strength, and the gleaming golden edge of the Fire Opal was visible just beneath his linen tunic and leather armor. I shuddered at the sight of the shining amulet, thinking of the shattered Sapphire I had tucked in my pocket and the insistent whispers I knew the jewels would soon be calling to me with.

Blaise finally found his voice, his lips curving into a nostalgic smile beneath his beard. "You look so much like your mother."

"People keep saying so," I replied awkwardly. I thought he would say something else sentimental, but he seemed to shrug off the weight of the past. Only the slight deepening of the lines between his brows gave away any emotion.

"Kaeleb tells me you have a Warding Stone in you."

"I...yes..." I was not sure why I felt so uncomfortable under his scrutiny.

"Once Gula has removed it, you will need a few days to recover. After that you can return to the mainland and we can-"

He was interrupted by the soft touch of a Tahitian woman's hand on his shoulder as she came up behind him to join us. "Blaise, please. This can all wait until tomorrow. Tonight is the Summer Moon."

It was Kaeleb's mother, Gula, the woman who would be my healer. She was pretty in a kind way, with a halo of curly black hair and a softness to her features that I liked. There was something tender in her voice as she spoke to the Fire Keeper, a gentle pressure, as if she knew she could persuade him to do whatever she asked. I could see why he had fallen in love with her, for she had a soothing presence that must have been a refuge for him, an anchor to hold him fast against the steady pull of his wrathful power. For a moment, my heart ached for them, and I hated that my aunt had forced them apart, destroying their small breath of happiness in this miserable world.

Gula turned her deep brown eyes to Kaeleb and her round face filled with delight. He leapt to his feet, wrapping his arms around her and lifting her into the air as he hugged her fiercely.

"My boy," she said, cupping his angular face in her hands as he set her back on the sandy ground. "You look well, but you are still too thin. You need to eat more. I am glad that Chaote has been looking after you."

Kaeleb snorted. "More like I have been looking after her! She would eat worms if I let her, and it is likely she would have gutted half the population of Imbria if I was not there to restrain her."

Blaise frowned, and it was obvious he did not approve of the relationship between his son and the halfbreed, though what exactly that relationship was I still had trouble ascertaining. I was not sure if their friendship was one of mutual respect, necessity, or something more.

Gula patted Kaeleb's cheek. "Did you get the planta cakes Noriah made? You know they will be gone soon. They are everyone's favorite."

"Ah, mother, do you think me a fool? Of course I did!" He leaned over to whisper conspiratorially to me, "You see, I told you the good food would not last long."

Blaise glanced down at the Tahitian woman and shook his head. "Eolande being here changes everything. We should not wait, we need her to tell us everything she knows. We need to know what happened in Veruca."

Gula saw the stricken look on my face at the mention of Veruca, the way my fists clenched at my sides. She leaned to Blaise, whispering something to him I could not hear. His amber gaze flickered over me and the shadow of regret returned to cloud his features. He looked away, down the beach to the drums and the dancing, but his eyes were seeing something much further, something that haunted his memories of the past.

"Enjoy tonight," he finally relented, then turned to Kaeleb. "But do not let Thyrr make a spectacle of her for his campaign to reclaim Lehar."

Kaeleb grinned and clapped his father on the back, and Blaise ruffled the young man's hair affectionately, matching his smile. The Keeper turned to Gula and held out his arm, and she hooked her elbow around his, leading him back to the throngs of dancers where they disappeared amongst the whirling bodies.

I stood where I was, rooted to the ground and wondering what I was expected to do next. Blaise told me to enjoy the night, but I did not know how. It had been ten years since I had celebrated anything. I felt panic rising in me, my mind shouting things at me that I did not want to hear.

You don't belong here you are not like them this is not real it will not last you should not have come but there was nowhere else there is nowhere safe you should have run just kept running.

"Eolande?" Kaeleb broke through my rampant thoughts. "We can just sit for a while longer, if you like. We don't have to join the others. To be honest, I don't much care for crowds. I only come to these things for the food."

"I..." my voice trailed off as I struggled with myself. The beat of the drums was invigorating, the pounding like the pulse of my heart, alive and beautiful. I wanted to move with it, to dance like the others were, like I had as a child before I learned that my life was not my own. But I was frozen with fear. I was afraid of living. I was afraid to hope that there could be something more for me. My fists clenched at my sides and I said the words before I could convince myself not to. "I want to dance."

He laughed and it was a beautiful sound, so full of joy that it nearly made my heart stop. He grabbed my hand, hauling me towards the nearest fire pit where we kicked off our boots and he spun me in a circle. My feet were still raw and sore from days of walking, but I barely felt it, losing myself in the rhythm of the music. Kaeleb danced around me, and I noticed he kept the other islanders from getting too close. He honestly looked quite ridiculous, and did not seem to have any sort of style or reason to his movements, but they were wild and free and joyous. I allowed a small smile to touch my lips and he beamed at the sight of it, spinning me faster.

I had no idea how long we danced. The fires were constantly replenished and the Tahitians were exuberant in their celebrating. Even when I was exhausted and could hardly bear the ache in my feet any longer, the islanders danced on, singing and hollering into the night, howling up at the silver moon in reverence. When we finally stopped, Kaeleb led me to the edge of the ocean, where the waves reached out to caress the shore and just before the beach ended in a rocky outcropping. His shock of pale hair was plastered to his head with sweat, and his shirt clung to the muscles of his chest, though I tried not to notice such things, averting my gaze and staring down at my feet as the sea swirled around them with its soothing embrace. I tucked my loose strands of white hair back into the braid Chaote had plaited.

"I wish it could be like this," I murmured. "My life, I mean."

Kaeleb sighed, digging his toe into the wet sand, watching the indentation fill with saltwater as the waves moved in and out. "At least you are free."

"Am I?" I had my doubts still. "I do not think my life will ever be my own. Maybe this is all I should hope for, a few moments where I do not have to be the Solvrei, where I can just be me."

"I know this is not what you want, but Imbria needs you. Maialen's power is destroying the world. If you saw the lands in the north and what she has done to them, you would understand. She tried to grow the forests back after Blaise burned them, but what came out of the earth is unrecognizable. In Samirra, there are acres of farmland that grow nothing but poison and thorns. Whole rivers have turned black, everything in them dying." He shook his head and his solemn grey eye transfixed me. "We have tried to stop her, but we are not you. We need you, Eolande."

I felt the panic flare once again. It returned, along with my irrational anger towards him. The voices of my mind that would not be quiet were telling me he was wrong.

Not me it is not me it cannot be me it is not possible why me why me why me I don't know how to save anyone I can't save anyone I could not even save myself.

"You don't even know me," I snapped bitterly, pushing past him and stomping back up the beach. It was foolish to stand in the moonlight with him, foolish to think that dancing or laughing would make things better for me. I was furious at myself for even trying, for thinking anyone would see me for who I wanted to be. To them, I was the Solvrei, nothing more.

I snatched up my boots, tugging them onto my feet as my uncle was making his way through the crowds of revelers. He spotted me, coming over and raising his eyebrows at the harsh glare I threw at him.

"Blaise told me you were to enjoy yourself tonight," Thyrr said, "Though you do not seem very happy at the moment. Perhaps this has all been a bit much for you. If you like, I can take you to Gula's home. She has prepared a room for you there."

Kaeleb was pounding up the beach behind us, a scowl on his face and looking just as furious as I felt. I accepted my uncle's proffered arm, wanting only to be away from the young man and his grey eye that saw too much of me and not enough of me at the same time. Kaeleb paused for a moment when he saw us, the lines deepening between his brows. He pulled on his boots and stood a few feet away, still scowling, waiting for us to go so that he could follow.

I felt a pang of guilt for my behavior towards him when he was still trying to protect me, but then I remembered he had been ordered by his father to do so. It had nothing to do with me or his desire to make sure that I was safe. I was a valuable commodity, one that each of them wanted to use.

"I would like to take you to see Lehar once Gula has removed the Warding Stone. It is your homeland and Cossiana tells me the Sirens are still there, wandering through the wreckage," Thyrr began, speaking as if he would be doing me a great favor.

I was silent, listening to the sounds of frogs and insects that filled the night as we walked up the beach towards the jungle path, away from the vibrancy of the festival. I could not help but notice the area where the vegetation was thinner, the trees smaller, for this was where I had flattened the island with the sea ten years ago. A shudder ran through me and I could not help glancing back at Kaeleb, my guilt swelling even more. He had tried to protect me that day, grabbed my hand so I could use my power, even though he knew it would hurt and it would cost him precious moments of his life. He had faced a Keeper, one of the most powerful people on Imbria, and a General who was twice his size and he had not hesitated. He had lost his eye that day because of me. But that was ten years ago. Kaeleb was a boy then, impetuous and unaware of his own mortality. It would be different now.

We passed through a wall of spiked bamboo poles, entering the village. The Tahitians had done their best to rebuild it just as it was before Maialen's attack, with a central clearing and rings of thatched huts forming a spiral that radiated outward. It was quiet, peaceful, and I tried not to think about the last time I was there, the night Akrin had taken me and screams had filled the air.

"Here you are," Thyrr said, releasing my arm and giving me a gallant bow. "I hope you will think about my request."

Kaeleb let out a heavy sigh, storming up and shoving his way between us. "You cannot let her go in there without making sure it is safe, you foppish dolt."

Thyrr looked mildly chagrined, but he let the insult pass, giving me one of his crooked smiles, and we waited while Kaeleb went inside, making sure that no one was lurking in the shadows waiting for us. The young man returned a few moments later and gestured for me to come in, closing the door abruptly in Thyrr's face. He had lit a candle, which he handed to me, pointing to the room that was to be mine. I went in, setting the feeble light down on a small table and squinting at my surroundings. It was a simple room with a small bed, the table that held the candle, and a large chest. Yellow curtains fluttered at the windows and there were strange little mementos littered about the space. There was a dried sprig of a plant stuck in a small clay pot, a scrap of parchment with the words *you are missed* scrawled on it, a leather pouch that looked as if had seen better days, and a small wooden carving of a frog with one eye open and one closed. I picked up the carving, turning it over in my hands. The edges were worn smooth and I ran my finger over the closed eye, realizing that I must be in Kaeleb's room.

I pulled off my boots, reaching into my pocket and taking out the broken Sapphire, shoving it down into the toe of one of them. I felt my breath catch at the sight of it, at the possibilities of what the next day would bring, but I was too exhausted to let my mind linger on it.

I went to the bed, taking the frog with me and cupping it in my hands, holding it close to my chest as I curled my body around it. The linens were soft and clean and smelled of the island, like salt and herbs. I breathed deeply, falling asleep almost instantly.

13

I awoke slowly the next morning, reveling in the unaccustomed comfort of waking in a bed. Sunshine filtered in through the window, stripes of warmth playing across my skin where the light slanted through the shadows of tall palms. I stretched my arms, sitting the carved figurine of the squat little toad I was still clutching on the table beside me. I could not remember ever feeling so peaceful upon the opening of my deep blue eyes, and for a moment, I allowed myself to relish the strange sensation. Then I remembered what day it was. The day I would have my Warding Stone removed.

Fear curled in my gut and prickled along my skin. For years in the darkness and silence of Veruca I had longed to hear the voices of the Keepers, for any sort of comfort or guidance, but now I remembered how much I had hated them and their insistent cries and demands. Even my mother's voice, not as harsh as the others, but conveying something I could not understand. I stood, noticing the sand and dirt I had left behind in the bed and quickly trying to brush it away, embarrassed that I had marred the clean perfection of the soft sheets. Then I walked to the door and opened it, banging into the back of Kaeleb's head. He leapt up with a startled cry, his sword in his hands, and I screamed, stumbling backwards and falling flat on my back. I grunted as the pressure of the Warding Stone slammed against my spine, glaring up at Kaeleb as he stood looking down at me. His pale hair fell over his empty eye socket as he rubbed the back of his head with one hand. He had been asleep, sitting in a chair he had pulled over to block the doorway to the room where I slept. Guarding me.

"I told him not to sleep there, but he never listens to me," Gula called out from across the hut where she was slicing fruit with a large knife. I swallowed hard and could not help but imagine her cutting into my skin with the knife, peeling it back like the rind of the fruit.

Kaeleb set his sword against the wall and reached out a hand to help me up, which I ignored, scrambling to my feet rather awkwardly. He narrowed his eye but moved aside, pushing the chair out of my way.

"Go and wash up. Then we will eat," Gula commanded.

I did as she told me, trying my best to smooth my hair back into the shape Chaote had plaited it in, but I had no mirror and no way of knowing if my efforts were bearing fruition. For all I knew, I looked like a wild woman who had been roaming across Imbria for days.

When I returned, they were seated at a square table and Gula motioned for me to join them, indicating the steaming dish of eggs and sliced fruit she had placed in front of me. I ate ravenously, trying not to inhale the food too quickly, for I did not want her to think I was rude. I liked her kind ways and I wanted her to like me as well.

"Kaeleb, slow down. You are not a goat," Gula chastised, clucking her tongue at the young man while her brown eyes sparkled with warmth. He rolled his eyes and continued to shove food into his mouth with hearty abandon. Gula turned to me. "Are you prepared for today, Eolande?"

I stirred the remaining eggs around on the dish, feeling the frown that pulled at my face. I shrugged, unsure of what to say to her. Should I tell her the truth, that I was terrified of her and of what would happen? That I had no desire to be the savior of the world and I was convinced I would disappoint everyone on Imbria. Should I tell her I heard the voices of dead Keepers yelling at me through the amulets whenever they were near, and I was terrified of what they would say after ten long years of silence?

"Eolande," Gula began, her voice low and soothing. "It is your body and you have a choice in what happens to it. If you do not wish for me to remove the stone, you can tell me so."

Kaeleb had stopped eating and was watching me closely. I tried not to look at him, feeling tears welling up in my eyes. Gula reached over, her strong, soft hand covering mine and squeezing.

"I will do it," I said finally, trying to sound assured, though I was not entirely convinced that I was making the right decision. "It is who I am, and I should like to be myself again. Even if that comes at a price."

Kaeleb returned to eating, his face clearing so that it expressed neither pleasure nor disappointment, seeming to be content with whatever I chose.

Gula smiled and patted my hand. "It will also be good for you to no longer be afraid and to know you have power of your own."

I wondered if she caught a glimpse of the emotions that flitted across my face in that moment. She popped a piece of fruit into her mouth, chewing happily, her round cheeks shining. We finished the meal in silence, and I regretted eating so quickly, for my stomach began to churn in anticipation of what was soon to come. Gula noticed my anxiety and she dismissed me and Kaeleb, telling us to go for a walk while she prepared for the impending task. I was grateful for the reprieve, for the last thing I needed was to watch the careful preparations for something I was already dreading. Though a decade had passed, I could still feel the stinging pain of the first cut Vishram had drawn down my back.

Vishram. I startled myself, suddenly remembering the advisor who should have been in Halig with Sybylla. I had not thought to look for his body, though it must have been there. No one in the town had been left alive, and I was glad I had not remembered before now. I doubted that Vishram's remains would have been treated with the same reverence as the Oracle's, and I had no desire to see his body hacked apart, despite what he had done to me as a child.

"Eolande," Kaeleb prodded, waving his hand in front of my face. I blinked, startled, returning to the present.

"I am sorry," I mumbled, standing up from the table and going to retrieve my boots. I slid the Sapphire into my pocket, my fingers trembling slightly. Of all the Keepers I could hear first upon regaining my power, the Air Keepers were not the ones I would have chosen. It was Astraeus, the last of them, who had killed my mother, and I was quite sure he would have no kind words for me. I could only hope that whatever damage Chaote had done to the amulet had severed the ties with the past, and perhaps the stone would be mercifully silent.

Kaeleb led me outside, winding through the village, nodding at people as we passed. It was quiet still, as most of the revelers from the night before had not gone to rest until sunrise and were still sleeping off their celebratory jubilations. He moved decisively, at a steady pace, and soon we were making our way through the jungle. We reached a tangled mass of thorny vines that towered above us and I saw Kaeleb's face pinch at the sight, though he kept going. He was not wearing any of his armor today and had strapped one sword at his waist. The leather eyepatch was back over his eye and I tried to avoid looking at it, finding the patch even more disturbing than the blackened darkness of his scars.

We stepped out onto the beach and I realized he had brought me to the place I liked to go to as a little girl. It was the place we had first met, all those years ago when we were still children. He had been haphazardly bundled in bright purple and yellow fabric, and I had been fascinated by the strange, wonderful boy who carried a sword. I could not help but laugh at the memory, and he looked at me quizzically.

"I was remembering the first time we met here," I confessed. "You looked ridiculous."

He chuckled, letting his smile ease the pinched anxiousness that had marred his features on our walk. "I was quite fashionable! And if I recall, you did not look your best in those days, either."

He gestured to my hair, which back then I had shorn off in a strange act of defiance. I still was not sure exactly what I hoped to accomplish with the rebellious cutting of my hair, but at the time it had made sense in my child's mind.

We sat on the sand and I watched the waves move in and out, matching my breath to them and enjoying the sense of calm that it brought me. His head was bent, but I could see him watching me out of the corner of his eye, through his long fringe of white hair.

"What if I can't control it?" I asked suddenly.

"My father will help you."

I sighed, digging a shell out of the sand and throwing it in the water. "His power is different from mine. He does not hurt people."

"We all hurt people, whether we mean to or not," Kaeleb said in response. "Our world is not one where we can live the lives we wish, so we must live the life we are given."

"Why don't you hate me?"

He turned to stare at me. The sun slid across his features so that he seemed to glow from within in the radiant light. "Why would I hate you?"

"Because it is my fault. Everything that has happened to you," I whispered.

"Ah, well, then I should be thanking you, not hating you," he said with a grin. "Because of you, I met my father and Gula. Because of you, I found a home where I am wanted, where I am missed when I am gone."

I thought of the slip of parchment in his room, those same words on it. *You are missed*.

"Do you not wish that you had a different life?" I asked him.

He shrugged, his toe digging into the sand. "No. There may be things I wish I would have done differently, but we cannot blame ourselves for the choices we made when we did not know any better. As long as we learn from the past, then it has served its purpose."

I sat for a long time thinking about his words. Had any of us learned from the past? Had we learned from the death of my parents? From the destruction of my homeland? If we had, there would be no need for me to exist. I opened my mouth to speak, but Kaeleb stopped me with a quick gesture, his hand gripping my forearm like a vise. His one grey eye darted around the beach, and he was on his feet just as a group of islanders pushed their way onto the sand from the snarled jungle path.

"There you are!" my uncle boomed, his voice carrying over the waves and shattering the peacefulness. Bacatha was behind him, in full armor, looking as terrifying as ever. Her hair was pulled back in a tight knot that accentuated the severity of her features, the net of pale scars on her face standing out in stark contrast to her tanned skin. She gave Kaeleb a brief nod of acknowledgment and he scowled at her as she ordered the guards they had brought with them to spread around the beach.

"What are you doing?" Kaeleb demanded.

"Protecting my niece," Thyrr answered smoothly. "I do not want anything to happen to her and although you may be a decent enough warrior, you are one man and it is foolish to think you can protect her alone."

"You nearly got her killed yesterday, traipsing through the countryside like a herd of addle-brained wild beasts!" Kaeleb retorted, his lips curling in disdain. "You are not even-"

"Enough," Thyrr practically shouted. "Your father would agree with me. The girl needs to be protected. She is vital to us and whatever foolishness this is, it is not as important as getting her powers back and restoring our kingdom!"

"You mean your kingdom?" Kaeleb practically spat. "Lehar has never done anything for me."

"Kaeleb," Bacatha cut in, her voice stern. "You know that is not true."

The young man eyed her in stony silence, but I saw the muscles of his shoulders relax slightly. I wondered what it was between all of them that made them so uneasy with each other.

"We need to be getting back anyway," Kaeleb muttered. "Mother will be ready for her."

He turned to glance at me, and I hoped I did not look as terrified as I felt. My stomach was a flurry of butterflies and my heart began pounding in my chest. I gave him a small nod, trying to be brave, and we followed Thyrr back into the jungle, Bacatha and the others surrounding us protectively as we went.

14

Damek sat with his elbows resting on the cool marble of the ancient table, his fingers steepled before him. His fingers were thin and bony, with knobby protrusions on the knuckles that ached horribly in the winter. To be honest, everything on his body ached these days. He knew he was growing too old, that he would not be long for this world, but he still had so much left to do.

The old advisor often sat in the empty Council Chamber, remembering what it was like when Chronus was alive, when the world still had order and the Edicts of the Gods were still followed. He could close his eyes and see the former Keeper, draped in the finest gold and green cloth, the Emerald of Earth gleaming at his neck. Chronus had been a true Keeper, one who respected the amulets and their power, until the Leharan Queen had corrupted him.

Damek felt his face wrinkle in disgust. Even Ursula, as awful as she was, had been relatively easy to deal with. Once the poison of the Fomori's bite begun coursing through her veins, she was no trouble at all, wasting away silently in her small prison amongst the trees of Kymir. It was her daughter that had been the problem. Orabelle was the disgusting result of an affair Ursula had with a halfbreed, and she was nothing but trouble since the day she was born. Damek remembered Orabelle as a child, precocious and stubborn. She loved to torment him whenever her mother brought her over from Lehar, running wild through the manor and wreaking havoc on the perfectly manicured royal gardens. All the while, Ursula would laugh indulgently, believing that none of them knew her secret. But Damek had known, even though he pretended to overlook the petty crimes of the willful child, secretly storing away his dislike for the mother and daughter. He kept it inside, even when Ursula was nothing more than a wasting bag of bones, dying from poison. Sometimes he would visit her, standing at her bedside and staring down at her as she struggled to cling to life. The island queen did not deserve a man such as Chronus. She should have worshipped at his feet instead of whoring herself with a halfbreed. She deserved every second of misery that was inflicted upon her. He remembered leaning over her once, shaking the cup of herbs that were supposed to help heal her.

"You will never leave this room alive," Damek whispered, silently adding the words in his mind, *and I am the one who helped make it so.*

Ursula's slow and painful demise had been a fitting end to the adulterous queen. The only mistake they made was not killing her daughter as well. Orabelle was just a child then, and it had seemed obscene to murder a child, but that was exactly what they should have done. She was the reason for everything that had happened, the reason Chronus was dead and Damek was forced to tolerate having Maialen, his youngest and most worthless daughter, rule in his place. Though Damek had to admit, it had been a source of great joy when Maialen had finally done something worthwhile and destroyed Lehar. He had always loathed the cursed island and its uncouth inhabitants.

Now there was another bastard descendent of Ursula's to deal with, and this one was even worse than her mother and grandmother, alleging to be the savior of the world. Damek knew better than to believe the fantastical tales of the Tahitians claiming that Eolande was the offspring of a deity. Having known her father, Tal, personally, the old advisor was certain that the man was no more divine than he himself was. Whatever the girl was, something had made her that way, and Damek needed to find a way to undo it. If he couldn't, then he needed to kill her before she could spread her poison any farther across Imbria.

Damek silently cursed Logaire. He never liked the woman, despised the way she threw her body around like a silken snare, using it to get what she wanted, but he never thought her to be such a fool. It was almost inconceivable that she was naïve enough to leave the child alive all these years, but then to compound that mistake by somehow losing her. Damek could not fathom the stupidity. He hoped Akrin had made a fine mess of the Verucan castle as he departed, and that Logaire was struggling to pick up the pieces. She no longer had an Oracle, or the terrifying General, or the blood of the Solvrei. There was nothing left to keep her in power, and she must be panicking, scrambling to hold on to the shards of her splintering reign. Perhaps Damek could use that panic to Kymir's advantage. He just needed to think about how it could be done.

Maialen already controlled Samirra. It would be easy for her to take Veruca, though not so easy for her to hold it. Having Akrin on their side would help. If they could convince Logaire to become a vassal of Kymir, then perhaps it could even be done without bloodshed. But the Verucans did not respect the Kymirrans, and with Blaise still living, there would always be rebellion fomented from his dark little caves under the desert. They needed to get rid of Blaise, but Damek feared Maialen was too sentimental. Her ridiculous obsession with the Fire Keeper was putting them all in danger. Over the years she had ample opportunities to kill him, but for some incomprehensible reason, she had not done it. Now she claimed it was the presence of her son, Aracellis, who was with Blaise in the Wastelands, that was keeping her from attacking.

Damek sighed, pinching the bridge of his sharp beak of a nose. Getting rid of Aracellis first would make the other pieces fall into place. Perhaps that was the key. If Maialen's son was dead, it would be easy to convince her to get rid of the Fire Keeper. And with Blaise gone, they could just kill the girl, Eolande, outright, which is what Damek preferred. Either way, he needed the help of someone among them, a traitor that he could bend to his will. But who could he recruit from the band of outcast buffoons? The Leharans were too motivated by their incomprehensible sense of honor and pride. The Tahitians were still under Cossiana's dominance and she would never agree, not after Maialen refused to help save her son ten years ago and instead waged war on the island realms.

Damek's eyes suddenly lit up and his dark robes shuddered with excitement. There was one person who came to mind, but it would take some careful manipulation on his part. Finding the right words to sway this person was crucial, but if he could do so, then Maialen would have complete dominion over all of Imbria. She would hold an empire greater than any the world had ever seen and Damek could finally rest, knowing that he had preserved Chronus's great legacy.

15

My eyelids fluttered open and I grimaced, the pain in my back stinging like fire. Gula was there, pressing a cup to my lips. I was lying on my stomach in bed, covered with a thin cloth, my hair loose around my shoulders. I reached up to push the pale strands back from my face, wincing at the pain the movement brought.

"You will need to lie as still as you can for a while," Gula told me. I sipped the tea, grimacing again, not with pain, but at the foul taste of the drink.

"Is it..." I hesitated to ask, terrified to hear the answer.

"It is right here," Gula said, her fingers hovering over the milky white stone that sat on the table beside the bed. "I left it for you, so that you could hold it if you feel you need to. I understand that it only works if you are touching it."

"I honestly do not know how it works," I admitted with a wan smile.

"I believe that is the way of it."

I closed my eyes again, listening, waiting to hear the voices creeping out of my boot where the Sapphire was hidden. There was nothing.

"Where is he?" I asked, trying to look around the room without moving too much.

"He thought you would not want him here when you woke," Gula said, knowing I was asking after Kaeleb, and there was a gentle reprieve in her voice. The sound of it made a knot form in my throat and I wondered if this was what it was like having a mother, where one slight change in the tone of their voice could shame you and bring you to tears.

"I am sorry I was unkind to him," I said. Earlier, when we had returned to the hut from the beach, Gula had taken me into Kaeleb's room where she had prepared everything. Then she explained to me what would happen, how she would give me some herbs to help me sleep and I would undress and lay on the bed while Kaeleb held me down and she removed the stone. My eyes had grown wide, and I shook my head in protest as she spoke.

"No! I do not want him here!" I had practically screamed, pointing at Kaeleb. I could not bear the thought of laying before him, unclothed, with the scars of my past on display for him to read like a cruel poem. He would know what they had done to me in Veruca, and I did not want him to see me that way. I did not want to see my pain reflected on his face. Kaeleb was startled by my unexpected reaction to his presence, his brows drawing together sharply.

Gula had tried to be patient. "I need someone strong to hold you. I cannot have you moving while I do this. Your spine is delicate and the stone is so close to it that one slip of my knife would be disastrous."

"I don't want him! Someone else, anyone. Bacatha! Get Bacatha. She can hold me, she is twice my size. I want Bacatha." I was adamant. I saw the hurt that washed over Kaeleb's face and it was like a dagger in my heart, but I remained insistent.

He can't be here he can't see me like that I don't want him to see me to see my scars all the scars he will know how I got them he will not look at me the same make him leave make him go away just go away don't look at me Bacatha is better she will know she will understand.

Kaeleb relented, leaving the room, and a short while later the imposing Leharan woman had taken his place at my bedside. Gula drew back the cloth that covered me and the two women exchanged a glance, seeing the marks I wanted to hide. There was something in their look, something that all women instinctively know about another's pain, and Bacatha laid her hands carefully on me, bracing one hand on my shoulder and one on my thigh.

"I will protect you," she promised me. I nodded, closing my eyes, knowing that she meant my secrets as well as my body. I drifted into the deep slumber that Gula's herbs brought about, trusting them with my life.

"Take another sip," Gula ordered, bringing me back to the present. "I understand why you did not want him to see you. But my son is not like other people. He will not care that you are scarred or broken. If anything, he will love you more because of it. His father, the Fire Keeper, was broken once too, but Kaeleb never cared about that. He never judged him because of his past, only for the man that he was in the present. In this way, Kaeleb saved him. He taught Blaise that he was still worthy of love."

"I am sorry that you cannot be a family."

She smiled, her cheeks rounding pleasantly. "So am I. But I am grateful for the moments we have."

There was movement in the corner of the room as Bacatha stirred from where she had been waiting. My eyes met hers and I wanted to thank her, but she gave a slight shake of her head. "You do not need to say anything. You are the daughter of Lehar, the child of Tal and Orabelle. It was my honor to help you."

Something in her demeanor towards me had changed, and I wondered what it was. She was almost reverent now, still protective, but in a new way, a way that reminded me of how Chaote had been. I wondered if it was because the Warding Stone was gone and I was the Solvrei again, or if it was something else, something we had all shared in that moment when Gula had drawn back the cloth that covered me.

Bacatha stayed near me as I recovered, sitting by my beside and telling me stories of Lehar and my homeland. At first, I had not wanted to hear them. I did not want to know about a mysterious place that no longer existed, dead just like everything else that mattered to me. But she had been insistent, and I was surprised to find her to be a gifted storyteller. She spoke of my father often, and it was strange to realize that I was hungry for knowledge of him, despite having avoided it so stubbornly.

She told me the story of how my parents first met, when Tal had come to Lehar on the day Orabelle was to choose a Guardian. My mother was young and fearless and bold. She had leapt down into the combatants, ordering them to face her and her power. But before she could wave her hand to defend herself, my father had been there, protecting her fiercely, as he had done every day until his death.

Bacatha's tales brought tears to my eyes, and it made me see my parents as real people, not just idols or abstract concepts conjured in my head. They had laughed and cried and made mistakes and had arguments, and they had truly loved each other. Enough so they had given their lives for each other, and for me. My mother died because she was trying to make the world safe for me. She could not have known that she would only make it worse.

With each passing day, the pain in my back became less intense. Gula peered underneath my bandages, slathering on a stinking poultice with nimble fingers. "You have healed well. You are able to do as you wish, my dear. Within reason, of course."

"I would like to see Lehar. My uncle offered, and if it is still possible, I would like to go before we return to the mainland," I said. Bacatha seemed pleased with my decision, and Gula simply nodded her head, as if she had seen it coming.

"Just remember that the Lehar you have heard stories about is gone. What remains is a haunting place to see," Gula warned.

I wanted to ask her if Kaeleb would go with us, but I felt foolish doing so and I remained silent. I had not seen him since I had screamed at him to go away, and neither of the women had mentioned him again. For all I knew, he had left the island and gone back to the mainland to his father. He was probably better off there, away from me. I had no idea what my power would be like after so long lying dormant. I did not even know if I had regained the use of my powers, for I had been too afraid to try. I had no desire to hurt Gula or Bacatha, or to take moments from their lives just to see if I could. My eyes strayed to the pair of boots, the silent Sapphire tucked within one of them. Chaote had warned me not to use it unless I had to, but what if I could not use it at all?

My uncle arrived early the next morning with his troop of Leharan guards to escort me to the island. Bacatha was with them, and she was holding her massive scythe, the wicked blade glinting in the sunlight.

"Do you like it?" she asked expectantly, seeing me eyeing the intimidating weapon.

"Um... yes, of course. It is lovely," I murmured, unsure of how to properly appreciate a piece of weaponry. Lovely did not seem to be the best choice of words for something you killed people with, but it was all I could think of in the moment and I did not want to offend her.

"It is quite lovely," she agreed proudly. "It is traditionally a farming tool, but it serves as an excellent weapon."

"Come, Eolande. We have a boat ready," Thyrr informed me, stepping forward and taking my elbow. His blue-gold eyes were bright and his jaw was clenched, the island breeze ruffling his golden hair. It seemed he was as nervous about seeing Lehar as I was.

"I will go with you," Gula announced, wrapping her shoulders in a brightly colored shawl that reminded me of a sunset. "Her wound is still fresh and I would like to be there to keep an eye on it."

I was pleased that she would be joining us, for her calming presence was comforting to me and I had no way of knowing what kind of turmoil seeing my mother's ravaged kingdom would bring to my mind. I looked past her for Kaeleb, but he was not there. Gula caught my searching look and she gave me a small smile, patting my arm affectionately as she joined us.

"Kaeleb is with Cossiana today," she told me.

I was glad to know he had chosen to remain on Tahitia, rather than going back to his father. I was not sure what business the young man had with the island's Elder, but whatever it was, it was surely more important than my nostalgic excursion to my homeland and so I could not fault him for it, though I still wished to see him and to apologize for screaming at him. Perhaps I could enlist Gula's help in doing so once we returned.

We followed Thyrr down to the long fishing piers where a small ship was waiting, creaking gently as it nudged against the dock. It was early, and the sun was still shrouded in mist, but the islanders were already bustling about, dumping piles of slippery silver fish into baskets. Beside the baskets stood Tahitians with sharp, curved knives. They reached into the baskets and flopped the fish down on large pieces of stone, fileting them with agile flicks of their hands. They worked with purpose, focused on their tasks and performing them as precisely as possible. I enjoyed watching them work, seeing the pride they took in a simple action like gutting a fish. I wanted to ask Bacatha if my father had learned to fish when he lived on Tahitia, but she was already ahead of me, stomping up the lowered ramp that led onto the ship.

I stood at the bow of the ship, the seawater showering me in cascades of shimmering droplets as we glided over the waves. The sun was still shrouded in a halo of fog, and as we approached Lehar I could see nothing through the misty ether that clung to the island.

"There used to be a clear view of the Citadel from here," Thyrr remarked, coming up to stand beside me as his golden hair was tossed about carelessly by the wind. The sea-spray clung to his face, catching in the light dusting of stubble that darkened his chin beneath his arrogant smile. He was wearing Leharan blue, just as I was, but he had donned one of the islander's silver breastplates and there was a sword sheathed at his hip.

"I wish I could have seen it. I have been hearing stories about the Citadel and the beauty of Lehar before my aunt destroyed it," I told him.

"Bacatha weaves a masterful tale, does she not?" he said with a grin. "I am glad that she has been telling you about our home."

I thought about his words. Home. Lehar was a fairy tale, the setting of the star-crossed love story that I happened to be the product of, but I did not think I could call it home. The only home I had ever known was the little cabin in the forest where I lived with Gideon. He was my father, not the romantic stranger from Bacatha's fantastic tales. I felt tears sting my eyes at the memory of Gideon I conjured in my mind, so vibrant and clear, as if I had just blinked and missed him standing before me. A brawny woodsman, strong and tender and smelling of the forest and moss. Suddenly, I had no desire to go to Lehar or see the place my parents once lived. It felt wrong. It felt like a lie.

"I want to go back," I told Thyrr.

He lifted his brows. "We are nearly there, Eolande-"

"I do not want to go!" I insisted, my voice rising. Gula noticed my agitation, rising from her seat and hurrying over to us.

"Is something wrong?" she asked quickly, lifting the back of her hand to my cheek to see if I was feverish. "Does your wound hurt?"

"No," I muttered, feeling ridiculous. "No, it is nothing. I just..."

How did I tell her what I was feeling? How could I tell anyone what I was feeling? I had spent years locked away in a dark dungeon, silently staring at four black walls, my only reprieve the few times I was sent to Halig. I was not prepared for everything that was happening. To meet people who were my family, who knew my parents, who knew what I was and wanted me to right the wrongs of a past that I could hardly understand. I was not prepared to use a power that I did not know how to control. It was overwhelming, the weight of it all threatening to crush me, and I just needed it to stop for a moment. I needed a moment to breathe.

Gula slid her arm around me, soft and warm, and tears coursed down my cheeks. Thyrr was upset, pushing a hand through his disarray of wild hair.

"Perhaps we should turn around," he muttered.

"No. It will be good for her to see," Gula said gently. "She is stronger than she realizes."

My uncle seemed doubtful, and I could not blame him. I felt weak, helpless, cowardly. I had been terrified of everything for ten years and now, even after I had escaped, I was still terrified of everything.

"I am not strong," I began to protest.

Gula gave me a rough shake. "Nonsense. Look at all you have survived, all you have overcome. You escaped Veruca, walked across half of Imbria, stayed alive and kept going when anyone else would have given up. Kaeleb told me about the villagers and what happened, how even after they beat you, you did not want them to die. That is not weakness, Eolande. That is strength. I see it in you, and it is not your mother or your father or anyone else you are descended from. It is you."

I wiped at my eyes, taking a deep breath, wondering if she was right. Thyrr gave me a questioning look, letting me decide if I wanted to proceed, and I nodded to him, giving him a feeble attempt at a smile.

Lehar was nothing like I expected. Even though I knew it had been destroyed, nothing could have prepared me for the shocking state of the island. The very land itself was broken and cracked, long jagged scars running through the ground like bloodless veins. There was debris everywhere, the crumbling remnants of a once vibrant kingdom, and all of it was tangled in snarls of vines and roots, as if the jungle itself was trying to swallow whatever remained of the proud civilization. There was nothing left intact, and the entire coastline was a pile of broken rocks and shattered coralstone.

"This part of the island got the worst of it," Thyrr said, holding my elbow as we waded through the shallow surf onto the rocky debris. "Your mother had her home here. The Earth Queen broke the entire island apart and threw it into the sea."

"Why does she hate my mother so much? They were sisters. Surely they must have loved each other once," I said, shaking my head at what my aunt had done. The extent of the damage was far beyond anything I could have imagined.

Thyrr frowned, his blue-gold eyes darkening with shadows. "I did not have the chance to know them before your mother died, but I believe Maialen was always the weaker of the two, and she hated herself for it. When her life fell apart, she turned that hate on Orabelle, rather than admit to her own weakness or faults. Her tryst with Blaise certainly did not help the situation, since he was in love with your mother. When Maialen realized he would never love her the same way, I believe it was the final breaking of her spirit."

"Yes, I have heard about that," I murmured.

"Sometimes the bonds of blood are not the ones that sustain us the most." Thyrr looked back at Bacatha with a brotherly fondness. "It is those we choose for ourselves that become our true family."

"You sound like a Tahitian," Gula interrupted with a smile. "We have always found family to be those you choose to love, not someone you are born indebted to."

Thyrr led us over the rocks, towards the ruins of what had once been the Citadel. Bacatha stayed with us, sending the other Leharans to spread out and keep watch. I was not sure what else there was for me to see on the island besides more wreckage, but Thyrr seemed to have a destination in mind, so we followed him curiously. The wound on my back felt stiff and sore and I was about to ask if we could turn back when my uncle stopped abruptly, nearly causing me to run into him from behind. I was so focused on not falling over Thyrr that at first I did not notice the men standing before him. He had stopped beside an enormous block of coralstone, a piece of rubble so massive that it could only have been part of the Citadel.

"Well, well. There you are."

I jerked my head up, my heart nearly stopping and my mouth going dry at the sound of his voice. Akrin. He was here. I wanted to scream, to run, to do anything except stand there and stare at him, but that is what I did. My blood pounded in my ears and I was frozen in place, watching him as he strode forward, breaking away from the group of soldiers he had brought with him. The soldiers spread around us, and one of them grabbed Gula, pinning her arms behind her. There were Kymirrans among them and I knew as soon as I saw them that Maialen had accepted an alliance with Akrin, and that the alliance was likely dependent on his capturing or killing me. He would not let me go this time.

"Eolande, get back!" Bacatha shouted, breaking into a sprint, her massive scythe lifted in her hands as she ran for Akrin.

"Not so fast!" Akrin said with a sound of rebuke. "We found one of your friends along the way."

He gestured to the men and they pushed a lone figure out in front of them. Chaote was tied by the neck, her golden armor smeared with dirt and blood, her lip swollen and bleeding. Two of the Kymirrans were grasping the end of the rope that was looped around her neck. Bacatha stopped short at the sight of her, narrowing her icy blue eyes.

Chaote spat at Akrin, disgust coloring her voice as she said, "You did not find me, you idiot. I walked right up to you and dispatched five or your men before you even realized what was happening. If it was not for the Keeper, you would all be dead."

My head was swimming. The Keeper. Was Maialen here? I looked around, searching the misty wreckage, but could see nothing. Then I heard it, the soft whooshing of wings. I lifted my eyes to the sky and I saw an eagle in the distance, making long, slow circles above us. Of course she would not get too close. Chaote had a Warding Stone in her still and the Queen's power was useless in her presence. So why had they brought the halfbreed here when they could have just killed her?

"This was not what we agreed upon. I said no one was to be harmed," Thyrr hissed at the sullen General. Bacatha spun to face him, confusion wrinkling her brow, and I gasped, backing away from Thyrr quickly, as if his very presence were poison. There were a million thoughts clamoring in my mind, but I could not make sense of them all. Everything was happening too fast.

"She is alive. That is more mercy than she deserves," Akrin retorted, pushing Chaote away from him. She snarled, snapping her teeth, and he leered at her hatefully.

"What have you done?" Bacatha demanded of Thyrr in a voice so cold that it sent a chill down my spine.

"Do not look at me like that. I have done what I needed to, for Lehar and for all of us," Thyrr said to her.

"I will kill you for this," the Leharan woman vowed.

"No, you won't. You will see that this is the best thing for everyone. We cannot keep living in the Wastelands. If we can return to Lehar, then we can-"

She cut him off. "I would rather die right here than live a single day with this shame! You have betrayed Lehar, and the Solvrei."

I reached into my pocket, feeling the edges of the Sapphire beneath my fingertips. Chaote was here. My power was worthless. That was why they had kept her alive and brought her here. I looked up at her and she was staring back at me, her gaze unwavering.

"Let them all go," I said, trying to sound brave but hating the way my voice shook. "It is me you want."

Akrin took a step towards me and Bacatha tightened her grip on the scythe, setting her feet wide. He laughed at the Leharan woman, but he proceeded no further, settling his attention back on me. "Come with us and they go free."

"She is not going anywhere with you," Bacatha said through her teeth.

She backed a step closer to me, and I realized what she was doing. Bacatha knew how my power worked. She was trying to get close enough to me so that I could draw from her. Akrin had also deduced this, narrowing his small eyes so they were nothing more than dark slits in his morose face.

"That is far enough, Leharan," he warned her. "Remember, your halfbreed friend over here has a Warding Stone in her. The girl's powers are useless, but she does have a choice to make."

A smile spread over his face, and it was more terrifying than any sinister words he could have spoken. Akrin's smile held nothing natural. It was a sick, twisted version of the expression that promised only pain. Gula made a noise behind me and I turned to see the man holding her press a knife to her throat.

"I will do what you want. Just stop hurting them!" I cried.

"Choose, then," Akrin commanded.

I shook my head, confused. "Choose?"

He plucked a knife out of his own belt, gesturing to Chaote with it, then waving at Gula. "Choose this one or choose that one. One lives and one dies."

"You said you would not harm them!" I protested, my heart practically beating out of my chest.

"Did I? I do not recall making that promise. I said they would go free. And what is more freeing than death?" he mused, toying with me, enjoying the stricken look on my face.

I shouted at the vague figure of the Earth Queen that hovered in the air, safely out of reach. "Why are you doing this?"

The Earth Queen was silent and Akrin laughed again. "Choose, Eolande, or they both die."

I looked at each of the women. "I can't!"

"Then you will kill them both," he taunted. He was practically salivating over my horror, relishing the pain he was causing. My eyes met Chaote's once again and she gave a slight nod, granting me permission to choose the other woman. I shook my head. I would not condemn her to death. I couldn't.

"Very well. Kill them both," Akrin ordered. Gula shrieked in protest as the knife started to pierce her flesh.

"Gula! I choose Gula! Please, let her go!" I shouted. The man with the knife released the healer and she stumbled forward, falling to her knees. I spun around just in time to see Chaote reach up and grab the edge of the coralstone boulder, flinging herself over the top of it. The rope around her neck caught and she dangled from the other side of the stone, her feet scraping above the ground. The soldiers clung to their end of the rope, choking her, and somehow I knew what she was trying to do. She was deliberately choking herself. She was going to make herself lose consciousness, and when she did, I would be able to use my power.

I reached into my pocket, pulling out the Sapphire and clutching it in my fist, praying that our blood would work and I could draw the power back to the amulet. Chaote's eyelids fluttered and then I heard them, the first whispers of the past coming from the amulet. I focused on the stone, gripping it as hard as I could, feeling it grow warm in my hand. The air around us stirred, the wind pushing away the fog. The whispers were louder now, more insistent, and I snarled at them to be quiet.

"What is she doing?" It was Maialen's voice that cut through the air above, shrill and sharp.

I flung my arm out, the force of the wind knocking the soldiers to the ground. Akrin sprinted behind the block of coralstone, and I saw Gula rush over to Chaote as soon as the men dropped her. I pulled the power further into me, feeling the cold rush of air as it swirled around us. Then I flung it at Maialen. The eagle struggled against the wind, rolling twice as it tried to get out of the way of the blast, but the Earth Queen held on. The sky darkened, clouds gathering and churning overhead, and I wondered if I was the one who had called them. Then the island began to tremble beneath me and the cracks in the ground widened and tilted down, so that everything was sliding into a yawning abyss.

Bacatha caught me around the waist, throwing me aside before I could be swallowed up by the ground. I landed hard on my back, crying out from the pain of my healing wound being split open again, and the Sapphire tumbled from my grasp. I rolled onto my stomach, stars bursting in my vision from the immense pain, groping desperately for the amulet.

It was then that Maialen dipped closer on her eagle, trying to see what was happening in the chaos, and my head was filled with shouts. They were overwhelming, a thousand voices from three different amulets, all screaming at me at once. I let out a cry, jerking to my knees and pressing my hands over my ears, trying to shut them out. Then one voice called my name, louder than the others, stronger. It was my mother.

Get up off your knees, daughter. Stand and face her. Remember who you are.

I screamed again, more to drown out the cacophony of voices than from pain, and did as she commanded, picking up the Sapphire and pushing myself to my feet. Akrin had grabbed Chaote and was dragging her towards the eagles, and Thyrr was right behind him. The General tossed the halfbreed's prostrate form over the eagle, then leapt onto the winged creature. Thyrr reached up to grab the tether of another, but before he could swing himself up on the eagle's neck, a keening wail pierced the air. A watery tentacle snaked around his torso and the Sirens were there, pulling him back, their rows of teeth bared as they hissed menacingly. Maialen shrieked at them, and the ground beneath Thyrr began twisting and buckling, but the Sirens refused to release him, sliding over the broken land and dragging him with them. Maialen whipped her head back to look at me and her face was distorted into a mask of rage. She moved her hand, and before I could stop what was happening, water arched over us in a monstrous wave. I heard my mother's voice again, bellowing in protest as Maialen used the Pearl of Water. The wave crashed down, and for a moment I was underwater, floating, still and silent. It was blissful, a blessed reprieve from the clamoring voices of the amulets. Then the wave receded and dropped me onto the debris-strewn ground, pieces of coralstone scraping my hands and knees. The taste of the water was bitter and putrid, causing me to cough and gag. Kaeleb was right, whatever Maialen was doing, it was poisoning everything she touched.

I lifted my head, coughing the last of the brackish water out of my lungs just in time to see Gula sliding into the cracked earth. Her brown eyes were terrified and I would always remember the look on her face at that moment, how her lips had formed a perfectly round circle of silent screams just before she disappeared. Her fingers clawed desperately at the crumbling ground, then the chasm closed around her and she was gone.

I ran to where she had last been, scraping at the ground, trying to dig her out even though I knew it was impossible. Maialen's eagle began to beat its wings in retreat, and I looked around desperately. I could have tried to stop the Earth Queen, but I had to save Gula.

"Bacatha!" I yelled, seeing the Leharan woman running after the retreating eagles. She skidded to a stop, her long blonde hair whipping around her head as she spun back to me. She knew what I wanted, sprinting and sliding to her knees beside me and gripping my hand. I hesitated for a fraction of a second, knowing what I would be taking from her. Bacatha pressed her lips together, closing her eyes, and I began to draw the power. She grimaced but kept her hand in mine, and the land beneath us moved, rolling up until Gula's body was churned out of it.

I let out a cry of relief, releasing Bacatha and scooting to Gula's side, pushing her curly halo of black hair out of her face. She was staring at something far away, her mouth still forming the shape of a circle, dusted with grains of sand and dirt.

She is dead she is dead she is gone her too everyone dies they all leave me it is my fault I could not save her I tried I tried I tried what will I say to Kaeleb how can I tell him it was my fault we were here I wanted to go back I should have gone back.

I screamed again, out of anger and frustration, out of sorrow, the sound drawing forth from the deepest place within me, the bottomless well of pain that was the loss of my parents, the death of Gideon, of Sybylla, and now of Gula. Everyone who attempted to care for me ended up dead and it was shattering me.

Bacatha gripped my shoulder. "You did all you could."

"But she is dead," I argued, tears streaming down my face. "And they took Chaote."

"The Earth Queen was never going to let Gula walk away from here, and that had nothing to do with you. As for Chaote, she can take care of herself until we can get to her. Come, Eolande, we must return to Tahitia. It is not safe here."

I suddenly remembered Thyrr. I stood and spun around to find him still gripped in the arms of the Sirens. He winced as they tightened their hold, their barbed tentacles digging into his flesh so that small rivulets of blood trickled down his arms. Their expectant eyes met mine, glistening with tears, as they sang a hauntingly mournful chord.

"Eolande, please understand," Thyrr began, and it took everything in me not to strangle him.

"No! You do not get to speak to her," Bacatha intervened before I could say a word, her voice harsh and thick with emotion. "Not after what you have done. You will carry Gula's body to the ship, and then we will take you back to Tahitia to decide what will be done with you."

"They told me no one would be hurt. All they wanted was Eolande..." Thyrr tried to explain. "And in return, she promised that we would have Lehar back. I had to try, Bacatha. I did it for all of us."

"You did it for yourself. You are a coward," Bacatha snarled.

His voice was pained. "Bacatha, please."

"Get the body," she ordered, ignoring the desperate plea in his blue-gold eyes. "Begging to me will not help you, so save your breath. I am not the one who will decide your fate."

16

When we reached Tahitia, Kaeleb was waiting for us near the docks. It was nearly dusk, and the sky was still heavy with clouds, the wind whipping across the ocean in frothy gusts that encouraged the waves to bombard the shore. I watched his solitary figure as we approached, knowing that we were about to destroy his world and wondering what words I could possibly say to ease the blow.

"I will tell him," Bacatha said from her place beside me. "He should not hear it from you."

"But it was my fault," I told her with a shake of my head. I could hear the whispers from the Sapphire, had been hearing them since I had drawn the power back into the amulet, and I was tempted to throw it out to sea.

"This was Thyrr's fault," she practically spat through her teeth. The scars on her face were muted in the grey light of dusk, but her icy blue eyes shone like cold fire. "The boy will need someone. Let me tell him so he will not have that memory from you, so you can be there for him."

I jerked my head up in surprise at her words, taken aback by the imposing woman's sentimental gesture. She cared about Kaeleb.

"I am sorry... for taking part of your life from you," I murmured to her. Guilt was eating away at me for everything that had transpired that day.

Bacatha shrugged, a small smile touching her thin lips. "I am a Leharan warrior. I never planned on growing old."

The ship was secured to the dock and the ramp lowered. Bacatha walked across it first, her jaw clenched and her back straight. She went up to Kaeleb and I watched as she gripped his shoulder, leaning close to him to say the words that would bring him so much pain.

He looked past her, his grey eye searching as if he did not believe what he was being told. Then his gaze met mine and there was something so desperate in it that it broke my heart. I felt tears spill down my cheeks and he began shaking his head. Bacatha turned back and gestured to the others, and they lifted the body, carrying it down as carefully as they could. As soon as Kaeleb saw his mother he was on his knees, his head bent so that his pale hair hid his face, his hands fisted against his thighs. Bacatha moved to stand behind him, staying with him while he was forced to accept what had happened. He reached out to Gula's body, his fingers stroking her cheek, and then he leaned forward, resting his head on her chest and wrapping his arms around the only mother he had ever known one last time.

He held her for a long while before he reluctantly let go, motioning for the Leharans to take her back to the village. A crowd was gathering on the beach, and word of what happened must have spread quickly, for the Elder herself was hurriedly approaching. Cossiana fell to her knees as the body moved past her, not out of grief, but out of respect. The other islanders quickly followed suit, kneeling and remaining there until the dead woman had disappeared along the jungle path.

"Where is he?" Kaeleb demanded, his voice as violent as I had ever heard it. "Bring him here!"

Bacatha returned to the ship and made her way to the bow where she had tied Thyrr to the railing. She cut his bindings, lifting him up and pushing him towards the ramp. He did not try to run or flee, but walked steadily before her down the pier, his face haunted and pale.

"Kaeleb, I did not kill your mother, Maialen did," Thyrr began.

"Because of you!" Kaeleb shouted. He stormed up to the man, Bacatha stepping back out of the way quickly. Kaeleb yanked one of his swords from its sheath, the blade gleaming in the fading daylight. The entire island was silent, waiting. Cossiana had gotten to her feet, but the Elder made no move to intervene, watching the scene with sorrow in her dark eyes. I felt my breath catch in my throat as Kaeleb lifted his sword, swinging it at the other man's neck.

He stopped just before the blade bit into the skin, the sharp edge hovering a breath above Thyrr's neck. He held it there, his face wet with tears, his arms shaking. I stepped onto the pier and Kaeleb's eye flickered up to me, raw with grief. His hands gripped the sword hilt with white knuckles, his muscles flexing, then he let out a roar, stepping back and throwing the sword down in the sand. He turned and stomped away down the beach, the Tahitians parting to let him pass.

Cossiana ordered some of the Tahitians to take the captive, then she spoke to Bacatha quietly. I walked up to them, not sure what I should do or say.

"Go and find him. He should not be alone and neither should you," Cossiana said gently. She lifted her withered finger and pointed to where the Sirens were bobbing up and down on the waves. "I see you have brought them back with you. They will watch over you both."

I looked out at the terrifying, beautiful creatures, their blue-green skin shimmering amongst the grey sea. Then I nodded to the two women, moving off down the beach and following Kaeleb's trail of footprints in the sand. The Sirens emerged from the sea, dancing along the edge of the shore as they followed behind me. The Sirens had held the Pearl for me as a child until Maialen had stolen it. Perhaps it was possible they would hold the Sapphire for me as well. I needed a moment of reprieve from the incessant whispers that had been ceaselessly gnawing at me since I first used the amulet. There was one who kept clamoring over the others, drowning out their cries by shouting *Harbonah* over and over again.

Once I was out of sight from the others, I stopped, waiting for the creatures to join me, pulling the amulet out of my pocket and fighting the urge to press my hands over my ears and scream as the voices grew louder.

The Sirens seemed to know what I was asking of them, and they made encouraging sounds, holding out one of their hands. I passed them the amulet and they dove into the waves, disappearing into the depths of the sea, taking the hateful voices with them. I took a deep breath, closing my eyes, thankful to no longer hear the shouts of the dead echoing in my head.

"Chaote gave you the Sapphire?"

I let out a startled yelp, nearly falling into the sea myself. Kaeleb was sitting on a boulder, just below a jutting ledge of rock that sloped up from the beach. The air around us was heavy with moisture and rain had begun to fall. It was not the quick, tempestuous rain of an island storm, but a gentle mist that coated everything in hazy droplets and soaked you through before you even realized it was there.

"Yes," I answered.

He nodded, not surprised. His pale hair was damp with rain and it clung to his forehead and neck. Water ran down his narrow, angular face, dripping from his chin and soaking his shirt. He continued to watch me, his one eye filled with a tumult of emotion. Suddenly I wanted to scream, to cry, to fall down and pound the ground with my fists, to yell and rip at my hair and tear at my skin. I wanted to do anything to escape what I was feeling, the guilt of who I was. I had not realized how numb I had become in Veruca. How everything in my heart had faded away behind the pain and fear until that was all that was left. Now, here with him, I could feel everything and I could barely contain it. It was almost worse than the whispers of the amulet because it was my mind, my soul, that was constantly screaming. I could not escape it and I was terrified that I would get lost in it.

"I thought you hated me," he said after a long moment.

I shook my head, feeling the clinging rain trailing over my face, following the lines of the high cheekbones that reminded people so much of my mother. He continued to watch me as if he were waiting for something, and I wished I knew what it was that he wanted. After a while he rose slowly, closing the distance between us, standing so close that I could see the droplets of rain caught in the thick fringe of lashes that ringed his eye and the dark shadow that swept along his jaw. I wondered if he could hear my heart beating, if he knew how it pounded in my chest.

"It was my fault," I began. "They came for me."

His eyes were no longer like steel, but clouded and grey, like the sky that rolled overhead. "No, it was mine."

"But you were not even there," I protested.

He sighed, looking out at the ocean. "I should have been. Was it quick? Her death?"

"I do not think she suffered," I lied, seeing the terrified circle of Gula's mouth again in my mind, even though I had tried my best to block out the horrible memory. "I tried to save her. Bacatha let me draw power from her so I could try, but it all happened so fast."

"Bacatha said Akrin was there, with the Earth Keeper. You tried to warn me he would go to her, but I never thought Thyrr would help them..."

"I am sorry my family has caused you so much pain." They were meager words in the face of all that had been done to Kaeleb. His entire life had been reshaped and distorted because of the choices my family made. Because of me.

He sighed, digging the toe of his boot into the sand. "Stop apologizing for everyone else's actions. You are sorry to have been born who you were, sorry for everything you think it has caused, but you cannot change who you are. Thyrr, Damian, your mother, my father, they all made their own choices that we were not a part of. We are just the ones who must suffer the consequences."

I stood in silence, thinking about what he had just said, wishing that his words would alleviate the guilt that was so heavy in my heart.

"There is something about Thyrr you need to know," he began, hesitant and once more rubbing the sand with the tip of his boot.

"Something worse than him being a traitor?"

Kaeleb let the ghost of a smile touch his lips. "Perhaps we should have seen it as a warning that he could become one. The truth is, he is not your uncle, Eolande. He is not Orabelle's brother."

I felt my blue eyes grow round and my mouth fell open in surprise. Emotions clamored for dominance within me and I struggled between confusion, relief, anger, betrayal and disappointment. Kaeleb lied to me. What was worse, not only had he deceived me, but he left me in the company of a stranger, someone I trusted was my family member.

"How could you?" I whispered.

He shoved a hand through his hair, pushing the damp strands out of his face. It was the first time I had seen his features so starkly displayed, even though his eye was still covered with the leather patch. "I wanted to tell you, but you were so terrified of everything. I thought maybe if you felt you had family here, it would be easier for you."

"But I did not have family!" I retorted angrily. "You let me go to that island with a man who was a stranger to me, who had no reason to care about me, and this whole time I have been blaming myself for what happened there!"

"Bacatha was there, and I never thought he would–"

"You should have been there!" I practically screamed at him, trying to hold back the sob that was tearing at my chest. "You swore to protect me and you should have been there!"

He dropped his head, the wet strands of pale hair sliding forward to shadow his face once more. "I know."

My anger towards him was gone as suddenly as it had appeared, and I realized I had flung the same words at him that he had admitted to me earlier. I did not mean to be cruel, but in that moment the rage was better than the pain and sorrow and I had latched onto it selfishly.

"I hate this!" I cried out, and everything that had been welling up within me since my escape from Veruca came boiling up to the surface. "I hate all of this! I hate how I feel, I hate that I am scared all the time, I hate what my life is, what your life is, that everyone around me dies! I feel like my very existence is a curse to anyone near me, that I destroy everything I touch! I don't want this! I don't want to live like this! I tried to save your mother. I tried so hard. I wanted to save her for you, but I couldn't. I can't save anyone!"

"Eolande." Kaeleb took my face in his hands, his perfect grey eye searching mine while his voice brought me back to myself, out of the dark chasm of my thoughts. I stared up at him with wide eyes, waiting, trying to understand what I wanted so badly from him. I felt his hands tighten and the muscles along his arms seemed to strain, his body taut, the way it was before a fight. Then he released me and stepped away, and the pressure within me eased so I could breathe again.

"I need to lay my mother to rest in the sea. After that, we will take Thyrr to my father," he said, his pale brows drawn together. I nodded, following him as he moved down the beach, back towards the village, towards Thyrr, Gula's body, and all that awaited us there.

17

Chaote smiled, revealing the pointed tips of her filed teeth and enjoying the way the Earth Queen grimaced at the sight of them.

"I have heard you have a particular dislike for my kind," the halfbreed said, feeling a drop of blood dribble down her chin. She turned her head briefly and spat, clearing the bloody saliva that had pooled in her mouth after Akrin had struck her.

Chaote was somewhere in Kymir's Royal City, her arms and legs shackled, secured to an iron ring on the floor of a dimly lit stone cell. Light slanted in through a narrow slit near the ceiling, just enough for her to see her captors as they stood watching her. Akrin was staring at her with a look she was all too familiar with, a deep and vicious hunger lighting up his beady eyes. She could see the tip of his tongue dart out along his lips and she knew that everything she had been told about him was true. He was cruel, and he would hurt her if she gave him the chance. Chaote chuckled to herself. She was not afraid of pain. It was worth it to get what she wanted.

"Is my dislike amusing to you?" Maialen asked, her voice dripping with disdain. "My father's life was taken by one of your ruthless blooddrinkers. He was torn apart in front of me, and it is a memory that I can never forget. Another of your cursed beasts ruined my Guardian, and it was one of you who bit my sister at the battle of Queen's End. The brutality of the Fomori knows no bounds and has destroyed many lives, so no, I do not prefer to be in the company of your kind."

Chaote shifted her attention from Akrin back to the Earth Queen. It was warm in the stone room, and the Keeper's cheeks were flushed beneath the scattering of freckles tossed over them. Maialen had lost the soft glow of her youth, and she wore a pinched expression on her face, as if the world around her was too loud.

"You cared so much about your sister's death that you bedded the man who killed her and bore him a son," Chaote responded, matching the Queen's tone. "You truly are your father's daughter."

"You did not know my father," Maialen retorted.

Chaote's smile widened, knowing she was getting under the other woman's skin. "I did not have to. The Fire Keeper told me all about him."

Maialen's big green eyes rounded, flashing with anger, and the lines on her face deepened. She lifted her hand and it hovered above her chest, where the two amulets rested against her skin, her gold bracelets shining. Chaote waited, tilting her head to one side, watching the woman like a child poking at an insect in the grass. The amulets were useless in her presence.

"I know what you are doing," Maialen said with a shake of her head.

"Do you? Then perhaps we should all stop wasting our time here. You want to see if your whipping boy can beat me into submission? Go ahead and let him try," Chaote encouraged. "He will fail."

Maialen threw a glance at Akrin, revolted by the way the man was leering at the chained woman. Even she had her limits. "Akrin, leave us. I wish to speak to her alone."

"But I am the one who-" Akrin began to protest, but he was stopped short when Maialen turned and banged on the door, her Kymirran guards opening it and hurrying into the chamber.

"Escort the General back to the manor for me. I will be along shortly," she ordered. Akrin frowned, the scar on his lip twisting into a lopsided arch. He threw a murderous glare at the prisoner, then stormed out, slamming the door behind him with a resounding thud.

"Thank you," Chaote conceded with a nod. She wanted nothing more than to rip the Earth Queen's head from her body, but it was not time for that yet. There was something else she wanted more. "I must admit, I find his company to be rather odious."

"We are not here to keep you entertained and Akrin is not a jester putting on a show for your amusement."

Chaote simply stared at her, waiting to learn what the Earth Queen did not want to say in front of the General.

"Why have you aligned yourself with him?" Maialen asked after a moment, her hands moving to smooth the rich fabric of her gown, pretending to be cavalier in her interest.

Chaote knew they were no longer speaking of Akrin. There was a change in the Keeper's eyes, a fleeting shadow that betrayed her attempt to conceal her emotions. "With the Fire Keeper? We are not allies."

Maialen's annoyance was growing, and she hated the jealousy that curled in her stomach at the thought of Blaise befriending such a beautiful creature. "I am not a fool. You have been roaming Imbria with that brat of his for years. If you are not his ally, then are you his babysitter?"

"You must be aware that Kaeleb is a grown man. He does not require someone to care for him," Chaote pointed out. She shifted, the chains tugging painfully against her shoulder blades. At least they had removed her armor, so she wasn't forced to sit there under the weight of that as well. She wore a tunic and pants, her feet bare and her shining black hair still pulled back in tight rows of braids.

"Why should I keep you alive? I could just kill you," Maialen suggested.

"Then do it."

The Earth Keeper sighed. "You really are quite unpleasant."

Chaote laughed, grinning at the other woman. "You think you can use me or else you would have killed me by now. I have a Warding Stone in me. I am a weapon against her. Your niece, Eolande."

Maialen's face darkened. "There is no proof that the girl is my niece. I have been lied to before concerning my sister's child."

"Tell yourself what you must, Earth Keeper. It does not change the truth of things. You hate Orabelle for the things she did. I can see it on your face when I say her name," Chaote observed, her voice low. "But Eolande is not her mother."

"You know nothing of me or how I feel," Maialen said waspishly. "Something changed when Orabelle's baby was born. All the Keepers felt it. That was why I went to Lehar, how I learned that she had given birth in secret. I wanted to help her, but Orabelle refused to even let me see the baby. I think she knew there was something wrong with it. If Eolande truly is my sister's child, then she is not like the rest of us. She is dangerous, and I will not allow my enemies to use her against me."

"You mean you will not let them take your power. You forget I come from a different time, a time when the world was still pulsing with divine blood and the Keepers were carving out their realms with the bones of their enemies. I have seen what power does to people, how it warps them. Especially the ones who are already broken."

Maialen's retort was like acid. "I am not weak or broken. Others have made the mistake of believing that about me. Do not add your name to that list as you sit here and try to lecture me on benevolence. It was not so long ago that you wanted to kill the child and drink its blood in order to gain power. What has changed?"

Chaote shrugged and the chains rattled softly. She tilted her head to one side, the golden light that streamed in through the narrow window radiant against her skin. "I like her."

"You like her?" The Earth Keeper's mouth fell open in surprise. Of all the things the ferocious halfbreed could have said, Maialen was not expecting that.

"Yes. I like her. I have no need to kill her. She will help me destroy the amulets. All I require is her blood and her power. I do not have to contain it within my own body for it to be useful."

Maialen thought this over, her hands still smoothing the folds of her gown. "You still have not convinced me why I shouldn't end your life right now."

"You could kill me now, take my Warding Stone out of me and try to find someone you trust to wield it, but who would that be? Who do you have left that would protect you? Akrin? He will turn on you in a second and you know it, especially with that kind of power at his fingertips. Logaire? Ha! We all know that snake would swallow her own tail to save herself. No, Earth Keeper, you have no one you can trust. You need me alive and you need the Warding Stone to stay in me. You know that Kaeleb and the others will not want to hurt me. They trust me. The boy trusts me." Chaote was watching the Keeper with her starry black eyes, seeing every movement, every twitch of the Queen's features and tremor of her hand. The halfbreed pressed on, "While your enemies may have reservations about killing me, they will not show the same restraint towards anyone else you decide to give the stone to.

As much as you may hate it, you need me alive, at least for now. But you cannot keep me too close to you, not when I dampen your power. I cannot remain here in Kymir. So what will you do, Earth Keeper?"

Maialen gripped the Emerald that hung from her neck, disconcerted not to feel the warm rush of energy she was used to. She hated the Warding Stones, the cold emptiness they carried around with them, swallowing everything. The halfbreed was right. Maialen needed to keep her alive, to keep the power of the stone contained within her, but she wanted the woman out of Kymir and as far away from her as possible.

"I will send you to Samirra where you will be Favian's prisoner," the Keeper declared. Maialen was pleased with herself, her eyes sparkling with satisfaction, enjoying the irony of the situation and how fitting it would be. Chaote and her army of Fomori had ransacked Samirra ten years before, taking the kingdom hostage and holding its inhabitants captive, including Favian, the man who later became her husband. Sending the halfbreed back there as a prisoner would be a fitting retribution for the atrocities Chaote committed in those days, and perhaps it would appease Favian's ceaseless whining. Maialen's confident smirk grew wider as she realized she had found the perfect solution to several of her problems, filling her with a sense of triumph.

Chaote stared at the other woman, her smooth ebony face carefully blank. Then she shrugged, lifting her chin stubbornly, as if being forced to stoically accept a punishment she could not escape. "Do as you must, Keeper."

18

I had never attended a Tahitian funeral. In Veruca they burned the bodies of their dead atop great funeral pyres, but here on the islands they entombed their dead in the sea. The morning after Gula's death, we gathered in small rowboats, before dawn had even begun to touch the world. I climbed into one of the boats to sit beside Cossiana herself and was handed a small pouch of flower petals. Each boat had a lantern at the bow and the lights bobbed in the darkness, creating filmy, opalescent pools of radiance that danced over the water. I strained my eyes to keep sight of Kaeleb's vessel, which also carried his mother's body, while the ethereal forms of the Sirens glided alongside us in the haloed light. They wove through the array of boats like guardians from another world, their long seaweed-like hair streaming behind them and shimmering on the crests of the waves. I smiled a little at the sight of them, comforted by their presence, knowing they would bring me the Sapphire if I needed it.

The men chanted as they rowed, low and deep, and the women hummed along at a higher pitch, their tones undulating like the waves beneath us. Tahitia was a tiny speck behind us when the islanders finally stopped rowing, forming a circle with the boats, Gula and Kaeleb in the center. The chanting grew louder and the men took out pouches of sand, spreading them into the water. The tiny grains glittered briefly on the sea, then disappeared, reminding me of what brief flickers our own lives were, shimmering so brightly for a moment, then gone forever, with only darkness left behind.

Kaeleb lifted his mother's body and I saw the Sirens reach out from the sea to take her. It was a sign of respect from the creatures, and an honor they rarely bestowed. I was pleased they awarded the merit to Gula, for she deserved it more than any of us. The creatures sank beneath the surface with the body, disappearing into the depths while the Tahitian women scattered their flower petals. I hurried to grab a handful of my own, so transfixed by the ceremony that I had forgotten I was part of it. I tossed the soft, velvety petals onto the water, watching them swirl and float, thinking of the woman beneath them and all she had done for me.

The chanting quieted once again, just as dawn broke far out over the ocean, the sky filling with bright pink bursts of sunlight. Kaeleb sat back down in his boat, and even from a distance I could see the tears on his face. He picked up an oar and began to row home.

"You will go with him to the Fire Keeper. You will need Blaise for what comes next," Cossiana informed me. She was sitting regally, her hands folded in her lap, watching me with eyes that were sharp and clear despite her age.

"What is it that comes next?" I asked her pointedly.

"You are the Solvrei, child, as much as you wish you were not. You know what comes next. Maialen is destroying this world and you must stop her," the old woman said and there was something tired in her voice, as if she had been fighting this battle far longer than I could imagine.

"My power hurts people. How can I fight with a power that I do not want to use?" I was hoping that if anyone could help me answer the thousands of questions and doubts that pounded in my head, it would be the Elder.

"You have the Sapphire. That will help. Chaote was wise to give it to you."

I scowled. "The Sapphire won't stop my aunt."

"You look like your father when you make that face," Cossiana said with a fragile laugh. "He used to make that same face when I would not let him have any saltfish."

My heart ached in my chest at the reminder of my lost family. "I forget you are my grandmother."

Cossiana shook her head. "No, child, I am not. I have never been a grandmother to you, and for that I am sorry. I have made many mistakes over the years and those mistakes have cost me dearly. They cost me my sons."

There was so much pain in her voice, and I somehow understood what she was trying to tell me. She had lost everything that mattered to her, and there was no room for anything else. For her, all I could be was the Solvrei, because that was all her shattered heart would allow. She could not bring herself to love me, and I would never be her granddaughter, not after all that had happened to us.

"I understand, Elder," I murmured, wiping at my eyes and the tears that were stinging them.

"When you are ready, we will send warriors to you. But only to you, Eolande. It is you who must ask us to fight," she said, and the fragile old woman was gone from her countenance, replaced once more by the proud and regal ruler of Tahitia.

Fear haunted my deep blue eyes as I stared at her. She still had not answered my earlier question. "My power.... You know how it works. I do not want to hurt anyone but to stop Maialen...."

"Find the Fenris."

"The dog?"

"You remember them, don't you? From when you were here as a child?" she leaned a little towards me, her dark eyes shining intently. "The god who walks the world in a mortal body that never dies. They will have all the power you need, and they have waited a thousand years for you to use it."

The dog the dog the god the dog it always goes back to the dog they are immortal but mortal they wish to die they told me so they want me to help them die my power can help them die I would not have to hurt anyone else but why aren't they here where are they why don't they help me maybe they have changed their minds they don't want to die I don't want to die I don't want anyone else to die I hate this I hate it I hate all of it I hate the dog.

"Eolande?" Cossiana prodded, her withered fingers gripping my wrist and jerking me out of the maelstrom of my thoughts. "We are back."

I climbed out of the boat and went up the beach to the village path, not looking back. I was stung by Cossiana's dismissal of me, even if I understood her reasons for it. I wanted someone to comfort me, to hold me and let me cry, to tell me that everything would be fine, to dry my tears. But I was the Solvrei, and what I wanted did not matter.

I went to Gula's house, sitting outside as the villagers streamed past. Kaeleb's long shadow slanted over me as the sun rose higher into the sky behind him.

"You are a mess," he said.

I could not help the short burst of laughter that escaped my lips, and it was good to see him smile in return. He was right, I was a mess. I had not bathed or cleaned myself since the fight on Lehar and my clothes were filthy, the cuts on my hands and knees still dirty and stinging. Kaeleb took my hand, lifting it so he could see my scratched palm and frowning at me.

"Come inside. We will clean you up. They will start bringing food soon, so we better do it now or you will not have a moment of privacy."

We went in and once I had cleaned myself and dressed in a fresh tunic and pants, he sat me across from him so he could tend to my wounds. They were superficial, mild cuts and scrapes, but he was surprisingly tender in his ministrations, wiping them with nimble fingers coated in oils and herbs.

"How is your back?" Kaeleb asked once my hands and arms had been seen to.

I wanted to lie and tell him it was fine, but the truth was it throbbed horribly, and I was worried that Gula's careful stitching had come loose. My former shirt had been caked in stiff, dried blood and though I had peeled it off carefully, I could not see what damage had been done to the injury.

"It hurts," I admitted after a while.

His brows drew together. "I know you do not want me to see you, but I need to look at the wound."

I felt the same panic flaring up, the same terror I had felt before when I shouted for him to get out of the room so he would not see my scars, and I tried to shove it down. He was waiting, patient, his eye filled with understanding. Before I could change my mind, I turned in my chair, motioning for him to pull my shirt up and look. Kaeleb moved quickly, pressing around the wound carefully, then slathering it in smelly herbs before patting it dry.

"I know something of what it is like when your body is not your own, Eolande," he said quietly. I was silent, struggling with the memories of the Verucan dungeon that were crowding my mind, and he went on. "You never have to hide who you are from me, and anything that has happened to you in the past is part of who you are."

He laid a bandage over the wound, then took a strip of cloth, passing the ends to me around my waist so that I could bind it tightly, tugging the tunic back down as soon as it was done.

"That was not so bad," he said.

"Thank you."

The islanders had arrived soon after, bringing steaming bowls of food and platters of fruits and nuts. Each of them wanted to speak to Kaeleb, to share with him some memory they had of his mother that was important to them, and he listened with a solemn expression, bowing deeply and thanking them for sharing. Between visitors, he shoveled some of the food in his mouth, nodding appreciatively when it was something good and making horrible grimaces when it was not to his liking.

"You should eat," Kaeleb had said. "There is no way of knowing when we will have a decent meal again after this. We leave for the mainland in a few hours. We need to tell my father what has happened."

I knew in those moments, while we sat eating together in Gula's quiet little home, that it had been the end of something for both of us. The healer had made us both feel safe, cared for. She had made a home that the world could not reach, a haven in the storms that were our lives. When we left there, Kaeleb and I both knew that we were leaving her behind forever, that it would never be the same and we would never know that feeling again. As we left the house for the final time, he reached out his hand to me, and this time I took it, lending each other the strength to move on.

19

The Fire Keeper leaned back at the table, bathed in the warm glow of torchlight that encircled the room. We were in a wide cavern in his underground lair, with sloping walls that were smooth like polished marble. The ceiling overhead was massive, a dome that rose at least a hundred feet over our heads, shrouded in a deep darkness the torches could not reach.

There were other men and women at the table, mostly Leharan, and Bacatha was among them, but my attention was fixed solely on the man who was Kaeleb's father. His face was relaxed, but his amber eyes gleamed as if it lit from within by his fiery Element. There was something disturbing in his silence, as if you were waiting for a sound that would not come, like a tree falling without a crash. He stared at Thyrr, and I saw his fingers twitch where they rested on the table.

I wanted to reach for the Warding Stone in my pocket, to quiet the insistent whispers that floated to me from the Fire Keeper's Opal and mingled with the voices from the Air Sapphire, but I forced myself not to. Most of them were faint, muted echoes from long before, but there was still that one, the one who was louder than the others, whispering *Harbonah* to me over and over like some kind of ghostly epithet. Before leaving the islands, I had reluctantly taken the Sapphire back from the Sirens. The Tahitians had fashioned me a leather necklace for the amulet, the best they could do on such short notice, but I still refused to wear it around my neck, hating the way the Element felt against my skin. I kept it tucked in my other pocket, wrapped in one of Gula's bandages.

I now stood watching the Fire Keeper with a gnawing fear in my gut that I was about to see Thyrr burst into flames in front of me. Kaeleb was beside me, but I made no move to reach for him or seek his comfort. I did not want to appear weak in front of the others, especially not Blaise. He did not seem the sort of man who appreciated weakness or hand holding.

Blaise continued to regard Thyrr thoughtfully, causing the younger man to squirm beneath his unrelenting scrutiny. Upon hearing of his treachery, the Leharans had immediately called for his execution, with Bacatha's gnarled old father, Brogan, leading the charge.

"It is our way," Brogan had insisted stubbornly. I knew that he was one of the members of the Leharan Guard who had served under my father, and although I was curious about him in that sense, most of my interest in the old man was centered around the fact that he had fathered the formidable warrior that was his eldest daughter. He was tall, like her, with long hair that had thinned and turned grey years ago. His face was deeply tanned and spotted with age, and he sported an impressive beard that hung midway down his chest. He still wore armor, but I could see that it was a light breastplate, more ceremonial than for any actual protection. He looked every bit the aging warrior, but he was still just an ordinary man. I expected someone like Bacatha to have been fathered by a titan, one of the legendary giants who had walked the world eons ago, colossal and savage and inhuman.

Blaise ignored the old Guard's insistent calls for the traitor's death, refusing to be provoked into a response. Finally, he shook his head, his curls of red hair falling back from his forehead. A hint of a smile touched the Keeper's lips, and it was more terrifying than any snarl or growl would ever be.

"We cannot kill him yet, old friend," Blaise said to Brogan. "We must find out what else he told our dear little Earth Queen."

"Nothing! I told them nothing," Thyrr insisted. I saw Bacatha's lips press into a thin line at the sound of his words, her icy gaze fixed on something far away to avoid looking at the man she had once believed in so wholeheartedly.

"Do you really expect me to believe that? Or anything else you say?" Blaise asked. There was an edge to his voice, like a sharpened knife was carving the words.

"The only thing I told them was that I had Eolande and would bring her to Lehar. I swear it," Thyrr vowed.

Blaise shrugged, his smile widening dangerously. "Even if I did believe you, we have to be sure."

"So, you will torture me? After all we have been through?" Thyrr cried.

Blaise was out of his seat and across the table before I realized what was happening, shoving Thyrr and sending him skidding across the stone floor on his back. "You have betrayed me after all we have been through! So, yes, dear friend, I will do what I have to in order to keep us safe. If you have told Maialen anything about Aracellis, then she will come here and flatten these caves with us inside them!"

I was startled to hear the name Aracellis, and I remembered what Kaeleb had said in the forest about him being Maialen's son. I glanced at the young man beside me and he gave me a small shake of his head, as if warning me not to ask, but I had to know if Aracellis was here. Thyrr had turned out to be a liar who had no relation to me, but perhaps I still had some semblance of family left alive.

"Is my cousin here?" I asked, my own voice startling me as it echoed through the chamber. Kaeleb groaned and threw Thyrr a scathing look, and Blaise looked at me as if I were mad.

"Your cousin?" Blaise echoed.

"Father, I did not want to tell her-" Kaeleb began, but it was Bacatha who interrupted him.

"Your cousin is dead, Eolande. He died ten years ago. It was an accident. He fell into that damned abyss his mother opened up between Kymir and Samirra. I was there when it happened, so I know it to be true."

"Oh," I said softly, feeling foolish, trying to understand why Kaeleb had lied to me again.

Blaise threw me a sharp look. "Favian knew we had taken the boy from Samirra. After Chaote relinquished her siege on their realm, he sent word to Maialen, asking after the child. She assumed we were hiding him from her, using him as a hostage so she would not attack us. We simply let her continue to think so."

"You let her..." my voice trailed off and I shook my head, trying to gather my thoughts, to understand. "You let her think her dead son was alive for the last ten years?"

"Well, when you say it like that, it sounds worse than was intended," the Fire Keeper snapped in annoyance. "We simply let her continue to believe the story she had already convinced herself of. We needed to protect this place, especially after we saw what she did to Lehar."

I had no cousin, no hope for a better family. He too was dead, just like the rest of them.

Death there is so much death everyone dies why why can't I stop any of it what good am I if I can't stop any of it the Harbonah will help you listen to me I am trying to help you.

I had to stop myself from covering my ears and shouting as the hissing voice from the amulet slithered into my thoughts. I bit down on my lip, then turned abruptly and walked out of the chamber. They would think I was angry about what I had learned of my cousin, but that was preferable to them discovering the truth, that I could not separate my own thoughts from the nagging voices of the former Air Keepers.

I hurried through the dimly lit corridors of the underground realm, not even sure where I was going. There were footsteps following me, and I wondered if it was Kaeleb or Bacatha who had been sent after me this time. Whoever it was, I was in no mood for their company and I abruptly stopped, whipping around so I could yell at them.

"Leave me alone!" I snapped at Kaeleb.

"Have you tried asking them what they want?" he questioned, leaning against the cave wall, his arms folding over his chest. He was wearing his leather armor again, his swords strapped to his waist and his pale hair falling over the patch that covered his missing eye.

"Have I tried... " It was obvious he was referring to the voices from the amulets, that he had discerned the cause of my unease. I wanted to shout at him some more, to punch him and hit him for lying to me about Aracellis, but there was no point and I knew why he had done it. I could not fault him for trying to protect his people and guard their secrets. I was a stranger to him when we met. It would have been foolish to tell me the truth. Some of the tension in my shoulders eased, but I could still hear the insistent whispers from the amulet clouding the depths of my mind. Perhaps he was right, and I should ask the irksome Air Keepers what they wanted.

"Ask them," he encouraged.

I shook my head. "I don't want to. I don't like them."

"You are just being stubborn now, Eolande."

There was a mild rebuke in his tone, and I narrowed my eyes at the sound of it. "Very well, I will ask them."

I reached into my pocket and let my fingers brush the cold, hard surface of the amulet. My skin tingled where I touched it, like I was standing too close to a bolt of lightning, and the whispers were louder, more jumbled, even harder to understand. I closed my eyes.

What do you want?

We want to help you destroy the amulets. They are poison, foul, foul poison. You are the Solvrei. We only want to help you.

Then stop yelling at me all the time. I cannot be the Solvrei if I go mad from your unending whispers!

We will be silent, but you must find the Fenris.

I looked at Kaeleb, waiting, testing the Keepers to see if they would keep their word. There was silence. I smiled at him, relieved.

"Did they stop?"

I nodded. "For now."

"My father is sending us to the north," Kaeleb announced abruptly, changing the subject. The smile faded from my countenance.

"But Maialen is in Kymir," I pointed out.

Kaeleb pushed a hand through his shock of pale hair. "She is, but we do not have the numbers to fight her. Just getting to her will take an army, even with you and my father working together. We need allies."

"What allies do you have in the north?" As soon as I asked the question, I knew the answer and my stomach turned. "You want the Fomori."

"Chaote has been taken. They will fight for one of their own."

I was incredulous, my blue eyes wide as I shook my own pale hair back from my face. While it was true that I felt pity for what the Keepers had done to the Fomori centuries before, I had no illusions about the ruthless beings they had become. "They are monsters."

"They are the fiercest creatures on Imbria and the Va'Kul is a strong leader. With their help, we could win-"

"At what cost?" I demanded. "I have seen what they do. I lived with Gideon and his useless arm and his constant pain. And have you all forgotten what happened at Queen's End? How my mother died? The Fomori ran rampant over the battlefield and one of them bit her! They had no control, their bloodlust was too great. You cannot take them into battle. They will slaughter everyone."

"I believe the Va'Kul can control them," he tried to reason.

"Even if she can, you cannot trust her! She is Fomori!" I argued. It had been years since I had seen one of the beasts, but I could still smell it, the foul odor of death that seeped from every pore. I said again, "I have seen what they do."

I was young when it happened. Gideon and I were on our way to the nearest town with a bundle of fish we had caught in the river early that morning. He wanted to trade our catch for fabric to make me a new dress. We were walking along, my tiny hand clasped in his, the basket of fish slung over his massive shoulder. His other arm hung uselessly at his side, the hand flopping against his leg as he walked, reminding me of the glassy-eyed fish we caught when they hit the rocks. I was humming, pleased with the tiny pink flowers that I gathered in the pocket of my apron. My scarf was tied firmly over my pale hair, hiding it, and atop that Gideon had dropped a puffy little yellow hat, a funny thing he had picked up for me to make me laugh and which I insisted on wearing everywhere. Yellow was my favorite color.

"Nearly there!" the big woodsman had announced, swinging me with his mighty arm so that I lifted into the air and squealed with delight. He smiled indulgently at me beneath his beard, and his warm eyes sparkled with happiness.

There was a sound of some sort, far off, and I no longer remembered what it had been. Perhaps a scream, perhaps a snapping twig. Something had alerted him and he stopped, the smile fading as he stared at the surrounding forest.

"Ew, what is that smell?" I had wailed, tugging my hand from his so I could cover my nose.

"Ssh. Quiet now, Eolande," he warned, stern and serious. He slid the basket of fish down from his shoulder, pulling me up in its place so that I was clutching him around the neck tightly, my legs wrapped around his torso. He crept forward, and from my new height I could see the edge of the town. I was about to shout at him that everything was fine and I could see the town, but then I saw one of them. The Fomori. They were on the road just before the town walls, and there was an overturned wagon, the ground littered with spilled baskets and barrels. The huge, grey-skinned creatures were bending over the wagon, their dark hair shining in the sun, when one of them let out a triumphant howl. It pulled something from the wagon. It was a man. He was still alive and he was writhing on the ground, crying for help. The Fomori fell on him, and blood sprayed across the wrecked wagon, soaking the dirt road. I let out a cry of terror, not loud, just a tiny mewl, but it was enough. The beasts lifted their heads, jaws dripping and their phantom yellow eyes darting around hungrily.

Gideon turned and ran, crashing through the forest while I tried desperately to hold on to him. My silly hat flew off my head and I squeezed my eyes shut, burying my face in his long, soft hair and trying to stop seeing the fangs and blood and horrible grey skin. Gideon waded out into the river so they could not follow our scent, and it took him hours to trudge home through the water with me clinging to his back.

"Gideon said I should always run from them," I said to Kaeleb, trembling at the memory.

"I know you are afraid, but we have to go to them. The Va'Kul has a Warding Stone. She can help us win," Kaeleb said gently. "If there were another way, I would gladly do it. But Maialen controls both Kymir and Samirra."

"What about the Verucans? Logaire no longer has Akrin to lead her army and the Oracle is dead. Blaise could take the realm from her, use the Verucans to fight. She is weak right now," I insisted.

"I will speak to my father about it," Kaeleb conceded. "But even if we side with Veruca, or take it back, we will need the Fomori if we want to win. The Va'Kul has the other Warding Stone and without Chaote we need it so we can control where Maialen will go and when she will fight. Eolande, I am doing this for you. I am trying to save you from having to fight her yourself."

I shook my head.

"Eolande, do you trust me?" he asked me, gripping my arms.

"No! You have lied to me at least a dozen times already!"

A sheepish grin fleeted over his angular features. "Let me rephrase that. Do you trust me to protect you?"

The humor was gone and his grey eye was fixed on me with a singular intensity that I found disconcerting. I knew what he wanted me to see in his eye, but I was afraid of it, afraid I was not worth the sacrifice, afraid that he really would die for me if it came to that. Suddenly I felt weak and shame washed over me like a hot wave. My mother had gone to the Fomori, and she had not been afraid. Her words echoed in my head. *Remember who you are.*

"Fine, we go to the Fomori," I relented.

"I will not let them hurt you, Eolande, I promise."

If I had only known what would happen to us in the north, I would never have gone.

20

Chaote would have preferred to be sitting on a horse, or at the very least walking on her own two feet. She wouldn't even have minded if they kept her chained. She had walked in chains before, a thousand years earlier, led by Rilian, the first Keeper of Water and the lover who betrayed her when he learned she was part Fomori. Rilian had her bound and beaten, paraded through the realms with the other Fomori prisoners on their way to the Wastelands. Chains she was used to. It was this damned wagon that she could not abide.

The wagon lurched to one side and she nearly fell over, bracing her forearms against the soft satin cushions that paneled the walls, her wrists tied together with a length of rope. It was the Queen's carriage, and it was completely ridiculous, an opulent display of wealth that the stark nature of the half-breed found obscene. Chaote curled her lip at the lavish gold trimmings, the rich fabrics and plush pillows. A pattern of ivy had been painted all along the inside and across the roof and Chaote rolled her eyes at it. Why not just look outside if you wanted to see a plant?

"You don't seem to be enjoying your accommodations," Akrin said. He was seated opposite her, leaning back into the corner, one arm outstretched along the back of the cushioned seat. Chaote ignored him, hating his nasal voice and the way it wormed into her ears. She was aware of him constantly, for she was no fool and men like him were opportunists when it came to inflicting pain. Since they had left the Royal City of Kymir, she had waited for the attack to come, never taking her eyes off him. His black armor and sullen face were so out of place amongst the velvety grandeur of the wagon that she found it jarring, but still she watched him.

He seemed aware of her trepidation and was enjoying it. He leaned forward slightly, breathing deeply. She had a musky smell, a warm scent that was almost inviting, except there was something more that lingered in it, something ancient and frightening. The scent of death and the Fomori.

"I know what you are afraid of," he said, smiling at her with his horrible parody of human emotion.

"I am not sure you do," was her quiet reply. She was beautiful, but it was a beauty that held no invitation for him. She was cold, like a statue or a being from another world, out of place amongst the rest of Imbria. The only thing about her exquisite features that appealed to him was the idea of carving them up into pieces and rearranging them.

Akrin lifted the little tasseled curtain to look out the window. "We are nearly to Iriellestra. Do not worry, halfbreed, I will not be stopping for a tryst."

Chaote let out a bark of laughter that caught him off guard. "Oh, you think I am afraid of that? Not hardly, Verucan. I am only afraid you will try, and then I will be forced to kill you and I will not get what I have come all this way for."

Akrin was unsettled by her words and her demeanor, shifting uncomfortably on the plush seat. He preferred it when women were afraid of him and he did not like the callous manner of this disgusting halfbreed. For a moment he was tempted to show her what he could do, but he remembered Maialen's orders. He had just recently earned the Earth Queen's favor and it would be unwise for him to disobey her so soon. Chaote was not going anywhere. There would be time to teach her some manners later.

Akrin leaned back again, staring at the foul woman. She stared back at him, her strange gaze unwavering. Her eyes were like the night sky, cold and hard, black flecked with bits of yellow. He wondered if the yellow was the Fomori in her. Disgusting. Perhaps it was best he did not touch her. Who knew what foulness she carried in her corrupt blood?

"Do you know what I had to do to become the Mother of the Fomori?" Chaote asked him, as if she could see into his thoughts. She could tell from the dull look on his face that he had never even thought about it. Here he was, sitting across from an enemy who he had not bothered to learn anything about, unconcerned in the way only fools could be. Kaeleb was right about him. He was a waste of skin.

"I suppose you are going to tell me," he said, trying to sound superior.

"It was not just the fighting. At first, it was only fighting, but then one day it was something more. We realized we were going to die in those dark tunnels the Keepers had trapped us in. There was no food, no way for us to escape. Have you ever seen anyone die of hunger? The mind is sometimes the first thing to go, and the Fomori were already ferocious and cruel. Hunger only made them worse. I watched one of the young get murdered over a scrap of leather. A group of them bashed his head in with a rock, all so they could chew on a filthy piece of leather."

Akrin shrugged. He was too callous to care that some child of the Fomori had died violently.

Chaote went on. "I was the one who suggested that we eat one another. The young one they killed was just lying there, his brains falling out over the rocks, and I thought, why are they fighting over that stupid piece of leather when there is plenty of meat right here? So I found a sharp rock and I cut him up, passing pieces of him around. I did not cry or vomit or scream or do any of the things that one believes one would do. I was calm. I made sure they were all fed, and that is when they began calling me Mother."

Akrin was disgusted, but she had aroused his perverse interest and he could not help asking her, "What did they taste like?"

"Like I imagine you would," she said without missing a beat. He glowered at her and she stared back at him, refusing to look away.

"Why tell me this?" he demanded to know.

"I wanted you to know that I will do whatever it takes to survive, and to win."

She was still staring at him when they reached the outer wall of Iriellestra, but something in her had changed. He saw the shadow that passed over her face and his curiosity peaked. He knew Chaote had left Samirra without the Fomori army, parting ways with her savage brethren. Everyone on Imbria knew that, but perhaps there was more to the story than he realized.

"What happened here?" he asked her. His tongue darted out over his lips and he was practically salivating. Whatever had occurred, it had caused this cold, mythical creature, a woman who could callously carve up and eat a bleeding corpse, to feel pain, and he was dying to know what it was.

"I lost someone," she said, and her voice was flat, emotionless. It betrayed none of the thoughts that were filling her head. The image of Damian rose in her mind, bringing back memories of being there with him. He was a good man, strong and proud and determined, but also kind and gentle. Too good for this world. Chaote forced herself to relive those last days, to feel his loss again as if it were the first time. She remembered him coming to her just before they were to leave the city, and how his dark eyes had shone with the promise of the future. He had believed in her, in what they could do together. Then Favian had murdered him, shot him in the back with an arrow as they were leaving.

Akrin's beady eyes narrowed, and he was suddenly wary of the change in her demeanor. They had passed through the outer wall and were now in the heart of the city. Chaote flipped back the curtain, looking out as they rumbled over the stone paths.

Iriellestra was as she remembered it. Dirty, crowded, wasting away. The buildings sagged, even more dilapidated than they had been ten years ago. The streets smelled of filth and too many bodies, and she wondered how the plague had not returned to devour what was left of the miserable kingdom. Up ahead, the palace rose above the inner wall, a shining beacon of gleaming marble and copper domes. Then she noticed the dark swathes along the facade. It looked as if someone had thrown tar or mud, dripped it off the soaring towers like icing on a cake. It had to be Maialen's doing. Her corrupt power was a blight that followed her wherever she went.

"The people look hungry," Chaote's comment was chastising, as if it were Akrin's fault that the Samirrans did not have enough to eat.

"Maialen can feed them," he dismissed with a flick of his fingers.

"Maialen is poison. Look at what she is doing to the palace."

Akrin was unmoved. "You think all Keepers are poison."

She turned her black eyes to settle on him once more and he wished she had stayed looking out the window. "Because they are."

"Then perhaps you should give us the girl. We can forget all this. You can go about your business, eating rats in the woods or eating your friends or whatever it is you do for fun."

She laughed again. "Is that what you think I do? Am I an evil hag from a children's tale, then?"

He scowled at her. He did not like being ridiculed, and he was growing weary of her constant derision. Perhaps he could hit her a few more times, remind her that he held the power, not her. His lips parted as he pictured it, his fist smashing into her perfect skull.

The wagon lumbered to a stop. They had reached the inner wall. Suddenly there were shouts from outside. Akrin tried to look, holding aside the ridiculous tasseled curtain with his cumbersome hands. He finally gave up with an annoyed growl, ripping off the dainty fabric and flinging it down at his feet.

"Get out," he ordered, reaching across her to push the door of the wagon open. Chaote did as he commanded, lifting her bound hands to show she was harmless and stepping out into the sun before him.

"No! No, I told the Queen this was a mistake, you were supposed to turn back!"

Chaote whipped around, her lips pulling back from her teeth to smile at the haunted, pale face of the Samirran Guardian. Favian. The man who had killed Damian, the man she had been hunting for ten long years. He had at least thirty soldiers with him and her grin widened, showing the filed points of her teeth.

"You thought you could hide forever, didn't you?" she asked him. Her voice was sweet, like honey, and Favian shuddered at the sound of it.

"Get her out of here! You have no idea what you have done!" the Guardian was yelling at Akrin, who was staring at him as if he were mad. "She wanted you to bring her here, you idiot! She orchestrated this whole thing!"

Chaote's throaty laugh floated on the air. "You should have brought more men, Favian."

21

"Tell me again why we cannot just take an eagle to the north," Bacatha muttered, holding up the torch she was carrying and trying to shake out the piece of parchment Blaise had scrawled his directions on. "Your father's writing is indecipherable."

Kaeleb peered over her shoulder. "Go left at the next fork. That should put us back on the right path."

"This is ridiculous. We are traipsing around like beetles in the dark, looking for a madman. We should be above ground, fighting the Earth Queen and rescuing Chaote," the Leharan warrior insisted.

Kaeleb raised a pale eyebrow. "Why are you so determined to save Chaote? Have you grown a little sweet on her, Bacatha?"

The severe woman glared at him. "Do not be an imbecile."

He laughed, shaking his head. "We cannot risk Maialen seeing us. The underground is safer, and that madman is the only one who knows the way to the north. He has spent ten years roaming these tunnels."

"I do not like it," she snapped.

I was quite certain the Leharan woman's foul mood had more to do with what she had learned about Thyrr in the last few days than her dislike of this strange man we were searching for. Blaise had not been bluffing when he threatened to torture the man. It had gone on for days, Thyrr's screams echoing down the long tunnels, reverberating through the caverns where we waited. People milled around us, some Verucan, mostly Leharans. It was a strange world, their dim, underground city. I had never thought that Leharans and Verucans could live together, but here they were, and it gave me hope for what the future held. If Blaise could bring people together to make these cold caverns into a home, then perhaps we could bring all of Imbria together, correct the mistakes that had been made.

Naïve sentimentality.

The voice of the dead Air Keeper had wormed its way into my mind as I sat there listening to Thyrr's cries of pain. Astus. The Harbonah. Apparently, Blaise had murdered him, an awkward bit of knowledge to have him screaming into my head every time I saw the Fire Keeper. I asked Kaeleb about it once, and the young man had curtly suggested that all the former Air Keepers were better off dead, especially the one who called himself the Harbonah.

Blaise is a foul brute. He will kill him, just like he killed me.

Be silent! I hissed at Astus. He retreated back into the recesses of the amulet, but I could feel his irritation like something chafing against my skin.

Thyrr let out another cry, sharper than before, and I flinched, glancing at Bacatha. She was sitting near me, her hands clasped together between her knees, her icy gaze fixed on the cave floor. She gave no indication that she was bothered by what was happening, aside from the thin slit she had pressed her lips into.

"Look at her! How could I risk the future of Lehar on her?" Thyrr shouted. My face flushed and I knew he was speaking of me. Thyrr was right. I was not the sort of person who looked as if they could save the world. I did not blame him for doubting me.

I heard the Fire Keeper's voice growing louder, more insistent, though I could not make out the words. I wished Thyrr would just tell him whatever it was he needed to know. Kaeleb was off gathering supplies, and I found myself glancing up at the entrance to the cavern every few seconds, wishing he would appear and take me somewhere else, any place where I could not hear the horrible screams. I was about to suggest to Bacatha that we take a walk when the door that had muffled Blaise's interrogation swung open. The Keeper strode out, wiping his hands on a cloth and leaving streaks of crimson blood on the fabric. His jaw was stern and his amber-colored eyes were shining so brightly they almost reminded me of the icterine glow of the Fomori. There was no joy in their brightness, only a deep rage, carefully maintained.

"Eolande, come with me," he had ordered, walking past us without stopping. I scrambled to my feet and hurried to follow him, Bacatha trailing after us. He took me out of the large cavern to another set of tunnels that led to the water chamber. He dipped his hand into the cool liquid that gathered in the bowl of rock, splashing it on his face and letting it run through his beard.

"Are you sure you have told me everything?" he asked me.

I thought of the Air Keeper's voice in my head, insisting that Blaise be punished for his murder. "There is something else."

Do not tell him about me!

Blaise was looking at me expectantly, waiting for me to speak. I could hear the whispers from his amulet, and they were drowning out the Air Keepers in their fury. The Fire Keepers wanted Veruca back, and they would do anything to get it. I shook my head, trying to clear it of all the different voices that were strangling my own thoughts.

Blaise looked sympathetic. "You can hear them when I am close to you."

I nodded. "They want you to take your kingdom back."

He sighed and shoved a hand through his hair, a gesture so much like the one Kaeleb often made that I found it disconcerting. He said, "I am going to Veruca. If what you say is true, if Logaire is truly as weak as you say right now, then I cannot let the opportunity pass."

"But what about Chaote?" I questioned.

Blaise regarded me carefully. "Chaote is the last person on Imbria you should be concerned for. She has a Warding Stone in her and she is our ally. Maialen may be foolish, but she won't risk hurting the halfbreed too badly, not when she can use her against us."

He rubbed his thumb over his knuckles and I saw they were scraped raw. I feared the answer, but I had to ask him, "Is Thyrr still alive?"

The Fire Keeper's face darkened. "Unfortunately, yes. I have what I needed from him. The Leharan Council will decide what happens to him now. From my previous experiences with your people, it would be safe to assume he is not long for this world. The islanders are not the most forgiving of Imbrians, and they despise traitors."

I felt a shiver crawl up my spine. As much as I hated Thyrr for what he had done and for his role in Gula's death, it was hard to imagine the brightness of who he was being snuffed out. For a moment I considered asking Blaise to intervene with the Leharans, then I glanced at his scraped and bloodied hands and realized that it might be more merciful to let the Leharans simply kill the man.

"Kaeleb tells me you wish for us to go north to the Fomori," I said instead.

"You fear them, but you are the Solvrei and you carry their blood. Remember that."

"Cossiana told me to find the dog." I wondered if I was just going to keep blurting out random facts to him. The Keeper made me nervous, and I chastised myself for being so ridiculous in his presence.

He arched one of his auburn brows, lifting his chin so that the torchlight danced over the stern planes of his face. The whispers from his amulet flared louder for a moment, then they quieted, as if they also wanted to hear what the Keeper had to say about the mythical dog-god. "Do not trust the Fenris, Eolande. They are the reason for all of this, and their aim is to rid the world of any and all divine powers. I would assume that also means you, my dear."

"But I need them to fight. Cossiana says they are the key to using my power without hurting anyone else."

Blaise snorted. "I trust the Tahitian Elder even less than I trust the damned dog."

He waved Bacatha towards us, and then he laid a hand on my shoulder, his powerful grip hot on my skin, even through the fabric of the tunic. The amber eyes flashed. "Whatever happens, protect my boy. Promise me you will do that. I can lose a lot of things, but I could not bear it if I lost him."

My lips had parted in a surprised circle at his admission, and I nodded clumsily. Bacatha gave him a deep bow in answer and he grinned at her, reminding her not to forget the new farming tool he had made for her. Then he strode from the room, leaving us standing there looking at each other.

Soon after, we began our journey. It was difficult to gauge the passage of time while underground. I had slept for a few fitful hours, so perhaps it was only a day or so since our departure. It had been quiet when we left, the bustling caverns nearly empty of inhabitants, and the stalls of vendors shuttered up for what I assumed was the night. It was eerie to pass through the realm as it slept, peaceful in a way that was unsettling, as if you were standing on the edge of a precipice and leaning out, watching the quiet darkness, aware that the first harsh sound would shatter it all.

"Who is this man we are searching for?" I asked for the third time. I had been staunchly ignored the first two times I asked, with Bacatha snorting in derision and Kaeleb shaking his head at her.

"My brother," the young man muttered, finally giving me an answer.

"Your... who is your brother?" I asked, confusion resuming its reign over my thoughts. For an orphan, Kaeleb seemed to have quite an abundance of family members. Though I supposed not so much anymore since Gula's death.

Kaden. He speaks of Kaden. It could only be him. He was an acolyte of the Harbonah, a worthy follower of mine.

"Kaden?" I asked aloud.

Kaeleb threw me a sharp glare and I gestured to my pocket where he knew I kept the amulet. His one eye narrowed. "Soon we will be far enough that you can use the Warding Stone without affecting my father. Then you can silence that cursed old maggot-eater."

"Who is Kaden?" I asked him.

"The man who raised me as a child. He was one of your mother's soldiers. Damian, Orabelle's Guardian, told him I was the Solvrei. He and Alita began grooming me as soon as I was old enough to walk," Kaeleb explained. "And Astus, your voice from the amulet who calls himself the Harbonah, helped them do it."

There was something rancorous in his tone when he spoke of Astus and I wondered what the old man had done to him to evoke such a response. The voice of the former Air Keeper was suspiciously silent on that matter.

"And Kaden just wanders around down here in the tunnels?" I asked.

"Ten years ago when Sister Alita took me to the Council meeting in Kymir, Brother Kaden felt he had fulfilled his duty and his promise to Orabelle. He came to the Wastelands and found Damian hiding there in the tunnels, and he has been underground ever since. He doesn't much care for people these days. He merely wants to be left alone."

"I cannot blame him," Bacatha muttered.

"Ah, Bacatha, but you don't want to be alone, you want to be with Chaote," Kaeleb teased, breaking off when Bacatha spun around and took a swing at him with her scythe. He ducked the blow, dancing away and laughing.

We lapsed into silence once more and continued to meander through the labyrinth of tunnels. I was completely lost, but I had a strong suspicion we were going in circles. Kaeleb must also have been concerned about this same occurrence, for I noticed that he began to rub his hand near the head of his torch, pressing sooty palm prints on the cave walls to mark where we had been. Sure enough, we walked into a long corridor that seemed eerily familiar, and Kaeleb sighed heavily, holding the torch up to illuminate the blackened smear of his palm.

"We are going in circles," he muttered irritably.

Bacatha stopped, shoving the parchment at him. "Then you try to decipher this mess, since you are so clever!"

"I never said you were not clever," he countered.

"You just did."

"No, I did not."

"Then what are you saying? Because it sounds as if you are saying I am too ignorant to read a map."

"Bacatha, you are angry because of Thyrr, not me or this map."

"Do not speak of him!" Bacatha's voice was harsh, but there was an underlying pain in it that made Kaeleb back off.

"I am sorry for what happened," he said softly to her.

"Why are you apologizing?" she demanded. "I am the one who is sorry. You lost your mother and I... I did not even see it coming. I failed everyone."

"It was not your fault, old friend," he told her, gripping her shoulder. Her icy gaze sparkled with tears.

"Are you two nearly done? Or would you like me to come back later?" An unfamiliar voice rose in the darkness and I let out a startled shriek at the sound of it. Kaeleb shoved me behind him, the pale strands of hair that floated around my face disturbed by the rush of air as he drew his swords.

"Brother Kaden?" he called into the shadows that lurked just beyond the edge of the torch's flame.

"You have been walking in circles for quite some time," the voice went on. A figure began to take shape, and I peered curiously at the man. He was younger than the Fire Keeper, but older than Kaeleb or Bacatha. His eyes were angular and blue, clearly Leharan, and he had such a perfect nose that I wondered how one feature could have been so precisely made. Perhaps the rest of him was just as finely sculpted, but it was impossible to tell beneath his straggling beard and long, unkempt hair. The man turned to me, sniffing at me like a dog would, and I shrank back behind Kaeleb, disconcerted by the strange behavior.

"Brother, please, do not do that," Kaeleb admonished.

"You should be less worried about this girl and more concerned with the fact that I could have killed you at least three times already," Brother Kaden muttered. "An earless slug could have outmaneuvered you here."

"She is the Solvrei," Kaeleb said quietly.

Brother Kaden's wild eyes widened and he closed the distance between us, peering at me over Kaeleb's shoulder. I noticed that his clothes were well made, if unkempt, and he had on a hodgepodge of armor, each piece looking as if it had been stolen from an ancient cemetery. He scratched at his head, looking me up and down as if taking stock.

"You look like your father," he mumbled. "But you have your mother's eyes. What are you doing down here?"

"We are looking for you," Kaeleb interjected. I was thankful when the man finally pulled his intent gaze away from me to focus on the young man.

"I do not wish to be sought out," Brother Kaden said, his tone souring.

"We need to get to the Fomori in the north, and we need to do so without Maialen finding out. We cannot risk going through Kymir. People would notice a group of banished Leharans running about the countryside," Bacatha said, trying to keep from wrinkling her nose in distaste at the disheveled state of the man who used to be a member of the prestigious Guard.

"The Fomori, eh? That seems stupid," Kaden said, squinting at her. "Did you bring me anything?"

"Did we... no, we did not bring you anything," the severe Leharan woman snapped irritably. "We are preparing for war, we need the-"

"War it is, then?" Kaden cut her off, swiping a hand through the air in a vicious gesture. "You know about war? You have seen it? No, no, I can see that you have not. You do not know war. I do. I have been there. I was at Queen's End. I held Orabelle's hand while she died, choking to death on her own blood-"

"Enough!" Kaeleb practically shouted, seeing my stricken face as the man rambled on about the gory details of my mother's death. "Eolande is her daughter and she should not hear such things."

Kaden seemed more annoyed than chastised. "If she is the Queen's daughter, then she should know war. The Solvrei should know war. You know war, little brother, because I have taught you the complexities of it, but you have not seen it for yourself, and seeing it is a far different thing. You cannot know the benefits of war if you have not yet learned the evils of it."

"I told you this would be a waste of time," Bacatha hissed at Kaeleb.

Brother Kaden spun on her. "You doubt me, Leharan? Your father would not doubt me. He has fought beside me."

"My father is an old man now," Bacatha retorted.

The man's fingers fluttered to his face, wriggling beneath his beard to feel the skin, as if she had revealed something to him that he had never imagined. "Are we old, then?"

"You are not old," Kaeleb assured him. "Please, Brother, we need to get to the Fomori. Can you help us?"

Brother Kaden turned his wild eyes back to me and I held my chin high, refusing to wither or squirm beneath his scrutiny. "For her, I will do it. For the Solvrei. Not for this other woman. She is rude and I do not like her at all."

Bacatha rolled her eyes and Brother Kaden snatched the torch from Kaeleb's hand, rushing off in a clatter of mismatched armor.

22

The journey through the tunnels was longer than I had anticipated, and colder too. The heat of summer did not penetrate the underground depths of the caves, and we were constantly shrouded in cold, stale air. Our food supplies dwindled rapidly, and Brother Kaden was quite annoyed that we had not been better prepared.

"There is no direct route," he said, shaking his head, his mess of hair tangling over his features. "The caves meander. They wind through the world like underground rivers. It takes longer to traverse Imbria in this way. You should have realized this, Kaeleb."

There was a rebuke in his tone, and a mild disappointment. I saw Kaeleb scowl out of the corner of my eye, though it was hard to see much of anything in the faint light of the torch. We were running low on oil and using it sparingly, trying to conserve as much as we could. Sometimes we walked in complete darkness, and it was on those occasions that I would reach into my pocket and touch the Warding Stone, wanting to be sure that my thoughts were my own and I was not going mad.

"We need to go to the surface and find more food before we proceed further north," Brother Kaden announced. "I know a way up, but we will be in Kymir."

The Earth Keeper's realm, the land where I had grown up. I wondered if we were close to the place where Gideon had built our little cabin. There was a river that ran near it, and an abundance of fresh fish and snails that were easy to catch and eat.

"Well, we cannot go to the Fomori half starved," Bacatha muttered. "The Va'Kul would love that. She would probably cut our arms off and feed them to us just to fatten us up before she killed us."

"Bacatha!" Kaeleb's warning was sharp.

"I'm sorry! It is this damned darkness!" she cried. "It makes me irritable."

Brother Kaden stopped, sniffing the air, his nose flaring out like a rodent's while he poked his head about. I could not help but giggle at the sight of it, and he cast me a heavy glower. I swallowed my laughter, looking down at the ground and waiting while he did whatever it was he was doing.

"This way," he ordered, marching down a tunnel that curved to our left.

We followed him, weaving through the maze of tunnels until I felt sure that he had no actual idea where he was going. I was just about to suggest that we stop and reevaluate our strategy when he spun on me again.

"You have an amulet?" he prodded, poking at my arm as if he would annoy the truth out of me.

"How do you know that?" I asked in surprise.

"I was following you for quite some time before I alerted you to my presence," he boasted proudly.

"You were spying on us?"

He glared at me. "Reconnaissance. Not spying. Though every good leader should have spies in the enemy camp."

"We are not the enemy!" I countered, shaking my head in disbelief.

"You could have been. That is why I did the reconnaissance," he said, as if my inability to grasp the situation was quite vexing to him. "Use your amulet and make sure we are going the right way. I believe it is the right way, but it does no harm to be sure."

"How do I do that?" I asked.

Brother Kaeleb gave an exasperated sigh. "You have the Sapphire, yes? You can use it to follow the air, to find where it flows into the cave from outside. Use your head, girl."

I pulled the stone out of my pocket, unwrapping the bandage that covered it. Brother Kaden peered at it curiously and I laid my fingers on the cool blue gem, closing my eyes and searching the air around us. I could feel it moving, sensing the long tendrils of breath that were inhaled by the dark cave.

"This way," I said, pointing. I put the amulet back in my pocket, eager to stop feeling the prickling sensation that crawled over my skin when I touched it. Kaeleb was watching me closely and I smiled at him, letting him know I was fine.

"Perfect! That is the direction I was going," Brother Kaden claimed. Bacatha appeared unconvinced, but we followed him down the tunnel. We entered another long cavern and I noticed a foggy haze in the distance.

Daylight.

Kaeleb let out a whoop and hurried forward, scrambling over the pile of boulders that blocked the way out. The rest of us waited to see if it was safe, and I held my breath, praying to the gods that we would finally be out of the mausoleum of caves. Kaeleb poked his head back in a few moments later, motioning for us to follow him.

The sunlight was dazzling, stinging my eyes as I clamored out of the dark hollows of the ground. I tilted my face up, relishing the warmth that beamed onto my skin. My eyes were watering and it took several moments before I could see what was happening around us.

"By the gods," Bacatha murmured. She was shading her eyes with one hand, staring at what had once been the abundantly beautiful forests of Kymir.

This was not the forest I remembered from my childhood. The trees were not the soaring towers of green that pierced the sky in their grandeur. Instead, they were blackened, charred remnants that had great bulbous protrusions jutting out of them. One trunk was twisted and bent in a way that reminded me of a person doubled over in pain. There was something odd about it, and I peered closely at the knotted bark. I screamed, hurtling myself back from the tree and the monstrous visage that was molded into the trunk. It was a hideous parody of a face, twisted and grotesque, frozen in pain. The rest of the tree was littered with oozing pustules that seeped like infected wounds.

"What... what is that?" I demanded.

"The Earth Queen makes them," Brother Kaden said.

"Makes them?" I repeated, horrified.

"I believe she is trying to create something like her sister did with the Sirens," he explained, disapproving.

"They are alive?!" I cried out.

"No. Not fully. Or not anymore, at least. Come, we need to find some food."

I could not tear my eyes from the warped face of the tree. How could Maialen have done such a thing? Why would she? I shook my head, forcing myself to look away, hoping there were not others.

"There isn't much to hunt in this part of the forest," Brother Kaden said, "but there are grubs and some wild mushrooms. Go ahead, scavenge away."

I did not care for the idea of eating grubs or any other insects, but I had done it before and searching for them was better than staring at the mutilated tree corpse. I squatted down, lifting up fallen logs and peering underneath them, careful to inspect anything before I touched it. I did not realize how far I had wandered away from the others until I found a fat little white mushroom, plucking it up and turning to ask Brother Kaden if it was edible.

I found myself face to face with a Kymirran man I did not know. For a moment, I had the irrational fear that the monstrous tree had come back to life and was attacking me. Then I realized that this was an ordinary man, not some sort of tree demon the Earth Keeper had summoned. The man leapt at me, knocking me to the ground and causing the air to burst from my lungs. I was gasping for air, trying to wriggle out from beneath the weight of his heavy shoulder, which was pressing me into the ground. He was sweaty and rank, and it was obvious he had not washed in days. I reached up and grabbed a handful of his greasy hair, yanking it back so I could try to twist out from under him.

"Not so fast," he hissed at me, grabbing my waist and slamming me back down. He pressed one hand over my mouth, the other wrapping around my neck and squeezing. I shook my head violently, clawing at his arms, trying to dislodge him. He was middle-aged, with yellowed teeth and swollen gums that stunk of decay.

You are the Solvrei! Get rid of this peasant and stop mucking about in the dirt. It is embarrassing. Use your power.

I stopped flailing in panic and wrapped my hands around the man's wrists where he held me. He licked his lips eagerly, clearly mistaking my intent and assuming I was surrendering. Then I called the power.

Yes, child, this is who you are! Show him what you can do. How dare he touch you! You are the Solvrei, the most powerful being on all of Imbria.

I felt the man's muscles tense as pain radiated through him, his eyes growing wide and round. He tried to release me, but I wrapped my legs around his sweating hips, pulling him closer. He began to tremble, his head snapping up and down on his neck as his body spasmed and blood seeped out of his eyes, crimson tears streaking down his panicked face. His mouth opened in a scream and I cried out, letting all the rage and fear inside me escape into his body. I could feel the world around us, every exquisite nuance of it, and it was incredible. The dirt beneath me, every leaf on the trees, the cool droplets of water high up in the clouds, and the deep, endless fire that raged far down in the depths of the world. I could feel all of it, since the beginning of time and far into the future, every breath that had ever been drawn, every raindrop that had ever fallen.

"Eolande!"

The man was flung back away from me and I cried out as the power was wrenched from my grasp. I pushed myself up onto my knees, trying to crawl towards the unmoving form, wanting desperately to take whatever was left in him.

"He is dead!" Kaeleb was shouting at me, grabbing me around the waist and holding me still. "You can stop now, Eolande. He is dead."

I froze, the roar of the power fading into the distance, leaving a stark emptiness in its wake. "Dead?"

"Yes. He is dead. You are safe," Kaeleb assured me and I clutched his arm that held me, clinging desperately to him as I started to cry. I could not tell if my tears were a reaction to the shock of what had just happened, or if I was crying for the absence of the power, wanting more than anything to feel the incredible rush of it once again.

"By the gods," Bacatha whispered for the second time that day. She was standing a few feet away from us, peering down at the man's body. "She practically turned him inside out."

"Cover him up," Kaeleb ordered, standing and pulling me to my feet. I was still clinging to him, overwhelmed by what I had done. "We need to get out of here. There could be more of them."

He led me back towards the entrance to the cave, and I tried not to look at the bloody mess I had made of the stranger as Bacatha kicked dead leaves over the body. Brother Kaden was watching me with a singular fixation that made me shiver, but he remained silent, following us back to the cave's mouth.

From the corner of my eye I caught movement, and I turned my head, seeing a man turn and glance back at us before ducking behind the twisted trunk of a blackened tree. Kaeleb saw him too, and he shoved me down to the ground unceremoniously, leaping over me and crashing through the underbrush after the retreating figure.

Bacatha snatched up her scythe, standing over me with the weapon ready, her cold eyes surveying the forest around us. Kaeleb had disappeared into the thick foliage, and I lay prostrate beneath Bacatha, craning my head and praying for him to reappear. He finally did, and there was a spray of blood across the chest of his leather armor. In his hand was the knife he had once given to me, the blade stained deep red.

"Get her underground," he ordered, his mood dark.

Brother Kaden was leaning on his sword, glaring at the surrounding woods. "If there are more of them, then word will spread that we are here. The Earth Queen will hear of it."

"It cannot be helped," Kaeleb muttered in response.

Bacatha stepped back so I could get to my feet, and I stood, picking bits of leaves and twigs from my loose hair. She took my arm, guiding me towards the hole that led back to the caves.

"Wait!" I said, pulling out of the Leharan's grasp before we could go back down into the darkness. "I need to see something."

I walked over to the mutilated tree, laying my trembling fingers over the knotted wood where the face had been. It was smooth, the lines of pain gone. A tiny green leaf was slowly uncurling on one of the blackened branches. I smiled at it, then turned and followed Kaeleb back into the cave.

23

Maialen frowned at the small wooden carvings that were scattered across the white marble table. She glanced up at Damek, wondering what on Imbria he was doing and if he had finally succumbed to the madness of old age.

"What is this?" she asked him.

He was a flurry of black robes rushing forward to demonstrate his intentions with long sweeps of his skeletal hands. "This is the battlefield of Veruca."

"What battlefield?" she questioned further, for he was making no sense to her.

"The one which will claim Veruca as your sovereign territory," Damek said, his voice as oily and persuasive as he had ever made it. This was the opportunity they had been waiting for, and Logaire and that idiot, Akrin, had served it up to them on a silver platter. He trailed his fingers over the carved blocks that were meant to represent the Kymirran regiments of archers. "Logaire is weak and the Oracle is dead. Now is the time to attack. Once we have taken Veruca, all of Imbria will be under your sway."

"You sound like the General," she said with a shudder. She was glad she had sent Akrin to Samirra with the halfbreed. His very presence was loathsome to her.

"Maialen, my dearest child, this is the opportunity we have been waiting for. With Veruca comes iron and steel. Weapons. You will be unstoppable. That ragtag band of Leharans hiding in the desert will be no match for you once you have the eastern realm. You will be able to crush them, and their false claims of the Solvrei."

The Earth Keeper pursed her lips, bending forward to peer at the mock battlefield. "Logaire has carefully maintained her neutral status throughout the years. What reason do we have for invading her lands?"

Damek wanted to shake her until her head snapped back. "We do not need a reason. You are the Queen of Imbria now, dearest."

"She did harbor that child," Maialen practically spat through clenched teeth. "She lied to me. To my face."

"She is a duplicitous and vile creature," Damek encouraged.

Maialen picked up the little carved totem that represented the Verucan queen, thinking of the last time she had seen her, years before. Logaire had traveled to Kymir to discuss trade, wishing to exploit Veruca's wealth of minerals for increased stores of grain from Samirra.

"Maialen, darling," Logaire had purred, her voluptuous body draped in golden silk and practically dripping with jewels. "You are as lovely as ever."

The Verucan woman had embraced her, pressing Maialen against her ample bosom in a gesture that was so motherly and inappropriate it made the Earth Keeper flush scarlet with embarrassment. Maialen had extricated herself from Logaire's maternal grasp, smoothing back the waves of chestnut hair that had been dislodged in the embrace. She noticed the other woman's golden gaze linger on the Pearl that hung around her neck just above the Emerald.

"I never thought it would be you," Logaire said, her voice light and playful. Her slender fingers delicately twirled a strand of coppery hair. There were touches of gray in her mane of curls, and the color was not as vibrant as it had once been. "But here you are, commanding two Elements and ruling over most of Imbria."

"I never asked for such responsibility," Maialen said softly, feigning reluctance. "I am only trying to do what is best for Imbria."

Logaire wanted to roll her eyes, but she managed to refrain, watching the Earth Keeper with veiled amusement. "Of course you are. Samirra must be quite the burden on your resources. Rebuilding a kingdom is a costly endeavor. That is why I am here, so we can help one another."

"Is my sister's child truly dead?" Maialen had asked suddenly, unable to refrain any longer from the question that was eating away at her.

Logaire's golden eyes sparkled. "Of course, and it is for the best. Imbria's destiny has been revealed by the Oracle, and a child such as that would only bring trouble."

Maialen nodded, feeling a lump in her throat. Logaire was right. It was best that the child was dead, but she could not help herself from feeling the lingering touch of the past and all that might have been. For a fleeting moment, she could picture her family still together, alive. Her parents smiling at each other, her sister holding her baby, showing her to Maialen who wiggled her precious tiny toes while Aracellis looked in awe at his little cousin. It was a sweet imagining, and one so far from the reality of her life that it left her feeling hollow. Her parents had hated each other, and Orabelle would not even let Maialen see her baby, let alone tickle her toes. Aracellis had forsaken her as well. Her own son had chosen to dwell in the Wastelands with the Fire Keeper instead of coming home to her, his mother.

Logaire brought her out of her reverie, pulling a tiny vial out of the bosom of her gown and displaying it proudly. The deep red liquid swirled within, coating the glass. "I did, however, save this from her before she died."

"Is it really hers?" Maialen demanded, skeptical that Logaire would display such a prize so casually.

"It is. The last of it, and my gift to you. It is important for us to maintain our alliance, and I want you to know how much I value your friendship," Logaire said, persuasive as ever. Damek was glaring at her from over the Earth Queen's shoulder, clearly displeased with Logaire's gift.

"Maialen, get rid of that vile substance immediately," the old advisor hissed. "It is an abomination to the gods."

Logaire laughed, her voice trilling in the air like a flute. "Nonsense, Damek. The blood is power. You could do incredible things with it, my dear Maialen, things your sister only dreamed of."

Maialen grasped the vial in her fist, her green eyes voracious. "Orabelle was weak. She could never have held two amulets. I have already surpassed her."

"Of course you have, dearest," Logaire cajoled. "Now put that away somewhere safe. You can use it when the time is right. Come, let us talk trade."

Maialen frowned at the memory, and the other remembrances that followed it. The metallic taste of the blood on her tongue, the thrill of power it had brought, and the burnt forest of her northern realm, writhing in agony as Maialen tried to restore it. Logaire must have known the blood would distort her power, make it sick and twisted, and the thought infuriated the Earth Queen. Damek was right. Logaire had always been a liar.

The Earth Queen's thoughts could not help but skip to Logaire's cousin, the Fire Keeper and the man Maialen had fallen in love with all those years ago. She could still feel the flutter in her stomach as she thought of him, the way he used to look at her with his amber eyes bright and a casual grin adorning the chiseled planes of his face. She had done everything to prove herself to him, but still he had thrown her aside. Blaise had used her, made a fool of her, all the while pining away for her dead sister. She had thought he would come for her when she married Favian, that he would object to the sham of a wedding and realize that she should have been his bride instead, but Blaise had been silent. He had not cared that she married another man.

Maialen recalled the wedding day with stark clarity. She had stared out over the gathered crowds below, her heart pounding, searching for him. She knew she looked beautiful, wrapped in green lace trimmed in gold, with her hair piled high on her head in the traditional fashion of the Samirran royal women. It was her second marriage to a man from their kingdom, and she knew with a despondent heart that it would be just as empty as her first marriage had been.

Favian took her hands at the direction of the binder, the woman who oversaw the pacts of marriage in the western realm. His skin was cool, almost brittle, and pale against her own. The binder entwined their arms with a long embroidered cloth and Maialen looked up at the face of the man who was about to become her husband.

Annoyance surged within her at the stricken look that adorned the former Guardian's gaunt features. He looked as if he were going to the executioner's block, not wedding the most powerful woman on Imbria. She knew Favian had no interest in her, or any other woman for that matter, for it was well known that he preferred the company of men, but he could at least pretend to be grateful for the gift she was granting him. The gift of Samirra.

"You could at least try to look happy," she had whispered to him.

He shifted on his feet, clearly uncomfortable. "I am sorry, my Queen. I am grateful. For Samirra."

Maialen's frown had deepened. "Then act like it. This is not exactly the greatest moment of my life, either."

Once more she had looked out at the crowd, watching for a telltale glimpse of red, searching for any shimmers of the Fire Keeper's raw power. There was nothing but slack-faced Samirrans with dead eyes.

Maialen had never forgotten how she felt that day, the deep and immense betrayal that curled in her heart when Blaise had not come for her. It was soon after that she became aware of his affair with the Tahitian woman, and the revelation had filled her with anger and heartbreak. Once more, he had made a fool of her. He was as devious as his cousin, and neither of them deserved a place in the new empire she was building.

The Earth Queen flung the totem down onto the table, scattering several of the other little blocks and causing Damek's black robes to undulate with surprise.

"Take Veruca," she ordered. "Raze the entire kingdom to the ground if you have to."

24

The Fomori were every bit as horrifying as I had anticipated them to be. I nearly gagged the first time I smelled their foul stench permeating the darkness, and I had not grown any more accustomed to it in the time since. The only benefit of the noxious odor was that it made me forget about the gnawing hunger in my gut. The sparse handful of mushrooms and worms we had collected during our brief foray above ground had not sustained us long. Brother Kaden had looked at our meager collection of food once we stopped to rest for the night, safely back in the depths of the underground tunnels. He had shaken his head, clicking his tongue in disappointment.

"This will not do. One must be prepared to survive in enemy territory. One must forage from the enemy. This is pathetic foraging," he announced. He shoved the food back in his bag and folded his arms over it. His wild hair hung over his face, but I could see that his lips were still moving as he muttered to himself. He was saying something about asking the Fomori for food.

"Don't the Fomori eat people?" I asked quietly, my stomach turning at the thought.

"Yes, yes, they eat people, that is true. But it is not all they eat," Brother Kaden assured me. "Since Kaeleb is so friendly with them, I am sure they will be happy to-"

"I am not friends with any of the Fomori," Kaeleb cut him off. "I was warned about the Va'Kul once, a long time ago. They told me her favor comes with its own set of horrors, and they were right. Whatever she agrees to give us, it will not be given out of friendship. She will take something in return."

Brother Kaden digested this bit of information, turning to stare at me once again, much to my discomfort. Then he opened his mouth and began to sing. It was a boisterous song, with bawdy rhymes from a sailor's adventures at sea. His voice echoed through the cave, so that it sounded as if an entire choir of tenors was singing along with him.

"He is mad as a loon," Bacatha leaned over to hiss at Kaeleb.

"I am in my right mind," Brother Kaden snapped, abruptly cutting off his jaunty song and giving her a sideways glare.

"Are you?" Bacatha challenged, raising a brow above her icy blue eyes.

"I am! Quite so! I am more in my right mind than she is," Brother Kaden said, gesturing at me. "She is the one who hears the dead. You cannot hear the dead without being a bit off."

I felt my face flush and I looked up at Kaeleb who was sitting across the cavern from me. He looked away quickly, heaving a sigh. He had been avoiding me since we had returned to the tunnels, and I could not help but wonder if it was because of what he had seen me do to the man in the forest.

"She hears the former Keepers through the amulets when they are near. She can hear the Air Keepers because she carries the Sapphire. Mostly the Harbonah, Astus," Kaeleb told the other man.

Brother Kaden seemed to perk up at this revelation and I let my fingers wrap around the Warding Stone that was hidden in my pocket, not wanting the former Samirran King to know what we were saying about him. The silent emptiness of the stone flowed over me, and I could not help but feel a twinge of longing for the power that lay sleeping within me.

"That is better than hearing his bastard son. Astraeus was a worthless twit who is surely still crying about how he could not control his own amulet. At least the Harbonah is a wealth of valuable knowledge. I suppose if you had to hear dead voices, his would not be the worst," Brother Kaden went on. "Though he was a bit obsessed with the boy here. I always found it odd, but Alita swore it was just his devotion to the Solvrei, even though it made me uncomfortable."

"Enough!" Kaeleb interrupted. "I do not wish to speak of that man."

Brother Kaden shrugged. "Knowledge is to be aware of the danger before there is danger, and to be aware of calamity before there is calamity. Know your enemy and know yourself. You should remember these lessons, my boy. You have a useful tool in that Sapphire. Do not let your emotions stop you from using it."

Kaeleb pushed himself to his feet with a scowl, stalking across the cavern and disappearing into the darkness. I stood, moving to follow him, when Brother Kaden reached out and grabbed my wrist. His eyes were wild, and he used his other hand to dig beneath the ramshackle breastplate that covered his chest, pulling out a pair of mismatched leather gloves and shoving them into my hands.

"You do not know what your power is yet, girl. We all saw that today. The boy feels something for you. You could hurt him if you are not careful," he whispered.

I stared down at the gloves.

He is right I am dangerous I don't know how to control it I don't know how to stop it I have the Warding Stone but I hate the way it feels I want to feel the power again I want to use it he is right what if I hurt someone what if I cannot stop myself I do not want to hurt him.

I yanked on the gloves, thankful that at least it was a way to protect the others that did not necessitate me grasping the awful emptiness of the Warding Stone. Then I hurried after Kaeleb, guilt eating away at me. Everything that was happening to him was my fault. Everything that had ever happened to him was my fault, and I had no idea how to atone for that.

I slipped into the darkness at the back of the cavern, straining to hear any sound of him. I could barely make out the steady inhalations of his breath, and I moved towards him. I reached out with my gloved hand, feeling in the darkness, startled when my fingers connected with his warm chest. I stood in the blackened cave listening to him breathe, trying to think of anything to say that would make him look me in the eye once again.

"I am sorry about the forest. About the man and what I did," I began softly. "And about the other man, the one you had to kill because of me."

He pushed the air out of his lungs with a heavy exhale. "Eolande, do not be sorry that you defended yourself from someone who wanted to hurt you. As for the other man..."

His voice trailed off, and I wished I could see his face, that I could see the expression in his beautiful grey eye. His tone gentled, was deeper and quieter as he said, "I would kill a thousand men to protect you. I care nothing about the life I took, as long as it meant that yours was safe. I do not know if that makes me a hero or a monster, or partly both, but that is how I feel."

I could barely breathe, and I was sure he could hear my heart pounding in my chest. His hands found my face, smoothing back the wavy strands of pale hair that had escaped my braid. His thumb moved across my lips, the lightest caress, and I stepped back, suddenly terrified, the voice in my head screaming at me to move away.

Do not hurt him do not hurt him get away from him before you hurt him what if Kaden is right what if you cannot control it use the Warding Stone you have the Warding Stone but I am too afraid I can't I can't breathe get away from him Eolande away away.

"I should not have done that," he murmured. "Come, let us get back to the others before Bacatha skewers us both for leaving her alone with the madman."

We had gone back just as Brother Kaden abruptly burst into another bout of singing, much to Bacatha's dismay. I could not help but laugh, and this time when I looked across the cavern in the meager torchlight, Kaeleb was looking back at me, a small smile playing at his lips. He gave Bacatha a nudge in the ribs and began singing along with the other man, horribly out of tune and causing the severe woman to press her hands over her ears and try to kick him.

I was glad we had laughed for a moment that night, for the horrors that followed I could never have imagined.

The Fomori found us, their stench rolling over me in putrid waves as Kaeleb called out to them in the darkness, demanding to have an audience with their Va'Kul. There were beastly grunts and I could hear them whisper, though their strange tongues were hard to understand. One of them ordered us to follow it, leading us out of the darkness we had been swallowed in for days and into a lit chamber. Fire burned in a massive pit dug into the floor. There was a draft of cool air, and the smoke curled upward, pulled towards an opening in the cavern far above our heads. Around the firepit were piles of gleaming bones, picked clean so they almost appeared to have been polished to a shine. The Va'Kul stood on the opposite side of the pit, her terrifying visage the stuff of nightmares. She was everything you would expect a Fomori to be, the embodiment of every savage tale you had ever heard about them. Her muscled form was swathed in pelts of fur and her eerie eyes glowed yellow, standing out starkly against the dull grey hide of her face. Her brow and cheekbones were large and protruding, and her lips were wide, pulled back in a terrible smile that showed her fanged teeth. Long, dark hair hung loose down her back and her inhuman gaze flickered over us with undisguised interest as her pink tongue darted out to touch the full lips.

"Boy," she said, the word elongated and reshaped by her strange accent. "You seek me yet again. Perhaps I was not clear the last time we met."

Kaeleb stepped forward and my heart was in my throat. I wanted to scream at him to run, that we should all run, we should not be there, but I was frozen, rooted to the ground and watching the tableau unfold helplessly.

"We need you to fight with us, Va'Kul. In two moons, we plan to attack the Earth Queen and take her power from her. She poisons the lands of Imbria and she cannot be allowed to continue," Kaeleb began.

The Va'Kul laughed, a brittle sound, like needles piercing my ears. "Save your speeches. What do I care about your wars and Keepers?"

"We know the land in the north is dying, and with it goes the food that sustains you as well. The Solvrei has returned, and she can restore the damage Maialen has done. I have seen her do it."

The Va'Kul swung her gaze to me again, stalking forward so that she towered above me. I knew my eyes were round with fear, but I forced myself not to cower beneath her gaze, lifting my chin and trying to face her scrutiny as boldly as I could.

"This little thing?" the Va'Kul poked a long talon at my chest. "What is this scrawny little thing going to do?"

"I can kill you all," I said quietly, my voice betraying me by wavering slightly.

The Va'Kul's lips once more pulled back into a smile. "Perhaps there is more to her than I thought. She reminds me of you, boy. I have seen the death of the land you speak of. The Earth Keeper has also poisoned many of the rivers that flow from these mountains we call home. We have to venture further for food, and there are less of your kind for us to hunt."

She paused, her heavy brows drawing together. "Where is Chaote? If this girl is the divine blood that you claim she is, I would expect our Mother to be in her presence."

"Maialen has captured Chaote," Bacatha interjected.

The leader of the Fomori whipped her head around to stare hatefully at the Leharan woman. "Chaote would not be captured by the likes of one of you. If she has been taken, it is because she chose to be taken."

"Will you fight with us?" Kaeleb asked, drawing her attention back to him.

"You must fight for me first. But only you. If you win, then I will come to your battle and feast upon your enemies," the Va'Kul decided, gliding back to stand among her fawning worshippers. She waved her clawed hand and the other Fomori in the room backed away, pressing against the outer edges of the cavern. Brother Kaden pulled me back, leaving Kaeleb standing alone in the center of the room, the fire blazing behind him so that he seemed to glow with a red-orange halo. He pulled one of his swords from its sheath, bracing his feet wide, his pale hair falling over the side of his face as he glared around the cavern.

The Fomori that stepped forward was the biggest creature I had ever seen. He was a nightmare of muscle and scars, growling ferociously and beating his chest. The other Fomori cheered him on, howling and screeching in delight.

"No, he can't do this!" I hissed at Brother Kaden. "You have to stop him!"

"Kaeleb knows what he is doing. I am the one who taught him to fight," Brother Kaden responded, as if that were all the reassurance I should need. I was anything but reassured. I looked to Bacatha, and her cold gaze was fixed on Kaeleb, a deep frown on her face as she watched his movements with the fierce intensity of a warrior who wishes they were the one fighting.

Kaeleb backed away a few steps as the Fomori advanced, never taking his gaze from the massive beast. The creature lurched forward, testing the young man's responses, seeing how he would deflect. This was no mindless beast. It was a trained fighter. My fists were clenched so tightly that I could feel my nails digging into my palms.

The Fomori charged, and Kaeleb spun out of the way, whirling back at the last moment and kicking the beast in his unprotected ribs. The Fomori stumbled, nearly toppling into the fire pit before he righted himself, letting out a long howl of rage. He charged again, his clawed hands tearing at Kaeleb's head. Kaeleb dropped to the ground, sliding out of the way on his back and swinging his sword at the creature's leg. Foul, black blood hissed from the wound and the beast tried to remain standing on the injured leg, but he was limping heavily and I could see the pink muscle where his flesh had been flayed open.

Kaeleb tossed his sword aside and was on his feet, running at the beast and ducking the blow that came for him, catching the Fomori's powerful arm and swinging himself up with it so that his legs wrapped around the creature's neck. He twisted his body, and the Fomori was thrown to the ground where Kaeleb wrenched the thing's neck, breaking it. He stood, panting, and I felt like my heart would burst with relief. He had won.

The Va'Kul let out a long hiss and lifted her fingers once again. Three more creatures stalked forward out of the shadows, surrounding Kaeleb.

"No!" I cried out. "He won!"

"Stay out of this, Eolande," Kaeleb warned me. The Va'Kul's terrible gaze was now fixed on me, and there was something so feral and evil within her eyes that it made me shudder.

"You have to do something," I whispered to Brother Kaden.

"The boy can take care of himself," he shook his head in response. "If he needs me, he will ask."

"What is wrong with all of you?" I screamed out. I pulled off my gloves, reached in my pocket for the Sapphire, grasping the amulet and ready to feel the cool spark of the Air Keeper's power. There was nothing. I lifted my head. The Va'Kul was still watching me, a smile playing on her lips. One clawed finger reached beneath the fur of her pelt and the shimmering white edge of a Warding Stone glowed in the firelight. I glared back at her. I did not need the Sapphire or my power, all I needed was to distract the Fomori who were closing around Kaeleb in a menacing circle.

I bolted forward and the Va'Kul cried out in protest. One of the Fomori spun around, throwing out its massive fist and connecting solidly with my face. Darkness exploded in front of me, and I fell backwards on the ground, the sharp fragments of bone bruising my body.

"Keep her out of this!" Kaeleb shouted. Bacatha grabbed my arms, dragging me back from the fight, but I had given Kaeleb the advantage he needed. He snatched up his sword and swung it in a wide arc, lopping off the head of the beast who had struck me. Then he turned, slicing towards one of the other beasts. The blade bit deep into the creature's shoulder and stuck there, the howling beast rearing back and dragging Kaeleb off balance. He stumbled, falling to the ground and letting go of the sword, which was still buried in the beast's shoulder. Kaeleb reached out, grabbing a piece of bone from the macabre piles that littered the floor. He was on his feet again and he kicked the protruding blade of the sword, causing the Fomori to wail in agony.

"Behind you!" Brother Kaden shouted and the Va'Kul once again hissed indignantly at the interference. Kaeleb spun around, stabbing the third beast in the neck with the bone. Blood spurted out in a high arc and splattered Kaeleb's pale hair. He darted around the creature, kicking it forward and sending it stumbling into the other one. They collapsed in a heap of blood and limbs, and Kaeleb yanked the sword free, stabbing downward into the final beast's heart and killing it.

There was silence in the chamber. The only sound I could hear was Kaeleb's heavy breathing. I watched the Va'Kul, staring at her fingers, waiting to see what she would do next.

"You interfered," she snarled.

"But you sent three in against him!" I shouted in disbelief.

"He agreed to fight. He knows our ways," she retorted in furious indignation. "You have violated our sacred ritual, and for that there will be consequences."

"Va'Kul, no, she did not understand-" Kaeleb began, but he was watching me and did not see the Fomori who charged from the shadows at Brother Kaden. Before the man could react, the beast had sunk his poisoned fangs deep into the soft spot on his neck, the vulnerable opening in his makeshift suit of armor.

Brother Kaden let out a cry, jerking away, the Fomori's fangs tearing at his skin. He pressed his hand to his neck and Kaeleb was staring at him in shock, his mouth dropped open. The beast grabbed Brother Kaden and dragged him over to where the Va'Kul stood, pushing him to his knees in front of her.

"I will take him as retribution for your violation of our ways," she announced.

Bacatha took a step forward, her scythe held across her body, and the Fomori hissed at her in warning. Kaeleb threw out his hand, motioning for her to stop.

"They did not mean to violate the sanctity of your ways," he promised the Va'Kul. "They were only trying to protect me."

She smiled at him, trailing her finger through the blood that dripped from Brother Kaden's neck, dragging it in a crimson streak across his cheek. "You know that begging will not help you, boy. Let us take this one, and you will have your army and your victory here. If not, we will kill all of you."

Brother Kaden shook off her hand, staring up at Kaeleb, his face set in determined lines. "I am already bitten. I will not survive either way. Let me go. Let me save the rest of you."

"No!" Kaeleb cried. "No, there must be another way! I will fight again! Let me fight again!"

Brother Kaden was resolute. "No. This is what must happen. Go ahead, then, beast. Get it over with."

The Va'Kul lowered her head to the wound in his neck, her fangs shining in the firelight as her jaws descended. More Fomori swarmed the man, and I could not stop screaming as they sank their teeth into him, a writhing mass of bodies gnawing at him. Pieces of his hodgepodge armor fell to the ground as the blooddrinkers ripped it away, seeking the soft, tender parts of his flesh. Brother Kaden opened his mouth, singing out the bawdy seafarers' song we had laughed at in the caves, but he only managed to get out a few of the words before he coughed, choking, blood dribbling over his lips. I watched his face turn grey, the brightness dying from his eyes, like the sun setting on a far horizon. From the corner of my eye, I saw Bacatha holding Kaeleb back, tears streaming down his horrified face as he watched his brother die slowly in front of him.

It seemed like an eternity passed before the Va'Kul stopped, stepping back and wiping her mouth with the back of her hand. She looked at Kaeleb, torn apart with grief, and something flickered deep in her eyes. I could not tell if it was sympathy or something far darker and worse, and I looked away, unable to stare at her inhuman face any longer.

"You have restored the sanctity of our arena with your sacrifice," she said. "We will join your fight, as agreed upon."

25

Logaire stared over the wall at the sea that raged against the blackened cliffs. The sky overhead was a dull orange, and she knew there was a song that seafarers would sing about the color of the sky and what it could portend, but for the life of her she could not recall the words. The wind lifted her coppery mane of hair from her shoulders, tugging it out towards the sea, as if the waves were beckoning her.

She turned her head, observing the man who stood beside her. He was different than she remembered, but then again, he had always been evolving, always reshaping himself into something that was better suited to the world around him. She envied him that gift. The gleaming edge of the Fire Opal glinted in the rays of the setting sun, and for a moment she felt a jealousy so keen and sharp that it was like a knife in her gut. No matter how powerful she was, she would never be a Keeper.

"You must stand with us. Together, we can take back Imbria before Maialen destroys any more of it," Blaise said to her, his voice low and urgent.

"Come now, cousin. I have no quarrel with the Earth Queen. It would be foolish of me to start a war against her,"

Logaire mused, her voice light and airy, as if they were discussing the rules of a game he wished to play.

"Now is not the time to be coy, Logaire," Blaise said. His amber eyes glittered with intensity, standing out even more brightly than usual against the auburn beard that now covered his face. It was not her favorite look of his, and she wondered if she should suggest that he shave it. She was finding it quite distracting to look at.

"What is it time for, cousin?" she countered, unable to keep the bitterness from seeping into her tone. "Is it time for you to finally end your ridiculous rebellion? Or for you to acknowledge me as the rightful ruler of Veruca? Or perhaps it is time for you to relinquish that amulet you are hoarding to your chest like a stingy old miser."

"Trust me, you do not want the Opal," he muttered. "It is nothing but misery."

Logaire scoffed. "Says a man who has wielded its power for more than twenty years. If it was so terrible, then why did you not give it up long ago?"

Blaise looked uncomfortable, his eyes roaming out over the sea. "Because I made a promise."

She could not help but laugh. "Since when do you care about promises?"

"I have always kept my word to you."

She pursed her lips, hating that he spoke the truth. "Does Maialen know about the girl?"

"She does. She and Akrin tried to kidnap the girl from Lehar. Thyrr betrayed us. He was bringing Eolande to them, in exchange for Maialen restoring Lehar and allowing him to rule," Blaise told her. "The girl escaped, but Gula was killed."

She could see the grief on his face, the dark shadow of it haunting his eyes. Blaise had always tried to be so emotionless, the cold, calculating soldier, but Logaire knew better. "I assume Thyrr is no longer among the living after his betrayal?"

"He is not. The Leharans were the ones to decide his fate, and you know how they are."

Logaire raised her eyebrows, hiding the twinge of sorrow she felt for the man who had once been her lover. Blaise was not the only one who had built walls around his heart, and hers were far taller and sturdier than his. "Well, well. I suppose I should not be surprised. Thyrr always was a little too amenable to coercion. And I am sure that Maialen dangled Lehar in front of him like a juicy carrot. Damek must have had a hand in that play. I am afraid your darling Earth Keeper is not clever enough to have thought of it on her own. If she had any wits about her at all, she would have killed Akrin the second she saw him."

"Says the woman who let him live long after she should have."

Logaire shrugged. "Yes, perhaps that was a mistake on my part. I should have killed him after what he did to Magnus. Now he has betrayed me and Veruca."

"Perhaps you should have learned something from his betrayal of me," Blaise suggested, unable to help the disdain that colored his voice.

Logaire glared at him, golden eyes flashing. "You must have something to offer me, Blaise. Surely you did not come here to beg my help with empty hands?"

"Do I need to bear gifts to have an audience with my beloved cousin?"

She laughed, the sound carried away quickly by the wind. "We are not beloved to each other, Blaise, not since we were children. There is no use holding on to that sentiment."

His voice was tender, surprising her yet again. "You don't really believe that. If you did, I would not be standing here."

"Then let us agree that we are both sentimental fools who should have killed each other long ago," Logaire said with a sigh.

He nodded. "That I can agree on."

They fell into silence once more, both watching the steady crash of waves as the sun bled into the water. Logaire wondered how different life would have been if they had run away as children, if they had followed through with their secret plans to escape the stifling black rocks of Veruca and make a home in the mountains. She remembered curling up beside Blaise as a child, his brother Bastion tucked on the opposite side and watching them both with adoring eyes. They would dream of a place far away from the misery of their lives, somewhere deep in the mountains where they could build a little stone cottage and hunt for food. There would be no one there to hurt them, no one there to drag them away from each other, or to punish them with sharp blows from a stick that was kept near the fireplace. Blaise would draw his finger through the air as he spoke of it, tracing the lines of the cabin he would build for them. Bastion would giggle happily, and they would have to stop him from leaping up and running to gather his things when his excitement overwhelmed him.

"You must stand with us, Logaire. You can atone for everything you have done," Blaise said, ripping her back from the memories of the past.

"I have nothing to atone for. Everything I have done has been for Veruca," she said, her voice cold. "Do not lecture me, cousin. You have done far worse things than I."

"You kept that girl chained in a dungeon with a Warding Stone shoved under her skin," he countered.

"I did the world a favor. You do not care about that girl. All you care about is appeasing her dead mother in case you still have a chance with her in the afterlife. You are pathetic," Logaire practically spat, knowing it would infuriate him and enjoying her taunts.

A shadow passed over the Fire Keeper's face. "Logaire, I am asking you for the last time, let me have the Verucan army to fight against Maialen. I do not care about the throne or about claiming Veruca. All I care about is stopping the Earth Queen."

"Does that boy really mean so much to you?" she asked in disbelief. "You would do all of this just to make Imbria a better place for him?"

The image of Kaeleb flashed through his mind. His son, the child he had raised as his own, the one he loved more than anything in the world. The boy had been an unexpected gift in his life, a beautiful purpose for being that Blaise had never thought possible to feel. Kaeleb was a better man than the Keeper could ever hope to be, and Blaise would do anything for him. "He does, and I would give my life for it."

Logaire tried not to feel stung by her cousin's devotion to a boy that was not even of his blood when he had never shown her that sort of fidelity. "I will think on it, then. Return to me in a week's time and you will have your answer."

Disappointment clouded his features. Of course, he could see through her ruse. He knew she was lying, that she wanted time to see what sort of offer Maialen would give her to betray him. Logaire would always do what was best for Logaire.

"I fear you will live to regret this decision," he murmured.

She smiled. "If I live that long, perhaps I will."

They were interrupted by a shout, and a man came running towards them, waving his arms frantically. He was a stout, stocky man built like a brick, with square features that were arranged like blocks of molded clay on his long face.

"Vishram, what has gotten into you?" Logaire questioned, frowning at her advisor.

"My Queen. There is word from one of the scouts. The Kymirrans have crossed the border into Veruca," Vishram said breathlessly.

If looks could kill, Logaire would have murdered Vishram on sight for blurting out his news in front of the Fire Keeper. The timing could not have been worse.

Blaise clasped his hands behind his back and let out a low whistle. "Well, cousin. It appears that my assumption was correct and Maialen will not tolerate your betrayal. Tell me, do you still wish for me to go?"

She wanted to scratch the smug smile right off his face.

"Are you certain?" Logaire demanded of Vishram.

"It has been reported by two different scouts, my Queen. I will send out another party to confirm, and to assess the Kymirran's numbers and intentions, but from the looks of it, the Earth Keeper plans to take Veruca by force."

Logaire spun on her cousin, jabbing a finger into his chest. "This is your fault!"

"You did this to yourself, Logaire. You should have killed Akrin a long time ago, and you can be sure that he is a part of this, which means Maialen will know everything about your defenses. Give me back Veruca, Logaire, and we can stop her together," Blaise said, persuasive and earnest. Perhaps he was telling the truth, and all he wanted was to make the world a better place for the young man he called his son, but Logaire could not afford to be so sentimental.

"Veruca is mine now, Blaise. I will not give it up, not to you or to Maialen. Fight beside me or leave us. The choice is yours." She could not help but notice the long look that Vishram gave the Fire Keeper, sowing the seeds of distrust she was already feeling for the stout advisor. Vishram had served her loyally for years, but she had recently begun to suspect that those loyalties might be divided. A few months past, one of Logaire's spies in the temple revealed that the advisor had been spending an increasing amount of time in Halig with the Solvrei and was even tutoring their pitiful little prisoner. Then Vishram had mysteriously turned up back in Veruca, the only survivor of the massacre at the temple that had claimed the Oracle's life. He swore he was already on the way to the castle when the massacre occurred and had no knowledge of what had transpired there. In truth, he seemed genuinely shocked to hear of Sybylla's death, but it was easy to feign surprise. She herself had pretended to be overtaken by a terrible fit of grief upon hearing of the murders, wailing and throwing herself down in a barrage of sobs and tears. Though it was not entirely a ruse. She felt genuine grief for the woman she had befriended for so many years. Sybylla had been a trusted confidant and ally, doing whatever Logaire asked of her with unquestioning obedience, until the Leharan girl started to sway her mind.

The last time Logaire visited Halig, she had walked through the temple gardens beside the Oracle, enjoying the warmth of spring after the long winter. Sybylla's pristine white robes had flowed around her, the sheer fabric caressing Logaire's arm as it fluttered in the breeze. Her hair was piled high on her head, in the fashion she knew Logaire preferred for her to wear, and her weak chin was relaxed, so that her face seemed to slope directly from her lips down to her chest in one smooth sweep.

"You are pensive, my dear," Sybylla had murmured, casting a sidelong glance at the Queen with her tawny eyes. "What is troubling you?"

"The girl grows older. She is harder to control," Logaire admitted. She considered her next words carefully, trying to appear nonchalant while she studied the other woman's re-action with veiled intensity. "Perhaps the time has come to dispose of her."

Sybylla stopped short beside a tangle of thorny rosebushes whose tiny buds were just beginning to form. "Dispose of her?"

Logaire shrugged her shoulders, the sun glistening off the cascade of rubies that draped her neck. "She has been useful, and her blood has brought us great wealth, but I worry it has gone on too long. The nobles who buy it have grown suspicious, even accusing me of deceiving them with ordinary blood."

Sybylla touched the tip of one of the rosebuds while birds sang in the nearby trees. "Perhaps you should have been a little more discerning in your claims of what her divine blood could do. You sold it to anyone who was looking for hope, whether it was to cure sickness or forego old age, or even to find a lover."

"Yes, and part of the wealth that I acquired in doing so has gone into maintaining this temple you reside so luxuriously in," Logaire snapped. She was not accustomed to Sybylla challenging her so directly. She and the Oracle had their share of disagreements over the years, but Sybylla had never been so openly critical. Logaire was fuming inside, but she forced herself to remain calm, smiling serenely. Perhaps she was being too paranoid, perhaps Sybylla's attachment to the girl was not as strong as Logaire feared, and she would still do whatever the Queen wished of her.

"If you are done with her, then let her go," Sybylla suggested gently.

Logaire kept her face unreadable, changing tactics. "There is something else I wanted to speak to you about, darling. Something we can do to strengthen my position here in Veruca."

The Oracle let a shadow of doubt fleet across her features. "Tell me what I can do for you, my Queen."

"Proclaim me to have divine blood," Logaire said, watching from beneath her thick fringe of lashes. She saw the Oracle's eyes widen slightly, the tremble of her weak chin.

"I do not understand," Sybylla stalled, shaking her head.

Logaire's voice was purring, persuasive, and her golden eyes shimmered greedily. "Maialen has been running around claiming to be the Solvrei for years and using it to amass a slew of mindless devotees, and her blood is no more divine than that pigeon's. If she can do it, why shouldn't I? You can grant me legitimacy. If you proclaim my divine heritage, then no one will question it."

Sybylla was aghast. "You want me to proclaim you a god?"

"Perhaps I am."

"Logaire, you cannot be serious. To do that would.... no, I cannot," Sybylla muttered, shaking her head. "I already have too many stains on my soul. I cannot add this one as well."

"Of course, darling, of course," Logaire had soothed. "Forget that I asked about it. It was a foolish idea, a musing thought, nothing more."

The Queen had linked her arm with the Oracle, steering her once more around the awakening garden and chattering on about the mundane details of life in the castle. She did not let her feelings show, wearing a pleasant smile like a suit of armor that hid the tumult of emotions raging within her. She knew in that moment, holding her friend's arm, that she would have to kill the Oracle. And Akrin would be the perfect fool to pin it on. It might even be possible to kill two birds with one stone. If Logaire allowed him to find Eolande, then he would surely kill the girl as well and she would be absolved of the entire cumbersome situation.

But, of course, nothing had gone as planned. Akrin had not killed Eolande on sight. It was likely the first time he had ever restrained his murderous instincts, and instead of solving her problems, he had come after Logaire and created a slew of new ones. Logaire had been forced to send men to protect the girl, otherwise Akrin would have realized something was off. Then those blithering idiots had let her escape.

Now Logaire had to weigh the risks of keeping her advisor alive. If he knew the truth about what happened in Halig, that it was not Akrin and his men who had killed the Oracle, but a group of hired mercenaries that Logaire had employed to the task, then he could ruin everything she was working so hard to protect. She had been toying with the idea of poisoning Vishram when Blaise had come to the castle, distracting her attention, and now there was this ridiculous confrontation with Maialen. Logaire wanted to scream in frustration.

"You know where to find me if you change your mind," Blaise said, interrupting her thoughts and turning to walk away.

Her mouth fell open in surprise. No one was behaving in the way she expected them to and she was sick of it. "This is your chance to rid the world of the woman who has been a pustulant thorn in your side for years, and you will refuse simply because I will not cower before you?"

"I know you too well, Logaire. Your manipulations will not work on me, and I will not be fooled by your empty promises. I take Veruca back, I lead its army, or you face the Earth Queen alone and may the gods help you."

"Bastard," she seethed, folding her arms stubbornly over her chest. She had to make a decision, and they both knew she could not stop Maialen on her own. Blaise had called her bluff, and she hated him for it. "Very well. You can lead the army against the Kymirrans, but the throne is still mine."

Blaise grinned at her, his amber eyes sparkling with anticipation. Logaire was not so eager. She understood what was coming, and she knew that one of them would not walk away from it. The final battle over Veruca would not just be fought against the Earth Queen, but against each other as well.

26

None of us were the same after Brother Kaden's death. For days afterwards, nightmares assaulted my sleep and I would wake up drenched in sweat, a scream caught in my throat. I would look over and see Kaeleb awake, staring into the darkness with his jaw clenched, his sword ready across his lap. We were still in the depths of the Fomori's underground world, waiting for the Va'Kul to organize her army of beasts to march on Kymir.

"We cannot trust them," Bacatha said for the millionth time one night. I sat panting beside her, torn from sleep yet again by the vicious dreams of a bloodthirsty Fomori ripping out my throat.

"I know that," Kaeleb muttered in response to her. "But we have no choice. If Maialen brings the armies of Kymir and Samirra together against us, we do not stand a chance without the Fomori. The island nations do not have the numbers or the food or supplies the Earth Queen has. We need something to tip the scales in our favor, and that something is the Fomori and the Va'Kul's Warding Stone."

"If your father can bring Veruca to the battle on our side-" Bacatha began, but Kaeleb cut her off.

"We do not know if he can. He will not kill her, and Logaire is wild, unpredictable. She has never done what is best for anyone except herself. For all we know, she could join Maialen against us."

Bacatha sighed. "That is true. With two Warding Stones, we can keep the Earth Queen from being able to destroy our armies with a sweep of her hand. She will be rendered useless. But so will Eolande."

Kaeleb looked at me, and I hated the shadows that lay behind his eyes. Shadows I had cast, for everything that was happening was because of me.

"Eolande has barely gotten her power back," he said. "The Earth Keeper has been wielding the Elements for twenty years. She cannot fight Maialen, not yet. But if the rest of us can destroy her armies, then we can take her amulets from her and Eolande can destroy them."

I picked at the edge of my sleeve, pulling at the frayed blue thread, deep like midnight out over the sea. I did not tell Kaeleb or Bacatha what I had felt in the forest, the overwhelming ecstasy that was my power and my constant yearning to unleash it again. I did not tell them how Astus whispered to me when the Va'Kul was far enough away that I could feel him again, encouraging me to accept what I was, to use the power I had been granted by the gods. I tried to ignore him, using my own Warding Stone to quiet him when it became too much, but I could not help hearing his words echo in my head.

You are the Solvrei. Your power can reshape the world. Do not let them dampen it. You could destroy the Warding Stones if you wanted to. I can tell you how. Your purpose is to rid the world of the amulets and the stones. Give us the peace we crave.

I knew what I wanted to do, the little seed of an idea growing in my mind, but I knew Kaeleb would not understand, not at first. I would need to show him. I looked at the steely grey eye watching me and I wondered if he could sense that I was different, or if he was too consumed by his grief to notice.

We began the march out of the caves soon after that. We had to walk, for the Fomori were not tolerated by horses, and I could not help the flutter of happiness in my stomach as we stepped out into the light after so many days in the darkness. I lifted my face, squinting my eyes against the harsh glare of the sun, feeling the warmth of summer on my skin. I could breathe again, the oppressive scent of the Fomori dissipating in the fresh northern air. Beside me Kaeleb smiled, the first time he had done so since Brother Kaden's death, and it was the same beautiful smile he had always worn. The sight of it gave me hope, for if he could still smile, unbroken, after everything we had been through, then perhaps I could make it through as well.

He reached out, taking my gloved hand in his. I was surprised by the gesture, but I did not pull away, sensing that what he needed the most was something to hold on to. His grip was strong, and I tried not to think about the army of demons that followed behind us. The Va'Kul was there, at the head of them, surrounded by her loyal inner sanctum of female Fomori. They hissed at the bright sun, ducking away from it and shading their eyes, and I could not help but feel a small twinge of satisfaction at their discomfort.

"I never thought I would be marching through Samirra with an army of Fomori at my back," Bacatha said. She glanced at our clasped hands, lifting one of her eyebrows and smirking. "Isn't that sweet."

"If we ever find Chaote again, you can hold hands with her," Kaeleb tossed back, causing the severe woman to glower at him. I tried to hold on to the lightness of the moment, but I could feel it slipping away almost immediately, his words reminding me that Chaote was still a captive and that Akrin had been the one to take her. I could only hope that she was safe, that she could hold on a little longer until we could get to her.

Any remaining joy I was still clinging to upon leaving the caves was soon leached away by the sight of the blighted lands below the mountains. Grey, chalky dust swirled around our boots as we walked, crowding the air in a dull haze, as if an ominous cloud was following our procession. Beneath our feet were the shriveled remnants of once fertile valleys, bisected with oozing rivers of dark sludge whose banks were littered with the pungent corpses of rotting fish.

"Is there any part of Imbria she has not cursed?" I asked, sorrow filling me at the sight of what Maialen had done to the beautiful land when she tried to expand Samirra's farming territory.

"Only the tunnels below," Kaeleb answered.

It was two days later that we reached the great divide that split the world between Kymir and Samirra. I looked down along the massive rift, stretching endlessly into the distance, and I was awed by the sheer scale of the immense chasm. Kaeleb was right, Mailen had been wielding her power far longer than I, and if she could do something like this, then I would be foolish to underestimate her.

"Can you get us across?" the Va'Kul's sibilant voice hissed near my ear, causing me to jump with fright. Her yellow eyes shone with amusement at my fear and her lips pulled back, revealing her fanged teeth as she smiled.

"Me?" I asked, confused.

"You are the Solvrei, are you not?" she queried, annoyed that I had not instantly done as she requested.

"I... I need someone to take from, to use my power," I mumbled. "And you have to remove your Warding Stone."

She let her gaze linger on me, her pink tongue darting out to lick her lips. Then she slipped the chain that held her stone over her neck, dropping it into the folds of her fur pelts. She made a motion with one of her clawed hands, and a male Fomori came forward, kneeling at her feet. She gestured to him impatiently.

"You... you want me to use him?" I asked, looking around at Kaeleb and Bacatha.

"Yes, that is why I summoned him here for you," the Va'Kul snapped. She also looked at Kaeleb. "Why is she so weak? I expected more from her."

"I am not weak," I said through clenched teeth. If she wanted me to drain the life from one of her beasts, then I would gladly do so. It would be one less of them the world had to worry about. I yanked off my gloves, shoving them at Kaeleb and laying my hands on the bare shoulders of the kneeling creature. His grey hide was smooth and soft under my hands, covered with a fine dusting of hair like the baby ducks I had delighted in seeing as a child.

I took a breath, my heart pounding, wondering if it would be the same rush of elation as before. Part of me was afraid to feel it again, even though I craved it.

The ground beneath us began to quake and I felt the huge muscles of the Fomori trembling beneath my hands. I stared at the divide, willing it to close, and then it came, the blissful rush of my power enveloping me. I could feel the dawn of the world deep below, the dark and fiery beginning of everything. The first grains of soil and the massive slabs of rock that had moved beneath the surface, shoving upward in a powerful thrust to create the mountains.

The beast began to spasm beneath me, and it let out a howl of pain. I released it, jerking myself out of the ancient beginning and blinking at the smooth expanse of earth that now bridged the gaping hole where the chasm had been.

"Impressive," the Va'Kul murmured. She reached out, grabbing my hand and peering down at my palm curiously, as if expecting to see thorny tentacles growing from my fingers, but it was just an ordinary hand. Then she flexed her razor-sharp talons and with a vicious swipe of her hand, she opened the jugular of the kneeling Fomori. She looked at me, her strange yellow eyes boring into me, wanting me to recognize her savagery. "You should have finished him off. He would only have slowed us down in the condition you left him in."

She gave the command to proceed, and the Fomori flooded into Kymir, disappearing amongst the camouflage of the mutated forest. My stomach turned at the sight of it, for though Kymir was Maialen's kingdom, it had also been my childhood home, and I hated seeing the menacing beasts loping eagerly amongst the trees.

A shadow slanted across the ground from somewhere above us and I threw my head back to look up at an eagle circling overhead. Fear knotted in my throat and my first thought was that the Earth Keeper had found us. The second was that I was not ready to fight her. Then I saw the black hair that streamed out from beneath the riding helmet, and my breath caught in my throat. The eagle dipped lower and the Va'Kul let out an undulating yell. The sound was echoed back to her, and I knew it was Chaote on the winged creature. She brought the eagle down, glaring around at all of us, her glorious countenance unreadable as she pulled off the riding helmet and threw it aside.

I wanted to run to her and throw my arms around her, but I knew she would not appreciate the gesture and so I remained still, staring at her in awe.

"You look like hell," Bacatha said, and she was right. Chaote's golden armor was gone and she was dressed in peasant garb, simple homespun clothing that was a dull, drab brown. One of her eyes was nearly swollen shut and there were bruises mottling the side of her face. Dried blood crusted a gash that ran along the side of her skull, and I could see the bright stain of crimson on her shirt from a fresh wound. That was when I realized I could hear the whispers of the Sapphire, that I did not feel the dampening emptiness of the Warding Stone which normally accompanied her presence.

"Are you..." my voice trailed off as I gestured to her chest, to the blood that was seeping through the bandage I could now see was tied beneath her shirt.

"It is gone," Chaote said, and her voice gave nothing more.

"Was it Akrin?" I asked softly.

She did not answer, refusing to say more. She turned to the Va'Kul and lifted her chin in greeting. The savage creature bowed low, but I could see the gleam of resentment in her eerie yellow eyes. These two were not friends, that much was clear.

"I assume you are trying to be seen? Because if not, this is the poorest attempt at stealth that I have ever had the displeasure to behold," Chaote said contemptuously.

Kaeleb grinned, throwing his arms around her and clapping her on the back while she stood stiffly beneath him, barely tolerating the embrace. He stepped back and I saw the hint of a smile on her lips, though it was quickly replaced with a scowl.

"We have no need to be stealthy. We want Maialen to know we are coming. It will draw her attention away from the coast, so the Leharans can surround the Royal City from the south," Kaeleb told her.

"Well, that is good, because I could hear you from halfway across Samirra. As for your plan, that might have worked, but the Earth Queen is not in Kymir," Chaote told him. "She has gone to take Veruca."

I saw Kaeleb tense, his pale brows drawing together. "My father is in Veruca. He is trying to convince Logaire to join our assault on Kymir."

"Then he will be facing Maialen alone."

Kaeleb shoved a hand through the shock of pale hair that hung over his forehead, his eye darting to the east, towards the black mountains of Veruca. "We must do something."

The Va'Kul was watching their exchange with interest, and she slipped the Warding Stone back around her neck, the emptiness of it flowing over me like a wave. Chaote's eyes flickered to the milky moonstone for a moment before returning to settle on Kaeleb.

"Take the eagle," Chaote offered him. "I know there is no point in telling you it is foolish for you to go."

He nodded and I looked between them, aghast. Kaeleb was just going to fly into a war in Veruca? And do what? Fight Maialen? Spirit Blaise away on the eagle? A thousand scenarios ran through my head, none of them ending with him alive. I practically shouted in protest, "You can't!"

Kaeleb turned to me, taking my hands. "I have to, Eolande. She has already killed my mother. I cannot let her take my father from me as well."

"But I can help you," I stated emphatically.

He shook his head. "Not this time. The eagle cannot carry us both that far, not if I want to get there in time. Stay with Chaote and Bacatha and take the Royal City as we have planned. We can use this assault on Veruca to our advantage, to cut Maialen off from her supply lines to Kymir and Samirra."

Chaote nodded, and Kaeleb crushed me against him, holding me so tightly for a moment that I could barely breathe. Then he released me and stepped back, vaulting for the eagle and soaring into the air before I could even gather enough air in my lungs to protest once again. My mind was screaming at me to do something, and I pressed my hands over my ears, trying to drown out my own voice.

He is going to die you will let him die don't let him die you should be with him he can't go alone she will kill him he will die and I will be alone again always alone alone alone.

Chaote stood watching me, her face carefully blank. The Va'Kul loomed behind us, her savage features twisted into a condescending snarl.

"You have grown soft," the creature hissed at the halfbreed.

Chaote lifted her chin. "Is that a challenge?"

The Va'Kul let out a resentful laugh. "I would never challenge you, Mother."

Even I could hear the lie in her voice, the taunting lilt of her words. Chaote shrugged, motioning for the Va'Kul to keep moving the army forward. She and Bacatha fell into step on either side of me, keeping a safe distance from the hungry stares of the beasts.

"What on Imbria happened to you?" Bacatha demanded. "How did you escape?"

Chaote scoffed at her. "Escape? I was never a captive, Leharan."

Bacatha narrowed her eyes as we passed into the forest. I could not help but shudder at our surroundings, at the dark and warped world Maialen had created in these woods. A bird cawed from somewhere in the trees, an angry warning, telling us to come no further. Even the Fomori seemed on edge, sniffing at the unnatural protrusions that sprouted from the deformed trees and letting out low howls of discontent.

"You came from Iriellestra?" Bacatha assumed.

Chaote nodded. "The Queen sent me there for safekeeping. She planned to use me as a weapon against the rest of you."

Bacatha grinned appreciatively. "And that was your plan all along. To finally get into Samirra so you could kill Favian."

"It was."

"So? Is he dead? Is Favian dead?" Bacatha wanted to know.

"No," was Chaote's flat reply. When Bacatha tried to get her to tell us more, Chaote refused, claiming that when we needed to know, she would tell us what had happened to her in Samirra. Bacatha finally relented in her questioning, and as we trudged through the forest, surrounded by an army of Fomori, on our way to lay siege to the most powerful kingdom on Imbria, I could not stop thinking of Kaeleb, praying to any god who would listen to me that he would survive what was coming.

27

Akrin stood beside the Earth Queen, staring out over the vast plains that sprawled at the foot of the black mountains. He had found Maialen just as she was crossing into the eastern realm, her army of archers marching smartly in organized regiments behind her. She had turned her head up to the sky, hearing his eagle screech, drawing her horse to a halt. The entire army ground to a stop behind her and she waited while Akrin brought the giant bird down to land nearby.

"I did not want eagles brought to this fight," she told him. "They are too easily spotted from the mountains."

Akrin thought for a moment she was toying with him and he almost laughed out loud. Then he saw that she was serious, her doll-like face solemn and stern. Surely, someone would have told her that the Verucans were just as likely to spot thousands of Kymirran soldiers advancing across the grassy flatlands as they were a bird in the sky. It was a wonder she had not gotten herself killed, and her soldiers slaughtered along with her.

"How are things in Samirra?" she asked when he continued to stare at her in silence.

"I delivered the prisoner and headed back to you as quickly as I could," he answered. It was not a lie, though quite a bit more than a simple prisoner exchange had transpired in the western realm, but Akrin saw no need to share those details with the Earth Queen just yet. He would worry about that mess later.

Maialen frowned at him, noticing the dried splatter of blood across the front of his armor. "Do not lie to me," she warned.

"I did not harm the halfbreed," Akrin swore irritably. Again, it was not a lie. He had not touched a hair on Chaote's head once she had gone berserk amongst the Samirran soldiers. He had run the other way as soon as she had leapt on the first one, jerking her arms down on either side of his helmet, using the iron crest that adorned it to sever the rope that bound her wrists.

Akrin had not thought twice about staying to help the Samirrans. He had no allegiance to the pale-skinned westerners, and he was unwilling to risk his life for them. He fled to the palace stables where the eagles were kept tethered. Chaote was Favian's problem now, if the man lived past the next few moments, and Akrin had bigger plans. He needed to get back to the Earth Queen as soon as possible and secure his place at her side. He also had no desire to be gutted by the enraged halfbreed, and from what he had seen thus far, she would probably take half of Iriellestra with her before they could stop her.

A skinny waif of a stable lad tried to stop him from taking one of the eagles, but as soon as Akrin raised his fist, the young man fled in terror. Akrin had climbed on top of the winged creature and lifted into the air, glancing back at the circle of carnage that surrounded the halfbreed and pleased with his decision to abandon the Samirrans to their fate. There were already several bodies littering the ground around her and she showed no signs of tiring.

Upon arriving at the Royal City, he was disappointed to discover that the Earth Queen was not there to greet him as he had anticipated. Fury boiled within him as the spidery old man who manipulated the Queen from the quiet corners of the Council Chamber came out to meet him instead.

"So, the halfbreed did not murder you on the way to Samirra? A shame," Damek sneered. "I would have staked the entire royal treasury that she would have."

Akrin wondered if the old man's brittle bones would crumble to dust when he ground them down. He could find out. The Keeper was gone. There was no one to protect the advisor. Akrin could take him down into the Council Chamber, pick him apart piece by piece. It had been so long since he had been able to relish killing someone. Old men were not his customary prey of choice, but he was willing to make an exception for this one.

"The Queen has gone to Veruca, to take that wretched pit of filth you call home from the whore who presides over it. You should be pleased to hear that," Damek went on, studying Akrin carefully. A brutish lout. Not much in the way of brains, but that was good. It was the clever ones that were always a problem. Like Logaire and her bastard cousin. Damek was practically salivating at the thought of Maialen crushing the Verucans, and this dolt could help them do it. Akrin would know everything about the Verucan defenses. It was a promising twist of fate that he had returned from Samirra so swiftly, still alive and breathing. Damek was no fool, though. He knew that leaving Akrin alive was a dangerous ploy. The man was completely deranged, and he could not be allowed to return to Kymir and wreak havoc upon their peaceful citizens. With any luck, someone would kill him in the coming siege once Maialen had gotten what she needed from him. Although the old advisor did not need luck. A purse of silver in the right hands would ensure that the General never returned from battle.

"When did she leave?" Akrin demanded.

"A few days ago. On horseback. You can catch up to them easily with the eagle you brought. The Queen will be pleased to have you return safely to her," Damek said, smoothing over the disgust he felt for the sullen man and playing to his ego. "With you by her side, Veruca will crumble."

"And Logaire will finally get what is coming to her," Akrin muttered darkly.

Damek rustled his black robes, wiping his sweating forehead with one sleeve. He detested the summer and its oppressive heat. "Allow me to see to your preparations so that you may leave as soon as possible."

Akrin nodded, satisfied with the old man's capitulation to his needs. Perhaps the waspish advisor had finally learned his place. Even Damek could see that Akrin was meant for greatness at the Queen's side. She would control all of Imbria, and he would be the sword that carried out her vengeance. He would be free to do whatever he wished, to whomever he wished, and the thought of such an unchecked ability to inspire fear and inflict pain made him giddy. He would be the most feared man in the four realms. As soon as Damek informed him that everything was prepared, Akrin wasted no time and departed immediately, eager to begin the siege on Veruca and claim his place in the new empire.

Now, Akrin stood beside Maialen at the head of her army, wondering at the cause of the satisfied glint in her big green eyes.

"It seems that Blaise has come to Veruca to beg Logaire's help," she confided, as if she had been dying to tell someone that juicy morsel of information all day.

"The Fire Keeper is here?" Akrin asked sharply. Something curled in his gut at the thought of facing Blaise, and he wondered how the Earth Queen could possibly be delighted about the prospect. It would make taking Veruca much more difficult.

"It appears so. Logaire has made an alliance with him. She knows she cannot defeat me on her own." Maialen's voice was arrogant, boasting. She lifted her chin high. She was wearing golden armor that looked suspiciously like Chaote's and Akrin wondered if the Queen had kept the halfbreed's armor for herself. It looked out of place on her, unsettling, like Maialen was playing a role she had not rehearsed for.

"They will meet us here, on the plains. He will not wait until we are in the mountains," Akrin said, squinting out over the stretch of land. "He will want us to have a way to retreat, and an open field where he can use his power more effectively."

"His power is nothing compared to mine," Maialen insisted.

"Be that as it may, Blaise is a strategist, and we will need to be careful. Send out a scouting party to see where the Verucan army is and how long we have before they reach the plains," Akrin said, used to commanding soldiers.

The Earth Keeper frowned, the lines that bracketed her mouth deep with displeasure. "I am the Queen and the Solvrei. I will give the orders here. Besides, you do not know what I know."

Akrin once again felt the longing to murder someone, and the Earth Queen was at the top of his list. He forced himself to relent, bowing and stepping aside in a gesture of obedience, but inside his blood was boiling. He knew the Fire Keeper's tactics better than anyone. He knew exactly what he would do and where he would attack. This was why Damek had happily sent him here to help the Queen. Now she was treating him like a nuisance, though it was obvious she knew nothing of warfare, completely unaware that she had already made several costly mistakes.

"My Queen!" a shout from a soldier interrupted Akrin's dark thoughts. The man came running up to Maialen, panting hard with exertion.

"The scouts have spotted the Verucan army! They are marching towards the plains," the man said breathlessly. Akrin could not help but curl his lip in smug satisfaction, though Maialen did not seem upset by what she just heard. On the contrary, she seemed eager, leaning forward in her saddle to peer out at the expanse of tall grass, as if hoping for a glimpse of the coming attack. The tall golden stalks waved in the breeze, and she thought she heard the faint rumble of an army mobilizing.

She turned back to Akrin. "General, prepare the army for defensive positions, then join me at the front of the line. I think you will enjoy what is about to happen."

It seemed like an eternity before the Verucans crawled into sight, like tiny ants marching in the distance. Their black-armored divisions spread out at the base of the mountains, banners flapping in the breeze. Maialen squinted harder, trying to find Blaise amongst the sea of men, but they were too far away and she could not tell one man from another.

"There he is," Akrin pointed. "With Logaire."

The two cousins were riding side by side on beautiful black horses, Logaire wearing a gilded breastplate over her shimmering gown. The fabric cascaded down over the sides of the saddle, glistening in the sun with every movement she made. Beside her was her cousin, in full black battle armor, his red hair shining like a beacon. They were resplendent, an inspiring sight to behold, and for a moment, Maialen felt doubt creeping up within her. Then she remembered the tiny scroll she had received that morning with a message from Veruca that would change everything.

Blaise lifted his hand, made the gesture for parlay. Maialen laughed to herself and lifted her hand in response. She would hear what he had to say, and it would force him to look her in the eye after all this time. She spurred her horse forward, galloping across the field to meet him. Logaire stayed back with the army, watching everything with her clever golden eyes.

"Maialen, do not do this," Blaise said as she approached him. He glanced over her, recognizing the armor she wore and grimacing. "You are making a mistake."

"You always underestimate me, Blaise," she said haughtily. "You are the one who made a mistake when you threw me aside like I was nothing. I am sure you regret that decision now. You could have been at my side all this time instead of squirreling yourself away underground."

"Why can't you let me go?" he asked her, and his voice was not angry or vengeful. It was soft, tinged with sorrow. A knot formed in his chest as he realized that the words he had just spoken were almost identical to the ones Orabelle had once said to him. The memory of that night crashed over him and he could see her as clearly as if she were standing before him. They were in Veruca and he had helped her wash her injured hands after the blooddrinker attacked her in the tunnels. He asked her why she did not want to marry him, pleading with her to tell him what she wanted from him, what he could do to make her love him. Orabelle's eyes had flashed, and for a moment he had seen a glimpse beneath the hard exterior that surrounded her heart, and there was pity and sorrow and pain. Then she asked him to let her go. Blaise felt a hot sweep of shame at the memory, and he regretted that he had been the one to cause her to utter those words. He could not help but feel that he deserved what was happening to him now.

"This is not about you, though I know you like to believe everything I do is because of you," the Earth Queen snapped at him, bringing him back to the present and the impending battle. "This is about Veruca."

"What you did to Gula was because of me," Blaise pointed out. Again, there was sorrow in his tone.

Maialen's big green eyes flared with emotion. She doubted that Blaise would have felt such sorrow if she herself was the one who died. She hated seeing the tears in his eyes, tears that were the manifestation of his love for another woman. It was practically unbearable, but she refused to let him see her hurt. "Your healer was in the wrong place at the wrong time and got herself killed. Do not blame me for her poor decisions."

"You know what you are doing is wrong," Blaise said, changing tactics, seeing that appealing to her emotions would get him nowhere. There was too much pain and anger between them now, and she would never see past it, just as he could not see past the things she had done. "You cannot continue to hold two Elements, Maialen. I have seen the forest, the rivers, what you have done to them. Your power has been corrupted and you are destroying Imbria."

"You would have done it yourself if you could have," she retorted. The one thing she was unwilling to give up was her power. It was all she had. The world had taken everything else from her and she would not let them take that, too. "Enough of this stalling. Send your army. We will see who is the most powerful Keeper."

She spun her horse around, galloping back to the line of archers who were poised, their arrows pointed high into the sky, ready to rain down havoc upon their enemies. Blaise lifted his hand, giving the Verucan ranks behind him the signal to attack while shouting the command.

Nobody moved.

He whipped his head around, confused by the silence that followed his command when he had expected to hear the thundering of horses and men charging forward. Logaire was there, the wind tugging at her gown, her hair fanning out behind her. She had the decency to look remorseful as she shook her head, her mouth forming the words, "I am sorry."

"No!" Blaise cried out, anger and betrayal nearly crushing his chest like a physical blow. Logaire had offered him to Maialen. His cousin never meant for him to walk away from this battle alive, and the pain of that knowledge was worse than a thousand arrows. The Earth Keeper lifted her hand and Blaise saw Akrin ride forward, a troop of cavalry soldiers with him.

"The Queen asks that you give up the Opal and surrender quietly," Akrin said, drawing the men in a circle around the Keeper.

"I will die first, and I will take you with me," Blaise snarled at him. He began to call his power, feeling the burning heat of it crawling up his arms. Akrin leapt off his horse, pulling his sword from its sheath.

Blaise threw a whip of fire at him, not wasting any more time with words. If they wanted to fight him, then he would fight them alone. A deluge of rain pelted down from the sky overhead, dampening the flames before they could devour the General. Blaise tried again, throwing the fire around him in a circle and causing the ring of Kymirran cavalry to break apart, but again Maialen countered his attack, and the fire slammed against a wall of corrupt water, showering Blaise in a spray of droplets and embers. Beneath them, the tall grass of the plains shriveled as the water touched it, curling into dry, lifeless stalks.

Blaise yanked out his sword, spurring his horse and charging at Akrin. Maialen intervened again, buckling the land beneath him and causing the horse to rear in fright, sending him tumbling to the ground. He rolled, righting himself, his sword somehow still in his hand. The men had formed around him again, drawing a tight circle, pressing him and Akrin within reach of each other.

"Maybe I will send the boy your eyes after I pluck them out, to make up for the one I took from him," Akrin taunted.

Blaise roared in fury, swinging his sword. The younger man dodged the blow but just barely, and Blaise swung again, the blade slicing into Akrin's arm. It was a shallow cut. It would not kill him, but Blaise grinned anyway, savoring even that small victory. He knew he was going to die. There was no way that he could walk away from the trap Maialen and Logaire had sprung for him, but he would take as many of them with him as he could. He gripped the hilt of his sword tighter. He would make them earn his death.

There was a screeching cry from overhead, but Blaise ignored it, lunging for Akrin once again. The dour general parried the blow, following it with one of his own. Blaise felt the sharp sting of steel scraping against his skin, twisting back before the blade could cut deeper. Suddenly one of the men who was circling them pitched forward, a dagger buried in the back of his neck. Another cried out, clutching his leg where a deep slash had severed his artery, dead in seconds. Blaise whirled around in confusion, wondering if Logaire had come to his rescue, unable to bear the thought of watching him die.

"Father." It was Kaeleb, and Blaise felt a moment of elation upon seeing the boy, but it was quickly replaced by an agonizing fear. The men were turning on Kaeleb, jabbing at him with their long swords. Blaise grabbed one of them, yanking him down from the saddle and throwing him to the ground while his horse reared in panic, crushing him beneath its powerful hooves. Kaeleb's eagle was flapping its wings in agitation, the cries of the horses making it uneasy. It bobbed its head up and down, poking its huge beak at the remaining riders and screeching like a banshee.

"What are you doing here?" Blaise demanded, yelling at his son.

"Saving you," was Kaeleb's blunt response. They heard Maialen shouting in the distance, felt the earth rumbling beneath them. Then it died away, and Blaise realized he could not feel his own power any longer. The boy had brought a Warding Stone. Kaeleb grinned at him. "Eolande slipped it into my pocket."

"You!" Akrin's voice tore through the melee, and he was staring, fixated on Kaeleb, his scarred mouth twisted in rage. "I will kill you both!"

"Go for the eagle!" Kaeleb shouted at Blaise. He rushed at Akrin, lifting his sword high as if he meant to strike an overhand blow. Akrin took the bait, lifting his own sword to block, and Kaeleb dropped to the ground at the last minute, sliding into him and thrusting upward. The sword pierced the man's stomach and Akrin screamed out in pain, falling to his knees. Kaeleb scrambled to his feet, running towards the eagle, where Blaise was shouting at him to hurry. There was a sound like a snap echoing in the air, and Kaeleb could see the volley of arrows arching towards them from Maialen's archers. He ran harder, his lungs bursting, throwing himself at the winged creature just as it lifted into the sky. Blaise caught him, holding his son tightly against him and cursing the boy for his recklessness and stupidity. He guided the eagle away from the archers, over the silent assembly of Verucan soldiers. Logaire's head turned to follow them as they moved, her full lips pressed into a thin line.

28

As we marched further south, towards Kymir's Royal City, my apprehension grew. It was clear the Kymirrans knew we were coming. Each town we encountered had been shuttered up and hastily abandoned, and I could not help but imagine the innocent people of the forest realm cowering in their basements and hiding from the savage invaders who were threatening their land. I still could not reconcile the Fomori being part of our battle, no matter what anyone said to me, and neither could I forget the look on Brother Kaden's face when he died. It was all I saw when I looked at the beasts.

Sometimes I thought the Va'Kul knew what I was thinking. She would stare at me with her eerie yellow gaze, her lips parted slightly and her savage features full of hunger. Chaote often walked beside me, and I was grateful for her company, which the terrifying Va'Kul could not seem to tolerate. The Fomori woman would glower at Chaote, slinking away into her sanctum of other females and giving me a reprieve from her constant stare.

"You should not antagonize the Va'Kul," Chaote said quietly to me. Branches of trees arched overhead, sheltering our path from the hot summer sun, though sweat still beaded on our brows. We were on the main road to Kymir's Royal City, and though we had not bothered to hide our coming, we had so far met with no resistance.

"How am I doing that?" I demanded, exasperated.

"Do not look at her," Chaote warned me. "She will not challenge you while I am with you, but you must still be careful of her. She is a cunning opponent."

"Why did you leave the Fomori?" I asked, curious.

She stared at the road ahead, not seeing it, for her thoughts were far away from the forests of Kymir. "When I was thrown into the prison of the Wastelands with the Fomori, I did what I needed to do to survive. I was forced to become one of them, to become the strongest of them, or else I would have been killed. I am not afraid of death, Eolande, but I must admit that I very much prefer to be alive. One cannot exact vengeance once one is dead."

"Something must have changed," I prompted.

"Damian changed me," she confessed, and I knew it was the first time she had said the words aloud. "He showed me there was a part of me that was still Tahitian, and I missed that part of myself very much."

"But then he died."

Chaote turned her starry gaze to me. "Yes, he died."

I could not help thinking of Kaeleb, of the constant fear I had that he would not return. I was afraid to care about him, afraid that if I did, I would be unable to bear his loss. I had lost so much already.

"You can try to hide how you feel, child, but in the end you cannot stop yourself from feeling it. I learned that lesson the hard way," she said.

Bacatha stopped up ahead, turning and motioning for us to halt. Chaote jogged forward to find out what was happening, and I hurried after her. We were at the top of a small hill, and below us the road sloped down into a walled town. From our vantage point we could see the town's inhabitants attempting to flee, hastily tossing their belongings into carts and herding their animals. Some ran on foot, dragging their children behind them.

"It is about time we had a decent meal," the Va'Kul murmured, coming to stand beside us and surveying the chaotic scene below. Her tongue darted along her lips and the icterine eyes were ravenous.

"No!" I protested. "You must give them time to flee. They have nothing to do with this."

The Va'Kul laughed, and the sound grated on my ears like breaking glass. "You are at war, girl, and these are your enemies."

"They are innocent people," I argued.

"There are no innocents. Every man in that town would pick up a weapon and strike you down with it if given the chance. Surely you cannot be this foolish. What has the Mother been teaching you?" the Va'Kul asked with a sneer at Chaote.

"Careful, Va'Kul," the halfbreed warned. Her hand moved to her side, but she seemed to have forgotten there was no sword there. Irritation flashed over her perfect features.

"We agreed to fight for the boy. We did not agree to take orders from your kind," the Va'Kul snarled at me before turning to Chaote. "You are still Fomori, Mother, and these people are the enemy. They are the spoils of war. It is our way, and you know it. Or have you forgotten our ways, spending all of your time with these weak bags of flesh?"

Chaote was silent, only a slight frown marring her features. The Va'Kul took this as her acquiescence, turning and letting out a long howl. The other Fomori howled back at her, the high-pitched cries sending chills down my spine in spite of the heat. In the town below, the panic escalated, and the air was filled with piercing screams as people abandoned their belongings and fled for safety. I saw one mother desperately carrying her two children, and she was so slow, painfully slow. She would not escape what was coming, but she kept trying, her terrified face turning to look back at the hillside that was littered with blooddrinkers. There was something in her dogged persistence that tore at me, and I knew I could not let her die.

The Fomori had gathered around us on the top of the hill, pressing forward with hungry snaps of their jaws. Bacatha moved her body in front of me, and I turned to Chaote, pleading with her to stop them. She was still staring at the Va'Kul, their gazes locked in a battle that only they could see. The Va'Kul touched her hand to her chest, where the pale Warding Stone glimmered beneath her fingers. Then she gave the order to attack.

The Fomori streamed down the hillside like a wave of death. I screamed, but it was drowned out by the savage roars of the beasts. I groped at the Sapphire, trying to call any tiny bit of the power that I could muster, but there was only the blanket emptiness of the Warding Stone.

Bacatha lunged at the Va'Kul, swinging the scythe at the blooddrinker's head. The Va'Kul caught the weapon in her strong talons, wrenching it away from Bacatha. The Leharan let it go, a movement the Va'Kul had not expected, and she was thrown off balance, stumbling backwards with a vicious snarl and dropping the weapon. Bacatha dove at her again and they rolled on the ground, the Va'Kul biting at her neck, trying to poison the Leharan with her putrid bite. Her long nails raked down Bacatha's face, bright streaks of blood running across the Leharan's cheek. I jumped on the creature's back, wrapping my hands around her neck, clamoring for the Warding Stone. If I could get rid of her stone, then I could use my power. I could stop them all.

The Va'Kul twisted, flinging me off her like I was nothing. I was no match for her size or her strength. I was nothing more than a skinny, underfed waif who had no idea how to fight, but I kept seeing the fleeing mother and her children in my mind, and I refused to give up. I landed hard in the dirt, ignoring the pain, shoving myself up and latching onto her once more, just before she could take a bite out of Bacatha's neck. The Leharan's icy blue eyes flared with hope, standing out brightly in her blood-stained face as she struggled to get out from underneath the massive Fomori woman.

"Help us!" Bacatha shouted, kicking wildly beneath the Va'Kul, whose murderous jaws were inches from her unprotected throat.

Chaote was watching, her face still impassive, the black eyes as cold as the night sky. For a moment, time seemed to stand still and I knew she was making a choice, one that would change our world forever. She would either stand by and let the Fomori kill us, or she would help us kill the Fomori. I felt a rush of pity for her, for the terrible choice that now faced her, and for a brief moment that stretched on for an eternity, our eyes met.

Chaote ran forward, kicking the Va'Kul under the chin and sending her flopping onto her side. I rolled with her, crying out as I was slammed into the ground beneath the beast. The Va'Kul was shrieking rabidly at Chaote, swiping at her with her vicious claws. Chaote snatched up the scythe where it had fallen, swinging it down and severing the Va'Kul's hands. The Fomori woman screeched in pain, black blood soaking down onto me from the stumps of her arms, and Chaote reached out, ripping the chain that held the Warding Stone off her neck.

I was still holding onto the Va'Kul, and as soon as the oppressive silence of the Warding Stone had lifted, I ripped the life out of her, gathering all of it within me. I could feel it radiating through me like a jolt of lightning, filling me until I thought I would split apart. The Fomori lived longer lives than the rest of us, and I had not been prepared for so much power.

I cried out, not sure whether it was from pain or ecstasy. Then the world around us exploded.

The Fomori who were running down the hill towards the town were flung to the ground, dead instantly. The ones who had gathered around us to watch the fight were violently tossed about like rag dolls, their bodies crushed under the immense force of the power I unleashed. A shock wave radiated outward, the trees of the forest bursting into showers of wooden fragments. The beasts that remained alive stopped their advance towards the town and fell to their knees, their heads lowered to the ground.

"She is gone. You can let her go now," Chaote said gently, peeling my hands from the corpse of the Va'Kul. I released the mutilated body, staring down at it in horror. Then I looked at the still form of the Leharan warrior laying nearby on the ground.

"Bacatha!"

"I am here, Solvrei," the Leharan gasped, opening her eyes. "I am alive. This damned armor makes it hard to get up."

I started to laugh, then to cry with relief and Chaote shook me gently, wiping at my face with rough strokes of her hand. When she spoke to me, her voice was harsh. "No. Do not cry, you must not be weak."

I looked over the grotesque corpse of the Va'Kul, at the prostrate forms of the living Fomori, still bowing their heads, and the realization of what had just happened dawned on me.

"You killed the Va'Kul," Chaote said. "You now lead the Fomori, Eolande."

Logaire sat astride her horse, the army of Veruca assembled behind her. She knew she was a dazzling sight, draped in jewels and golden fabric, her gleaming breastplate shining in the summer sun below her mane of copper hair. Her eyes were fixed on the center of the field, where half a dozen men lay dead. Maialen was walking towards them, motioning for the Kymirrans nearest her to come and collect the bodies. The Earth Queen stopped as she reached Akrin, who was sitting upright on the ground, leaning against the carcass of a dead cavalry horse. She bent towards him, saying something that was carried away by the breeze wafting through the tall prairie grass. Logaire wondered if Maialen would still grant her request, or if the Earth Queen would renege on her promise to give the General back to Veruca. It was a reasonable doubt for Logaire to harbor, since Maialen had not gotten what she had accepted in return, which was Blaise.

The Verucan Queen felt a smile tug at the corners of her mouth. Her cousin truly did seem impervious to death, no matter how hard they tried to kill him. She had not been surprised to see the boy come to his rescue, and a small part of her was relieved, even though she knew Blaise would never forgive her for this betrayal and it would be better for all of them if he was dead.

Maialen straightened her back, looking up at Logaire, her face set in hard lines. Then she turned and walked back to her army. The other bodies were collected, and Logaire's smile widened as Akrin was left alone in the middle of the bloodied field. Logaire waited until Maialen had disappeared amongst her divisions of archers, then she spurred her horse forward, the men of her personal guard following close behind her.

She pulled at the reins, halting her mount just before she reached the wounded General. He glanced up at her from the corners of his beady eyes, his dull, obscene face twisted with rage beneath the close-cropped auburn hair. She slid down from the horse, blocking out the sun and casting him in shadow as her eyes skimmed over him, seeing the deep wound in his belly.

"It is a painful way to die," she commented, her purring voice full of amusement. "Perhaps I should leave you here. Let your wound fester while the vultures pick you apart."

"Take me to a healer," he snarled.

Logaire arched her brow. "You are in no position to be making demands, Akrin darling."

"The Earth Keeper told me you wanted me back. Surely, it was not just to watch me die," he spat at her, pain distorting his features as he clutched harder at his bleeding stomach.

"No, it was not simply to watch you die," she agreed, and she stepped one foot across him, lowering herself down so that she straddled his lap. She saw the surprise on his face, the dark, sinister thing within him that imagined her doing this thousands of times. She laughed. "It was so that I could be the one to kill you."

She pulled a knife from the sheath that was fastened around her waist. He recognized it as one of his own and he jerked beneath her, but her weight had pinned his legs to the ground and he was in too much pain to throw her off. The horse behind him was as solid as a wall. There was no getting away from her. She was smiling, her full red lips wide, her golden eyes dancing with pleasure. She did not seem to care about the blood that soaked her glorious gown, or the dirt beneath her knees.

"I will have vengeance for the murder of my beloved Oracle," she said, laying the edge of the knife against his cheek, wondering how many people he had killed with the hateful weapon, how many helpless men and women had begged for their lives as he toyed with them. She thought of Magnus, her friend, carved up into little pieces and tossed at her feet. She could still hear the horrible tapping of his severed finger against her door when Akrin had come to tell her of his death. Logaire had waited so long for this moment.

"I did not kill your Oracle!" he protested, spittle flying from his mouth.

"Well, yes, darling, we both know that. But no one else does, and they never will," she told him. "You will be remembered as the vile traitor who murdered the divine Oracle, and I will be the Queen who brought you to justice. I will give the people the blood they are calling for. I will deliver them their retribution for your reprehensible act, and they will love me even more for it. I will be revered for generations to come while you will be forgotten, your name never uttered again. People will remember you as nothing more than a weak man who slaughtered an innocent woman, and who was killed by Queen Logaire herself. I should thank you, really, for this is quite the gift you are giving me."

"You are witch! A cursed demon woman from-" he raged at her but stopped abruptly as pain twisted in his gut. He looked down, seeing the knife as it began to slide into the wound in his stomach, slowly, then halting while she looked down at him, her lips parted breathlessly and triumph shining in her eyes.

"You deserve every moment of this," she whispered. The blade slid in further and he bucked beneath her. She turned her head, addressing the soldiers who were waiting nearby, her voice carrying across the silent field. "The murder of the Oracle has been avenged! I have promised Veruca that I would not let her death go unpunished, and here is her murderer, taking his last breath before your very eyes!"

Logaire shoved the knife in up to the hilt, grunting with the effort.

"Say hello to Magnus for me. I am sure he will be waiting for you in whatever hell awaits you," she whispered in Akrin's ear. Blood poured over her hand, hot and sticky, and she kept smiling as his head lolled forward, beady eyes empty and silent as death finally claimed him.

Logaire sat for a long time, staring down at the corpse beneath her, relishing the warm embrace of vengeance. Finally, it was done, and for a moment, peace flowed over her. She heard a rumble in the distance, whipping her head up just in time to see Maialen emerging from her ranks of archers, her delicate hand clutching the Emerald that hung around her neck. Logaire had the sensation of falling, then she realized the world was turning. The ground was lifting up around her, sliding apart. She clutched at the body below her, trying to keep herself from falling, watching in disbelief as the entire Verucan army was swallowed by the earth in a matter of seconds. The air was thick with dust, the plains eerily silent in the aftermath of the destruction. The grass was dead for miles around them, withered and dried up as if the life had been choked out of it.

"What are you doing?" Logaire screamed at Maialen.

"Making sure that you do not betray me again," Maialen called back. "Veruca belongs to me now, Logaire."

"I gave you Blaise! I did everything you asked of me!"

Maialen shrugged, the movement awkward in the heavy golden armor. "I have learned from you that promises do not have to be kept. Do not worry, dear friend, I will not kill you. You have proven your loyalty to me enough to spare your life today, but I will only let you continue to rule Veruca as my vassal. I will be the queen of this realm from now on. The Queen of Imbria. Our entire world belongs to me now. You can submit to me, or you can forfeit your rule and your life."

Logaire let go of Akrin's corpse, her mind working frantically for a solution, but she could see no way out. She could never fight Maialen, that was the reason she had offered Blaise to the Earth Keeper in the first place. Logaire could not help but feel that she had made a mistake, chosen the wrong side. She should have fought beside her cousin, but it was too late to change what had happened. All she could do now was try to save herself, for one wrong move, one mistaken word, and she would be as dead as the soldiers who were now buried in the field behind her.

Logaire smiled, pushing herself to her feet and bowing low, hating every second that she had to capitulate to Maialen of all people, and hating herself for underestimating the other woman's ambition. She still saw Maialen as the mousy little thing she had been twenty years ago and failed to recognize just how much the world had changed her. "Of course, darling. Veruca is happy to serve the Queen of Imbria."

30

I laid my gloved hands on the carved sigil that was emblazoned on the door of the Council Chamber. My fingers traced the curving lines of the burning sun at the center of the seal, and my thoughts strayed to Kaeleb, praying once again that he was safe and trying to ignore the gnawing voice in my head that was telling me he should have returned by now.

Bacatha reached past me, pulling open the ancient doors. I glanced at her. The fresh claw marks that bisected her scarred face were swollen, crusted with dried blood. She caught my look, giving me a wry smile in return. I stepped through the doorway, descending the stairs into the chamber below. I could not help but think about my mother, the last Keeper of Water to hold Council here beneath Imbria, in this ancient chamber forged by the gods centuries before.

"So you are the bastard of the bastard," a small, spindly old man practically sneered at me from the shadows. "You have the arrogant look of your mother."

From his tone, it was clearly not meant as a compliment.

"This is Damek," Bacatha explained. "Maialen's closest advisor. He is the one who surrendered the Royal City to the Leharans."

"Only to prevent you barbarians from destroying it!" Damek snapped. He was pale for a Kymirran, with grey hair that slunk over his forehead like withered fingers holding his skull in place. His dark eyes roamed over us, his frown deepening as he looked from me to Bacatha, then to Chaote. "I always knew you islanders were nothing but mindless savages."

"The Earth Keeper is the one destroying Imbria, old man, not us," Bacatha said, her voice slightly muffled as the pain of her wounded face kept her from fully shaping the words. It was her father, Brogan, who had led the islanders' attack on Kymir from the south. As soon as his ships had approached the docks on the mainland, white flags of surrender had fluttered all over the Royal City. They had taken the city without a single casualty. We joined them soon after, marching in from the north with our army of Fomori. The Fomori that I now commanded, a circumstance that I would never have foreseen and one that I was in a hurry to rid myself of. It was only a matter of time before one of the blooddrinkers was brave or stupid enough to challenge me. And all it would take to remove my head was one well-aimed swipe of their massive, clawed hands.

"Lies!" the old man countered belligerently, bringing me back from the worries that shadowed my thoughts. "Maialen is the Queen of all Imbria now, and when she returns here, she will deal with you."

"We do not plan on allowing her to return," Chaote said to him.

Damek shrank away from her, disgusted by her very existence. "Do not speak to me, you foul beast!"

Chaote let out a warm, throaty laugh that filled the surrounding air with the honeyed sound. "I have been called much worse."

"No doubt you have!" Damek concurred. "And I am sure it was well-deserved!"

"You are still as pleasant as ever, Damek."

I turned at the new voice in the chamber, and Cossiana was descending the stairs, wrapped in regal blue cloth, her long braids wound around her head like a crown.

"Cossiana," the old advisor greeted her. His voice was dripping with disdain. "I should have known you could not keep yourself out of this. Though I suppose with all of your children dead, you no longer have much else to occupy your time."

My eyes widened at his cruel words and I saw the tightening of Cossiana's jaw, though she made no other indication that she had heard him. She went on as if he had not spoken, turning her attention to the rest of us. "The advisor knows everything that is happening on Imbria. He will know what happened to Kaeleb and the Fire Keeper."

"Perhaps they are dead, lying on a field somewhere between here and Veruca with vermin picking at their bones," Damek offered, fluttering his black robes around him as if enjoying the thought so much that he could hardly contain his exuberance.

Cossiana sighed. "We both know if that were true, you would have been shouting it from the manor when we arrived. We also know that if Maialen had the Opal, the Solvrei would have felt the change in the Elements. The Fire Keeper lives."

I felt hope tighten in my chest, keeping me from being able to breathe. I realized in that moment that all I wanted was to hear the old man say Kaeleb was alive, that somehow, miraculously, he had escaped whatever snare the Earth Queen had set. He had the Warding Stone. I had slid it into his pocket when he had held me against him, and I had to hope that he had found it in time to use it. If Blaise was alive, then surely Kaeleb was with him. I had seen for myself how much Blaise loved the young man he called his son. He would not have saved himself if Kaeleb had been killed.

"Since you know so much, Cossiana, you have no need of me," Damek's oily voice sneered.

"I am growing tired of this!" Chaote announced, folding her arms over her chest. She was still wearing the drab peasant's garb she had arrived in from Samirra, refusing to don a suit of armor that was not her own, though as of yet she had not found the golden warrior's attire that had been taken from her here in Kymir. "Where is my armor?"

Damek looked at her as if she were mad. "I thought you were keen to know what happened to that brute you have allied yourself with."

Chaote shook her head, irritation sweeping over the perfection of her features. "The boy can take care of himself. If they were dead, you would have been the first to gloat. Cossiana is right, they live, and therefore we have no reason to be concerned for them. What I am concerned for, though, is my armor. Tell me where it is!"

She reached forward, yanking the advisor by the front of his robes so that he stood trembling before her, twisting away as if her very breath was poison.

"I do not know what happened to it!" he cried out, slapping ineffectually at her hands. "Let me go, you feral beast!"

She released him with a disgusted grunt, throwing herself down in the carved mahogany throne that was seated at the head of the Council table. Damek nearly gagged at the sight of her in the Earth Keeper's chair, turning to Cossiana and plastering a sycophantic look of pleading onto his pale face.

"Please, Elder, you must control your people. She cannot sit in the Earth Keeper's chair at Council! There are Edicts that strictly state-"

Chaote cut him off with a snarl. "Edicts your Queen abandoned when she took a second amulet!"

"Get out of that chair!" the old man wailed at her, his eyes growing wild.

"Make me," she taunted him, running her hands over the carved arms of the throne in a possessive caress.

"Enough, you two!" Cossiana interrupted. "You are acting like children!"

Chaote stared at the older woman in petulant silence, one finger still rebelliously tracing along the lines of the heavy chair. Cossiana frowned deeply at her, then turned back to Damek.

"This is getting us nowhere. Unlike the Earth Keeper, we have no wish to destroy a realm, not even this one. We have accepted your surrender peacefully, now tell us what we wish to know. Or do you forget there is a legion of Fomori waiting outside your precious city? If they are let loose, then someone sitting in the Keeper's chair will be the least of your worries."

I had been silent since we had entered the chamber, observing all of them quietly from the back of the hallowed room. Damek spun on me once again, stabbing a bony finger in my direction. "This is your doing! You and your whore mother did this! You ruined Imbria with your disgusting, foul presence! You are an abomination. They should have murdered you while you were still in your mother's womb!"

Bacatha stepped behind him, hitting him sharply on the back of his head with her gauntleted fist. His eyes rolled back and he crumpled to the ground, blissfully silent.

"Is he dead?" Chaote asked, leaning forward curiously.

"No," Bacatha answered, bending to make sure his heart was still beating. She lifted her cold blue eyes to mine. "You should not have to listen to such things, Solvrei."

His words would not stop clamoring inside my head.

Abomination abomination that is what I am I should not exist I am a monster look at what I do to people I tear them apart with my power I steal their life from them he is right I should not exist I am no savior where is Kaeleb if he lives why is he not here where is he I need him I should not be here I am an abomination a monster he should stay away from me perhaps that is why he does not return he knows what I am he is disgusted by me they all are.

I turned and fled, running up the stone steps and shoving the door open with a resounding boom that echoed through the chamber below. It was late in the day, and the light was fading from the sky overhead. I pressed my hands against my ears, still hearing Damek's hateful voice, unable to stop hearing it. I shoved past the group of Leharans that were guarding the chamber and they stepped aside, letting me go through them. I was not sure what I wanted in that moment, but I knew that whatever it was, it was not here in Kymir. I stopped as I reached the intersecting paths that spread outward from the Council chamber. To the south was the ocean, the fleet of ships the Tahitians had brought, and the Sirens. To the north were the Fomori, camped along the edge of the forest, waiting for me to tell them what to do. To the west was Samirra, and whatever mysteries remained there that Chaote would not speak of, and east was Veruca. Logaire. Maialen. Everything that had destroyed my life.

I stood there, helpless, with nowhere to go and nowhere to turn, tears running down my face. I was trapped, constrained by a world that I had no hand in forming, by a life that I had no choice in living, by a power that I could not rid myself of and an overwhelming desire to use that power again. I wanted to scream, to fall to the ground and beat the hateful dirt with my fists. I yanked off the gloves I wore, balling them up and throwing them into the carefully pruned topiaries that lined the path.

You have done well.

My eyes flew open, startled by the deep baritone voice that echoed in my mind. Whoever was speaking, it was not one of the dead Keepers. Chaote now held the Va'Kul's Warding Stone, and I could still feel its foggy emptiness surrounding me. There was something vaguely familiar about the rumbling tone, something that tugged at the back of my mind, though I could not quite place it. Then I remembered where I had heard it before and I whipped my head around, searching. There was a clamor of activity in the direction of the Council Chamber and I took a step towards the noise, but a cold, wet nose pressed itself into my hand, stopping me. I stared down at the mongrel dog and it lifted its eye to me, its mangled tongue lolling out over the side of its misshapen mouth.

"You," I whispered. I jerked my hand back from its muzzle, and the dog sat on his haunches, his head turning to alert me to the presence of the two men behind him. I remembered the brothers, Seff and Vayk, and they had not aged a day since I had last seen them, more than ten years ago. Their reddish-brown skin was still smooth and unlined, their hair long and brown without even a strand of grey. The one with the scar, I forgot which one he was, leaned over to sniff at me curiously, as if I were an oddity on display. Then he wrinkled his nose in displeasure.

"Stop staring at me!" I snapped at him, pushing the loose strands of pale hair back into the braid that was supposed to be holding them. I glanced down at my clothing, soiled and torn from everything that had transpired. Stiff, dark stains blotched the blue fabric, remnants of the Va'Kul that had washed down on me after Chaote had removed her hands. I cringed at the memory, shaking my head to clear it from my mind.

"You should bathe," the one with the scar said. "You have taken the Royal City. Surely you can at least bathe yourself. The Earth Keeper has a bath chamber fed by hot springs from beneath the ground."

"I am not concerned with bathing!" I practically shouted at him, my face flushing scarlet.

"You are just standing here. You might as well be bathing," the other brother chimed in. The dog was silent, staring up at me while he panted happily.

"How did you get here?" I demanded, ignoring their pleas concerning my personal hygiene. "And where have you been?"

The one with the scar shrugged. "The Fire Keeper has brought us. We have been waiting for you to be ready."

My heart leapt into my throat. "The Fire Keeper is here? Is Kaeleb with him?"

The brothers looked at each other, perplexed by my insistent questioning. "The boy is with him, yes."

I shoved between them, running towards the Council Chamber where I had heard the commotion coming from moments before. It must have been Kaeleb and Blaise arriving. I squeezed through the Leharans that were clustered around the chamber door, breaking through the circle of islanders and shouting his name, not caring who heard me or what they thought of it. All I cared about was seeing him again.

Kaeleb was standing at the open doorway, about to step down into the long corridor. He stopped at my shout, turning his head, his shock of pale hair falling over one side of his face as he grinned. It was the most wonderful sight I had ever seen and I could not decide in that moment if I wanted to hit him or hold him or scream at him. In the end, I threw myself at him, nearly knocking him off balance as he caught me.

"I told you I would come back," he murmured into my hair, holding me against him. I started to cry again, great heaving sobs that shook my whole body, my fists clutching at the fabric of his shirt beneath his leather armor.

"I am the leader of the Fomori now. I killed the Va'Kul," I blurted out.

"Yes, I just heard something about that," he said softly. "I am sure that whatever you did, you had no other choice."

"Is your father here? Is he safe?"

Kaeleb nodded. "He is wounded, but the Tahitians are here, and they are the best healers on Imbria."

"You brought the dog? How did you find him?" I knew I was rambling on, babbling questions at him just so I could keep hearing his voice, keep feeling the warmth of his arms around me. I could have stayed there forever, safe in his embrace, filled with gratitude that he had somehow managed to live through whatever happened to them in Veruca.

"She has not rested," Bacatha interrupted us, stomping out of the underground chamber in a clatter of silver armor. She looked just as bad as I did, and Kaeleb grimaced at her appearance, his eyes straying to the jagged claw marks that marred her cheek.

"You both look like you could use some rest," he said. "Bacatha, take her to bathe. I will find you after."

Bacatha glanced back down into the chamber. "If you want to get anything accomplished here, I suggest you send Chaote with us. She just found out from Blaise that Maialen stole her armor and wore it into battle, and she is trying to kill the old man for lying to her about it."

I released Kaeleb reluctantly, knowing he was right and at the very least I needed a bath, since everyone seemed to be constantly mentioning it. I followed the Leharan woman to the bathhouse at the foot of the Earth Keeper's grand manor. As we passed through the winding garden path, I noticed the twisted and distorted weeds that were spreading over the ground, the brittle flowers whose blackened petals crumbled in the breeze. The earth itself was a dull shade of grey, as if the soil had been leached of everything in it that brought forth life. It was like a strange parody of death, a play of decaying plants that symbolized the Keeper's foul reign. I shuddered, happy when we left the deformed gardens behind and reached the bathhouse. It was a square stone building with several deep pools inside. Short, fat candles ringed the pools, their light flickering over the bubbling water. A terrified Kymirran woman stood inside, trembling with fear at the sight of us as we entered.

"We wish to bathe," Bacatha told her imperiously. The woman stared at the towering Leharan warrior as if we had just asked her to give us her first-born child. Bacatha groaned irritably and motioned at the water. "We wish to bathe! We will need scrubbing sand and fresh clothes."

The woman nodded furiously, hurrying into a smaller room and reappearing with a bag of scrubbing sands. Then she darted out into the night, disappearing into the darkness. I heard a startled yelp from the direction she had gone, and Chaote's throaty voice growling for the woman to get out of her way.

"Do not scare her!" Bacatha called out. "We need her to bring us clothes!"

"The Earth Queen has my armor!" Chaote snarled, stomping into the stone room and tossing her clothes to the ground in one quick motion. She flung the pale moonstone around on her neck so that it hung down her back, then she peeled the bandage from her chest, dropping it on top of her pile of clothes. She stepped into the nearest pool, sinking down into the warm depths of the spring and folding her arms angrily over her scarred chest. "Why would she need my armor? She is a Keeper. She can get her own armor!"

"Perhaps she finds yours incomparable," Bacatha teased, sliding into the pool beside the other woman after peeling off her own silver armor. I hesitated, unsure what to do with the Sapphire that I kept tucked in my pocket. I looped it around my neck, mimicking Chaote, then hurried to join them, feeling the blissful heat sting for a moment as it touched my cuts and bruises.

"It is incomparable! There is no other like it. She cannot just take it and wear it! She is doing it to taunt me," Chaote spat out. "I will cut it off her in pieces if I have to!"

"The dog is here," I interrupted, blurting out the thoughts that were racing through my mind. "Blaise and Kaeleb, they brought the dog. That is why they took so long to return."

Chaote continued to glower at nothing. "Yes, I heard the Fenris was here. Though I do not consider that to be any better news than the theft of my armor. Do not trust him, Eolande. He is a liar and he will do anything to get what he wants. Question anything he tells you to do."

"He told me to take a bath," I confessed with a small smile.

Bacatha snorted with laughter. "Nothing like a living god showing up and telling you that you stink too much to save the world."

"Stop amusing me! I am trying to wallow in my rage against the Earth Keeper," Chaote said, unable to stop the smile that was tugging at the edges of her lips.

It was a strange moment to share laughter with the two women, though I was happy to have a reprieve from the constant misery I had felt since we had found the Fomori. Kaeleb had returned, my friends were with me, and we had taken Kymir without so much as a scratch. We would be sleeping in the Queen's manor that night, and I could not wait to feel the softness of a real bed beneath me. There was much to be grateful for, but there was also much to be afraid of. We were carving out a small piece of happiness, a moment of laughter and ease, but all around us the shadows of war loomed, like beasts stalking us in the night.

I scrubbed myself with a handful of sand, watching from the corner of my eye as Chaote tended to the angry wound on Bacatha's face. Her fingers were quick and nimble, cleaning the deep scratches and rinsing them gently, her brow furrowed in concentration. It reminded me of the time I had showed her the Warding Stone on my back, and I wondered for a moment what sort of life she would have led if fate had not intervened. Perhaps she would have been a mother, and I smiled to think of her tending to a flock of beautiful children beneath the Tahitian sun. Bacatha, on the other hand, was born to be a warrior. She sat unmoving, not flinching as the wound was cleaned, though it must have been painful. I could never imagine her choosing another path for herself, and no matter how many scars she collected, I knew she would never regret a single one of them. She was noble, honorable, a protector above all else.

"What are you staring at?" Bacatha asked me, interrupting my musings. "Thinking of Kaeleb?"

Chaote smiled, shaking water from her hair. "You could do worse, Solvrei."

"I... I am afraid of him," I admitted, avoiding their eyes and staring down at the dark water that swirled around me. "Not of him, I mean, but of the way I feel. Of feeling things at all, really."

"I told you before," Chaote said. "Your fear will not stop you from feeling. It will only stop you from living."

"Ahhh, wise words from the sage Mother of the Fomori," Bacatha said. "She is not wrong, Eolande. There is a battle coming, one that will be far deadlier than any that has ever been fought on Imbria. Perhaps it is time to tell the boy how you feel. At least you will be clean when you do it."

The Kymirran woman had returned then, setting down a basket full of clothing. She was older, about the age my mother would have been had she lived, with greying-brown hair and a hesitant disposition. The woman's eyes met mine and she took a step towards me, holding out her hand, fingers outstretched. Bacatha grabbed her scythe from the edge of the pool, ready to slice the woman in half if she made a wrong move, but the Kymirran did not seem hostile.

She whispered reverently to me, "Are you really the Solvrei?"

I nodded my head and her face flushed. She stroked my wet hair, her fingers trembling. Then she snatched her hand back and hurried from the room, leaving us staring after her. Bacatha set her weapon back down, but the spell of the evening had been broken and we climbed out of the baths. Chaote glared at the offered clothing, for it was three long gowns, each simple in design with a long muslin skirt and a corseted top.

"I am not wearing this," she muttered. Chaote threw the gown back into the basket and strolled out of the bathhouse, naked as the day she was born except for the gleaming Warding Stone that hung down her back.

I had already donned one of the drab gowns and I stared after her in shock, my mouth hanging open. I could hear startled cries from the manor, and I was quite sure that Chaote would soon have whatever clothing she demanded. Bacatha laughed, shaking her head, plucking at the long dress with distaste. She pulled it on, grimacing at herself and gathering her armor. I helped her, for it was quite heavy and cumbersome, and we followed after Chaote and the trail of startled Kymirrans she had left in her wake.

I was shown to a room by two of the Leharans who now guarded the manor, and I went inside, locking the door behind me and praying that it was not Maialen's personal room. The last thing I wanted was to be haunted by my aunt and the mementos of her life. It was easier for me not to see her as a person, not to pity her or learn the reasons why she had changed so much from the woman I had briefly glimpsed as a child. If I was going to destroy her, then I needed to keep hating her, and I was afraid if I knew too much about her, then I would not be able to. Already, the threads of empathy were creeping into my mind. I knew what it was like to lose everything that mattered to you, and to feel the terrible pull of power, to yearn constantly for it, afraid you could not control it, but still longing for it with every fiber of your being. I pitied Maialen, for the innocent girl she must have been once, before that innocence was ripped away by a cruel world.

The room was thankfully bare of personal items, and it was clearly a bedchamber reserved for guests of the Queen. I wondered who she would have kept it ready for, who would have visited her that was close enough to her to be invited to stay in the manor. Did she have any friends? I shook my head, refusing to think of her and pushing the thoughts away so I could focus on my surroundings. There was a large canopied bed with an elaborately carved headboard and it was piled with plush blankets and pillows. I took one look at the bed and forgot about my aunt and everything else except my exhaustion. I crawled up into it, curling around one of the pillows and falling asleep instantly.

I was not sure how long it had been since I closed my eyes, but suddenly I was torn from sleep by the savage nightmares that haunted me. I lay awake, panting, my eyes wide open and staring at the strange room, trying to calm the panic in my heart. I knew Bacatha was in the room beside mine. All I had to do was shout and she would be there.

I tried to close my eyes again, but muffled voices forced them back open. I thought I heard a low chuckle of laughter and I slid out of the bed, moving to the door that led onto the terrace. The manor had balconies that wrapped around the entirety of it, each level connected by roped bridges that spanned between the massive tree branches that cradled the estate. I opened the door as quietly as I could, peering out into the dark night.

I was not expecting what I found out there, and I narrowed my eyes, confusion marring my sleepy thoughts. Kaeleb and Bacatha were sitting upright on a pile of bed coverings they had dragged out onto the terrace, trying to stop laughing at

Chaote who was sitting smugly across from them, lounging on a mountain of plush pillows and wearing an elaborate gown of green and gold lace that cascaded around her like a sea of gilded moss. The night was warm, with a slight breeze in the air that ruffled the edges of Kaeleb's pale hair. He and Bacatha were both wearing clean leather pants and long tunics, their feet bare, and I could see a bottle of Kymirran wine beside them.

Kaeleb looked up at me, grinning, motioning for me to join them. "I hope we did not wake you."

"What are you doing out here?" I asked, coming and sitting next to him.

"Enjoying Kymir's finest wine and fashion," Bacatha snickered, waving her hand at Chaote.

I looked at the Tahitian woman and she was breathtaking in the gown, more beautiful than anyone I had ever seen. In that moment, there was no doubt in my mind that she was descended from the gods, for no mortal creature could have been made so perfect. The silver light from the moon illuminated the deep ebony of her skin, like something magical crafted from the night itself. She plucked at the delicate lace she was swathed in, swirling it around her and chuckling.

"It is the Earth Queen's wedding dress," Chaote informed me, and once more Bacatha and Kaeleb fell into fits of laughter. "If she can take my armor, then I can take her dress."

"Do not worry, Eolande," Bacatha added, "We will find you suitable attire in the morning. We cannot have the Solvrei running around looking like a milkmaid."

"We could not sleep," Kaeleb said ruefully, as if that explained everything. I noticed his eye patch was gone, and I was sure that it had been removed to show solidarity for Bacatha's wounded face. He passed me the bottle they had been drinking from. "And then I found this. Apparently Maialen has accidentally destroyed most of the Kymirran vineyards with her corrupt power, so this is one of the last bottles we may have of it for a while."

"There were pastries, but Kaeleb ate them all," Chaote added.

I had never tasted wine. I sniffed at it curiously and it smelled awful. I passed it back to him, shaking my head to decline. He set it aside, then he leaned back, pulling me with him so that I was nestled against his side. I was caught off guard by the gesture and tensed, unsure how to feel about his proximity. He was warm, the muscles of his body hard and firm, and I saw Bacatha give Chaote a knowing wink. The Tahitian rolled her eyes, snatching up the bottle and taking a long swig.

"Kaeleb was just showing us some of his more ridiculous compositions in the stars," Chaote said, waving the bottle at the night sky that stretched out above the canopy of trees.

"Apparently, there is a cow over there wearing a crown," Bacatha chimed in.

"Eolande will see it!" he exclaimed. "Even if you two are lacking the imagination!"

"Tell us if you can find it, Solvrei," Chaote ordered, her words slightly rounded and soft from the wine. "In the meantime, I may close my eyes for a bit."

Kaeleb lifted his hand, pointed at the cluster of shimmering fragments that glittered in the dark. I tried to see what he was pointing at, but all I could think about was his closeness, the smell of his skin and the warmth of his breath. He turned his head, his lips brushing my forehead, and I thought it was possible in that moment to die of happiness. The rest of the world faded away and there was only us, beneath the stars, surrounded by the warm night and our friends. I found myself wishing in that moment that it would never end, that we could stay there forever. But I had already learned that nothing lasts forever.

31

We woke as the sun rose, the golden rays slanting through the trees and drawing us gently out of sleep. Birds chirped happily around us, flitting between the branches of the trees in quick bursts of color. It had been a long time since I had slept so soundly, undisturbed by the turbulent nightmares that usually haunted me. I was still curled against Kaeleb, my head resting in the hollow of his neck. He shifted his body beneath me so that he could look at me, his fingertips reaching over to trace along the edge of my jaw where the remnants of a bruise still marred my skin. His hand curved around to the back of my head, lifting me closer, and his lips touched mine. It was a brief, gentle kiss and I pulled back from it, overwhelmed by everything that was happening within me. Chaote was still sleeping nearby, which meant her Warding Stone would not be working.

"I am afraid I will hurt you. My power... what if I cannot control it? What if I accidentally hurt you?" I whispered.

"I would give a thousand days of my life for this moment with you, Eolande. I am not afraid of you."

He leaned in, kissing me once more, and I let myself savor the moment, the way he tasted, the smell of his skin, the way his hair brushed against my face. It was the closest I had ever come to feeling the same rush of energy that I felt when I was using my power, and it was nearly as unbearable.

Chaote stirred from her pile of pillows and I jerked away from Kaeleb, sitting upright and blushing furiously. The Tahitian woman lifted her eyebrow in amusement, grinning so that she showed the sharpened points of her filed teeth. "Am I interrupting?"

"Yes," Kaeleb said, returning her grin. She rolled her eyes, throwing a pillow at him. He batted it aside with his arm so that it hit Bacatha's sleeping form, and the Leharan jerked awake with a startled cry, leaping up, her hands fisted and ready to fight.

"Relax, Leharan," Chaote said. "No one is trying to fight you."

Bacatha stretched out her arms and looked around, yawning. "We need to get moving. The Earth Queen must know by now that we are here, and she will be marching this way. We need to plan for the battle. Kaeleb, where is your father?"

"With the Tahitians on the ships. Come, I will take you to him," he offered, standing up and reaching out a hand to help me to my feet.

"Could we please get her some decent clothing?" Bacatha asked, gesturing at my wrinkled gown. "I cannot bear it any longer."

"Come with me, child. We will see what else the Keeper has for us. We will meet the rest of you at the ships," Chaote said, also rising, the cascade of her lace gown tumbling around her long legs. I followed her into the manor, and she strode down the hallway, throwing open a door at the end and leading me into my aunt's private chambers.

"I was afraid to come here," I admitted. "I do not want to know her."

A shadow passed over Chaote's features. "Those of us with the most power must often do terrible things with it. If it is possible, I will kill Maialen for you, so that you do not have to do it yourself."

It felt strange to say thank you for an offer to murder a member of your family, so I remained silent, looking around the room. It was eerily juvenile, a room that one would expect a little girl to have, not a tyrant or a Keeper. The bed was draped in ruffled coverings, with a canopy wrapped in flowers and vines. There was a stuffed doll tucked into it, old and well-worn, clearly a beloved memento, its face smiling with a curved line of pink thread. A chair was placed near the paned windows that overlooked the terrace, a blanket balled up on the seat of it, as if someone had just stood up and left. Opposite the window was a massive wardrobe, and Chaote was tossing its contents out onto the floor with a cold detachment.

"Stop!" I practically shouted at her. "I... I cannot wear her things! I just can't."

My thoughts were racing in my head, so confused, and I could not sort through them.

She is like a child but she killed Gula you saw it do not feel pity for her she is evil she was not born that way the world made her that way it does not matter why she will kill you she will kill everyone you care about she has tried to kill you already she is destroying the world you have to stop her do not feel pity for her even though she is so pitiful is she scared is that why she holds a doll at night does it comfort her is she afraid the way I am afraid.

Chaote shook me gently, snapping me out of the dark spiral of thoughts. I was still shaking my head stubbornly as I repeated to her, "I can't. Find me someone else's clothes. Anyone else."

In the end, I ended up with a pair of dark blue breeches and a white tunic that Bacatha procured from one of the smaller Leharan lads. She also managed to gather a few pieces of armor for me, claiming that I would not be able to move in a full suit, and I put them on, unsettled by the heavy weight of them. She was right. There was no way I could support a full suit of armor like she and Chaote wore. The Sapphire hung around my neck, tucked beneath the breastplate, and my hair was pulled back in a short braid. I could hear the faint whispers from the amulet, which meant that Chaote had removed the Warding Stone from around her neck, most likely at the behest of the Fire Keeper, who refused to allow them in his presence.

"Maialen most likely knows that we have taken the Royal City. Damek would have made sure of that before surrendering," Blaise was saying. He was leaning over the navigation table in the ship's galley, one hand braced on the side of a large map of Imbria. He was dressed in all black, and his red hair curled around his shoulders, just above the large bandage that was wrapped around his right arm, holding the limb tightly against his chest.

He lifted his head as we entered, giving me a brief smile of greeting. Kaeleb was already beside him, staring down at the map intently, and Cossiana was on the other side of the table next to Brogan, Bacatha's father. The dog was in the corner of the galley, the two brothers standing silent behind it.

"What do you think she will do?" the Tahitian Elder asked.

The Fire Keeper sighed heavily. "I am not sure. We have heard rumors that she has destroyed the entire Verucan army. It could be possible she will hole up in Veruca and wait for us there, but it would be foolish. We could lay siege to the kingdom and simply starve her out. As long as Samirra does not come to her aid from the west."

He lifted his amber eyes and looked at Chaote. "I have been told that you came from Samirra, and Favian still lives."

Chaote stiffened beside me in my aunt's leather archery uniform. "He lives. But he will not be joining his wife in any of her conquests."

"Care to elaborate?" Blaise prompted.

Chaote darted a quick glance at the Fenris. "No."

Blaise also glanced at the dog, the lines between his brow deepening slightly, and he seemed to understand that whatever Chaote wanted to tell him about Samirra, she did not want to say it in front of the dog.

The Fenris! He is here!

The eager voice of the Harbonah practically shouted with joy in my head and I winced at the jarring exuberance of the thought, noticing the dog turn his one eye to look at me.

Be silent, or I will throw your amulet back into the sea with the Sirens.

But we have waited so long for his return.

You are dead. You no longer wait for anything.

The Harbonah fell into petulant silence and I focused my attention back on the conversation at the table. Blaise was motioning at the open space that stretched between Kymir and Veruca.

"Where she is now is the best place for an attack," he said, his amber eyes shining with intent. "She is between the mountains and the forest and it is likely that she is gathering food and supplies from Veruca, which will give us time to get there. We cannot let her return to the forest. Maialen and the Kymirrans are at a disadvantage on open ground, but her soldiers are trained to fight amongst the trees. They could pick us off one by one."

"Which means we must move immediately," Kaeleb said quietly. "And we abandon the Royal City."

"Any Kymirran soldiers that are still here should be put to death, so they cannot attack us from the rear when we move out," Blaise said matter-of-factly.

My mouth fell open in shock. "You cannot do that!"

The entire room turned to look at me, and I squirmed beneath their collective gazes.

"I know it seems callous," Blaise began, "But this is how wars are won."

I lifted my chin, taking a deep breath. "My mother would never have condoned the murder of innocent people just to get what she wanted."

Blaise gave me a long look, an easy grin stretching beneath his beard that was at odds with the fire in his eyes. I wondered if I had gone too far by using my mother's memory to convince him I was right. When he finally spoke, his words were slow and deliberate. "I will not risk the lives of people I care about to save a bunch of wretched Kymirrans. I will not risk Kaeleb's life. If you have another way, then by all means, share it with us."

"I... I do not know much of warfare," I stammered quietly, hating that everyone in the room was still staring at me. "But I command the Fomori. We can put them at the rear of the army. The Kymirrans are terrified of them. They will not follow us if they know they will be facing the blooddrinkers. Especially not if we have taken all of their eagles and horses and they would be on foot."

I didn't say what else I was thinking, that I was remembering the Kymirran woman in the bathhouse who had touched me with such reverence. It was possible that the Kymirrans, at least some of them, had no desire to take part in Maialen's war or to harm me.

"That is a gamble. You cannot be certain," Blaise pointed out.

"I am certain that murdering people will make us no better than the Earth Keeper!" I threw back at him. He raised an eyebrow and his smile widened.

"I quite like her," he murmured to Kaeleb, who beamed at his father's praise. "Very well. We will have you lead the Fomori in the rear. Chaote can help you."

Chaote smashed her fist into the galley wall, splintering the wood. "I do not want to hide behind your motley little army! I want the Earth Queen's head and I want my armor back!"

Blaise tapped his fingers against the map. "You have one of the Warding Stones. I will take the other, and I will lead the assault while you stay to the rear. The Fenris tells me you and Eolande can move power between the other amulets. If you are together, then you can remove the Warding Stone and do this as soon as the battle begins. Hopefully, it will catch Maialen off-guard and you can take her power away from her before she realizes what is happening. Once her power has been pushed into the other amulets, she will be weakened and we can stop her. Eolande can then draw her own power from the Fenris, or she can use the Sapphire."

Chaote threw a sharp look at the Fenris. The dog was panting happily at her. "If this is their idea, then I do not trust it. If the dog wants to die, then I think we should just cut off its head right now and be done with it. "

Kaeleb sighed. "We have been over this. If you cut its head off and it does not die, then you will have a headless dog running around Imbria for all eternity and nobody wants to see that."

"We can at least try. Eolande can take the head to battle and use it-"

"No one is cutting off heads!" Blaise shouted, slamming his uninjured hand down on the table.

Chaote folded her arms over her chest, glaring at him.

"Are we in agreement?" he asked, turning to Cossiana and Brogan.

The island leaders nodded their heads, and Blaise dismissed the meeting after giving orders to prepare the armies to depart. I saw his sidelong glance at the Fenris as they left, and the quick shake of his head he directed at Chaote. She lagged behind the others, waiting until it was just Kaeleb and me standing in the room with them.

"The Fenris cannot be trusted!" she claimed once again. "They are the reason for everything that has happened, and they are responsible for all the deaths that have resulted from their meddling."

"What do you mean?" I asked, stepping forward.

"It was the Fenris who helped the Keepers imprison me all those centuries ago. They knew my blood would be needed to destroy the amulets, and so they made sure the Keepers turned against me. My family was slaughtered. My life was stolen. Then they left me trapped in that ice until they were ready to use me." She was practically trembling with anger and I had never seen her so upset. When she spoke again, her words were directed at me. "The stories the Samains tell on Tahitia are just lies fed to them by the Fenris. Your father was not a god, any more than I am. The Fenris bred him over the centuries, manipulated generations upon generations of your ancestors, looking for the perfect combination that would create a being such as you. They did this to your grandmother, Ursula, pushed her into the arms of your grandfather. It was the same for Orabelle. With her, they came close to having the powerful child they craved, but she was still not you, and so they had to keep going. The Fenris is the reason your father, Tal, went to Lehar and met your mother. They orchestrated the banishment of the Tahitians, knowing that the Leharan boy would one day be forced to leave the island, and they made sure that he went straight to Orabelle. You were never an accident, Eolande. You were not a divine child born of love. The Fenris made you."

I was staring at her, my mouth open, my stomach twisting into knots at her words. I felt a pain that I had not known I could feel, a deep, endless pain that stretched back genera-tions, for hundreds of years and hundreds of lives. If what she said was true, then nothing had been our choice. Every twist and turn we encountered was not a matter of will or circumstance; it was all connected to the Fenris, a manifestation of their desires. My life had been filled with misery because of them.

Blaise sat down at the table, staring into the distance. I knew he was thinking of my mother, wondering if there would have been a life where she could have loved him if the Fenris had not intervened. Kaeleb reached out, grasping his shoulder and squeezing it. The Fire Keeper seemed to shake off whatever melancholy gripped him, and he looked up at the young man who stood by his side.

"I will never regret anything that brought you to me," he said to his son. Kaeleb smiled at him and I felt a knot in my throat watching them. At least something good had come out of what the banished god had done.

"That is all very touching," Chaote interrupted. "But I hope that you now understand why we need a better plan than just trusting the Fenris."

"And I suppose you have one?" Blaise asked her, arching his brow.

"Yes, cut off its head and see if it dies."

"Let's see if we can do better than that," the Fire Keeper suggested. We spent the next hour debating ideas, though nothing we thought of seemed to be enough to save us all. In the end, we would just have to wait and see what happened on the battlefield, to learn who would betray us and who would stand with us. It left me with a bitter taste in my mouth, and as soon as I could, I snuck away from the others, trying to find a quiet moment to think, to breathe. I went into Maialen's tortured garden, shuddering at the monstrous carnival of horrors she had created.

I heard the dog coming before he reached me, the soft padding of his paws along the ground. Seff and Vayk were with him, and I could not keep my gaze from drifting to the wicked array of knives the brothers had belted around their waists.

"We know you do not trust us, Eolande, but we want the same things," Vayk said. His voice was as dull and bland as the rest of his countenance.

"My father was not a god." I said it bluntly, a statement, not a question.

"Are you disappointed?" Seff asked. The dog let out a low whine.

"No," I answered, looking at the gnarled animal. "I am relieved."

"Will you still destroy the amulets?"

I was still looking at the dog, not sure which of them had spoken, though it did not really matter. They were all the same being. "How can I hear the dead Keepers?"

The dog whined again, sitting down on its haunches, his tongue lolling out of the mutilated snout. Seff answered for him, "You do not hear the Keepers. Those who have gone before are no longer here. You hear the echoes of them, fragments of their soul they traded when they used their power. When the amulets are destroyed, those fragments will be destroyed with them."

"No one ever told me their power costs them part of their soul."

"That is because no one knows. No one has ever heard the past Keepers until you, so they have never thought to ask. They were always too hungry to have the power to consider that there might be a cost. Our kind prefers balance in all things. Harmony. You cannot gain something without giving something up, but it is merely a fragment of their being, inconsequential."

Inconsequential to you, I wanted to say. I had a feeling the Keepers would have felt differently had they known. I looked up at the brothers. "Why tell me now?"

"So you will not hesitate to free your world," Vayk said.

"And to free you from this world," I pointed out.

He shrugged, as if it were another unintended consequence of no significance, like losing part of your soul. "It is true we wish to leave this mortal realm."

"Because you are disappointed?" I asked, mimicking his earlier question to me.

"Your kind has been a great disappointment to us, yes."

I wanted to hit him in the face, but I just stood there looking at them, thinking of all that Chaote had told me, all the Fenris had done just to save himself. Finally, I told them, "I want you gone just as much as you want to be gone. You do not deserve to live in this world any longer. I will do what you ask."

I turned and walked away from them.

32

Maialen was pacing the ground beneath the large tent that served as her chambers on the fields between Kymir and Veruca. She had been waiting all day to hear something from Samirra, but so far no messages had come, by eagle or by hawk, and she was growing more agitated as the day wore on. The last word she had received from Favian was a cryptic message that she had been unable to decipher the meaning of.

Samirra will only stand for Samirra.

She was tempted to take the single eagle she had with her and go to the wretched western realm herself and wring Favian's neck, but a rider had come from Kymir, telling her that Damek would surrender the Royal City to keep the Fomori from ransacking the kingdom. Maialen had been furious at the news, screaming in rage and frustration, ripping the message into tiny pieces and grinding it beneath the heel of her boot. She gripped the Emerald that hung from her neck, trying vainly to calm herself while the rider fled from her presence. She could feel the wild, tempestuous pull of the Pearl, longing to be used, heightening her emotions. More than anything, she wanted to throw the wretched amulet into the great divide and rid the world of it forever, along with the memories of her sister that it conjured.

Maialen hated thinking about Orabelle, and ever since her sister's child had returned, she had been forced to think of little else. The girl even looked like her, despite Maialen's denial of her birthright. When she had seen Eolande on Lehar, she had known in her heart that it was her niece. The sight of her had dredged up memories from their younger years, memories filled with laughter and innocence, memories the Keeper had tried to forget. Orabelle, small and stubborn and untamed. Orabelle, who had always been stronger, always been more clever, always more beloved. Maialen had adored her sister and looked up to her, but she had never been anything like her, no matter how hard she tried to be. Being loved was the one thing Maialen had always craved more than anything, but her mother had never loved her as much as Orabelle, and neither had Blaise. Her father was the only one who had ever chosen her over her sister, but even his affections came with the condition that she behave as a dutiful and obedient daughter. Chronus had not truly loved her, for he had never truly seen her for who she was. She was nothing more than a pretty doll to him, a blank face that resembled his own enough for his legacy to carry on.

In her youth, Maialen had mistakenly believed that her sister genuinely cared for her. It was only after their father's death that she realized the depths of Orabelle's selfishness. It was her sister's fault that Chronus had been murdered by the Fomori, and as if that were not enough, Orabelle had taken Gideon from her too. She used Maialen's Guardian to hide her bastard child, not caring that it ripped away the one person Maialen could still trust in this world. It was Orabelle's fault Gideon was dead. It was her child he had been trying to protect the night Maialen had accidentally killed him.

The Earth Keeper squeezed her eyes shut as tears stung them. Even her son had been stolen from her. It was because of Orabelle that she was all alone. She wanted to shred the memories of their past the way she had shredded the message from Damek, and the only way to do that was to rid the world of the abomination that was her sister's child.

"There is another messenger for the Queen," one of her guards called from outside the tent.

"Finally," she muttered, relieved to have something to divert her attention from the lingering memories of the past. She hastily wiped away the tears streaming down her cheeks. Hopefully, this new message was from Favian, saying that he would soon be arriving with more eagles and reinforcements. She wanted to crush the rebellious islanders, to put an end to them once and for all. She could not believe they had the audacity to attack Kymir. She would make sure they understood the magnitude of their mistake. "Send them in!"

The tent flap was pulled aside and a man shuffled in. She recognized Logaire's stout advisor as he bowed low, despite his cumbersome size.

"Vishram," she said, her voice holding no warmth or greeting. Inside, she was fuming that it was not someone from Samirra and Favian's irksome silence continued.

"Queen Maialen." Vishram straightened up from his bow, looking around at her meager furnishings. The tent had a bed, a chest, and a wooden stand to hold her golden armor, but there was little else in the way of comforts.

"I was not expecting to be here long," she told him.

"Yes, yes, of course. That is what I wish to speak to you about, my Queen. Logaire has instructed me to tell you about the food supplies in Veruca."

"And?" Maialen prodded, annoyed by his presence.

"There are none."

Her big green eyes widened slightly. She whipped the folds of her long gown aside, storming up to him angrily. "What do you mean, there are none?"

"Samirra has not been producing... there has been hardly any trade this spring. I am afraid that we have little in the way of sustenance to provide you and your army," the advisor informed her, rubbing his large nose in a gesture of agitation.

She wanted to murder Favian. Whatever that little weasel had been doing with all of her grain, he had not been sending it where she had ordered him to. The next time she laid eyes on the wiry Guardian, she would remove his head from his shoulders. He had gone too far this time.

"You must have something," Maialen said, trying to appear calm. "Veruca is not starving. From what I have heard, your Oracle brought in plenty of silver over the years."

Vishram looked extremely uncomfortable, rubbing his nose harder. "Logaire says there is nothing."

"Send Logaire to me. I want to hear it from her own mouth."

Vishram lifted his hands in a helpless gesture. "I am afraid that will take some time, my Queen. Logaire has gone to Halig to pay her respects and oversee the burial of the Oracle."

"You cannot be serious!" Maialen exploded. "Who let her leave?"

Vishram shrugged. "No one. She just left."

"She just left," Maialen repeated. "Well, find her and bring her back here!"

"You have disposed of the Verucan soldiers. Who would you have me send after her? Is there a Kymirran division that can be sent?"

"Of course not, you idiot. I am fighting a war here! I need my men!" Maialen shouted. "Get out! I do not care who you send after her! Mercenaries, the castle cook, I do not care, but send someone and get her back here, now!"

Vishram bowed low, backing out of the tent hurriedly before the Keeper turned her wrath on him. He wiped at his forehead as the tent flaps closed behind him, breathing hard and grateful to be out in the sun once again and still living. It had been his idea for Logaire to flee to Halig, though it had not taken much convincing. As soon as he suggested the idea, she had leapt on it, and with her out of the way, Vishram was free to do as much as he possibly could to stop the progress of the Earth Keeper. He needed to slow down her return to Kymir, to give the Solvrei time to prepare. The battle was finally upon them, after all these long years of waiting.

His thoughts flashed briefly to the girl they had kept hidden for so many years. Had he done enough for her? Had he taught her enough to survive what was coming? Had he prepared her for the harshness of the world, prepared her so that she could stand against the Earth Keeper? Regret crept over him at the vision in his mind of the sweet little girl, her hair shorn off and her blue eyes red-rimmed from crying as she tried to be brave. She had not deserved any of it, but her life had never been her own. She was the Solvrei, born to change the world. She was never meant to lead an ordinary life.

He thought of her escaping from Veruca, walking across half of Imbria, weak and hungry and alone, somehow surviving. Now she led an army of warriors. Her resilience was incredible and no matter how hard it had been, the lessons she had learned in Veruca had saved her life.

Vishram looked back at the sea of tents and the swarms of soldiers that wove between them. Soon this field would be bathed in blood, and the fate of their world would be decided. He could do no more. He took a deep breath and turned away, plodding along the long path back to the Verucan castle.

33

I did not know what to expect in a battle. I had never been in one, never seen one. It seemed silly to me to line up on opposing sides of a field and wait to slaughter each other, but apparently that was the way of it. I could see dawn wrestling its way over the mountains in the distance, long fingers of ashen light stretching between the tall peaks.

"Are you ready for what comes?" the brother with the pale scar asked from beside me. His name was Seff.

"We are ready," Kaeleb answered, taking my hand in his. He looked at me, his steely grey eye shining in the clinging darkness of night. His hair fell over his forehead, shadowing the missing eye, and his jaw was clenched, his whole body tense. My breath caught in my throat and I felt fear crashing over me like a wave. I was not afraid for myself. What frightened me the most was losing the ones I cared about. Losing Kaeleb.

"Good," was Seff's blunt reply and he strode forward through the ranks of soldiers, the dog trotting behind him.

The Fomori were massed behind me, most of them still hidden amongst the trees. I could feel their eagerness like a hot breath on my neck, their blood-thirst for the coming battle. Before we had left Kymir, I had let them slaughter a herd of cattle to satiate their hunger, but it was not sustenance they were after, it was fear and death. I felt a queasiness in my stomach at the thought of what was to come, and I prayed for the thousandth time that somehow Maialen would surrender and we would not have to fight.

Kaeleb was straining to see what was happening near the front of the army, where his father was. Blaise had ordered him to stay and guard me, and we all knew it was the Keeper's way of protecting his son as much as he could.

The Leharans were shining like silver jewels, their armor reflecting the breaking dawn in a dazzling array of shimmering light. Bacatha was at their lead, tall and proud astride her horse, her father beside her. Blaise was near them, his black armor blending into the shadows that still clung to the morning and his blood-red hair glinting like a beacon amongst the sea of pale-haired Leharans.

The Tahitians were further south, bodies gleaming, pounding the ground with their long spears in a steady beat that sounded like drums. They moved with the sound, their bodies swaying as one in a rhythmic wave. Cossiana was behind them on an eagle, draped in bright blue, looking over her people with the careful eye of a matron. Behind the warriors and Cossiana were the healers, wrapped in white, their baskets of herbs and bandages ready to tend the wounded and the dead.

The sun rose higher in the sky and we could see movement across the plains in the Kymirran camp. The archers were lining up in their neat divisions, and in the center of them was a glittering sun, their leader, clad in gold armor and holding the tethers of an eagle. It was the eagle Akrin had flown on and I searched for him amongst the endless rows of Kymirrans. Perhaps Kaeleb was right and the wound he had inflicted on him truly had been fatal, though we had no way of knowing for sure if he was alive or dead.

"She is still wearing it," Chaote muttered darkly, coming to stand with us. She had not been pleased when she had been forced to wear Leharan armor, and even now she tugged at the edges of her breastplate as if it was chafing her.

"Hopefully, you will soon reclaim it," Kaeleb said.

I could not share their eagerness for the Earth Queen's death, no matter how much I tried to. All I felt was sorrow, deep and endless. Maialen was my only living relative, and as much as I wanted to hate her, I had already let pity for her take root in my mind. She was like a broken bird, a delicate thing who had fallen from the safety of her nest, whose fractured wings had never mended. I could not wish her dead, but I also knew that unless she relented and gave up the amulets, one of us would have to kill her. I could only hope that it would not have to be me.

Chaote had finally told us what had happened in Samirra, how she had attacked Favian and his men, how he begged her not to kill anyone else, to fight him one on one. She agreed and they had gone to the steps of the palace, to the trampled ground that had once been her arena a decade before. There, they had beaten each other to a bloody pulp. Chaote had not expected the aging Guardian to be so skilled, and his determination not to give up seemed endless. By the end of it, they were both grappling on the ground, neither of them having enough strength to stand, gasping for air, their bodies screaming in protest with every movement. Chaote had been thrown to one side, taken advantage of the opportunity and wrapped her legs around Favian's neck, using his arm to pull her towards him so she could watch him die. Her legs were shaking, too weak to keep their hold, and he took in huge gulps of air as her muscles spasmed and she released him.

"I did not mean to kill him," Favian said, as they lay on the ground, close to death, too weak to keep killing each other. "Damian was my friend."

"But you did." There was so much pain in her voice and it made his heart ache with the echoes of his own loss.

"I was trying to kill you, not Damian. I wanted to avenge Hovard."

"The man from the arena? I did not mean to kill him," she said, repeating his own words. She tried again to squeeze his neck and he gripped her thigh, pressing into one of the delicate pressure points and causing her to cry out in pain, releasing him again.

"Your beasts killed him after the boy's escape. He did not even fight back. He was hiding in the cells and they just cut him down like he was nothing. Like he did not matter."

Chaote could hear the grief that still laced his voice. He had loved this man, Hovard, and it was because of her that he had lost him, whether she was the one to inflict the fatal blows or not.

"I am sorry for what was done," she said, still keeping her hold on his neck. She had to kill him, for the only alternative was that she allow herself to be killed.

"I do not want any of this," Favian said, panting desperately. "All I ever wanted was to help my people."

"Then you should have helped me kill the Keepers and destroy the amulets," she said irritably. He tried to kick her, his boot thudding ineffectually on the ground.

"I still can. Maialen is destroying Samirra. Let me live and I will keep my kingdom out of your war."

Chaote snarled at him. "Trying to bargain for your life now?"

"No. I am trying to atone for what I have done."

She stopped, releasing her hold on his neck and flopping back onto the ground, staring up at the blue sky overhead. She was exhausted, her entire body aching. "Very well."

"In return, I only ask that you give me the Warding Stone. If you lose, then I must have a way to defend Samirra against

Maialen. She will know I betrayed her." The wiry Guardian was sincere, his cool blue eyes fixed on her as blood dripped from his nose and mouth onto the ground.

Chaote had agreed, and they had laid together beneath the Samirran sun, staring up at the sky, both wondering if the ones they had lost would agree with their choices. Chaote had recounted the events to us in a cold voice, but I could see the emotion behind her eyes, how much it had cost her to give up her revenge to help us, and I would always be grateful.

It was already afternoon when the Tahitians on the battle-field began to chant, their voices echoing out over the grassy expanse. Cossiana glided before them on her eagle, settling to the ground so she could address her warriors.

"Tahitians! Leharans! We have waited too long for this day, but it is finally here. The Solvrei is among us!" her regal voice boomed out and the warriors quieted their chanting, listening intently to their Elder.

I could not help the flush of doubt that stained my cheeks. Thyrr's words echoed in my head, the last words I would ever hear him say.

Look at her! How could I risk the future of Lehar on her?

He was right. I was nothing, the product of a manipulative god whose only purpose was to breed a weapon that could kill them. I was no hero, no saint, no divine being. I wanted to run away, to hide, to flee from the battle before it began, but then I looked around me and I knew I had to stay, to fight for my friends and our dying world. I took deep breaths, trying to find the courage within me to be what they needed me to be. The Solvrei.

Cossiana went on, her fervor increasing with every word. "The Earth Keeper has violated the laws of Imbria. She destroyed your homeland, Leharans. Forced you to live in brutal conditions in an unforgiving desert while she grows wealthy from the spoils of your pain! Now she seeks to grind all of

Imbria beneath her boot, but we will not be so easily silenced! We will not allow this tyrant to defy the gods and desecrate our lands any longer! We will rise up, we will fight for what is ours, and we will win!"

I felt my heart beating faster and I gripped Kaeleb's hand tightly. Then everything was chaos. Maialen's archers moved forward, the first line of them firing their arrows into the air, then retreating through the ranks so the next row could take their place. Volleys of arrows showered down on us and I saw the Earth Keeper gripping the Emerald that hung around her neck, furious that our Warding Stones were sapping her power. The Tahitians let out their blood-curdling war cries, streaming forward and tossing their long spears into the ranks of archers. The Leharans also charged, their curved swords flashing in the sun. Eagles lifted into the sky, filling the air with screeching cries.

I turned to Chaote, and she slid the edge of a knife across her thumb, reaching out and smearing her blood across the Sapphire that I held in my hands. Then she cut my thumb, pressing it into the jewel, one of her hands wrapping around mine. She handed Kaeleb the knife and pulled the Warding Stone over her head, dropping it on the ground between her feet.

The cacophony was instant. I could hear all the amulets, all of Imbria's Keepers shouting at me, screaming at us to stop what was happening. I cried out, nearly falling to my knees under the assault of their enraged voices. Kaeleb caught me, holding me against him, his gentle voice in my ear telling me he was with me. I searched through the screaming voices in my head, trying to find one to focus on, to drown out the others. The Harbonah was the loudest, crying out for me to destroy the amulets, but he was not the one I sought. I was looking for her. My mother. Orabelle.

You must stop her. I know you want to save her, daughter, but she is beyond saving. You must stop her.

I felt tears on my face and my heart ached at the sound of her. I gripped the Sapphire tightly just as the ground began to tremble beneath us. Maialen had realized the Warding Stone was no longer sapping her power.

"Now, Eolande!" Chaote shouted. I reached into the amulet with my mind, pulling on the tendrils of power with all of my strength. I could feel them stretching between the Elements, connecting everything. The Sapphire brightened, seeming to glow from within, and wind whipped around us, tearing across the field and flinging back the rain of arrows from the Kymirrans. I pulled harder, feeling the amulet strengthen as it drew power from the others.

Then it stopped.

I opened my eyes, staring down at the stone as the brilliant shimmer of blue faded from it, leaving it dull and grey.

"What is happening?" Kaeleb demanded.

"I don't know!" I cried, panic seeping up in me.

There was a loud howl and then the dog that was the god Fenris was beside me, circling my legs in agitation. Seff and Vayk were running up to us, their bland faces for once showing an emotion as they looked extremely displeased.

"What did you do?" Vayk asked me, staring at the useless grey rock in our hands.

"I did what you said! We used our blood and-"

"Does Maialen have your blood?" Seff questioned. "Does she?"

"I don't know! Logaire used to take it from me. She might have given some of it to Maialen," I answered, shaking my head.

"And you were her captive," he spun on Chaote. "Did she beat you, make you bleed?"

The murderous look in Chaote's dark eyes was all the answer he needed. "She is using your blood to draw the power back to the Emerald."

Chaote let go of the Sapphire, bending down and snatching up the Warding Stone from where it had fallen. Seff was shaking his head. "It is not enough. She is too powerful and you are too far away. For the stone to work now, you must be closer to her."

I heard screams of terror, the bellows of the warriors from the front lines where the armies were clashing. The ground was dissolving beneath them, the earth crumbling away as Maialen used her power. Cracks spread across the field, and the tall grass began to twist and bend, wrapping around the islanders and dragging them to their knees.

It is time.

I looked at the dog, his one eye fixed on me, tongue hanging out of his mouth and his scarred tail wagging.

Send Chaote and the boy to use the Warding Stone on Maialen and help the Fire Keeper. We will let you draw your power from us.

I could not stop hearing Chaote's warning not to do what the dog wanted, and I looked around in panic. People were dying. What choice did I have?

"Go, get closer to her with the stone!" I shouted at them. Kaeleb shook his head, unwilling to leave my side, and Chaote turned back to face the savage band of Fomori.

"Give them to me," she said.

"Follow the Mother!" I screamed at them. They poured forth around her and she sprinted towards Maialen, disappearing amongst the chaos of the battle.

It is time.

I lowered myself to one knee, wrapping my arms around the dog, feeling his mottled scars beneath the brindle fur. Then I closed my eyes, bracing myself for what would come, though the instant I felt it I knew I could never have prepared for it. It was like nothing I had ever felt before. Nothing had ever even come close. I could see the beginning of everything, the beginning of the world, the hands shaping the mountains, carving out the seas. I could feel every piece of Imbria, every grain of dust, every breath of life, every moment that had ever existed. It was too much, and I felt my mind fracture, splintering like the fissures that crisscrossed the ground beneath us.

You are strong. Fight it. Do not give up! I am here.

It was my mother. I shook my head, crying out for her, begging her to help me. I could not do it. It was too much. I wanted to give up, but my mother's voice was there, urging me to hold on.

You are my daughter. You are stronger than everyone else. You must not give up, Eolande. Fight. You are strong and you are loved. You are so very loved, my sweet girl.

I cried out again, a sob tearing from me as my heart broke. I had wanted to hear those words my entire life, had never thought I would. The dog was howling beneath me and I gripped him tighter, trying to focus on the amulets, to find the threads that connected them to me. I found the Pearl, my mother's amulet, the one that held her beautiful voice within it, and I crushed it, sobbing harder, feeling the power fade away, knowing the last echo of her that remained in the jewel was now gone forever.

"Eolande!" It was Bacatha's voice calling for me and I ignored it, searching for the Emerald amongst the millions of threads that held our world together. "Eolande, behind you!"

I spun around, still holding onto the dog, feeling a sharp pain in my back, just below my neck. I cried out, letting go of the animal and groping behind me to find the source of the burning pain. A knife was sticking out of my skin and I yanked it free, feeling blood course down from the wound, staring at the blade in my hand in shock. I lifted my eyes and Seff was pulling another knife from the belt of weapons that were wrapped at his waist just as Kaeleb caught him, grappling with his wrists.

Seff pushed Kaeleb off him and Bacatha charged between us, kicking the dog as hard as she could and sending him rolling away with a howl of protest. She swung her scythe, severing Vayk's leg as he rushed at me, the limb falling as he took one more step before realizing it was gone and crashing down on top of it. Kaeleb bolted after Seff, who was running after the dog, and Bacatha grabbed my arm, hauling me to my feet. Vayk was writhing on the ground, blood spurting from the wound and we jumped over him and ran through the press of men, towards the fiery inferno I could see rolling over the Kymirran soldiers. The Fomori were everywhere, and all I could hear were the screams of the dying. A man fell between us and Bacatha's hand slipped from my grasp as I was shoved aside in the melee. I tried to wrench my way back to her, but there were too many people, too many bodies. I could feel them under my feet, slick with blood, pressing all around me. I was knocked to the ground once again, pinned down by the enormous weight of a fallen Fomori. I tried to shove the beast off me, but it would not budge and I could feel it crushing my chest, my breath coming in desperate gasps. I reached out, grabbing the ankle of the person nearest to me and calling my power. Wind filled the space between us, lifting the Fomori and tossing the body of the beast off of me. I gasped, my lungs screaming, taking in great heaving breaths.

I got to my feet in time to see Bacatha hacking mercilessly with her scythe at a group of men who were surrounding her. Her father was near her and he lifted his sword, an arrow piercing his throat. I heard Bacatha's cry just as someone slammed into me, throwing me to the ground once more. The man lunged at me, sword slashing down, and I twisted out of the way, kicking his feet out from under him. He landed on the ground beside me and for a moment our eyes met. He could not have been much older than me, and he looked so frightened. I touched his face gently and his eyes widened. I ripped the life out of him, throwing a surge of power at the Kymirran army and watching for a moment as it tore through them. Then something crashed against the back of my head and darkness flooded over me.

34

The sky overhead had darkened, bloated clouds of ash cloaking the last hours of sunlight from the horizon. Darkness crept at the edges of the battle like a looming monster waiting to pounce. I pushed myself up to one knee, wiping blood and dirt from my eyes. I was breathing heavily and I could feel the pulsing wound in my back with each beat of my heart. But at least my heart was still beating. I tried to stand and cried out with the effort, falling back to my knee.

Get up!

I could not tell where the voice had come from amidst the chaos. The war churned around me, a violent mess of blood and bodies. Everywhere I looked there was death. The ground was soaked with it, the air fouled with the cries of it, my senses assaulted by it. These were my friends, my companions, everyone that I had ever cared about, and they were being strewn about, torn apart callously like discarded, broken toys.

I tried again to stand, struggling unsteadily to my feet even as the pain threatened to engulf me. I reached to unclasp the breastplate that protected my heart and I let it fall to the ground with a heavy thud. A steady pulse of blood ran down my face and dripped from my chin, and I watched its rhythmic cadence as it fell upon my discarded armor. It was too much. It was all too much. I turned my head away from the sight of my own blood and squinted through the thick blankets of smoke and fire. I thought I saw the figure of a wolf leaping, strong jaws snapping at its enemies' neck. I took a step towards it and it was gone, either swallowed by the fight or perhaps it had never existed at all, a trick of the flickering flames and my battered mind.

You have to stop them.

Was the voice in my mind? I could no longer tell. I looked about frantically and there was only the battle, the awful clamor of weapons against armor, the cries of the dying.

Stop them, it shouted again.

"I can't!" I screamed back, shrieking into the premature night. "I can't! I tried and I could not stop any of it!"

You are the only one who can.

I hung my head, my matted hair falling over my face. I could smell the burnt flesh that clung to me, carried on the air, and I tried to breathe, to find the strength to go on.

"I can't," I whispered. A tear slid from the corner of my eye, painting a golden streak down my stained cheek. I wanted to stop, to fall back to the ground and close my eyes and let the darkness overtake me. I did not want to face the pain, the awfulness of afterward, of knowing they were all gone. I did not want to feel the loneliness again, and part of me longed for the numbing nothingness that would come with death. All I had to do was stop, to fall back down, to let them have their broken world and let them burn it to the ground.

Something cold touched my face. Then again. I tilted my head to look up. There was a break in the heavy curtains of smoke and far above us I saw grey storm clouds rolling across the sky. Another raindrop fell and it ran over my cracked lips, tasting bitter in my mouth. Silvery light bathed the landscape and for a moment, the horrible redness of the flames dimmed.

My throat knotted with emotion and I felt my lips turn up into a smile as more tears fell from my eyes and mingled with the falling rain. Something inside me stirred and I bent forward, screaming out with every muscle of my body, my lungs burning with the sound of it, my fists clenching. I felt the strength gather within me and I screamed again, the sound echoing over the ravaged field. I would not let them have this world without a fight. In the distance, I heard a name called out in fury and terror and my smile widened. The name of the one who had changed everything all those years ago, the one who started it all.

Orabelle.

I ran towards Maialen's voice, the one who had screamed out my mother's name. She was facing Blaise, a wide chasm opening in the ground between them. Chaote was on the ground at the Earth Keeper's feet, wounded and clawing her way towards the pale shimmer of the Warding Stone where it lay in the dirt.

"It was always about Orabelle!" Maialen was screaming at the Fire Keeper. The golden armor she wore was tinged with soot and splattered with gore, her long chestnut hair billowing out behind her. Her face, so much like a doll's with its smattering of freckles, big eyes and delicate features, was eerily out of place amongst the carnage, like a child who had gotten lost and wandered amongst a pack of wolves.

"Maialen, you must realize now that you are not the Solvrei! End this and we can all live, we can all walk away! Let her destroy the amulets. We can be free of all of it," Blaise was shouting at her. Blood coated one side of his head and his injured arm was hanging uselessly at his side.

"Stop trying to save me!" she shrieked back at him. "You only want to take what is mine. You don't care about me! No one cares about me! She is not the Solvrei. I am. Imbria is mine now!"

Where is Kaeleb I don't see Kaeleb where is he is he dead he can't be dead he can't be where is he I need to find him where is the Fenris were they trying to kill me why why why I was doing what they wanted where is Kaeleb where is he?

My thoughts were racing, as chaotic as the battle that raged around us. The rain was pelting down now and it soaked the bloody ground, making it slick with mud. Maialen lunged forward, stepping on Chaote's outstretched hand with her booted foot and grinding her heel against the splayed fingers. Chaote yelled in pain, swinging her other arm at the Earth Queen, but a tangle of grass twisted around the limb, pinning the halfbreed to the ground. The Warding Stone disappeared in one of the deep crevices Maialen was slicing into the ground around her. She sneered at Chaote, gloating, twisting her boot over the halfbreed's crushed hand. That was when I saw Kaeleb running at her, sliding to the muddy ground and swinging his sword. She whirled at the last second, lifting her hand and causing a row of sharp rocks to jut up out of the ground, surrounding her. Kaeleb crashed against the hard rocks, his sword flying out of his hand, and Maialen laughed, looking back at Blaise as he threw a surge of fire at her. She flung her wrist, dirt dampening the flames before they could reach her.

"That boy is the only thing you care about. You can watch him die last, after I destroy the rest of your pathetic army." Maialen lifted her hands, the world shifting beneath her. I ran for Kaeleb, trying to help him to his feet, pulling him away from the enraged Earth Queen.

"No!" he protested. "We have to stop her."

I looked around frantically. The field of soldiers was crumbling, the ground collapsing beneath them. I could see the Tahitians desperately trying to clamor onto the remaining eagles and get off the ground before it swallowed them.

"Where is the dog?" I asked Kaeleb. "I need the dog!"

It was Chaote who shouted back to me from the other side of Maialen's jagged barrier of rock. "You cannot kill the Fenris! If you do, they will kill you!"

I remembered Blaise's words, that the Fenris wanted to rid the world of all divine powers, and that included me. It must have been their plan all along for the two brothers to kill me after he was dead, or close enough to dead.

"It has to be me."

Kaeleb grasped my hand, but I shook my head, my entire being rebelling at his suggestion. "No. Not you. It can't be you."

"She is killing everyone. We have to stop her," he said, gripping my hand tighter. I looked into his eye, his beautiful grey eye, and I could not do what he asked.

Fire surged overhead and dirt rained down on us. The world was unrecognizable, a tortured, twisting plane of existence. Kaeleb was pleading with me, his angular face set in determined lines. "Please, Eolande. This is the only way. You don't have to take everything. Just enough to stop her. If you don't, we will all die."

I nodded, my heart aching in my chest. He was right. I did not have to take everything. I held his hand, closing my eyes, not wanting to see the pain on his face that I knew I would cause. Then I turned on the Earth Queen. I found the thread that was her Element and pulled on it, but she was stronger now that the Water and Air amulets had been destroyed, and she fought against it.

I pulled harder, calling on the rain to help me. It drove at her in torrents and she cried out as the droplets stung her face, lifting her arm to shield herself. I tried not to feel the elation the power brought, hating the way I savored it even though I knew I was stealing the precious days of Kaeleb's life with every second that passed. I felt Kaeleb start to tremble, opened my eyes to see his face distorted with pain, the blood vessels bursting in his eye. I was killing him. I let out a scream of frustration, shoving everything in me at Maialen, trying not to take too much from Kaeleb, fighting desperately to find that delicate balance that would destroy her and save him, but it was not enough and still she was fighting me.

He is going to die I am killing him I have to end this please help someone please help I am killing him help us help me I can't I can't I can't please please please.

I saw a flash of red behind Maialen, and Blaise leapt over the chasm that separated them, wrapping his arms around her from behind. He called out the words and Maialen's big green eyes widened in surprise, finally hearing the one thing she had always wanted to hear from him, from anyone. I used that moment, pulled as hard as I could, shoved all of her power into the last amulet. Blaise's amulet.

"I love you."

Maialen could not see his face, did not know that he was looking at Kaeleb, that the words were not meant for her, but were for his son, a father saying goodbye to the child who meant everything to him. Maialen's lips parted and a look of joy fleeted across her face, then they burst into flames.

"No!" Kaeleb ripped his hand from mine, throwing himself at the burning bodies, but it was too late. The fire that Blaise had called forth had the power of all four amulets behind it and it had killed them both instantly, destroying the Fire Opal along with them. There was nothing left but ashes floating in the air. Kaeleb was on his knees, fists pounding the ground as bloody tears streamed down his face. Rain slanted down, dampening the last of the flames as he cried for the loss of the first person who had ever loved him, and the one who had given his life to save him.

It took a while for Chaote to pull herself around the jagged rocks, and when she finally did, she leaned against them, panting with exertion. There was a deep gash on her side, and blood was soaking one of her legs. She cradled her mangled hand, staring at the mound of damp ash that had once been the Earth Queen. "There goes my armor."

I could not help the brief burst of laughter that bubbled in me, and even Kaeleb, in the midst of his grief, shook his head at her with a teary smile, asking her, "What is wrong with you?"

"Is it over?" Bacatha limped up to us, covered in blood and mud, the cuts on her cheek dripping dark crimson stains down her face. She grimaced at Chaote, then knelt beside Kaeleb and laid her hand on his shoulder. He shook beneath her, crying softly, and my heart ached for him. I wished more than anything that I had not failed him, and I wondered if he would hate me after all that had happened today.

He reached back as if knowing my fearful thoughts, groping for my hand, pulling me towards him and wrapping me in his strong embrace. His tears were hot against my cheek and I held him, rocking back and forth on the ravaged ground. Then he tried to stand, and I helped him up, Bacatha catching him under his shoulder and supporting his weight from the other side. Chaote sighed, looking at us with a frown marring her perfect features, then she pushed herself up against the rock, standing beside us. We stood looking out over the destruction, battered and broken, scarred, torn, filled with grief and loss, but somehow still alive and together. As night descended over the desecrated field, we made our way back to whatever was left of our people.

35

I let the last grains of dirt slip through my fingers, watching them as they fell upon the soft mound of earth. The sun was high overhead, the sky brilliantly blue. Around us, the land was still scorched and scarred by the battle that had taken place. I looked over my shoulder at the two women who stood watching over me, one silver, one gold, their polished armor dulled with dust and their skin glistening with sweat.

They waited in silence, and I could hear the faint howl of the wind as it curved through the deep chasms that threaded the land. My fingers clenched in the dirt and I knew I needed to stand up, to walk away, but I could not bring myself to do it.

"I am sorry," I whispered to the two women.

"We will stand guard until you are ready," Bacatha said, her stern, scarred face pressed into determined lines. I saw the glitter of tears in her icy blue gaze and how she clenched her jaw, her knuckles white where she gripped her scythe.

Chaote simply nodded, the perfection of her dark eyes filled with understanding and the shadows of her own losses.

"Will it ever stop hurting?" I asked her.

"Time does not heal all wounds, Eolande. There are some that will bleed forever. But eventually you will learn to live with the pain."

I turned back to stare at the dirt beneath me, the fragile barrier of death that would forever be between me and Kaeleb. I wanted to see him one more time, to hear his laughter one more time, to feel his arms around me just one more time, but I knew that even if it was possible, I would still want one more and one more after that and there would never be enough. If we had all of eternity together instead of one brief year, it would never be enough.

I remembered the day we had walked away from here, away from the battlefield. I had known then that we would return, that this is where I would bury him, the boy I had loved and I had killed. We never spoke of it, but I knew he would like to be buried here, near his father, who was also somewhere beneath us, the ashes of his body part of the land.

We had not known how long he had. There was no way of knowing how many precious days were left of his beautiful life or how much I had stolen from him that day. I vowed to spend them all with him, whatever was left, and that was exactly what I had done. We had sacrificed more for this world than should ever have been asked of us, and all I wanted was for him to have a life that was his own, even if we both knew it could not last.

We had taken an eagle and found a house in the woods, away from everyone, a place that reminded me of my childhood home with Gideon. Chaote and Bacatha had understood, and they had gone to do the things that needed to be done, trying to tend to the chaos we had left behind in the aftermath of the battle that changed our world forever. They would come by on occasion with news and to see how Kaeleb was faring, and he always looked forward to their visits, showing them around our meager homestead with pride. I had done my best to make the little cabin into a home. Bacatha brought us colorful fabrics from Tahitia, bright sunny yellows that were his favorite color, and I hung them over the windows and made cushions for the chairs. I kept sprigs of wildflowers in clay jars and hung his father's sword on the wall, where he could walk by it and smile, sometimes touching the cool metal with his fingertips.

We spent our days laughing, peaceful, gathering food, and hunting. We managed to collect some chickens and Kaeleb mocked my efforts to care for them, doubling over with laughter as I chased them aimlessly around the cabin, cursing them thoroughly. At night we lay before the fire, or sometimes out on the ground so we could see the stars. He loved to find shapes in the stars, to point out his ridiculous compositions in the heavenly orbs. He told me wild stories about his adventures before I had known him and I read books to him, which Chaote sometimes brought to us. He would stare at me as I read, his one eye watching the movement of my lips in fascination. I would blush, tell him to stop staring, and he would laugh and pull me against him, kissing me softly. In those early days, I had allowed the idyllic life we had created together to lull me into believing it would last. Kaeleb was not as strong as he had once been, but he was fine. He was alive and healthy.

Then he had taken that step. That one fateful step that I would never forget. I closed my eyes and I could see it, over and over, echoing in my head. We were walking down the path that led to the river and he was in front of me, singing heartily, a wooden bucket swinging in his hand. I had lifted my voice to join him in the song, and he glanced back, grinning. Then he stumbled. He had fallen to his knees, his breath coming in heaving gasps. I ran to him, helping him to stand, and when I touched him, his skin was flushed, feverish. I looked in his eye and I knew. He had known it was coming, had tried to hide it from me as long as he could.

I sent our eagle to the islands, to tell the others that it was time, hoping the creature understood what I wanted and remembered the whistled commands we had taught it. Bacatha would know what it meant when the bird appeared riderless. She would realize that I could not bring myself to leave Kaeleb's side. I stayed with him, still praying for a miracle, praying for the gods to help me, even though I knew in my heart there was no one to hear my fervent pleas. They never came, never answered, and there was only silence, broken by his fitful coughing and labored breathing. I tried to ease his suffering, giving him the herbs Chaote had left for me, knowing that one day we would need them. I stroked his pale hair back from his forehead, staring at the lines of his face, trying to memorize them so I would never forget. I did not know what would become of me in this life without him, but I was determined to keep him in my memory, to hold him in my heart. I would always be thinking of him.

The last day I had with him, he had pushed himself up out of the bed. It was still dark out, but the sun would soon rise and he wanted to see it. I wrapped him in a blanket and let him lean on my shoulder, and he was so light, so thin by then. We went outside and sat on the ground, and he smiled, watching the golden glow as it rose between the trees, long fingers of ruby and rose streaming across the sky. In the soft morning glow, I could barely see the dark smudges under his eye or the gauntness of his hollow cheeks. He was the Kaeleb I remembered, the man who was strong and brave and fearless, fiercely protective and unshakably loyal. He looked at me with so much love on his proud face that it broke my heart. He whispered quietly, "You are my beautiful dawn, Eolande."

I had not answered, the knot in my throat choking me, making it impossible for me to form words. Tears streamed down my face and I held his hand tightly as he rested his head on my shoulder and took his last breath.

I felt it again as I knelt on his grave, the overwhelming grief that I did not think I could bear. It crushed my chest, made me want to scream and cry and rage against the world until I had exhausted the tireless pain. I wondered if this was what my mother had felt when she lost my father, and in that moment I forgave her for everything she had done afterwards.

I finally stood, turning to face the two warriors who were waiting patiently, paying their own silent homage to the brave and selfless boy who had saved us all.

"I am ready."

Chaote nodded her head, her starry eyes bright with emotion and her new suit of armor gleaming. "Where shall we go first?"

I looked out over the wreckage we had left behind, the deep scars that wounded both the land and me, scars that would never heal. Then I looked back at the women who stood watching over me, the women who had become my sisters, not by blood or by birth or by any ties other than those we had chosen for ourselves. We were bound by our scars, by our losses and our pain, and also by the unshakable bond of knowing that we had chosen each other, that we were the family we never expected to have. No matter what happened, we were not alone. We would always have each other.

Bacatha turned her face to the east, and I nodded. Veruca.

"Logaire thinks I have forgotten about her. Let us go and show her that we still remember. Perhaps we will find a lost dog along the way," I said, and we began to walk.

About the Author

Jenna Barrett is an award winning author who writes fantasy novels and is currently at work on the Keepers of Imbria series following the release of her debut novel, Orabelle. She weaves complex emotional dichotomies and breathes life into strong female heroines and villains that you love to hate. Jenna is a recent breast cancer survivor and currently resides in Texas with her three-legged dog, Artemis. When she is not writing, she spends her time doing freelance photography and is an avid adventurer who enjoys anything outdoors, especially rock climbing and mountaineering.

Visit her on the web at www.jbarrettauthor.com
on Twitter and Instagram @jbarrettauthor
or on Facebook J Barrett Author